S0-DMX-100

FOUR WENT TO
THE CIVIL WAR

To Rob Dunn

FOUR WENT TO THE CIVIL WAR

BY
LOIS E. DARROCH

Lois E. Darroch
" 1994

Preface

This book is the saga of a central Ontario family during the years 1855-1865. The hundred or so letters that have provided the springboard for this novel is the longest, possibly the only, series extant in Canada from the forty thousand Canadians who were involved in the American Civil War.

The letters were written to and from the family of four Canadian brothers who were at school in Cleveland, Ohio, when the war broke out. Because they were caught up in that conflict, 1861-1865, it is also a tale of the progress of that war, the memory of which still burns in the minds of humankind.

First names of the persons in the central family have been retained, but because the events in the letters are bound together by fiction, the family name Wolverton, has been changed to Harding.

The author acknowledges with gratitude the use of primary sources such as family letters and diaries; similar letters and diaries in Yale University, and the Glenbow Museum, Calgary; the libraries of Case Western Reserve University, Florida State University, the Bentley Historical Library, University of Michigan; the archives in Ottawa, Toronto and Washington; and the pertinent volumes of the seventy that comprise *The War of the Rebellion; a compilation of the official records of the Union and Confederate armies,* published under the direction of Stephen B. Elkins, Secretary of War, Washington, 1892.

Otherwise, because her main object was to introduce unique Canadian letters to the public, not to engage in primary research in the American Civil War, she relied strongly on secondary sources such as *Reveille in Washington,* Margaret Leech, Harper & Brothers, 1941; *This Hallowed Ground/The Story of the Union Side of the Civil War,* Bruce Catton, Doubleday & Company, 1955; *Canada and the United States/The Civil War Years,* Robin W. Winks, The Johns Hopkins Press, Baltimore, 1960 and *The Blacks in Canada,* Yale and McGill-Queens, 1971; and many others.

Certain events such as the times of the building of the church and school in Wolverton, Ontario, and the months of the deaths of Daniel and the wounding of Alonzo have been manipulated for the purpose of the narrative. No references have been given for the use of various stories such as "Just enough for another killin'" for they are already legend in the annals of the war.

Copyright© Lois E. Darroch, 1985

Published by:

AMPERSAND PRESS
2009 - 33 Elmhurst Ave.
Willowdale, Ontario
(416) 221-3625 M2N 6G8

McBAIN PUBLICATIONS INC.

70 Otonabee Drive
Kitchener, Ontario N2C 1L6
(519) 894-4000

ALL RIGHTS RESERVED

No part of this book may be reproduced in any form without permission in
writing from the publishers, except by a reviewer who may quote brief
passages in a review to be printed in a magazine or newspaper.

Canadian Cataloguing in Publication Data

Darroch, Lois, 1912—Four went to the Civil War

ISBN 0-920469-01-9

1. United States - History - Civil War, 1861-1865 - Fiction.
I. Title.

PS8557.A77F68 1985   C813'.54   C85-098995-7
PR9199.3.D26F68 1985

Cover idea by Peter Waldock

Cover design by Ray Banks

Cover photos courtesy Bentley Historical Library, University of Michigan

Engravings on pp. 38, 128, 220, 264 from **Michigan Men in the Civil War**
by Ida C. Brown (University of Michigan: Michigan Historical Collections,
Bulletin No. 27, Sept. 1977).

Manufactured in Canada by Allprint Company Limited

To my late parents
William Franklin Darroch
and
Leonora Wolverton Darroch

and

To Rosa Parks
who on December 1, 1955
in Montgomery, Alabama
refused to surrender
her seat in a bus
to a white man

Contents

Chapter 1

Red Velvet Lined

Enos Harding stood at his ease, appraising the half-finished carriage in the middle of the Weir carriage works in Ayr, Canada West. Five excited sons clustered behind him. Only partly concealing his pleasure at the thought of owning a carriage at last, Enos lifted his hat and re-settled it on his head.

"How long will it take to finish it, Jake?"

Old Jake contemplated his crumpled shoes. "Don't rightly know. Everybody's gone home for dinner and I'm just caretakin'. I'd say in about two months."

"Just right; just about right. Britain's war in the Crimea* has sent the price of wheat sky high. I was right when I planted every acre I could. A cash crop at bumper prices—three dollars or more a bushel; twenty bushels to the acre. That's enough to keep us and buy a $200 carriage."

Two younger sons clamored to climb in. "Stand aside, boys, and let yer pa git in first." Old Jake looked negligible for he was baggy and craggy, one enormous wrinkle of face and clothes, but he knew protocol.

Enos stepped up, dusted the seat with his handkerchief, lifted his coat-tails and sat down. Four sons leaped in and pulled the fifth in after them. "I'll have it lined with red velvet. Don't tell your mother and sister yet. Keep it a secret, lads. Out you get."

Jubilant and noisy, they jumped out of the carriage and into the waiting surrey. Their father flicked the reins over the trotter's back. "Giddap, Phoenix," piped eight year old Newton from the front seat

---

*1854-1856.

1

beside his father, and the horse's haunches gleamed and settled into their lively rhythm.

A carriage with red velvet, the sons murmured among themselves.

"We've the carriage, boys, and I'm about to commence a big house to go with it. Two months to finish the carriage, two years to build the house. And soon there'll be a town around us. I'll be Enos Harding of Harding Hall, Harding, Canada West."

Old Jake shifted his tobacco quid from one side of his mouth to the other. On legs like walking parentheses he moved towards the door of the carriage works and spat a brown splotch into the dust eddies Harding had left behind him. "Nothin' uncommon about red velvet for a carriage. It's the carriage that's uncommon around here." He pulled his plug of tobacco from his pocket and then his pocket knife. "A few here in Ayr and one over on the Blenheim town line. Mackey offered to buy that one—give fifty acres for it, he said, but Jordan wouldn't sell. Said there was lots of land around but not many carriages. Wouldn't sell. Now Harding's gettin' one. Red velvet lined."

He could not have told why there came to his mind just then, "Red can be glad or red can be blood." Old Jake was given to formless musing but not to poetry or prescience.

The Hardings bounced over the rutted road to the two-hundred-acre farm where the wheat was already turning to the colour that would bring the cash to build the house that would satisfy Enos' ambition. Four storeys high, it's going to be, he told his boys, with a glass cupola that will be higher than the tops of the maples that were left when the farm was cleared.

Now they had reached the crest of the hill that sloped into the valley through which the Nith River meandered. "Steady, boy," said Enos as he pulled the reins to slow Phoenix to a walk. "Slow, boy, take her easy down the hill," he coaxed as the horse's hooves slid on the stony road.

Then, "Look at that, lads," he said as the wide valley with his farm came fully into view. The farm was bottom land. The river nosed its way around it, held to its course on the east and south by the high banks that rose in places to the height of cliffs. In springtime it was brown with silt and so powerful in flood that rapids and deeps shared the same mighty flow. In summer, cattle, with their owners' marks cut into their ears, would wade across the rapids to feed on the lush river grass. Or they rested in the shade beside slower green-brown ruminant depths that, moving silently, reflected the great willows that held the muddy banks

2

with their roots. The river valley was cupped in its hills. When the children played, the sound of their voices hung like bells in the clear air.

"This won't be farm much longer, boys. I'm going to break it up into lots for houses and make a village. Maybe it'll grow into a town. I'm going to claim my water rights, and build a dam right here." said Enos, pointing to a spot on the river to the north of the bridge they were now rumbling over. "MacPherson from over on the seventh concession wants to build a gristmill on one side and I'll rent him half the waterpower. But I'll keep this side for myself for a sawmill. Jim Currey will move in with his horses for hauling, George Bautenheimer will come as blacksmith, John Edger will be the shoemaker and a couple of carpenters and coopers will come in no time."

Sixteen year old Alfred gasped. "When is all this going to happen?"

"You saw me talking to John Meigs the other day? He's ready to buy a lot and build a small hotel. We'll find a tanner and there can be a flax mill near the pond on the south flats where the flax can be laid to ret."

"Are you going to retire, pa, when the farm is all sold?" asked Daniel, the second oldest son at fourteen.

"Like ducks I'll retire. I'll build a store and have a post office in it. We'll get a branch of the railroad to come through here. We'll have mail every day, maybe twice, on both the noon and night trains."

"Can I pick up the mail at the railway station?" begged thirteen year old Alonzo. "I can drive Phoenix by myself."

"I get to read the postcards before we give them out," eleven year old Jasper called out.

"You and Newton will have your hides tanned if you touch the mail. Mail is government property till it reaches the owner and is not to be played with." Enos lapsed into visions again. "There'll be a school here in the valley and a church to please your mother. And our new house will be just south of the bend in the river. And the cupola will be high enough so that we can look over the whole valley, right to the hills. But mind, sons, don't tell your mother or Roseltha about the carriage. Keep it a secret."

Phoenix quickened his pace as they approached the barn. Enos reined him in sharply as they came abreast of it. "Open the door, Newton, and Daniel and Jasper, fetch the cows for milking. They're bawling at the gate. And Alonzo, see if there are any more eggs. I hear some hens clucking." As Enos slapped the horse into the barn, its whinny echoed over the valley.

Alfred and Newton leaped across the long verandah into the house where their mother Harriet was playing the melodeon in the parlour. Roseltha, the boys' nineteen year old sister, was singing alto to the

3

soprano of Sarah, the governess from England. Five Harding sons and their sister constituted a class in themselves and the nearest school was five miles away. Bursting with their secret, but keeping it, the boys joined the singing.

> There's a church in the valley by the wildwood,
> No-o lovelier place in the vale.
> No-o spot is so dear to my childhood
> As the little brown church in the vale.

This was Harriet's dream, a church nearby. She wanted a church when Enos built the town he had been talking about to her. Only the church would be white, not brown, white as the souls of those washed clean by baptism, clean as the boys' mouths after Enos had washed them out with soap if his sons' words offended.

The church they would worship in would lead them all to their goal of eternal life. They turned the pages of the hymnbook and sang:

> "O Beulah Land, sweet Beulah Land,
> As on thy highest mount I stand
> I look away across the sea
> Where mansions are prepared for me,
> And view the shining glory shore,
> My heaven, my home, forever more."

The rays of the summer sun pervaded the parlour, little dust motes dancing in its beams in spite of ardent housekeeping. The light shone on Harriet's smooth cheeks, straight features and heavy brown hair pinned close, hair that touched the hem of her long skirt when released. Roseltha's face bore the same sweet expression as her mother's but her hair and cheeks gleamed with the deeper colour of youth. Alfred and Alonzo resembled their mother too, but Daniel, Jasper and Newton looked like their father with less handsome features than they and with silkier brown hair and slender frames. Perhaps when they were older they would share their father's taut, decisive stance, the firm angle of his head and the quick blue eyes that could plumb a situation at a glance. Enos Harding was forty-five years old, at the peak of his energy. His height was medium but he had presence. He was relaxed now as he rested his hand on his wife's shoulder.

Harriet was angelic by nature and she drew her family to her faith, to her hope that they would never be parted except for a few earthly years before they would meet in the heaven that was their final goal. Each one who sang around the melodeon believed it with her.

Enos believed in heaven too, but pragmatically he figured there was no reason he ought not to have a bit of a mansion on earth while he waited for one higher up. He didn't think Harriet would mind it either.

4

Next morning Enos called to his youngest son, "Get me the axe, company coming for dinner."

"Which one are you going to kill, pa?" quipped young Newton.

"Scat, boy, and catch a good big hen, not a skinny one."

Newton stalked a fat chicken in the chicken run till he cornered it squawking against the fence. One hand grasped its feet and he turned it upside down to quiet the flapping wings. "You may be a chicken but your goose is cooked," he shouted as he raced with it to the chopping-block on top of the cinder-sifter beside the woodshed.

Harding lifted his axe and severed the head, scraping it to the ground. The cat caught it and immediately began to crunch. Enos flung the body to the grass where it flopped about grotesquely, its reflexes still operating. Newton jumped behind, screeching as he followed the frenzied flopping of a bird already dead and leaving bright splotches of blood ruby against the grass. It was half beautiful, half horrible. Newton partly enjoyed, partly hated it, but the thought of chicken and dumplings for dinner eliminated all distaste as he picked up the carcass after its final flop.

Sadie, the maid, came out with a kettle of hot water to use to pluck the feathers and clean it. Newton loved to watch the drawing. It was fascinating—all those mysterious jumbled insides. The gleaming purplish gizzard with its gritty green contents. The slithery brown liver that the Harding family never ate—he didn't know why, for the German family on a nearby farm ate the liver, he knew. Eggs all ready to be laid. Sadie set aside the largest for baking, and threw out the masses of red-veined little ones cheated of their turn to grow.

Jasper came along just as Sadie was wiping her hands. "What's this, Sadie?" he asked, pointing at the "Pope's nose" from which she had cut the oil sac.

"What's this, Sadie?" Newton continued the teasing, pointing at something unidentifiable.

"Get along with you, question-bags," and Sadie gave Newton a push with her fat elbow.

By this time the boys were ready to run off, for the hot smell of the liberated innards was not one of the delights of chicken for dinner. Away they ran, dodging the blood stains brilliant upon the grass.

The visitors were Enos' older brother Asa and his wife Juliet from the little town of Paris, eight miles away. Asa had built his own house high on the banks of the Nith just above its convergence with the Grand River. The main part rose, imposing and pillared, two storeys high. The big windows front and back in the spacious parlour surveyed both road

5

and river. To the left a cobblestone wall enclosed the flower and vegetable gardens that Asa had laid out with walks in formal rectangles and with a cobblestone root house on the river side. To the right a one-storey coachman's quarters adjoined the house and continued to the high-doored carriage house with a stable behind. The servants' quarters and kitchen beneath the house were windowed towards the river, not dungeoned underground. It was a fairly impressive establishment. Enos, younger than Asa by five years, was busy chasing him in achievements, a little friendly sibling rivalry.

Today the coachman who halted the carriage in front of Enos' house was a negro, soft-spoken and very black. Jasper and Newton stared compulsively at him for they had never seen a negro before. As soon as they had kissed their uncle and aunt they escaped outside to have a better look at him. Alfred followed. He had never seen a negro either but he knew about escaped slaves coming from the United States to Canada for freedom. The Bible he read daily with his mother told him that the sons of Ham were destined to serve their brothers but it also said that all men were equal in the sight of the Lord. He found the contradiction a little perplexing. The newspaper they read, the Toronto *Globe,* had occasional reports of the activities of an Anti-Slavery Society, and his mother believed in its work. He followed the younger boys to the barn where the coachman was unhitching the horses. Then he ventured to speak.

"My name's Alfred Harding. What's yours?"

"George Washington Jones," the name rumbled from the big man's chest.

"How long have you been in Canada?"

"Two years."

"Where did you come from?"

"Kentucky."

"Were you a slave?"

"I was but I ain't no more. Now that I'se here I'se a free man."

"How did you get here?"

"A Quaker in Cincinnatti, name Mr. Levi Coffin, he'ped us git to Cleveland. Me and my wife follow de North Star to Canada. That was our freedom star. We hide by day and travel by night."

"Weren't you chased?"

"We'd few bad time but now we'se safe we'se forget de bad parts."

"Is Canada all you expected?"

The black face flashed a contented grin. "I ain't complainin' yit." The horses drank noisily from the bucket and the negro sang half under his breath:

"Farewell, old massa,
Don' come after me.
I'm on my way to Canada
Where coloured men are free."

Alfred returned thoughtfully to the house. Jasper and Newton pointed, "There's oats in that bin for the horses," and ran.

Behind the lilac clump they paused. "At last I've seen a nigger," said Jasper.

"Do you think his tongue is black too?" breathed Newton.

"Come and see where I'm planning to build my new house, Asa," said Enos, rising from his chair when the women began to compare crochet patterns. "We'll go out by the front door."

The men walked towards the river. "I think it should be here," said Enos.

"Nice location for it, and high enough from the river, but you're planning pretty big, aren't you? Three storeys and a cupola is a whopper of a house."

"I don't think so. I don't like war but this rumpus in the Crimea will keep up the demand for wheat and send the price sky high. And Edger, the carpenter, will buy the house we're in now as soon as we've moved into the big one. He has some cash and can work out the rest."

"Counting a bit much on the price of wheat, aren't you? I see you've planted wheat in every acre you could and it looks like a good crop. But this war in the Crimea won't last long. Not enough reason for it."

"It'll last longer than Britain and France figure. The generals are so old they're still fighting the battle of Waterloo."

"They have the new Minié rifle and bullets and the Russians are still fighting with smooth bore percussion muskets. Those new rifles can kill at more than a quarter of a mile," Asa said.

"Winter's coming on. The Russians are used to winter and the French aren't. Winter defeated Napoleon in Russia and it may do the same again. My wheat will sell. And Asa, I've more than wheat. I've bought some Great Western Railway stock, twenty shares for £500. It costs three shillings to get a barrel of flour from here to Hamilton by hauling it, but it will cost only sixpence by railroad. Besides, Great Western is paying six per cent dividend now and some people say it will go up to eleven and a half."

"Better be careful, Enos. Stocks are always risky unless you make them your whole life. I think they're planning so many railroads in so many

7

different directions that they'll soon run themselves into bankruptcy."

"I don't know what your Brant County Council is doing now but Oxford County holds £25,000 in stock and debentures, not without opposition, you may imagine, but the ayes won out."

"Suit yourself. I know the railroad will bring business to Paris but I'd hate to see you get stung. I'm sticking to straight building now."

"I may go into building too, more than my house. Take a look at this map." Enos straightened out the roll of heavy paper tucked under his arm. "This farm will soon be a town. It'll be called Harding after me." He leaned the map on top of a rail fence. "This is the plan I've laid out for lots and streets. I'm going to build a saw mill next summer. A tanner, blacksmith, two teamsters, two coopers and two more carpenters have already said they want lots and are going to build. I may put up a store as well as the mill and the boys and Roseltha can help run it. I'll build it facing the street between the new house and the barn. I'll sell all the livestock except one cow for our own milk and two horses for driving."

"If you build a church for this village you're proposing, I hope you do better than I did with the Baptist church in Paris. They ended up owing me eighty-five dollars, and to close the books I just said, forget it, count it as an extra contribution from me."

"You can afford it, Asa. Wish we could get a legacy from somebody in Scotland the way your Paris church did and I'd begin a church here tomorrow. When I'm finished building in the village I won't build any more. I may contract for a few roads though, plank roads. Time they were planking the Governor's Road west of Paris. Room for a toll road between here and Princeton. Enough traffic now."

"I hope you're right, though the time for toll roads is passing now that railroads are being built."

"More need than ever for toll roads, I think, for the farmers have to get their produce fast to the cars. And I'm going to try to get the Buffalo and Lake Huron line to come through here and Ayr. Look how my village would grow then."

"Too much trouble getting the engines up and down the hill, but it's worth a try. Well, time to tell George to put the horses to the carriage and call Juliet."

"I don't like it, Asa," Juliet said as the horses climbed the hill out of the valley. "Harriet doesn't look too well. I think moving will be hard on her. The house they have is big enough."

"Nonsense. She'll love a bigger house. More room for that big family."

"More steps, too. Four storeys!"

"Don't worry, my dear. They don't have to cook in the cupola."

8

The wheat was in and threshed and sold. On the first day of September the carriage would be ready to be picked up in Ayr. The secret had been kept so well that neither Harriet nor Roseltha had any suspicion of the surprise in store.

"Think we'll visit Asa and Juliet in Paris towards the end of the week if the weather looks right," announced Enos carelessly a few days before the end of August. "Get your Sunday-go-to-meetin' clothes ready."

Roseltha began to sparkle with the thought that she could visit the bonnet shop on the main street as well as dine in Uncle Asa's lovely dining-room that overlooked the river. "It'll be a tight squeeze with us all in the surrey," she said, "and I hope it doesn't rain."

Friday morning, combed and polished, the boys settled themselves innocently in the surrey. Big brother Alfred poked young Newton in the ribs to stop his giggling. Over the bridge and up the hill they went, the grass on the roadsides bright with dew, the crispness of early morning in the air. Past the quarter town line, on to the town line between Blenheim and Dumfries townships they went, but turned north to Ayr instead of south to Paris.

"What are you doing, father?" said Roseltha, almost seizing the reins to turn the horses.

"What are you doing, pa?" chimed in Jasper and Alonzo, stifling laughter.

"I've a little errand in Ayr and then we can take the Back Road and the Keg Lane Road to Paris. Won't take much longer."

"Too bad," said Daniel, "I was hoping we could go by the Crooked S road. Maybe we can come back that way."

"Or else by the Alps Road where we go down and up and down and up," added Jasper, putting in his two-bits worth to the deception.

"Don't be silly. That's out of our way."

The horses began to trot along the town line, better kept than the eighth concession. A mile along, they crossed the Nith again and drove through the sun-dappled, cedar-lined road on the ridge above it till they crossed the bridge into town.

"Now where are you taking us?" Harriet was anxious to reach Paris and stop lolly-gagging around.

"Hold your horses. We'll only be a minute now." Enos turned a corner with a flourish and stopped in front of the carriage works.

"Look at that carriage sitting beside the road, lined with red velvet." Harriet was a little envious in spite of herself.

"Want to sit in it for a minute? Weir won't mind."

Enos put his hands around Harriet's small waist and swung her and then Roseltha to the ground. "Come on, don't be afraid." He took his wife's hand. "Just put your foot on the step and up you go. My, but you look nice there. You, too, Roseltha."

Harriet and Roseltha spread their skirts and clasped their hands in their laps, enjoying the sensation of sitting in a carriage. Then they stroked the red velvet lovingly. The boys could not keep quiet any longer. "It's ours, it's ours. Surprise, surprise."

"You're fooling us. You wouldn't fool us, would you, Enos?"

Enos jumped in between his wife and daughter, knocking their bonnets crooked. "It's true, it's ours. We've no coachman like Asa but the carriage is ours. We're driving to Paris in it. I've hired another horse and we'll pick up the surrey tomorrow."

Roseltha handed her mother a bouquet of toadflax and purple asters that she had gathered by the roadside while the horses were being hitched. "Flowers to celebrate. These will have to do."

"They're beautiful. I hope we always have flowers to go with the carriage." Harriet pulled out a toadflax and set it saucily in Enos' buttonhole. "Thank you, my dearest Enos."

"Alfred, you drive. Daniel, get up front with him and the rest come under the top with us." The carriage rolled off. The exuberant boys began to improvise a song.

> "Yankee Doodle went to town
> In a brand new carriage
> All the girls they looked at him
> And then they thought of marriage."

"Let's see how she rolls when we gallop. Paris, here we come."

They reached Paris a little faster than usual. "Sorry the horses are in a bit of a lather, George," Enos said to Asa's coachman. "Better rub them down and blanket them for a bit. Now, let's show the carriage to Asa."

When dinner was finished, the young ones were excused from the table as the grown-ups drank second cups of tea. "Come and look in the store windows with me, Alfred," coaxed Roseltha, swinging her bonnet by the ribbons and turning her oldest brother down the hill into the town.

Thirteen year old Alonzo wandered across the road to look at the cobblestone houses that an American mason from Rochester had built. He liked their neat appearance. One of the houses had a cobblestone wall around the garden like his Uncle Asa's. He heard a strange chanting coming from beyond it and then he saw a girl hopscotching along the garden path beside the hollyhocks in time to her words.

"Persicos," she hopped her feet together. "Odi," she hopped her feet apart. "Puer," together. "Apparatus," apart.

Then her words became recognizable. "Bring me a chop and a couple of potatoes." Four more hops with that line too.

Then strange words again, "Displicent," hop, "nexae," hop, "philyra," hop, "coronae," hop. She paused, out of breath, and ended with a rush of words and a frenzy of jumping, her long curls bobbing, "If I can't have that, I'll have cheese and macaroni."

"What kind of crazy nut is this?" said Alonzo to himself. Then, as the girl came closer out of curiosity to see the boy leaning over the wall, he spoke to her. "What was that you were saying?"

"Oh, that. Just something I picked up in school. Guess you wouldn't know. It's Latin."

"I haven't been to school. The school's too far away. But we have a governess and I've heard her say she knows some Latin."

"We don't learn Latin now for that teacher left. He taught us some Latin roots and said that the old Romans wrote poetry as well as prose and this was a way to remember some." She rattled off, no hopping this time:

> "Persicos odi puer apparatus
> Bring me a chop and a couple of potatoes.
> Displicent nexae philyra coronae
> If I can't have that I'll have cheese and macaroni."

"I don't know what it means except that "puer" means boy and "coronae" a crown of flowers and "Persicos" is Persians that the Romans didn't like."

"Why do you bother if you don't know what it means?"

"I just like the sound of it, and it's something to hop to. I know some more too. Amo, amas, amat, amamus, amatis, amant." She hopped from one foot to the other as she chanted. "They're verbs."

"What do they mean?"

"Ha, ha, won't tell. Do you live around here?"

"No, we're just visiting Uncle Asa. I have to go now. I see George harnessing the horses. That's our new carriage, red velvet lined."

"Oh-h, it looks nice. Wish we had one. What's your name?"

"Alonzo. What's yours?"

"Leonora. You can call me Lee."

"Goodbye, Lee." Alonzo ran across the road, stubbing his toe on a stone. "My turn to ride up front."

Enos tipped his hat grandly as they drove off, not trying to conceal his pleasure in the carriage. Harriet looked back at Asa's house, shining white with its stucco-over-board finish, the cobblestone wall around it setting it off. "What kind of house is our new one going to be?"

"It'll be brick, red brick from the Drumbo brickyard. I'll have the foundation dug next month ready to begin building in the spring. Harding Hall, here we come. Giddy-ap, Phoenix, giddy-ap."

Chapter 2

Harding Hall

In Blenheim Township, Canada West*, his golden wheat turned into cash at the peak of the boom caused by the Crimean War, Enos Harding began to build his house. Brick by rosy-coloured brick the walls of the big house were going up. It had no southern-style pillars like brother Asa's house in Paris. It was Georgian with casement windows and a centre recessed doorway surrounded by glass lights. People came from miles around to see the brick house that was a novelty in this township, for many still lived in log cabins and even a frame house was considered a sign of prosperity. They slowed their horses to a walk as they rounded the corner and leaned from under the buggy tops to peer upward at the third floor semi-circular windows in the wide gables, and the crowning glory of the cupola. Privately, maybe enviously, some called the house Harding's Folly, but not one failed to admire.

By the time the first snow fell the house was enclosed, even to the glass in the cupola. As the winter cold gave way to March winds and the snow turned brown from the dirt blown onto it from the bared fields, Enos planned that the plastering would begin in April. As each room was finished, its fireplace was lit to assist the drying; and when the windows could be opened the sickly odour began to dissipate. In August 1856 the Hardings moved in. The furniture was in place, with the new Jacques and Hay suite in the parlour and upstairs a new bedroom suite for the master and mistress. The old fourposter with the ends of branches sticking out to

*Ontario was called Canada West from 1841 to 1867 when four provinces united to form the Dominion of Canada.

be used as pegs for clothes was relegated to the third floor attic for Sadie.

But there was no staircase, for it was no common staircase that Enos had in mind for his house. It must be spiral, curving right to the cupola. Night after night the family climbed a ladder to the second storey bedrooms and Sadie climbed another to the third while Enos waited to find a carpenter who could fashion it. No local carpenter would undertake the job.

A year later a millwright from Brantford stopped in; said he could build the staircase, use dovetail and dowels, all wood, no nails. He'd use cherrywood for the bannister and pine for the rest. At times the whole family watched with awe as he cut and steamed and measured and fitted until the stairway was finished to the first storey. On that day Harriet walked proudly up the stairs and instead of having to go through one bedroom to get to another she could walk around the circular hallway and enter each bedroom separately.

"I've never told you, Enos," she confided that night, "that I've wanted this spiral staircase as much as you. My grandmother Elizabeth in New Jersey lived in a house with a circular staircase. She used to tell us that she housed General George Washington and some officers during part of the Revolutionary campaign, and General Bray, who collected boats for them to cross the Delaware, was a cousin by marriage. She said that their swords sometimes clanked against the balusters if they came running down."

"You've been keeping secrets from me, Harriet."

"No, I just didn't want to raise my hopes in case the stairs couldn't be built your way and the way I wanted them too." The dying fire spoke softly to itself as they slid contentedly into sleep.

The day came when the completed staircase spiralled four storeys up, unfolding like a flower as it rose. The whole family gathered to celebrate. From the ground floor hall they took turns peering up the twisting newell post to the ceiling in the cupola. From the cupola, where the balustrade curved around in a wide concluding flourish, their gaze reached straight as a plumb line four storeys down. They looked out to the north over the willows where they could see the cedars where Black Creek gurgled through the swamp. They looked to the south where the village was already taking shape, where the roof of the sawmill lay long and low, and the foundation for a one-room school was already laid. Then down they all raced to gather at the melodeon.

The sound of their singing floated upward through the house like a benison. "O Beulah Land, sweet Beulah Land." The song echoed their earthly happiness as the darkness of a late spring night closed around them.

"Time for bed, Jasper and Newtie."

"Don't forget that *Uncle Tom's Cabin* book, Jassie," Newton whispered. "Shove it under your jacket. We can read it in bed."

The boys bounded up the stairs. Jasper went up with his hand on the bannister on the wide inside tread of the steps. Newton scrambled up the hazardous narrow side.

Harriet heard subdued noises from their bedroom. "Daniel, run up and see what those boys are doing. They should be asleep."

Daniel took the steps two at a time. "Come on, you two, blow out that candle. It's dangerous to read that way."

"Don't blow it out, don't. We have to find if Eliza gets across the river with her little boy. They'll take him from her and sell him south if they catch them."

"She gets across. I've read the whole book. Bet you cry when you get to the part about little Eva. Now settle down. You can read some more tomorrow."

The ties that bound this family together were close and loving but the parents knew that the children could not be held at home forever helping in the mill and store. The family was maturing and their ideas were beginning to diverge. Roseltha was twenty-one with beaus clustering around. Alfred at eighteen was already a man. Enos regarded him critically, thinking, "A handsomer lad never walked, but he's dreamy, like his mother. Loves his Bible. Memorizes whole chapters. Would make a good minister, but a minister's life is a hard one. I should know, for my father was an itinerant one and if Preacher Harding hadn't had more irons in the fire than the Bible—like boiling salt or processing potash—we'd have gone without pretty often."

He continued his assessment of his family. "Daniel's getting restless, wants more schooling, and with Sarah gone to be a governess in Hamilton after the new school opened here, he's at a standstill.

"Alonzo's voice has already changed. He'll be wanting to strike out somewhere, although he likes the mill. He's fifteen, too old to be in the little schoolhouse another year.

"Jasper—let's see, he's nearly fourteen and still a harum-scarum, and Newton at ten is twin to a grasshopper. Well, I'll let things ride for a time. Plenty of work for everyone here, although now that the Crimean War ended in February, my wheat may be hard to sell and there's bound to be some kind of slump."

It was Daniel who made his wishes known first. "I'd like to be a teacher. I want to go to the Normal School* in Toronto."

Harriet was startled, for the announcement had come rather suddenly. She tried a delaying tactic. "How do you know they'll accept you?"

"I've found out what the qualifications are. I met a fellow in Ayr last week who's going. You have to be sixteen, know how to read with expression, write legibly, employ the four simple rules of arithmetic, and be of good character. I was seventeen in January and I guess my character is as good as anybody's. So what's to stop me?"

"Not so fast, Daniel, how much will it cost?" asked Enos.

"Just room and board. The tuition and books are free and the school helps to find us a boarding-house."

"Toronto is so far away. There's a county board that will qualify you to teach in the county." Harriet was loathe to lose her son.

"But mother, I might want to teach outside Oxford County. When I get a Grade A certificate I can earn $320 a year and there might not be a position in this county. If I go to the Normal School of Upper Canada I can teach anywhere in the province." It seemed that Daniel had all the answers.

"We want the best for you, my dear. Better send for an application form." In her heart Harriet almost wished he might not qualify, then she thought, "When he gets his certificate, maybe he could teach right here in the new school."

Daniel was accepted. The next term at the Normal School would begin in May and run till November.

There was a flurry of preparation and then Daniel's trunk was hoisted into the surrey. "If it weren't for the trunk, we'd take you to the cars in style in the carriage."

As the big black engine with red and green stripes followed by canary yellow cars smoked into the Great Western railway station at Princeton, Enos thought scornfully, "It looks like a circus. If I had anything to do with the railway, I'd order less gaudy colours."

Daniel trembled a little as he clutched his carpet bag. "Shut your eyes till the engine's passed so you won't get any cinders in them," warned his mother, squeezing her own to fight back the tears, as she clung to her son's arm.

"Oh, mother, I'm too big for that now," said Daniel, squeezing nevertheless.

---

*The former name for Teachers' College.

16

The conductor placed a stool on the platform to help the passengers step up. Daniel waved from the window. The great shafts on the engine wheels began their slow revolutions. He saw Phoenix paw and whinny uneasily. His mother and Roseltha fluttered their handkerchiefs, close to tears. Enos looked stern, Alfred and Alonzo a trifle envious. Jasper and Newton turned cartwheels on the platform and shouted, "Yahoo". The train speeded up and Daniel was off into the world on his own.

"Dear mother and father," he wrote the second Sunday after his arrival, "I am becoming used to Toronto, although when I stepped off the cars at the station I felt bewildered. It is easier to become lost on city streets than in the woods at home. Over thirty-one thousand people live here, I have been told.

"I like my boarding-house fine and think it worth the $2.50 a week you are paying for me. This afternoon after I attended church I walked across the city in an hour. It took me longer coming back for I took a few detours to see some of the landmarks. You were fortunate to buy your Jacques and Hay parlour suite when you did, mother, for the factory was burned down last year and is not yet in working condition. There are so many taverns on the main streets that I stopped counting. Never fear, I shall not enter them. I saw the place where a Mr. Hutchinson sells those new sewing machines you talked about but I understand why his business has failed. I guess women want them but can't afford to buy them.

"Much of our lesson time so far has been used to teach us grammar, spelling and mathematics so that we may teach those subjects correctly. I have not had as much difficulty as some because of the good instruction Miss Sarah gave us in the past. However, I must be careful not to be too conceited for out of 183 scholars in the first year of school only eighty-seven passed.

"Life is pretty serious here. We have to work hard but now and then we get a laugh. Last Thursday when a scholar hesitated to give an answer in class, the headmaster said, "Come, come, if you do not answer we shall think you do not know." "Sir, if I do answer then you'll know I don't know."

"I must close now and as the Sabbath is nearly over I think it would not be wrong if I should look at a reading lesson for a while before bedtime.

"Your loving son, Daniel."

Alfred watched as his mother read and re-read the letter. He wished he could have something in his life settled as Daniel had. "I'm nineteen," he scolded himself. "Father needs me, I know, but I've three younger brothers to help if I should strike out somewhere. Wish I knew where, but it's a bad time now. They say 1859 is going to be a worse year than last."

The Crimean War had ended in February 1856. Both sides had retired ungraciously, leaving memorable only the suicidal charge of the Light Cavalry Brigade into the mouths of the Russian guns, the terrible winter siege of Sevastopol and the work of a nurse named Florence Nightingale. One year and a few months later the sweet taste of the economic boom was already beginning to turn sour.

Uncle Asa and Aunt Juliet came for tea soon after Daniel had left for Toronto. Alfred stayed in the store that had recently been built a short way from the house, and Roseltha went to the parlour to help pass the cake and cookies. Alonzo took his tea out to the north verandah where he amused himself by curling his little finger away from the cup in imitation of the ladies. Jasper and Newton escaped to the barn where George, the black coachman, was no longer a curiosity but a friend.

"You were right, Asa, I may have spent a bit too much on the house, but anyway we're enjoying it," said Enos a little defensively. "Times *are* getting a little harder. Seems the only golden thing about my wheat, now that the war is over, is the colour. But I'm selling a few lots. The sawmill goes pretty steadily. We sell our surplus butter and eggs in the store or trade them for meat. The post office salary is cash. I'm doing all right."

"Anything coming in from your railway stock?"

"Last year the Great Western paid eight per cent dividend. The Grand Trunk is supposed to pay eleven and a half. Of course, they keep on building instead of paying it all out in dividends, but it's a solid investment. I guess the banks will watch their money."

"M.P. Francis Hincks promoted railroads and look where he is now— out of office and in Barbados, more or less forced to resign because of financial irregularities—which is the government term for incompetence."

"I'll hang onto the stock rather than sell right now."

"We're better off here than they are in New York," said Harriet. "I read in the paper about bread riots there not so long ago. The poor said the flour was being hoarded for speculation. Prices went sky high. They say five thousand businesses failed and more riots were prevented only by opening soup kitchens."

"The bank foreclosed on Jake Weldon's mortgage on his farm near Princeton."

"I hope it made them happy for the bailiff's sale only brought enough to cover costs." Enos was belligerent at the thought. "Don't worry about me, Asa. Maybe I did count a few chickens before they were hatched but I'll pull through. You can't stand still in business."

There was a great commotion outside and Jasper and Newton burst into the room. "Pa, guess what we just saw."

"Boys, boys, don't be so rambunctious. Calm down."

"Ma," shouted Newton, "I was walking past the field where we put the pigs yesterday, that low place with rocks where the rattlesnakes sun. The big black pig rooted up against a snake. The snake reared and rattled but the pig didn't care. It just walked round and round till the snake nearly went crazy. Then it pounced and smashed it to death with its feet. I saw it myself and so did Jassie."

"Heavens to Betsy, let's leave the pigs in that field till the rattlers are cleaned out," said Harriet. "I'm always afraid when I go into our garden that I'll meet one. Have another cookie, both of you. You deserve it."

Next morning as Alfred sorted the mail there came another letter from Daniel.

"Dear mother and father, Already a third of my time at Normal School has passed. I'm still liking it. This is the sixth year that the school has operated in this building. Before 1852, the year it opened, classes were held in old Government House, corner of King and Simcoe streets and the Model School was in the former stables. The first year, they say one young man named Edward Dewart was so anxious to become a teacher that he walked one hundred miles from his home in Peterborough. There are women here too. I understand that the Normal School is the first public institution in Canada West to admit women to higher education. This will please you, mother, for you have always maintained that in the sight of the Lord women are as worthy of education as men.

"There are seventy-five scholars this term, forty-two men and thirty-three women. Yes, father, I may be only seventeen at home but here they call me a man. I think some rules are too strict, for men and women are not allowed to mingle. The women sit on one side of the classrooms and the men on the other, but sometimes notes are passed around in spite of the rules. One young woman recognized a man who had come from her old home in Argylleshire, Scotland. They wanted desperately to talk to each other. Mr. Robertson, the headmaster, gave them permission to meet in his office. There was great glee among the scholars to hear that they spoke in the Gaelic which Mr. Robertson could not understand.

"I study, study, study grammar and mathematics and seem to be doing very well. We have little time for levity but last Hallowe'en they say three young women decided to play a prank. They dressed up in cloaks to which they had sewn cabbages for heads which made them appear faceless. After dark they walked out hoping to frighten people. Who should they meet but Mr. Robertson. When they saw who it was they fled shrieking to their boarding-house. A few Sundays later they received an invitation to dine with Mr. Robertson and his family. When the cover was removed from the soup tureen, there was a head of cabbage, boiled whole. Mr. Robertson's eyes twinkled merrily as he carved it, pretending not to observe the blushes of the three young women.

"I'm already wondering where I'll be teaching when I finish in November. I like Toronto but I miss you all. What mischief has Newton been up to lately?

"Your affectionate son, Daniel."

The bad times after the war's end were worsening. In spite of his confident talk to his brother, Enos was more than a trifle worried about his prospects. People were saying that soon you would have to use a search warrant to find a dollar in Canada West. Some of his merchant friends were reverting to barter but, Enos told himself, it doesn't do to put all the blame on postwar depression after the Crimea. There've been wars before and people have come through the depression afterwards. I'll just sit tight. Wonder what Silas will say about times in Kentucky when he comes for his visit.

Silas Harding, Enos' oldest brother, had returned to the States to make his living after their father had brought the family to Canada in 1826 in search of land nearer than the Alleghanies. Silas was doing very well running stage coach lines and mail routes. He brought presents for his niece and nephews. Newton's gift was a pair of red cowboy boots.

"Quick, let me try them on." He pushed and tugged. "I can't get them on. They're too small," he wailed for he wanted them so much.

"Never mind, Newton, at least Uncle Silas didn't forget you, and you can show them to your friends anyway. Tell us about your journey, Silas."

"I travelled from Lexington to Cincinnatti by stage. Then I took a canal boat to the terminus of the Miami canal near Sandusky. There I took the regular boat across Lake Erie to Port Stanley where I sent a telegram to Princeton for you to meet me there two days later."

20

"What a lot of trouble you had, but we're very glad to see you."

"I rather enjoyed the trip, seeing the country and meeting people, and being back home. How is business in Canada West now, Enos? There was gloomy talk as I waited in Princeton. I could likely put you in touch with something good in Kentucky."

"Silas, come into the hall with me. You see that coat of arms above the front door? That's the Queen's coat of arms. "Dieu et mon droit" it says, even if I have trouble pronouncing it. I don't want to change the Union Jack for the Stars and Stripes. I know our family came from the States and we're still called Dirty Yanks by the U.E.L.'s* but thank the Lord there aren't too many of them around here. You may be doing all right in Kentucky but don't forget the Bread Riots in New York. There are more hard times in the States than here."

"You might try lumbering some place else. Not too many trees left here in Oxford County but I saw some fine pine stands near Port Stanley. Another passenger said the pine was even better around Walsingham Township a little to the east. The pine is straight and tall and spaced well. Easy to cut and not too many lumber mills either, he said. Deblacquey's is the biggest, he told me. And believe it or not, we saw some dogwood with leaves turning red. Didn't think there would be any this far north."

"That part of the province is the farthest south in Canada, the same latitude as California. Maybe I could try lumbering there, Silas. I'd like to try a steam sawmill. You can't depend on water power. The Nith here is low part of the summer and sometimes it's hard to get up a head of water strong enough to run the mill. I saw a steam sawmill in London a few months ago. I'll travel with you as far as Walsingham on your way back to Kentucky and look it over. You said that you would return by way of Detroit instead of crossing the lake."

"I hear feeling between slave states and free is becoming more bitter." This was Harriet's concern when thinking of the land to the south of them. "There was a court case a little while ago that said negroes were so inferior to whites that they had no rights that the white man was bound to respect. I disagree. In the sight of God, I say there is no colour to a man's soul. In the sight of God all souls are the same." Harriet's large, expressive eyes flashed as she spoke.

"Yes, feeling between slave and free states is becoming more bitter and I don't know how it will end. As a Kentuckian I'm somewhat in the middle as far as location goes. Henry Clay, an Ohio Representative, is

---

*United Empire Loyalists who left the Thirteen Colonies during the revolution.

21

definitely anti-slavery. He's Speaker of the House. And a little while ago when one of the Illinois Republican candidates for the Senate was campaigning, he said he did not believe that a government could endure half slave and half free."

"Who was that?"

"A man named Abraham Lincoln. I think things will turn out all right if we just keep calm."

Enos was never one to take too long to make up his mind. "I think I'll go as far as Detroit with you, Silas, on your way back. I'd like to see that pine in Walsingham but I'll go a little farther to the settlements where the escaped negroes have been living. They call them Dawn and Buxton. How would you like that, Harriet?"

"That would please me, Enos. I'd like to know more about them. I've heard that the negroes are so happy when they cross the border that they kiss the ground of freedom. You know, Silas, this country banned slavery in its very first parliament; way back in 1793, I think it was."

Silas broke in. "I've no slaves myself. My negroes are free men, but they can be uppity if you give them a chance."

"Nobody is perfect, Silas. I'm uppity too sometimes. Ask Enos."

Alfred came in from the post office. "Here's a letter from Daniel. Maybe it will say when he's coming home."

Harriet seized the envelope. "Dear mother and father, I am well and hope you are too. Our days are long. It is a good thing that one day has been set aside for the Sabbath otherwise I am certain that the school would have classes on all seven days. On Sunday afternoons some of us go walking. I have twice seen the fire reels rushing by with bells clanging and horses galloping. The firehall is between Toronto and Church streets on the north side of Adelaide. There is a library funded by the Mechanics' Institute on the second floor of the Court House at Church and Adelaide. Once I went into the library though I am not a member. Members pay five shillings a year. It must be wonderful to belong to it for they have a vast number of books. It made me realize how little I know even though I am nearly qualified to teach others.

"I see a number of negroes on the streets here, and one named James Rapier was attending the Normal School at the beginning of the term. Unfortunately he had to drop out for lack of money, but as he is a determined person I am sure he will finish somehow. He says that negro children share the same schools in Toronto as white children but they are segregated in Chatham and Windsor. He wants to teach in his home town, Buxton. He says it is true that negroes are not slaves in Canada but neither are they entirely free if they cannot attend the same schools.

"I am looking forward to having a school of my own and hope to obtain one in Blenheim township. I know that you are satisfied with the teacher in the new Harding school and I shall have to go farther away to obtain one. I am employing my time diligently so that I may be as good a teacher as possible and make you proud of me. I can hardly wait to be home. Only two more weeks. Why not meet me and my teaching certificate with the carriage?

Affectionately, Daniel"

Harriet smiled as she folded the letter. "I'll be so glad to have Daniel home again." As she gathered the teacups she burst into song:

> "This is my Father's world
> And to my listening ears
> All nature sings and round me rings
> The music of the spheres."

"You'd better let me tidy up, mother," said Roseltha. "You're so happy you might forget and feed the cream to the cat."

"That's an idea! Here, Chippy, why shouldn't you be happy too?" And Harriet emptied the cream pitcher into the cat's dish, humming to herself.

As soon as Daniel was back in Harding Hall he waved his certificate at them jubilantly. "You should have heard the poem that was read at the closing exercises. I memorized part of it.

> Learning then was fortune's favour,
>   to the poor by fate denied;
> Now the gates of Truth and Knowledge
>   unto all stand open wide;
> And the poor man's boy, with only
>   honest heart and brain,
> May evince his native kingship
>   and the highest place attain.

So you see, mother, now that I am a teacher I can teach others to better themselves."

"Ignorance enslaves but knowledge emancipates. That I believe," said Harriet.

"Now you can look for a school," Enos added, "Maybe there will be some openings when the new term begins after Christmas."

A few days later Enos accompanied Silas as far as Port Burwell and then hired a horse to take him to St. Williams and farther north into the township. There he found 750 acres with Venison Creek flowing through it before it joined Big Creek that flowed into Lake Erie. The creek in spring was big enough to float logs and squared timber down

23

to the wharf on the lake. The rest of the year the slabs and edgings would furnish power for the steam sawmill Enos had already made up his mind to erect. There was only one other steam sawmill in the township. The rest were water power operations doing mainly local business, for they were dependent on the vagaries of the weather. With a mill run by steam Enos would have enough lumber for export. George Reade, the customs officer in Port Rowan, told him that close to fourteen million board feet of lumber and twenty-five million feet of logs and spars had been shipped through that one port alone the previous year. There was good communication from Port Burwell across the lake to Cleveland, and from Port Stanley steamers went regularly on alternate days.

Enos' mind moved fast. He could sell his lumber across the lake in Cleveland, duty free, for the recent Reciprocity Treaty with the States meant free trade for ten years. Cleveland's population was increasing daily. He was told that a minor building boom there meant a market hungry for lumber.

Quickly he decided to run two operations. He would keep Harding as his headquarters and travel to Walsingham when necessary. Alfred could run the sawmill in Walsingham while his father was in Harding. Daniel could obtain a school in Walsingham and Roseltha could keep house there for her brothers. Alonzo, who had stopped attending the one-room school in Harding, could help in whichever place he was needed. Jasper and Newton were old enough to assist in the store and post office in Harding after school. It would not be difficult to manage operations in both places.

He made a quick trip to see the negro settlements at Buxton and Dawn while he thought things through. Then he returned to Walsingham and put a down payment on 750 acres in the north of the township near Venison Creek. He could hardly wait to tell Harriet as he caught the train for home.

He hired a driver at the station in Drumbo and urged the horse to go faster. With a flourish he drew up in front of his big house, his beautiful house, his dream come true. He leaped out of the buggy and bounded through the recessed doorway as exuberantly as if he were one of his own sons. No depression can keep me down, he said to himself, and wait till I tell Harriet that I saw a shingle-making machine in the negro settlement at Buxton—why couldn't I have one too and ship shingles as well as lumber to Cleveland? And that I listened to a debate there on the question, "Which have suffered most from the hands of the white man—the Indians or the coloured men?" And that I met her beloved Uncle Tom too.

The house that was usually bustling was unnaturally quiet. As soon as he was through the door, the stillness hit Enos like a slap in the face. Where was Harriet? Why didn't she come to greet him? What was their bed doing downstairs in the north parlour instead of upstairs in their bedroom? Who was coughing uncontrollably?

Roseltha glided from the parlour into the hall. "Sh-h, mother's sick. It's diptheria. They had it at the Smith's over on the quarter town line and she caught it when she took them soup."

He went in beside the bed. The only times his wife had ever been confined to bed before, there had been a baby beside her in the crook of her arm. She lay alone now, inert, propped up on pillows, face flushed, her long braids crooked on the covers. "Enos," she started to say but the coughing seized her. The paroxysm nearly strangled her till it ceased with her exhaustion. She did not dare try to speak again, just reached out her hand. No soothing syrup could cope with the galloping diptheria that was slowly and inevitably strangling her. There was no medicine known to man to stay its progress.

Three days later Harriet Harding was dead. Her children moved about the house like shadows. Neighbours brought in food. Her bed was moved upstairs again and a coffin replaced it in the parlour. They bathed her face with saltpetre to keep its colour. On the third day the Baptist minister from Drumbo came to take the service.

The family sat unbelievingly in the parlour while friends gathered in the hall and living room and outside as well. The church in the wildwood was still only half-finished. The minister spoke of the virtues of the dead one. He prayed for the consolation of those remaining. "The Lord giveth and the Lord taketh away." Then the coffin was closed.

It was carried out and laid in the black hearse behind black horses. The family climbed into the red velvet lined carriage behind it. A long procession made its way to the cemetery on top of a rise of land overlooking the river. "Ashes to ashes and dust to dust."

When the buggies and surreys had departed, old Jake climbed over the fence from the field where he had stood quietly chewing a straw while the minister said the benediction and the family struggled to contain their sobs. Bandy-legged, unhurried, he shovelled in the earth, humming snatches of a tune. "O Beulah Land, sweet Beulah Land." The earth thumped in. "For this is heaven's border-land." His Adam's apple bobbed. He stopped for breath and thought, "If anyone should reach the glory-shore, it would be Harriet Harding. But I think they'd rather have her back with them than up there waiting, and her only thirty-seven years old."

The red velvet lined carriage drew up in front of Harding Hall. Neither house nor carriage gave any enjoyment now. Enos helped Roseltha step down. Mechanically they greeted people and choked down some funeral food. Then they closed the door on the last to leave.

No woman was singing as they were left alone. The big clock at the foot of the stairs boomed the time, one tone for each of the four storeys. The circling stairway lifted the sound, one, two, three landings upwards. Aimlessly the family looked about, then like the sound they began to climb till they stood in the cupola, level with the trees, and looked over to the hill they had just left with its lonely mound beneath the chilling sun.

Enos jingled the coins in his pocket and whistled tunelessly through his teeth. Roseltha let the tears roll down her cheeks unheeded. Alfred put his arm around her shoulders. The younger boys shuffled restlessly.

Then Enos spoke. "I don't think I can stay here without her. We'll rent the house and business here and go to Walsingham. We'll start new there."

No one was singing in the house as they circled their way downwards.

Chapter 3

Walsingham Township

Early in the new year of 1859 Enos, Alfred and Daniel set off for
Walsingham Township to begin organizing the operation there. Roseltha
remained in Harding to look after her three younger brothers and the
house till it was time to rent it. Lonesome as the house was now, she
dreaded the move. In miles it was not so far, only seventy-five or eighty.
In strangeness it was worlds away. When she went into the kitchen in
the morning to stir up the fire in the stove for making breakfast, she took
no pleasure in the frost pictures on the windows traced by the zeroing
cold.

Now it was she, not her mother, who trimmed the rind off the side of
breakfast bacon and dropped the bits to the tortoise-shell tabby-cat
mewing eagerly at her feet. Now it was she who struggled with the
washing, for Sadie had gone to work for Uncle Asa, knowing that the
family could not take her to Walsingham with them.

"Pull the tub-stand over here and carry the boilers in from the stove,"
she called to Alonzo and Jasper from the back kitchen. "And then help
Newton shovel a path under the clothes-lines so that I can hang out the
sheets. It's going to be a sunny day."

"Aw, Rose, they only freeze stiff as boards. Why don't you dry them
inside?"

"Freezing keeps them white. Now please do as I ask you."

Sometimes at night, when her work was finished, Roseltha wrote in
her diary. It was too cold to go up to the cupola where she sometimes
went for privacy in the summer. She snatched a few moments to write
when her brothers were not around to tease her. They minded her
pretty well, but she was only twenty-two and they were sixteen, thirteen,
and eleven, each with ideas of his own. She wrote:

27

"If only mother were here. I feel so inadequate. She was so remarkable as she lessened my father's cares and influenced and encouraged and restrained my brothers. Oh! That I could supply to them the place of elder sister and mother. Please God, I will try.*

Alonzo's job was to mind the mill, and Jasper the store and post office. Newton was attending school. The teacher was a young woman who was good with grammar, spelling and reading, but poor in arithmetic. Newton was poor in spelling but good at arithmetic and the two did not agree too well at times. He came stamping home one day at noon.

"What's the matter, Newtie?" asked Roseltha.

"She gives us questions that are too easy. Any stupid could do them."

"Maybe you're just conceited."

"I am not. Listen to this one. If A can saw a log in three hours, and B can saw a log in two hours, and C can saw a log in one hour, how long will it take them to saw a wagon-load of twenty-five logs?"

"Well, couldn't you do it?"

"It was too easy. I didn't even try. I told her if A and B were so slow, why not let C do it?"

Roseltha burst out laughing in spite of herself. It was good to laugh again. She tried to mollify the situation. "Now you put yourself in your teacher's position. A teacher in a one-room school who has to teach everything to all ages has a pretty big job to do. Eat your potatoes."

Newton swallowed his potatoes, grabbed a tart and flinging himself out of the door, pulled on his coat and toque as he went, his breath blowing white around him. "He'll be cooled down by the time he gets to school," said Alonzo. "Come on, Jas, we should be back at work."

In mid-February Enos returned from Walsingham to see how things were going in Harding. He travelled on the Great Western Railway, paying his way on the road whose stock he held. As he looked around at his fellow passengers, he thought, "Maybe now I'll get some returns from my stock for the train is filled. Just my luck I couldn't get the railway to go through Harding."

---

* *Passages taken from original diaries and letters will be identified by italics.*

As he walked up the main street of the village after a visit to the hotel to see what travellers were there, he could see through a break in the willows the noon train crossing the trestle bridge over Black Creek where in summer the children picked watercress and pulled sunfish out of the shallows. At night the moaning whistles of the freight trains reminded him how close he had been to having the railway bring the growth he hoped for when he planned the village. Because of one railway mile of distance it was unlikely that Harding would ever be the thriving town he had foreseen on paper. And now he was moving away.

But that was not all. He was beginning to think that dividends from his railway stock were just as much a dream as his town. The Great Western was in financial trouble and so was the Grand Trunk. The previous year the government had asked for sixteen million dollars of public money to save the Grand Trunk. The Toronto *Globe* would soon call the continual requests "the annual thunderbolt." Where was all the money going? Not into railway ties; into someone's pocket, you can bet. Back in Walsingham Township they had formed a corruption committee to investigate the frauds and jobbery between politicians and contractors. Negotiations for road contracts were often questionable enough, Enos knew, but were nothing compared with railroads. He resented having tied up money in unsaleable railway stock but had to content himself when people came into the store complaining about hard times with tirades against "this darn depression triggered by the end of the Crimean War."

The financial crisis was bringing forth all kinds of criticism of the government. The Reformers had held a Great Reform Convention in Toronto the previous November to popularize their panacea which was the confederation of five provinces. The Clear Grits favoured 'Rep by Pop' to redress the discrepancy between the populations of Canada East and West. Enos had chatted with "Wandering Willie" MacDougall, elected for the North Riding of Oxford County. The former Grit was now on the editorial staff of George Brown's Reform paper in Toronto, the *Globe*. Some were saying that the cause of the current depression was the releasing of the clergy reserves money into the hands of the munici-palities—too much too quickly had led to too much expenditure on credit. At mail time little knots of men congregated in the post office as Enos sorted mail. Politics was a consuming subject.

"Lots of things need changing. Now take this so-called union between Canada West and East. First they tried to shunt the capital between Toronto and Kingston, then it was Toronto and Montreal, or Quebec. Who'd try to run a business by moving offices like that—only a durn-fool government."

"It's these confounded coalitions that make me mad—both sides trying to lick the other's boots. What do you think of the latest Macdonald one?"

"I'm sick of coalitions. Baldwin-LaFontaine, Hincks-Morin, Macdonald-Taché, Macdonald-Cartier—it's like trying to team a trotter and a pacer."

"Yah, Canada East and Canada West—they're still French and English, as far apart as they were before the Union and as far apart as slave states and free."

"They're beginning to say it would be better if the Maritimes would join in. Then there'd be five provinces instead of two."

"You mean there'd be three more to squabble instead of two. Why not be just Upper Canada. Now that the Family Compact's dead, it ought to be all right."

"We need Rep by Pop. And vote by ballot. I'm a Grit. We say that the last election rolls weren't made up properly. I hear that in Canada East in the last election they counted votes from Julius Caesar, George Washington and Judas Iscariot."

A roar of laughter met the last sally. Enos put in, "That might happen in Canada East, but there wasn't any hanky-panky like that around here."

"No, just railroads. They say there's as much water in railroad stock as there is in Lake Erie."

Enos finished pigeon-holing the letters. The men picked up their mail, pulled their scarves tight and went out into the brilliant cold.

The bell over the door tinkled and a young man entered. It was Will Goble of Goble's Corners, eight miles distant on the Governor's Road east of Woodstock. His parents had come from the same northern New York community as the Hardings. In the new country the two families continued their friendship through mutual respect and various church gatherings. Their twenty-two year old son, Will, with his sandy hair and freckled face, his easy manner and good-humoured smile was always a welcome visitor.

"Hello, Will, what brings you so far on this cold day? What's the weather like around Goble's Corners?"

"Cold, cold." Will walked to the stove, rubbing his hands together. "But the old dogskin coat works pretty well for a drive in the cutter. Little hard on the face, that's all. How're things in Walsingham?"

"I left Alfred to supervise three teams of horses. The men are cutting and skidding logs ready for the sawmill when we get it going in the

30

spring. Daniel has been lucky. The teacher in the Houghton school took sick at Christmas and he was asked to take over."

"Lucky for him and lucky for them. No reason why he shouldn't do a first-rate job." Will shifted on his feet and cleared his throat. "Must be hard for Roseltha here with you away most of the time and Mrs. Harding gone."

"It's hard for all of us, Will." Enos looked away for a moment as he swallowed the lump in his throat. "But Roseltha is doing a fine job of keeping house. Why don't you go in and cheer her up. It's Tuesday. She'll be ironing today."

Without bothering to wonder if Enos had read his mind, Will was out of the store and ringing the bell at Harding Hall before his breath had time to disappear behind him.

"A good lad," noted Enos. "Nice that our folks know each other. Baptists like us, too." He resumed working on his account books, then looked up as a thought came to him. "I wonder now? Hmm, well, I won't put any stones in his way."

Roseltha blushed with pleasure when she saw Will. "Come into the kitchen. It's warmer than the parlour on a day when there's a north wind."

She almost wished her father would not come in to share the conversation, but come he did and talked business with Will. "I might as well have kept on ironing," she raged a bit to herself as they talked, then found she was strangely tongue-tied anyway for Will was glancing her way pretty often. Her cheeks were pink as she handed him his fur hat when it was time for him to leave. "Are you sure you've enough coal oil in your lantern? It'll be dark before you get home."

After Enos returned to Walsingham, Will appeared again, going to the house first for it was Sunday.

"I'll come and help you move when you're ready," he said as he left, then jingled down the road in his cutter, leaving Roseltha with bells in her heart.

"Courting, I guess," drawled Alonzo, coming in from feeding Phoenix. "Want to use Newton for a chaperone? No one disappears faster than he does."

"You're just imagining things." Roseltha tried to be tart in her answer. Secretly she was beginning to hope that her father would be a long time finding a house in Walsingham.

As usual Enos was trying to shelter his family better than the average. There were two frame houses in Walsingham Township, the rest being log. Soon he was able to rent one of them, the storey and a half one, and before the spring melting would render the roads impassable, he and Alfred came with two teams and sleighs for whatever furniture they were not leaving for the two families who were taking over the house. They would fetch the carriage later when the roads dried.

The night before they were to leave, Roseltha and Alonzo climbed to the cold cupola to take a last look at the valley. The sun was setting with a magnificence that made her feel with the Psalmist, "My soul doth magnify the Lord." Its beauty was almost enough to cheer her. Some clouds showed a silver lining and some feathered out in red and coral.

"I wonder what the clouds would look like if you could go above them," Alonzo thought out loud. "Someday I'd like to be above the clouds. They say you can if you climb a mountain."

"Mountains are far away from here and just as far from Walsingham. What a queer idea to want to go above the clouds, but I hope you get your wish someday."

They fell silent as they watched. The silver lining faded, then the flames, then the whole sky became mauve-blue as the evening star came winking out.

"Come, let's go down before it's too dark to see. We should have brought a candle. I wish I could forget that this is our last night here and that other people are moving into our house next week. It doesn't seem right somehow."

"Never mind, Rosie," said Alonzo, "maybe there'll be a silver lining in Walsingham."

They were up at dawn to stow the furniture in the sleighs. They had barely begun when Will Goble drove up.

"Surprised to see you, Will," was Enos' remark. "Good of you to want to help."

Now that he was there, Will fetched and carried, and exchanged a few glances with Roseltha, then it was time for them all to drive away, after Will had tucked the buffalo robe around her, saying, "I'll write. Please answer my letters."

"Don't look back," Enos said as he urged the horses up the hill and out of the valley, hoping they could make it without unloading some of the heavier furniture, and looking to see if Alfred was having trouble with the second sleigh. The horses set down their heavy hoofs and strained hard.

"Good-bye, old school," chortled Newton. "I won't have to go to school in Walsingham. None close enough."

32

"Don't brag too much. I could send you to Houghton with Daniel, or else when he comes home on weekends he can set you lessons to do."

"Good-bye, River Nith," thought Alfred, looking at its frozen course. "All we have in Walsingham is Venison Creek, a poor trade. Even Big Creek isn't much better."

Roseltha looked at the far hill where her mother lay, then hung on tight as the sleigh mounted a drift and slid down the other side. "I hope spring comes early this year. Wonder what it will be like in Walsingham?"

It was not easy for the newcomers to fit into the new locality. There was a Baptist church in neighbouring Houghton Township but the community around them was largely Methodist. However the Hardings were not Hardshell Baptists too ingrown to recognize other denominations, and one night Enos, Roseltha and Alfred drove with some friends to a Methodist meeting. Roseltha described it in her diary:
May 1859:
"We drove about four miles over the wildest road I ever saw. I really enjoyed the ride. The moon and stars were very bright causing the majestic pines to cast sombre shadows. The stillness was unbroken save by the carriage wheels and an occasional remark from some of our party. "O! there is much solemn grandeur in this dim deep forest."

Alfred too was keeping a diary.
"We went yesterday evening to a noisy, crowded Methodist meeting. The house was very small and exceedingly crowded. They seemed to think God was asleep, or gone on a journey, and they must needs make a great noise to excite his attention. I do not believe in so much noise. Paul says, 'Let everything be done decently and in order.' I thought of Elijah, for it was not in the rushing wind nor in the sound of many waters, but in the 'still small voice' that he heard God speak. Yet I fain believe there were many sincere devoted hearts, earnestly seeking to know what they should do, and desirous of the favour of the High and Holy One. I fear there were too many acting from the exciting impulse of the moment, like the seed that was cast on a rock and when it sprang up it withered, for it lacked moisture."

That ended Alfred's entry, for Jasper and Newton came up with whoops of repressed spirits and took him outside to play catch.

The sawmill was now working full time. Enos had bought his coveted steam engine from a man near London who had given up his work because of illness. Hour after hour, the logs that had been skidded during the winter were sent screeching through the saws and the pile of cut lumber rose higher and higher. They had already shipped some to Thatcher & Burt, a firm in Cleveland whose business reputation Enos had investigated during a recent visit.

"There's a demand in Cleveland for shingles as well as lumber. I think I should buy a shingle-making machine too. George White and Company in London is starting to make them. They cut two hundred shingles an hour. It's silly to rely on shingling hatchets any longer," said Enos as he stirred the pot of navy beans simmering on the camp stove ready for their noon meal at the mill. Beans, Roseltha's home-made bread, and milk from their own cow kept cool in the creek, were a feast for outdoor appetites as they set their plates on the rough-hewn table.

When he had finished, Enos rose. "Think I'll go into St. Williams to get the mail this afternoon. There should be money from Thatcher & Burt for that last shipment. I'll pick up Roseltha on the way past the house. She needs a little outing. You boys keep on working."

It did not take Rose long to tidy her hair. Even St. Williams, or Walsingham as it was sometimes called, was a change after their isolated house. It was a little bigger than Harding with the usual assortment of buildings—store and post office, hotel, mill, blacksmith shop, tannery, livery stable, a bakeshop in the front of a house and an English cabinet-maker named Kirk who made furniture from the walnut and oak cut on local farms. As yet, Roseltha knew few of the people living in the houses but it was a change to be there. She listened as Enos chatted with the men in front of the store.

"Deblacquey's shipping his lumber to Windsor and Hamilton," said one.

"I'm shipping to Cleveland," said Enos firmly. "The market is there, the price is good, and when the weather's fine the boats can go straight across the lake. Save shipping costs."

"Guess you want to take advantage of this free trade the government's put over on us. Reciprocity, they call it to make it sound good."

"Why not? As long as we keep reciprocity with the States the pine trees here will help me weather the depression."

"Who cares if Harding weathers the depression?" muttered one man as he climbed into his democrat. "Trading with the damn Yankees is no good. Trade with Britain, that's what, or sell it here in Canada West."

"Father," said Roseltha as they drove away, "some people don't like you shipping to Cleveland."

"They're still living in the past. It's nearly fifty years since the American army came through here in 1813. They're just jealous of my steam engine. Can't stand anything new-fangled. Wait till they see the shingle-making machine I've made up my mind to buy. That letter held a remittance from Thatcher & Burt and an order for shingles if I can supply them. We'll use cedar from near the swamp and turn out shingles by the hundreds. You'll see."

Enos' steam engine was a portable one on skids made of squared timber with the noses shaped up in front so that it would slide over bumps. Its novelty had worn off by now but when the shingle-cutting machine arrived, neighbours gathered around to watch it perform, powered, of course, by the forty horse power steam engine. With everyone watching, it seemed to take an age to get up steam, though it was only half an hour.

"Feed some more wood into the firebox, Newton. Jump, we can't wait all day."

Newton heaved in more wood and the turn valves on the steam engine speeded up and the black balls on the demand governor started to whiz around like mad.

Alonzo was standing on the operating platform. "Close the valve, Alonzo, too much steam. Steady her down. Now she's ready."

The men had already cut a pile of eighteen-inch blocks, shingle size, so that Enos could demonstrate the cutting. "Hand me a block," he ordered, relishing the situation. "The block is on the feed rollers like this, far enough in so the teeth can catch it. Now the pawl dogs, those round teeth with ridges, roll the teeth lines forward to the saw. You see this metal frame that holds the block? This elliptical cam tips the block back and forth so that it saws the shingles thick at the top and thin at the bottom alternately." He pulled the lever to start it up and the shingles dropped down, slick as slicing bread. The sawdust went sailing down a belt away from the cutting saw to gather in a pile away from the machine.

"Jumping Jehosophat! That's pretty neat. Here, put in another." Jasper handed his father a block.

"We can fill any number of orders with this." Alfred was jubilant.

Enos set in a fresh block and became more technical in his explanation. "You see, it's elliptical control with an eccentric type of wheel."

Roseltha was fascinated by the ease with which the shingles were cut. She inhaled the fragrance of the cut cedar spreading through the sunny air. The newborn leaves cast dimpling shadows around the clearing. It was a day for happiness. "I'll just take some of these shavings to put in the blanket chests to keep away the moths," she said. "Time to get home and set the bread to rise. Too bad Daniel isn't here but he'll see the new machine when he comes home from the school next weekend."

It was lonely for Roseltha when the men were away working. She thought of Will often and cherished his letters, but was afraid to reveal what was in her thoughts. She used her diary for solace as she longed for her friends back in Blenheim Township.

"As today was Sunday Father, Newton and I went for a walk in the afternoon. We went about two miles through the woods to a Mr. Mabel's. They live in a small rough shanty in the woods. I wonder how they got in there for I could not see any way a waggon could possibly be taken in. They seem quite contented and happy. I believe there is far more happiness in some of these backwood huts than in many a stately mansion. I like the woods better than the huts. I would like a lofty Gothic castle with numberless windings and intricate labyrinths, with massive doors and gates, a dim grand irregular mass such as the Middle Ages produced in a deep forest, the winding paths and circuitous roads which none could find but those accustomed to them."

"Dear me, I might just as well wish for a castle like that as wish to be back in Harding Hall."

The woodsy isolation did not prevent the family from following the familiar routines that somehow served to fill the emptiness left by their mother's death. Every morning after breakfast they pushed their chairs back from the table for family worship before the day's work was begun. They took turns reading the day's lesson from the Bible, then knelt at their chairs as Enos prayed, remembering the mother whose sweet voice no longer sounded in the house.

Enos had fetched the melodeon on one of his journeys back to Harding to see how the rented house and mill were faring. In the evenings now Roseltha played for them to sing again:

> Safely through another week
> God has brought us on our way;
> Let us now a blessing seek,
> Waiting in His courts today.

Or perhaps the hymn would be:

> I have heard of a land on a faraway strand
> ... 'Tis a land where we never grow old.

The melodies brought comfort.

They needed comfort. A letter from Harding said that MacPherson might not want to rent the mill much longer as money was too scarce for him to make a profit. "Well, never mind, we'll get someone part time. Come on, everybody, early to bed and early to rise, makes a man healthy, wealthy and wise."

Next morning Roseltha walked part way to the mill with the men, leaving the dishes for a change. She dawdled back through the leafy summer woods, picking a few daisies and buttercups, savouring the cool shadows and the warm sunny patches. Reaching home, she drew out her diary:

I passionately love nature whether the green plain, lofty mountain, gentle rivulet or foaming cataract. All alike are beautiful—the birds tuning their sweet songs, the soft breeze whispering among the trees. Every plant and leaf seems to have a voice and they all unite in one harmonious song of praise to the Great Giver of every good and perfect Gift.

So she wrote to assuage her loneliness. She looked over what she had just written. "Mountains! You've never seen any and probably never will, but I can like the pictures I've seen of them, can't I? I can even wonder, as Alonzo did, what it might be like to go above the clouds."

She dipped hot water from the reservoir in the stove and began to wash the dishes. She did not dare write how she wished that the young man who had been springing through the door of Harding Hall before she left would come racing up the road to her now. "If I were writing to Will now, I would describe the woods to him. I would try not to say that I am often lonely and weary of the wilderness here. How I wish I could ask him to come for a visit and we could all go for a picnic to the Sand Hills. How I wish we were back in Harding where we knew everybody."

Disconsolate, she picked up some quilt patches and began to hem.

Chapter 4

The Knot In The Pine

A picnic to the Sand Hills near Lake Erie was one of the delights of several Lake Erie townships. There were the Little Sand Hill and the Big Sand Hill, but the Big Sand Hill was the more popular, for years of winds had hollowed the top into an amphitheatre that could be used for a baseball diamond. The merchants and mill-owners of Walsingham and Houghton Township where Daniel was teaching were having a Saturday picnic and baseball game there in two weeks. For the occasion, Roseltha made a new dress, white muslin sprigged with pink and red roses, and covered a parasol to match.

She was excited as her brothers hitched the horses to the carriage. "Let's pick up the mail as we go through the village."

The stage had arrived a short time before they drew up in front of the post office. A young man was standing uncertainly outside wondering if he should hire a horse or a horse and buggy at the livery stable. After a startled glance, Roseltha saw that it was Will Goble. With a cry of recognition and blushing as she put up her parasol, she was helped from the carriage and they all greeted him.

"I just suddenly made up my mind to come to see you for the weather was good. I hope you don't mind."

"Mind? We're delighted." Enos shook Will's hand heartily. "Come to the picnic with us. Put your carpet-bag here and sit beside Roseltha."

Roseltha chattered to hide her pleasure. "Isn't this a nice little village? We live a few miles north but I can tell you a bit about it. See that house? A widow named Andrew lives there. Her husband was coming home a few winters ago with a load of lumber. There was a small incline with frozen ruts and it was beginning to get so dark that he couldn't see to keep the runners in them. The sleigh overturned, pinning

39

him under the lumber and the horses went home without him, dragging the empty sleigh."

Will looked into her bright happy eyes. "Poor Mrs. Andrew. I'm glad nothing like that has ever happened to either of our families. I guess we were born lucky."

Roseltha smoothed her dress, glad there was so little room in the carriage that every bump in the road sent her a little closer to Will. She looked up at him, silent now because of her secret throughts.

Daniel looked back from the driver's seat. "You know that Laura Secord who warned the British that the Americans were going to attack at Beaver Dams? The Secords used to live here before they moved to Niagara."

"That happened over ten years before our families moved to Canada," said Will, "We're such good neighbours now that there'll never be another war between us."

"You're right there," said Enos. "Anyway it's unthinkable that brother should fight brother. I'm here in Canada and Silas is in the States. No way would I fight against a brother, no matter what our government would say."

"I agree with you, Mr. Harding."

Roseltha leaned against the red velvet cushions, drowning in contentment because her father and Will were getting along so well. They were driving down the Plank Road towards the lake. "Look up that road, Will. It's the first concession. You can't see the house but a Dr. Troyer lives there. He's a Tunkard, not a Baptist like us. He believes in witches. He sets traps to catch them in case one should come in the night."

"I hope you don't think he believes in witches just because he's a Tunkard, not a Baptist," Will bantered.

Roseltha was not to be put down. "I'm not that silly. Oh, there's Lake Erie already, Isn't it lovely, Will? So blue and sparkling."

Will leaned close. "I can see something nearer that's blue and sparkling," he said softly as he looked into eyes fringed with long dark lashes. At a loss for words, she captured a strand of brown hair caught by a breeze and tucked it into place.

"Lake Erie looks peaceful enough today," said Enos, "but it can be treacherous because of changing winds. They say that on some days when a ship goes by you can see its smoke blowing in four different directions in half an hour."

"That's a little different from rowing on the Nith river. Remember the family picnics we used to have there?" recalled Will.

"We had such good times then and mother would make a chocolate layer cake with date filling and thick icing." Roseltha's voice choked a little, so quickly she began another story about the neighbourhood as they had turned along the Broken Front Road. "If we were a little farther along, we could see Long Point. It's a great sandpit jutting several miles into the lake. It's called the graveyard of Lake Erie because the winds are always shifting its shores so sailors can't keep track of them."

Jasper leaned forward. "Right now it's an island but it used to be joined to the mainland. Five years ago, that would be in '54, a three-masted schooner was wrecked on it in a violent storm. It was loaded with lumber going from Amherstburg to the Welland Canal."

"I know the rest of that story," interrupted Newton. "Jeremiah and Abigail Becker were living in a hunting cabin near the east end of the Point but Jeremiah had gone to the mainland and Abigail was alone with the children when the storm blew up. When she saw the ship in distress, she risked her life by wading into the breakers and helping the exhausted men to shore."

Alonzo broke in. "The cook couldn't swim and they lashed him to the mast till they could rescue him in the morning."

Alfred knew more. "Queen Victoria sent Mrs. Becker a letter praising her bravery. I've seen it because she lives on the seventh concession near us. They call her the heroine of Long Point."

Enos was more practical. "The Queen sent her more than a letter. She sent her £50 and she used it to buy a farm."

They were passing the mouth of a creek. "Look, there's a muskrat," shouted Newton. "I thought they were all hunted out. Can we come back tomorrow and get it?"

"No, leave it, maybe it has babies somewhere."

"Any deer in these woods?" asked Will.

"No, not any more. No elk either."

"Any Indians?"

"No, this used to be Neutral land but the Iroquois from New York state practically wiped them out."

Roseltha had still another story to tell. "See that house over there, Will? There was a family there that stole a horse. When the owners came to search for it, the people hid it upstairs in the house. Then they couldn't get it down."

Will looked innocently into the distance where, because it was a clear day, the Ohio shore could very faintly be seen. "Must have made quite a smell if it died upstairs." In their holiday mood they all laughed at Roseltha's discomfiture.

Soon Big Sand Hill came into view on the left. The Hardings had seen the sand hill before but Will regarded it with awe. Aeons ago Lake

41

Erie and the winds had united to deposit those enormous piles of sand.

"Lucky there's no wind today to blow the sand around," said Alfred. "Now that all the trees are being cleared off, the dunes are beginning to shift. All we need is a camel to make it look like Egypt."

They left the horses under the trees, and slipping and sliding, laden with picnic paraphernalia, they joined the other picnickers at the top of the Sand Hill. Here the baseball game would be the main feature of the outing. People had played rounders till recently but now baseball was the rage. Sand Hill games were no ordinary games. Sometimes the homers hit the slopes and rolled down erratically till they were scooped up by the fielders. Luck, rather than prowess, often decided the winners, but the unpredictability only added to the fun.

"Come, Will, join the team," suggested Daniel. "You're a crack player."

"Not today. Anyway I don't belong to either township. I'll just sit here on the blanket with Roseltha and watch."

The game over, the people began to mingle. Ensign Aquila Walsh, J.P., and Walker Powell, member of parliament for Norfolk, were shaking hands all around as people settled around their baskets of food. After the Hardings had finished their meal, the men went off visiting, but Will helped Roseltha put the remaining food into the basket.

Some of Enos' business acquaintances stopped to chat. Mr. Peter Cline and his daughter Neridia lingered. Enos had met them both on several occasions. Enos regarded the daughter admiringly. "She's almost as pretty as my Roseltha, and as well-mannered. Quieter though." Then the two moved away and Enos went off. Daniel walked around with Mr. Jonathan Bridgeman, the store owner with whom he was boarding on the Lake Road South in Houghton.

Roseltha settled her skirts primly around her on the blanket but did not allow her parasol to shield her from Will's gaze. Now that they were alone, Will began to speak more openly.

"Miss Harding, you're just as pretty as I remember you." The colour rose in her cheeks.

"I've tasted your cherry pie too. Miss Harding, your cheeks are getting as red as the cherries," he teased. The colour deepened.

"Miss Harding, I hear from Jasper that your handwriting won first prize at the local fair. Maybe you could write more often to me when I return home." Roseltha drew a deep breath, too happy to flirt.

"Yes, I'll write often," she managed to say. "I'm glad you came to see us."

Will watched her thoughts beautify her face. He already knew what he wanted. "If only, on the way home in the moonlight, Roseltha and I could sit beside each other again. Maybe I could put my arm around her shoulders where no one could see. I wonder if she'd mind?"

As they drove home with the moonlight brightening the road, Roseltha sat between her father and Will. By the time they reached St. Williams, Will's arm lay along the back of the seat, and by the time they reached the house it was resting lightly on the lady's shoulders. Roseltha was not chattering now. She was too filled with wonder and contentment.

"Sir," said Will to Mr. Harding the next morning, "May I have the honour of courting your daughter?"

Enos thought of his motherless family, soon to be daughterless as well if he said yes, but he had seen the glow in his daughter's eyes. "You have my permission, William. Why not stay a couple of weeks if you can."

At the end of the two weeks Roseltha had set her wedding date for Christmas. Will would visit once a month till then. It seemed an eternity to Roseltha.

Again she resorted to her diary.

August 15, 1859. I came up to the mill about five o'clock this morning. I wish I had time and energy to take such a walk every morning. I believe it would do me good.

August 18. It is pleasant cool weather. My Forest Home is very beautiful these long bright summer days, but sometimes I get lonely and weary off here in the wilderness.

August 31. The last day of summer. This is a beautiful bright morning. All nature is uttering a morning hymn of praise to the 'Author' of so much beauty.

September passed and Will was coming for his October visit. Roseltha woke that day with the first crow of the rooster. Phoenix stamped in his stall. The birds gathering to go south began their first tentative twitters. Roseltha tied her apron and sang as she stirred the fire.

> Can she bake a cherry pie,
> Billy boy, Billy boy,
> Can she bake a cherry pie,
> Charming Billy . . .

"Singing so early, little Rosie?" Enos took the porridge spoon from her and began to stir. "When your mind is elsewhere, you might burn our breakfast. But don't stop singing."

Yes, she made for me a pie,
But she threw it in my eye,
O my Nancy tickle my fancy,
O my darling Billy boy.

Oldest brother Alfred harnessed Phoenix and he and Roseltha drove through the reddening woods to meet the stage coach. The sun itself was not more bright than the light on Roseltha's face.

"Hurry, Alfred, can't the horse go faster?"

"Not unless he turns into Pegasus, or we get him a magic carpet, and even then I don't think you'd be satisfied."

The stage drew up in a cloud of dust. Will jumped out, a great wide smile on his face. Seizing his fiancée by the waist he whirled her till her bonnet bounced off her head and hung by its ribbon. He didn't dare kiss her in public but his happiness was obvious. "Let's go," he said, "I'm starved for one of your dinners."

"We're eating later than usual, all for you, Will. How is everybody at home? Hurry, Alfred, you can talk to your friends some other time."

Phoenix set off briskly as if he were hungry too. He shied a little as a groundhog sat up on its haunches not far from the road. They drove swiftly along through scarlet maples, and poplars like great yellow candles. The leaves took their own sweet time in drifting through the golden air. "I guess we know why autumn is called 'fall' around here," Will said contentedly as he savoured the beauty of the day beside the one he loved.

"Alonzo and Jasper, help me with the dinner while Will rests after his trip," called Roseltha as they arrived at the house. Will followed her into the pantry to steal a long-awaited kiss. "Only two more months till we're married."

"Quick, someone will see us. Here, carry out the bread."

"Did you bring us any papers, Will?" asked Enos after dinner. "You know I like to see something different from the *Globe* that I subscribe to."

"Sure thing. I brought some *Leaders*. I know they're Tory and you like the Liberal papers, but that's the paper my parents get."

Alfred opened one and after a moment he exclaimed, "Listen to this. 'On one side stands the white man, dominant in his mind, his energy, his genius and his intellect. On the other the negro. He is inferior intellectually as he is aesthetically. Is it possible, is it desirable, that the two races, for now they are so, should intermingle?' That's quite a narrow stand, isn't it?"

Will looked up from his place beside Roseltha on the couch. "I hear there were anti-slavery meetings over a year ago in Chatham. They say

44

that a man called John Brown was there to organize help for a real struggle against slavery in the States. I'm glad we don't have slavery here."

Enos looked over his glasses. "I saw John Brown in Ingersoll about that time. He was a tall, gaunt man with a shock of white hair and a long beard. He was walking along with his hands under his black coattails and there was something about him that compelled attention—you couldn't walk past him without wondering who he was. Some people said he was a mite touched, or at least peculiar. Well, they say we Baptists are queer because we think we're saved after being dipped in a river, but we don't think it's queer. It's a symbol that we're dedicating ourselves to a purposeful life. So maybe there's nothing queer about John Brown."

"I don't think a man is queer because he wants to get rid of slavery," broke in Roseltha. "Mother said she heard a black woman named Paola Brown when she lectured in Canada West. Mother praised the Anti-Slavery Society of America for giving women as well as men a place on the lecture platform."

"I remember some of the things mother told us about Paola Brown's lecture," said Alfred. "She said, 'Slave-holders! I call God, I call Angels, I call Men, to witness that your destruction is at hand, and will be speedily consummated unless you repent."

"Will, I wish you'd change your paper to the *Globe* if the *Leader* says things like that. I don't think negroes like Uncle Asa's George were born inferior. The editor of the *Globe*, George Brown, is a member of the Toronto Anti-Slavery Society."

Will winked at her. "I'm thinking, I'm thinking. I don't like that Fugitive Slave Law that claims it can reach into Canada and seize any slave who's escaped here. Sounds as if they think they can do whatever they want in Canada. They may own slaves but they don't own us."

"Some slaves commit crimes when they're escaping, like stealing a coat or a horse. They say there's a man hiding out near Brantford who murdered his master who had come to take him back after he visited his wife on a neighbouring plantation."

"Stealing a horse is one thing, but murder is another and should be punished, no matter what the circumstances." This was Daniel's opinion.

"Selling human beings is just as wrong as murder, almost." This was Alfred's.

"It's wrong to plot against the government, as they say John Brown is doing, maybe even stock-piling arms, to get rid of something wrong. Law and order must be upheld." Enos was firm in his opinion.

45

"Milk and water protests will get you nowhere," said Alonzo. "A little action will."

Newton tried to enter the conversation. "I think the slaves are right to do anything to get away from slavery. How would you like to be sold like a cow or horse?"

Jasper mussed Newton's hair. "You're too young to know what you're saying."

"No I'm not. I'm nearly as old as you are, and I'm better in arithmetic."

"All right boys," admonished Enos. "I'm just afraid that the Southerners are so determined to keep slavery that there might be bloodshed over the matter."

"I guess John Brown's back in the States by now so we don't have to worry what he does," said Daniel.

Jasper disagreed. "Maybe we should worry. In 1813 the Americans came right through here burning houses and taking prisoners. It would be dreadful if they came in to get their slaves."

Roseltha jumped up, pulling Will after her. "This talk is too gloomy. Come over to the melodeon and let's learn a new song, ready for Christmas. It's called, 'O Little Town of Bethlehem', and was written by a man in Boston a few years ago."

A week later the news reached Canada. On October 16, 1859, John Brown scized the government arsenal at Harper's Ferry. There, at the junction of the Susquehanna and Potomac Rivers, where the railroad passed over a bridge across the gorge where the two rivers converged, there where the wild mountains of western Virginia were no wilder than the light in John Brown's eyes, John Brown and twenty-two followers who believed in his cause seized government arms and barricaded themselves in the engine-house by the river. Two days later they were forced to surrender to Colonel Robert E. Lee who was sent with government troops to quell the armed rising. On December 2, the man who said he was God-commanded to free the slaves was hanged for treason and murder.

"He was right," said Alonzo. "Now everyone has to begin to think about slavery. Now maybe it will be forbidden."

"He was wrong," said Alfred. "He that lives by the sword shall perish by the sword."

"That's pretty old-fashioned, don't you think?" said Jasper.

Roseltha was thinking out loud. "I wonder if John Brown *was* wrong? Sometimes it is hard to know what is right and what is wrong. His ideas were right. Then why was he wrong if he was right?"

"There's no real answer to that, is there?" said Enos. "But I hope this isn't the beginning of something nasty."

The Harding mill had received an order for squared timber and they were hurrying to fill it and get it shipped over the lake before winter set in. Daniel had come home from his school in Houghton for the weekend and was helping Alfred at the mill till dusk, for on Saturday the hired men left early.

"Let's do two more logs, Danny, and call it a day." Alfred hoisted two logs into place on the sawhorses. He picked up a small hatchet to lop off the few remaining boughs, then took the big broadaxe to begin squaring. As he worked, he began to think of the Sunday School lesson he would be teaching next day in the Houghton Baptist church for he would drive Daniel back. He began to say a Psalm to himself, for he loved to memorize the Bible.

"Lord, remember David and all his afflictions," he began. Then he thought whimsically, "Wonder if David ever had to square logs at the end of a day when it's beginning to snow? Looking after sheep was a cinch to this."

He finished the Psalm and started reciting another favorite to himself. 'I will lift up mine eyes to the hills, from whence cometh my help.' "There are no hills around here to help me. Nothing bigger than a good-sized mound. Guess I'll just have to score this log by myself. No help from the hills here." The rest of the Psalm ran through his mind. 'The Lord is thy keeper . . . The sun shall not smite thee by day nor the moon by night.' "Too cloudy for a moon tonight," he thought inconsequentially. He laid down his axe after a last score. "That finishes mine, Danny. It's getting dark. Leave that log and let's go home. I'm hungry."

"No, I'll finish this one. You go ahead and I'll be along in a few minutes." Daniel hefted the big broadaxe and took a swipe at the wood. "Murderous-looking thing," he grumbled as he looked at the axe with its great wide blade. He swung his leg over the log and stood astride, French-Canadian fashion. "Father said to work from the side, but I'll finish this way. I get a better swing." He sent the big chips flying.

He brushed a fluff of new-fallen snow off the log. He hurried his strokes. He straightened his legs that were bestride the log. In the gathering dusk as he lifted the axe he did not see a knot in the log. The broadaxe slipped off the side of it and gashed into the calf of his leg.

He shrieked as the blood gushed out. He grabbed his leg to halt the spurts. "Help," he cried into the December gloom.

Alfred came running. He too shouted for help but there was no one near to hear. He tore off his shirt and made a tourniquet above the gash but Daniel was already weak from shock and loss of blood. Alfred cushioned him with his coat, tied him on a nearby toboggan and set off for home as gently but as fast as he could.

47

After three weeks of nursing and conquering infection, the great gash was beginning to heal. Daniel had even hopped about a little on one leg. Tomorrow, he thought, I'm going to see if the leg will stand my weight, maybe with a cane. That night, comforted by the thought that he would soon be walking again, he blew out his candle with a feeling almost of cheer. He relaxed fully for the first time since his accident and fell into a deep sleep. He turned and stretched both legs luxuriously. The movement opened the wound where it was poorest knit. Slowly the blood oozed out, then a little more. He stretched again uneasily in his sleep. The blood flowed a little faster.

In his bedroom on the ground floor Enos woke with a feeling of apprehension. The house was night-still but something was wrong, he sensed. In his nightshirt he climbed the stairs to Daniel's room, stood over the bed. Daniel seemed very quiet. Enos looked for breathing. He bent closer. No sound, no movement. Then in the rising morning light he saw a dark wet stain on the floor beside the bed. It was his own son's lifeblood that had drained away while he slept.

"Daniel," he cried out. Enos' despairing cry brought the rest of the family running but it was too late for help. Eighteen year old Daniel was dead.

The friends came, braving the December winds—the Bridgemans, the Clines, with daughter Neridia to keep Roseltha company till Will arrived from Goble's Corners.

They took Daniel home to Harding, to the cemetery on the hill that they could see from the cupola of Harding Hall when they had lived there, the place where their mother lay. Once again the long procession climbed the hill that overlooked the river cupped in the valley. The grave Old Jake had dug was waiting. He climbed over the fence, out of the way of the mourners, leaning on his pickaxe as he watched them gather round.

"I am the resurrection and the life, saith the Lord: he that believeth in me, though he were dead, yet shall live, and whosoever liveth and believeth in me shall never die."

Then a song trembled thinly into the cold wind over the river and over the valley:

> Abide with me; fast falls the eventide;
> The darkness deepens; Lord, with me abide . . .
> Heaven's morning breaks and earth's vain shadows flee;
> In life, in death, O Lord, abide with me.

The red velvet lined carriage rolled quietly away. "Do I have a curse upon me that I should lose wife and son like this?" thought Enos. "Surely this is the end of my afflictions."

When the cemetery was alone again, Old Jake climbed back over
the fence to finish his work. A few snowflakes fell on his sleeve. He
looked sadly at them, seeing in their intricate forms nothing more than
three months of winter. He picked up his shovel and hummed as he
worked:

> O-o, come to the church in the wildwood
> To the trees where the wild flowers bloom;
> Where the parting hymn shall be cha-anted
> We shall weep by the side of the tomb.
> O-o, come, come, come, come
> Come to the church in the wildwood . . .

The earth thudded on to the coffin. "Heard them singin' that song often
as I passed the house. Never thought I'd live to be singin' it fer young
Daniel."

> No-o spot is so dear to my childhood
> As the little brown church in the vale.

He hitched his collar around his ears, picked up his tools, hoisted
them to his shoulder, and walked bandy-legged and unhurried down the
hill to the village as darkness closed in.

Chapter 5

Cleveland

No one sang "O Little Town of Bethlehem" in the Harding house that Christmas. Roseltha and Will postponed their wedding day till Easter when they were married quietly. Only the two families, a few close friends like the Clines and daughter Neridia, and thoughts of absent mother and brother were present.

But it was spring and the April sunshine warmed them as they left the little church in Houghton township and settled themselves on the red velvet carriage cushions. The horses strained and splashed through the softening ruts. The chickadees balancing on the bushes trilled out their spring songs and the bluejays shrilled through the treetops. The ice was melting and runnels were purling and glinting everywhere. As the stage drew away amid goodbyes and rice, gladness prevailed.

Who was to prepare meals in the motherless and sisterless house when the wedding goodies were gone? Five pairs of masculine eyes looked lost and gloomy at each other.

"Shall we engage a housekeeper, father? She could sleep in Rose's room."

"Not right now, Alfred. I've spoken to Annie Hopton about coming in by the day. That will tide us over for a while."

"Ho, ho, pa." Newton's fourteen years did not allow him to remain serious for long. "I hope she has more sense now than when she first went into service. She was telling us last summer that when she first began to work she was just my age. She had only one dress made of deerskin. It was so smelly that when the family went off for the day they told her to wash it while they were away. She took lye to it and it made the dress so stiff she couldn't get it on. There she was, nearly naked, and it was time for the family to come home."

"What did she do?" interrupted Jasper.

"She hid in the root cellar under the kitchen. When the Porters came home, there was her dress, standing upright beside the washtub but no Annie. Then someone went down to get potatoes for supper and found her crying behind the apple barrels."

The story broke the gloom. "She knows more than that now about keeping house. And mind you don't tease her, boy, or we'll give you the washing to do."

The move from Harding to Walsingham was already seeming a good thing. The Harding mill was now worth about $15,000. In addition to his sons, Enos employed twelve men and six horses. Together they produced two million board feet of pine lumber yearly valued at $60,000. This was a sizeable chunk of the fourteen million board feet that George Reade, the customs man at Port Burwell, told Enos he calculated had been shipped the year before. Enos was proud of his output but marketing it and collecting his money was requiring as much effort as producing it.

As they set out for the mill one morning soon after Roseltha's marriage, Enos spoke to eldest son Alfred. "I want you to come to Cleveland with me next week to see if we can collect our money for the shingles we shipped to Thatcher & Burt and pick up some more orders. I want to use the machines to capacity. With wages for twelve hired men at fifty to fifty-five dollars a month and the horses to feed, I'm getting short of money to meet the payroll."

"Great, father, I've always wanted to go to Cleveland with you. It's bigger than Toronto and I've never even been there, like Daniel."

"This is no pleasure trip. Look at those piles of logs we skidded this winter and that lumber. They have to be sold."

It was too early in the year for them to cross Lake Erie the short stormy way by steamboat from Port Stanley so they travelled by the Great Western from Port Burwell to Buffalo and then to Cleveland. It was the first time Alfred had seen so large a city, nearly 44,000 people. Business was moving faster than in Canada but the effects of the 1857 paralysis were still being felt. Thatcher & Burt made only a token payment but they picked up another order for lumber and shingles. As they walked around the town they passed West High School, recently built in West Cleveland on that side of the Cuyahoga River.

Alfred looked longingly at the new three-storey brick building. "Father, Daniel went to Normal School in Toronto and Roseltha had music and painting lessons. I'm nearly twenty-two years old and I don't want to work in the woods forever. Why can't I go to school here?"

"There's a grammar school in Norfolk County and one in Woodstock. You could go there."

"This school is better and Cleveland is bigger."

"There'd be board to pay away from home but wait a minute, maybe you could look after some business here better than I can from Walsingham. And now that I think of it, there is no reason why you couldn't start building a house in your spare time. That'll use some of our lumber profitably. Let's go into the school and see what they say. Mind, you might not like it for you'd be in a lower class with gaffers much younger than you."

"I wouldn't mind, if only I could be getting somewhere."

A.G. Hopkinson, the principal, looked doubtfully at the handsome young man with the curling brown hair, straight features and hazel eyes for he was much older than the pupils he would have to share classes with. Nevertheless, sensing Alfred's eagerness, he put him through some quick tests.

"You've gaps in your knowledge according to a formal curriculum but you're very good at what you can do. I've never heard anyone, not even a minister, recite whole chapters of the Bible the way you can. Your mathematics aren't too bad and you can catch up in history, logic and other subjects. If you could come now and study in the public school till June, I am sure you could easily pass the examinations for entrance to high school next fall. I would be proud to have your son attend this school, Mr. Harding."

Alfred was jubilant. Enos was thoughtful. He knew his sons' education had been sporadic. So had his own schooling in upper New York state before his father had brought his family to Upper Canada. With his boundless energy and enthusiasm he felt no lack of education himself but he knew his sons should have what changing times required. He began to assess each of them mentally. Alfred soaked up books as the earth soaked rain. Alonzo had a practical turn; he liked the mill. Sixteen year old Jasper's aptitude was indeterminate. Fourteen year old Newton was by turns bright and erratic. He needed discipline. I think I should send Jasper and Newton as well as Alfred to school, he concluded swiftly.

"If you go to school here, I'll let Jasper and Newton come too. You can keep an eye on them. Alonzo can stay with me at the mill. You may get ready as soon as we reach home."

Enos regretted another break in the family even though it was for the best. Now he would have a household in Cleveland to keep an eye on as well as the Walsingham business and the property in Harding. "It'll keep me plenty busy but that's the way I like it."

Alfred and Jasper packed in a double-quick hurry and were off to Cleveland before Enos might change his mind. Newton was to stay behind till the older boys had found a boarding-house that would accommodate them and a volatile fourteen year old.

They were catapulted into school work but their first letter arrived before the end of April.

Cleveland 1860

*Dear [Father]**

*I should have written sooner but if you knew how hard we have to study, you certainly would excuse my delinquency; . . . the term was one third gone, and I have hard work to keep up with the class. Jasper and I are trying **very** hard to get in the high school at the close of this term. We study, with all our might, from four in the morning until eight at night, and then take an hour's exercise before retiring. Last week I was very unwell and was afraid I could not hold out till the close of the term but I feel better this week.*

[Your son]
Fred

Jasper added a note in the same envelope:

Dear [Father]

This is Saturday and as I have a little spare time I will improve it by writing to you and put it in Alfred's letter. At the end of June we will be examined for the high school. You will be surprised to learn that we get up every morning at four o'clock, but the reason for it is that we cannot get our lessons if we do not. It is nothing but study from morning till night, mostly practical arithmetic, and as one of the scholars told the teacher, they worked in figures all day and dreamed about figures all night. I sometimes think I would rather be in Walsingham and working hard there than to be here poring over my books, but if we do not get in the high school now we cannot have another chance for a year. We changed boarding houses a week ago and have a cleaner room and better folks. When we get our two month vacation we will have time to begin building a house.

J. [Harding] Esq.

6153281	*563459265*	*76235*
		565
		15

Brackets around words in letters indicate changes from the original letters. Original spelling remains uncorrected.

54

When their sister heard that her brothers were on their own in a strange city, she was perturbed, and wrote them.

My dear Brothers

I have been trying to find time to write to you. You know there is four of you boys to write to while I am only one . . . I am so glad you are getting on well with your studies. Alonzo wrote that you were head of your class and Jasper of his. Father was much pleased when he was here that you and Jasper are doing so well. He is doing the best he can for you, do all you can for yourselves. It will not be long before you will be men and have something else to do. Improve the present opportunity to the best of your ability. I think of you every day; and would like very much to see you. I feel very anxious for my dear **Motherless** *brothers. Be a good boy and do all you can. Be very careful of the boys you go with and try not to get any bad habits. It is much easier to acquire bad habits than to get rid of them. You cannot be too careful . . . If you knew how often I think of you and how much I want to hear from you and Jasper you would both of you write me a long letter as soon as you get this. Tell me about your studies, troubles, hopes, aims and pleasures. Do you get lonesome and want to come home? Or are you satisfied where you are? Do you go to Meeting and Sunday School . . . read good papers. Among all your reading and studying do not forget your Bible, but read it often with careful earnestness. May God bless you all My Dear Brothers and make you happy.*

Your own dear sister

Rose

When the two boys read her letter, homesickness overcame them but they passed off the feeling quickly. Then Alfred said, "I wish she'd try to remember that I'm a man, not a boy. Well, here goes for a letter to her so she won't worry."

When Enos read their letters he was happy to know that his sons were taking advantage of their opportunity, but figured that he would wait to hear Newton's report after his arrival before he believed the story of such amazing application.

"Pack your clothes, Newton, I'm sending a load of lumber to Buffalo on that little schooner, the *Oak*, that will leave the day after tomorrow. They've room on deck for about 25,000 board feet. You can ride free on board and then take the cars from Buffalo to Cleveland."

"Holy mackerel, a ride on the cars at last!"

There was a lump in Enos' throat as he said goodbye to his youngest son at Port Burwell. "Thank God for Alfred. He'll look after you as well

55

as I can since your mother is gone and your sister is married. Be sure you mind what Alfred says."

The wind was rising but he thought little of it as he supervised the loading of his lumber on the deck of the stout little *Oak* and waved goodbye. "Pull your cap down over your ears," he shouted to Newton from the dock. "That wind's cold."

The little ship bobbed into the wind and soon Newton could no longer see his father on the dock. "I'm not staying on deck any longer," he said to one of the deckhands as they were well under weigh. "I'm going into the cabin where it's warm."

Lake Erie beats up waves fast. The little *Oak* pitched and lumbered till Newton's stomach churned with it. All night he retched. In the middle of the night, over the sound of the wind, he heard a great shouting on deck and a series of horrendous crashes. It meant nothing to him as he struggled to keep from being thrown off the bench to the floor, or tried to replace the lid on the slop pail that the captain had hastily set beside him.

In the morning the wind subsided. Newton sat up shakily and put on his cap, preparing to go outside. Suddenly the ship lurched and pitched him sideways. He saved himself just in time to prevent himself from falling against the stove but his cap fell onto the red-hot top. By the time he made it back to the stove, crawling on his hands and knees for safety, the cap was burned through. He was almost too miserable to care.

His cap was gone. So was the lumber Enos had loaded on deck the day before. The crashing in the night had been the lumber going overboard, loosened by the storm. Harding lumber from the Harding mill—a dead loss. Enos still owed money on the shingle machine and could ill afford this set-back.

There was another day and night of queasiness before Newton felt his stomach settle as soon as he stepped on solid ground at Buffalo. He saw the captain tell the man who came for the lumber what had happened to it, and then, ashamed of his hatless head (even a tramp had a hat), he trudged to the station to take the cars on the new railroad to Cleveland.

"Where's your cap, Newton?" Alfred asked as he met him at the station.

"So the lumber's gone too. Poor father. Come on now, don't cry over spilt milk or you'll commence school tomorrow red-eyed. Mr. Hopkinson says he'll start you in the third class and advance you when you're ready. I'll buy you another cap, and father will survive the loss of the lumber somehow."

The three lads were studying hard, but there were business details to attend to as well if they were to start building a house as soon as school was out. Alfred wrote to Alonzo, June 8, 1860.

56

*Dear brother, I received yours of the 20th inst. We have left Paines and gone to Johnsons. We could not longer stand the filth and bedbugs, . . . We paid them on settlement $32.98 and we settled with them on the 2nd of June. Our school had a picknick today. They start at 8-1/2 o'clock. We have not done anything with the horses yet. The cream mare has shed her coat and looks as streaked as a leopard, the result of Shepherds whip. They are in pasture at present as horse-selling is at a discount. I have been all over the city looking for a good situation for to build. The lots spoken of by Captain Cartwright are all sold; but there are others near them for $240, a small payment to be made on purchase, and the remainder at six pr.ct. per anum interest. There are some very good lots on Erie Street between Ohio and Eagle Streets but I have been unable to learn their price. It will probably be about six or eight hundred dollars each. I would not like to purchase a lot for father as it would not suit him. I could not suit myself. If he brings over lumber to build he can purchase them, to good advantage, and probably better, than I could now. By what I have said about the lots he will know very nearly what can be done. I have had to buy a good many clothes for the boys. . . .I never received the "papers" you spoke about, they must have miscarried. Our lessons are hard now, we get up between four or five in the morning and study incessantly until between nine or ten at night. We are doing our best to get in the high school. . . . In two weeks we are to be examined, and we do not expect to lose much time before that. . . . I received $25 from Burt a few days ago. I went down several times to settle with him but they never **have time,** but they promised to make out the act, and give it to me in a few days. . . . Business is very dull and times are very hard here this summer. Common lumber sells at $7 per thousand. Shingles are quite brisk at $2.50 for thousand. I would like to hear all about how things get along at home. . . . Are you comming to Cleveland on the fourth? I do not think there will be much going on that day. How are you doing, and what do you intend doing. How do the Williams boys get along with the mill? They can sell here for $2½ without any trouble, but I do not think they could do more. Are they going to saw lumber, if so what are the terms? Can you get any money from Bloughton Star? Is John Scrivers at work for Williams, if so, try to collect the $4 comming to me. . . . Does Father intend comming over soon? Write all about everything. I believe I shall have to stop as time and paper, pen and ink, fail me.*

Your Brother
A.P. [Harding]

Enos wrote:

Dear Boys

I hope you are all trying to improve your time to best advantage you can in learning your opertunities may not last long. But if it is possible to keep you through another summer and winter at school I should be glad to do so you must write and let me know the best plans you can think of to effect it . . . I was in Blenheim last week all well there can't sell anything for mony I send you $25 spend nothing but what is absolutely necessary write me if there is any prospect for the shingles write the perticulars of your prospects.

from your Father
Enos [Harding]

Because of her deep concern, Roseltha wrote often.

My dear Brother

Your letter proved very acceptable . . . for I was anxious to hear from you. I am so glad you are attending what I think will prove a very good school. You must improve the opportunity and lay away a store of useful knowledge for the years to come. Should it please "our Father in Heaven" to spare you. The acquisition of knowledge is one of the noblest **aims** *of* **this** *life. "Knowledge is Power." Strive to improve, Strive to be wise. And in all your strivings, strive to be good, for there is no true greatness without goodness. You will need to be both industrious and persevering to succeed in your studies. Perseverance will overcome a host of difficulties. It is the Key to success in every undertaking.*

We were down to Walsingham the Friday after you left. We were very disappointed in not seeing you. . . . Father was here . . . He bought goods and groceries in Hamilton. Mrs. Montroy, Mrs. Gregg's sister is **dead.** *They brought her here yesterday and we were at the funeral. Mr. Newlove and one of the Boughnier's came up with them so you see I hear quite often from Walsingham. The Mill is running. They are all well; and everything is going on about as usual I guess. . . . I had a letter a few weeks ago from Uncle Silas they got home [to Kentucky] safely. . . . We were out to [Harding] . . . The place is improving considerably I think. We took dinner with Aunt Eliza and spent the evening at John Currey's . . . Another year with its good and evil is passing away. How many have passed away with it. And among the number our own dear brother. And we are yet spared. . . . God grant if any of us are called we may be ready. I very often think of you, my dear brother. You do not know how anxious I feel for your soul's welfare. Beware the corruptions of city life.*

Never be persuaded from doing what you know is right. Be careful in choosing your companions for much depends on that. Do your duty. And may God bless and make you happy is the fervent, sincere prayer of
Your own dear sister
Roseltha
Will sends his kind regards. **Write soon.**

Newton wrote home to say that he had outgrown all his clothes and needed money for a new suit. The new colour for men's nether garments, he wrote cheerfully, was "subdued mouse." It would make me very elegant, he concluded. When Alfred looked over his shoulder as he was writing, he added a postscript: "Forget the subdued mouse. Newtie spends more time roaming around than trying to look elegant. What he needs is a good strong tweed which can be had for $5. He needs shoes too. If his feet grow much bigger he will soon have to go to an intersection to turn around."

There was a deal of difference between life in Cleveland and life in Harding or Walsingham. "The women go about much more freely here than in Canada," wrote Jasper. "Some even work in offices and in New York they work in factories too." And Alfred wrote, for Roseltha had queried him about fashions: "We see many women wearing hoop skirts. The papers advertise them as available in steel, gutta percha, brass or reed. Daniel said that in Toronto the only women he saw wearing hoops were elderly women or visitors from the southern States."

They bought Newton a tweed suit. He wrote importantly about it to Roseltha, and to show her how intellectual he was becoming, he asked her opinion about the effect produced when an irresistible body came into contact with an immoveable one, and if the cars, in the case of a tunnel, went through the mountain or the hole in the mountain. Jasper added to the letter: "Newton is very good at arithmetic. He wonders where the figures go when they are rubbed off the blackboard. He drives us to distraction by punning Bible quotations. The other day when it was cold he said, "Never mind, many are cold but few are frozen."

It was exciting to be in Cleveland after little Harding and sparsely settled Walsingham. They saw the trains passing through the city en route to the west with its multiplying homesteads and California gold. "Maybe when we finish school we could go to California too," they thought. They saw other trains laden with the iron, coal and oil from nearby areas, the material that would make Cleveland continue to increase in size. When Alfred visited Thatcher & Burt's office at the corner of Bank and St. Clair in the first stone-front block of buildings in the city, he wondered if Wall Street could be any grander.

On their way to school the lads passed Franklin Circle with its new fountain and pavilion. They marvelled at the new medical school the Western Reserve University had opened in the city. They listened to the sound of fife and drums when the Cleveland Grays paraded with their ten companies of Light Artillery and their six twelve-pounder cannons on their caissons. They laughed at the words of *Plain Dealer* writer Artemus Ward, when he said that Cleveland's main thoroughfare, Euclid Avenue, more than equalled the well known "Unter der Sauerkraut" in Berlin and the "Rue de Boolfrog" in gay Paree.

Sometimes, after dark, they fancied they saw discreet flashes from the belfrey of St. John's Episcopal church that told runaway slaves when it was safe to continue on the road to freedom. Sometimes they thought they heard the bell ringing on the Stone Church that told when the professional slave hunters were in town. A school friend said that one station-master was said to have helped one thousand slaves to freedom in Canada. They read in the paper about Lucy Bagby who had escaped from her former master in Wheeling, Virginia. When her master came to seize her out of a free state, some Cleveland citizens demonstrated in the street outside the jail where she was being held for trial. They offered her master double her price to release her, but Lucy Bagby was taken back into slavery.

"It's a queer state of affairs," commented Alfred, "when they want to save a slave from slavery and allow the negroes here to be educated in the same schools as whites, but they won't let them sit with them in the churches."

Difficult as it was for the Harding young men to concentrate on their studies with so much going on around them, before they knew it the June examinations were over. Alfred and Jasper passed into the high school and Newton into the fourth class.

Now they were free for two months to begin to build a house. Again they went to Thatcher & Burt for money. They were given part payment and used it for the down payment on a $240 lot on Franklin Street in West Cleveland, the same street where the principal of the high school lived. Enos sent Alonzo over to help with this major undertaking, and from dawn to dusk the hammers rat-tat-tatted as the house took shape.

Chapter 6

It Will All Blow Over

As the Harding sons hammered and sawed in Cleveland, and Enos managed the mill in Walsingham and Roseltha enjoyed being Mrs. William Goble of Goble's Corners, their letters crossed and crisscrossed so that at times no one was quite certain what the others were doing. In mid-July, 1860 the boys opened a letter from their father.

Walsingham
Alonzo I received your letter of the 20th last week it having been some time in the office. You say you hire your bord it may be the best way you write that you are quite out of money I send you a letter for Thatcher Burt Co. you will take it to them and do the best you can with them and send me back an answer. I did not mention anything about the shingles try to sell to some other party if you can without too much loss You ask me what I am doing the mill has been standing still Mcombs attempted to start it and make shingles the pump broke and he quit . . . I have halled some 80 thousand ft to Pt Rowan some 50m more to hall my debts press hard it costs a grate deal to keep the teams I have just commenst halling a contract of timber for Deblaque of 9 or 10 hundred $ from the lot Wiley give down the Venison some 5 miles I have to hire several teams . . . I send you $25 Canada you will write on receipt of this and tell me all about the boys . . . and how they prosper.
    Jasper you must be a good boy and work hard and gain knowledg while you have an opertunity it may not last long. Be shure to abstain from bad habits encourage Newton to be a good boy write to us and let us know all about the School and how you get along atend Church and S.S.

61

*Newton my son you will remember you are now forming your
caracter for the rest of your life and that you have no mother to watch
you nor father to look after you but God sees you Do what Alfred tells
you and try to make your self respected spend your time dillegent in
your studdies keep yourself tidy and clean and be a good boy atend
Church and S.S. and write and let me know all about your situation we
are all well in Canada so farwell*

Enos Harding

*See if the shingles shipt from Alwood is sold or what become of them
he wants his pay.*

Now that Alfred had finished school he had time to indulge himself in
a little outside reading. He bought a book that one of his teachers had
recommended, a book of essays called *Walden* by a new Englander
named Henry Thoreau. He treasured it for he had had to argue with
himself over the purchase of something that seemed frivolous in the
face of all the necessities they required. He wrote about it to Roseltha
for he knew there were things he could write to her that his father might
be too busy to read:

"Henry Thoreau was a great lover of nature for he said she fed his
imagination as well as his body. For two years he lived in a hut beside a
little lake to prove that a man could live with very little money and
without the organization that accompanies urban life. His descriptions
are beautiful, the result of his having time to think, a luxury in which I
cannot often indulge myself. I will copy a small passage for you.—"I
was as much affected by the faint hum of a mosquito making its
invisible and unimaginable tour through my apartment at earliest dawn,
when I was sitting with door and windows open, as I could be by any
trumpet that ever sang of fame. It was Homer's requiem; itself an Iliad
and Odyssey in the air, singing its own wrath and wanderings. There is
something cosmical about it"—I might have swatted the mosquito
rather than calling it cosmical but I like the way he writes. He seems to
be a spiritual man but I find it odd that he never refers to the Bible. He is
fiercely anti-slavery and once went to jail for refusing to pay taxes to a
government that allows slavery.

Last Sunday at a baptism in the Cuyahoga river the minister was
trying to immerse a woman wearing hoops. Every time he tried to
submerge her he was swallowed up by her skirt. When he tried to force
it down it only flew up in another place. He only succeeded in baptizing
her when the skirt was too wet to billow, and then it was so heavy he
could hardly help the poor woman to shore. It was hard not to laugh.

Fortunately Newtie was not present or I should likely have had to choke him to keep him quiet.

We are all well and working hard at the house. I am looking forward to going back to school.

Your Brother

Alfred

Though summer with its gardening, gathering and preserving kept Roseltha busy she always found time to write to her brothers.

Goble's Corners

. . . Times are hard but we are managing. Toronto papers report that city finances are so tight that they are turning off every second light in the streets and permit none on moonlit nights.

Father was here, and I went home with him staid in Walsingham a week and then we went with the ponies and carriage to visit "Sister" Lissa. It rained before we arrived. The roads were very bad . . . And you know Talbot Street is all the way a clay road so you can imagine something of what it was like . . . [They are] about 38 miles west of Fingal we were two days and a half getting there. We found them all well and getting along comfortably these 'hard times'. [Sister] Lissa has her hands full, three babies to take care of. Arthur does not walk yet. She has named the babies Ida and Eva. Heman preaches twice Sundays and several times during the week. I came back with Father to St. Thomas and took the cars to London and then to Princeton. James Dawson was here two or three weeks ago from [Harding]. Things are well there.

*I am sure I have filled two pages and have not written much either. I do not feel much like writing this morning. . . . Granpa Towl is **dead** . . . I had a letter from Aunt Celestia containing the intelligence. . . . I suppose you will come home a Yankee. When do you expect to come home? . . . There is a very good school in Paris I expect now. I have not seen Uncle Asa or Aunt Juliet since I came here. James Dawson said Aunt was coming to see me. . . . Which do you like best, Canada or Ohio. When I say Canada I do not mean Walsingham by any means.I received a paper from you and send you a Flag today. I wish you would send me a paper occasionally if you have them. . . . you must try and improve the opportunity and have the boys do so too especially Newton. He did not use to be so fond of study. Be very kind to them for they have no one now to look after them but you. . . . I feel very anxious and think very often of my Motherless brothers, especially Jasper and Newton.They are young and do not feel the necessity as much as they will when they are older of forming good habits, learning to be industrious and laying up*

63

a store of knowledge to use when they grow to be men, should it please the "Great Giver" to spare them so long. . . . I would like to be near enough to spend an evening with you now and then. How we are being scattered. A few years has made a great change in our family. Two are lying in the cold ground and I often wonder if those left will ever all meet again. . . . Try to look after the boys clothes see that they are mended in time and kept clean. Best love to you all. Goodbye.

From your own dear sister
Rose

The summer passed as swiftly as sheet lightning. The roof was on the house and the downstairs was livable. To save board money the boys moved into the house.

Cleveland, Sep. 16, 1860

Dear Rose

*It seems almost like an age since I heard from you; but I suppose it is my own fault for not writing. Mrs. Grimes is here keeping house for us. . . . The new house which we expect, after we get it finished and everything in order, will be worth about three thousand dollars. We have got my horse here and a buggy and harness and are building a good sized waggon house. . . . We commenced going to the High School two weeks ago, and are **determined** to stand second to none in our class. During the last vacation our school was deprived of a faithful and devoted teacher. After four years of toil and weary labor, she wished again to return, for a short season, to her "childhood home", little dreaming of the fate that awaited her, but prepared for whatever might befall her. She went. Kind friends and loving parents welcomed her back to the scenes of her youthful associations—welcomed her back but to see her die. But a day elapsed after her arrival home ere she was stricken by disease and in a few short hours, she crossed death's dark river—entered the shining gates of the "City of Gold", and, we fondly believe, was clothed with the robes of Paradise, unfading and immortal. Undisturbed by scenes of earthly strife and far from the field of her labors in a quiet sunny vale, on the beautiful banks of the broad Connecticut, she sleeps the sleep eternal. Cleveland mourns her early death. One of the most lovely and beautiful examples of female perfection has passed away; but she has left behind her the character of a Christian—and the example of a life of gentleness and piety in all its spotless purity. Think not that I speak too highly of an almost stranger. Her loss is felt in every throb of the great heart of the Cleveland public.*

The tenth of September has passed away with its crowd of one hundred thousand, and the monument to the memory of the gallant [Commodore] Perry*, a fine specimen of artistic skill, occupies a prominent place in the park. We attend Sabbath school every Sunday morning at 9 o'clock at the Baptist church. I teach a class and the other boys are in the Bible class. I must close as it is time to go to church. Write soon for I long to hear from you.

From your ever loving brother
Fred

If life was settling into a pleasant routine for four brothers, their father was beginning to feel the effects of the business slump and the growing knowledge that free trade with the United States would not be renewed. Some of his men were suing him for $100 in back wages.

"Just give me a little more time to get my money from Cleveland," he asked them, but promises would not put turkey on the table. It was disheartening all around. Roseltha wrote to Alfred:

"When Father was here last . . . he was thinking of breaking up in Walsingham and leaving there as soon as he could get through with his law-suit. He did not know whether he would send for you to come as a witness in consideration of the expense and your having to be out of school. . . . He spoke of their being a quantity of shingles he hoped you could sell. . . .

"We are keeping bachelors' hall," wrote Alonzo to Roseltha, for their motherly housekeeper had returned to Canada. He had commenced school in September along with the others but was chafing at being in the same class as young Newton. He was more interested in adding finishing touches to the house than in poring over arithmetic problems. "I can figure enough to measure what I need for house-building," he said when Alfred urged him to study more. He did not lack interest in everything though. "Here, give me that ancient history book. I'll read about Leonidas and how he and 300 men held the pass at Thermopylae against the Persian army. Now, there's a man."

"If you like the story that well, better learn to spell Thermopylae right," Alfred teased, for spelling did not come naturally to Alonzo.

---

*In 1855 Commodore Matthew Perry negotiated a treaty with Japan that opened two ports to American ships.

They were feeling at home in Cleveland now and were learning the meaning of the intense political talk with which the city was filled as two Illinois men, Democrat Stephen A. Douglas and Republican Abraham Lincoln, battled for the presidency.

"I think the 'Little Giant' will get in," said Alonzo as they walked to school. "After all, Douglas beat Lincoln when they were running for senator."

"That doesn't matter now that he's split his party over the question of squatter sovereignty," countered Alfred. "Lincoln may have lost the race for senator but he hasn't split the Republican party."

"What's squatter sovereignty?" asked Newton. "You've lost me."

"I know," said Jasper. "It means that each state can vote whether or not it wants slavery instead of asking the federal government in Washington for permission. That's known as local autonomy. Look it up in the dictionary if that one goes over your head, or else call it states' rights, the way most people do here. And it also means that Kansas and Nebraska and every new state coming into the Union can be slave in spite of the Missouri Compromise."

"But," Alonzo broke in, "there's that Supreme Court case about Dred Scott—you know the slave who claimed he was free because he'd lived in the free state of Louisiana and they tried to make him a slave again when he went into a slave state. That means that if Uncle Asa's George went back to Kentucky he'd be a slave again."

"I remember what Lincoln said about the Dred Scott case," said Alfred. "He said, 'Accustomed to trample on the rights of others, you have lost the genius of your own independence and become fit subjects of the first cunning tyrant who rises among you.' Put that in your pipe and smoke it."

"Trust you to memorize somebody's old speech. We can't even vote, so why get het up about it. Come on, let's run or we'll be late for school and we'll be behind in all that valuable old ancient history. Canadians can't do anything about who gets elected president."

No one could live in Cleveland in 1860 without being caught up in some part of the slavery question, whether academic or not. Besides stories of flashes in the night and ringing of bells, there were speculations about the amount of money certain lake captains were being handed for taking fugitives across the lake at dead of night. Without any desire on their part, the Harding boys were caught up in one such situation.

They were just getting up one morning when they heard a rustling outside and then a subdued tapping at the door. Two negroes, gaunt and wet, stood outside. "We suppose to fin' a house wid a red door but

66

we los' our way in de rain. Please don' turn us in." They stood tall but there was apprehension in their voices. For a moment Alfred hesitated to become involved, then he remembered his mother's words: "I say there is no colour to a man's soul."

"Come in, we'll get you some breakfast. Quick, Newton, stir up the fire." They all sprang into action. The look of relief on the two black faces was sufficient reward, but what had been only someone else's problem was now on their own doorstep.

They could not be certain of the sentiments of their new neighbours. "Eat fast and then hide behind that pile of lumber we're going to use to finish the floor upstairs. Here are some quilts and be careful no one sees you," they said as they left for school with a feeling of mingled trepidation and righteousness.

"What'll we do with them now?" asked Jasper.

"I think Captain Cartwright could help us. We'll go to him after school." Two nights later they found the negroes free transportation across the lake.

"Where we go w'en we gits dere?" asked one.

"Why not tell them to go to father for work?"

"No, father can hardly pay the men he has now. Besides those Sutherlands close by have never been too partial to negroes. I think they should head for Dawn. That's a settlement of free negroes," Alfred told them. "They'll be able to give you the best advice."

Political talk about abolition of slavery often turned to war talk these days. Ohio Senator Benjamin Wade in a speech in December predicted that there might be a brief war with the slave states if the northern states tried to force abolition on them. Secretary of State William Sumner talked of annexing Canada by force to compensate the northern states for the loss of the South if secession came.

"Do you think Canada will ever be part of the States?" asked Newton.

"Just let them try to take us," said Jasper.

"Well, here we are living in the States and we don't mind it. But Britain wouldn't stand for it and neither would most Canadians," was Alonzo's opinion.

"What will it matter? We'd enjoy life just the same. And we'll be able to sell our lumber for a good price. Look how father sold his wheat during the Crimean war."

"Let's hope there won't be war, no matter what the reason," said Alfred. "War is murder and war is wrong. Surely civilized people can find some other way of settling differences. We'll ask Rose to send us some Canadian papers to see what they say."

"If she and Will would stop taking the *Leader,* we'd find out more. Let's ask father to send us the *Globe."*

In December 1860 the *Globe* was busy with news more exciting to Canada than an analysis of the American position on slavery. It was describing in detail the visit of the twenty year old Prince of Wales, Albert Edward, who laid the cornerstone for the new Canadian parliament buildings in Ottawa, watched Blondin cross Niagara Falls on a tightrope, dedicated the new Victoria railway bridge spanning the St. Lawrence river at Montreal, and danced with the daughter of the American consul at Halifax when she requested a dance with "Mr. Wales."

Then he proceeded to cross the border into the United States. This was the first time since the American Revolution that a member of the British royal family had visited the States. Albert Edward was greeted at Detroit with a flotilla of illuminated steamers and 300 torch-bearing firemen. When he visited Boston he shook hands with the last surviving soldier of the battle of Bunker Hill. What could be more cordial than British-American relations at this very moment? Annex Canada and offend Britain? Pish tush.

"Wish we could have been at Detroit to see the fun," said the Harding boys. "Come on, let's go to the post office to see if there are any letters."

"My dear brothers, you will excuse my poor writing but I am feeling poorly. The great excitement here now is the trial in Brantford of the negro Anderson who murdered his master while escaping. He was working incognito near Brantford but someone found out who he was. He was jailed by a magistrate, released, then re-arrested on a warrant sworn out in Detroit and sentenced to extradition by Chief Justice John Beverley Robinson who is noted for his harsh sentences. There had been a great uproar over the decision and the papers reported that armed police were present during the trial. A few days ago there was a mass meeting in Toronto led by D'Arcy McGee to protest the sentence. As you know I cannot condone murder but as long as a country allows slavery it is difficult to blame a man bred under that criminal situation for taking violent means to free himself. Those who support Anderson's extradition say that Canada will become a refuge for criminals favoured simply because they used to be slaves but many others feel strongly about the court's decision. I find I am becoming more politically minded since you have gone to Cleveland for I sometimes fear that what may happen there may affect you. Those southern states sound as if they are getting very angry with Washington.

*Alonzo you speak of being done going to school in April. I had inferred from Alfred's last letter you did not intend returning soon to Canada. When Father was here last he said he wanted you all to stay in Cleveland some time . . . If you do not attend School . . . cannot you get employment in Cleveland go into a lumber yard or something of that kind. If you do not make much in a pecuniary point of view it would be better than going home unless father really needs you. When he was here he did not intend doing business in Walsingham again. I do wish he would get out of that miserable place and be comfortable somewhere. He has worked hard enough all his life to begin to rest now. . . . What church do you attend? . . . I had a letter from Uncle Silas not long since. . . . Be careful, my dear brothers . . . many promising characters have been ruined by evil companions. . . . Mrs. Goble wishes to be remembered to you all. My love to you **all.***

> *From your dear sister*
> *Rose*

Alonzo answered.

Dear Rose
    You must pardon me for not writing sooner but better late than never, I received a letter from you some three weeks since and I answered it but yesterday as I was turning over papers in my "Desk" I found the letter I had forgot to put it in the office. I sent you a paper today the "New York Weekly". . . . It does not seem to be more than four or five weeks since I came here and yet it is nearly seventeen. "Time waits for no man." The boys are getting along well, especially Jasper. Newton does better than I had any idea he could do. Jasper is head of his class and so is Newton in his. . . . The boys send their love to all.

> *I remain your affectionate*
> *Brother Alonzo*

Soon after there came disquieting news from Enos. Enos Harding of Harding Hall was fighting for his existence. More than $100 in wages was at stake now.

Dear Boys
    . . . White has comenst a suit again by suing me for £1600 cy on the Bond sued it in Wall's name as before in the queens bench in the spring if I loose the suit . . . it will take some time to close up in Canada which I

shall do as soon as possible I send you $25 save what you can write the perticulars of your prospects.

from your Father
Enos [Harding]

"That's over $4,000," Enos' sons calculated when they read the letter. "Even if we sold the house tomorrow it wouldn't cover that much. If we weren't going to school we could finish it faster and find work somewhere."

"Father wants us to stay in school so we'd better do it. If he could only collect the money owing. . . " The words died on their lips and they pulled their school books towards them.

Alonzo was restless. "Father's in trouble. I think I should go back to work for him this winter. I'm pretty good at running the mill and he wouldn't have to pay me wages. And it's pretty lonesome all by himself," he told his brothers the day school closed for the Christmas holidays.

"It will have to be your decision, Lonnie. Do what you think is best for you." Alfred was the first to speak up.

Just as Alonzo was trying to decide what he should do, South Carolina withdrew from the Union, December 21. On the previous November 10, Abraham Lincoln, Republican, had defeated Stephen Douglas, Democrat, and was now president-elect of the United States. The predominantly Democratic South saw this as a victory for the North with its growing anti-slavery attitude and its policy of tariffs that hurt the interested of the planting aristocracy of the South. The South was beginning to think that the situation was the same as the one that had prompted the Boston Tea Party, only this time the outside repressive power was not Britain but a Northern-dominated government based in Washington.

This was a nice situation. Did a state have the right to secede? Could you force South Carolina to come back, and if so, with what measures? War talk filled the air, and speculations whether any other states would follow South Carolina in seceding. The government prevaricated for President Buchanan was merely a caretaker till Lincoln would be inaugurated the following March.

The Harding boys wondered what they should do in case war should come. "I think we should all go back to Canada," Alonzo urged. "No telling what will happen."

"We're staying in school," the others declared, "and we have to see about selling the house when it is all finished. There's no danger of war. It will all blow over as it has done before."

Chapter 7

No Danger At All

The winter of the secession crisis had begun. South Carolina had taken the first step towards bringing the long-standing feud to a decisive stage. Would the right to hold slaves, which the South claimed was its inalienable "peculiar institution," become a federal institution recognized by every state? If that were so, claimed William Cullen Bryant, the whip and the fetter would then be the country's proper symbol—the true device on the American flag—not the stars and stripes. Would Washington say to South Carolina, "Go in peace, my friend," or would it be the beginning of "a dialogue of guns?" Would the new Republican president, Abraham Lincoln, the man whom the party machine thought it could manipulate with ease, be able to deal with South Carolina's defection and stop this move from turning a country to blood?

What was the new president's stand on slavery and state's rights? Did he have one? Was he a fence sitter as well as a rail splitter? He had said a few years before that "if all earthly power were given to me, I should not know what to do as to the existing institution." If slavery, according to the principle implied in the constitution, was to be restricted and ultimately abolished, what would he do about not only South Carolina's secession but also western Kansas where southern slave-holders and anti-slavery northerners were already clashing as they grabbed for land? In Kansas now, men went about armed, and even in Brooklyn the clergyman, Henry Ward Beecher, declared that a Sharpe's rifle was a greater moral agency in the crisis than the Bible.

"Beecher's Bibles, they call a Sharpe's rifle now," said Alonzo as he packed his clothes to return to Walsingham to help his father. "Alfred, what do you think of a minister of the gospel advocating violence?"

"Not much," answered Alfred laconically, refusing to be drawn into an argument as his brother was departing. "Lucky we don't have to decide. Feel sorry for those who do."

"We had to decide what to do with those two negroes we helped get across the lake."

"We Baptists have usually been against slavery. Some Baptist churches won't even let a slave owner take communion. Come on, let's get to the station. I almost wish I were going with you. Write and let me know all about father and Rose. There's lots of war talk but I don't think anybody's going to fight. It will all blow over."

It did not blow over. In quick succession six more states followed South Carolina's example and early in February, 1861, seven seceded states met in congress in Montgomery, Alabama. They elected Jefferson Davis provisional president of a new country, the Confederate States of America. Four more states joined when the Republicans in Congress refused to compromise on the question of allowing slavery into the western territories, one of them Kansas. How was the impasse to be resolved?

Just outside the harbour in Charleston, North Carolina, the Stars and Stripes blew in the wind over federal Fort Sumter. The work of this little island garrison for the last hundred years had consisted in peering periodically out to sea for a foreign enemy that fortunately never came. Now suddenly the garrison had to change the direction of its vigil and keep a lookout towards the land. Confederate guns in the city of Charleston were pointing towards the fort. Fort Sumter was under seige. Guns, not words, were about to enter the issue of state sovereignty.

A young negro slave, one of the pawns whose fate hung in the balance, idealistically anticipated a change in his status. He stole a canoe and paddled away from his master to the fort and Freedom. The commander did not know what to do with him. He sent him back to the mainland for he was a military man, not an initiator of a new social order.

When President Lincoln called his first cabinet meeting on March 9, 1861, the main item on the agenda was how to get food into the fort. On April 12 the matter was taken summarily out of his hands. Southern guns from Charleston fired on Fort Sumter and forced its surrender.

In the state capital at Columbus, Ohio, in the midst of an otherwise normal session, a member rushed from the lobby into the chamber. "The secessionists have bombarded Fort Sumter," he shouted.

"Glory to God," screamed a woman in the gallery. "It's an end to slavery." The question of whether secession or slavery was the main issue in the war that had just begun would remain as close as those two cries unto the end.

When the news reached Cleveland, the Harding boys surged uncertainly into the street to mingle with the cheering, flag-waving people mad to avenge the affront to the central government, mad to put an end to slavery, the crux of the South's defiance. The wild enthusiasm that swept the whole North surprised even those who had generated the situation, for at last, come what might, the long suspense was over. In Union Square, New York, a huge crowd saw the flag of Sumter on the stump of its shot-off staff placed in the hand of George Washington's equestrian statue. On April 15, Lincoln called for 75,000 militia volunteers to join the federal service for ninety days. Was it to keep order or to fight battles? At the moment, no one was sure.

In Cleveland, in quick order, the old fairground at Woodland and Forest streets became Camp Taylor, and Camp Wood was set up on Seneca Street hill. On April 22, six companies of the Cleveland Grays took six guns with their caissons to Columbus. The Grays had been founded in 1839 by the sons of the best families in the city. They had built the caisson for their first gun with their own hands. They were now the 1st Ohio Volunteer Light Artillery as they started for Washington. Tears and cheers sped them on their way.

It was all very well to talk of passing exams. How could anyone concentrate on lessons when the school was in a ferment of speculation and action? Newton wrote in his diary:

April 18, 1861. Thursday. Rained in afternoon and evening. At School. Was dismissed to see Grays off to Washington at 2 p.m. At home in the evening.

Friday. Fair day. At School. After school staid to meeting for organizing military corps and was appointed chairman of committee to draft a constitution. In evening went to Lyceum.

April 27. Saturday. Fair in forenoon and shower in afternoon. Drilling with Union Cadets in forenoon. At Camp Taylor in afternoon.

April 29. In the evening drilling with Home Guards.

May 11. Drilling with U.C. in forenoon . . .

There were equal quantities of excitement and indecision in the air. At a meeting on April 19, Cleveland's coloured citizens pledged themselves to organize a military company without delay. "Resolved that today as in

73

the times of '76 and in the days of 1812, we are ready to go forth and do battle in the common cause of our country." Their offer, paradoxically, was refused. If there was to be war, it was a white man's war.

A fugitive negro, escaped from Alabama, wrote, "You can imagine my feelings on hearing that Fort Sumter had been bombarded. I listened to the sounds and though many miles away I fancied I heard the cannon, in thunder tones, say,'The year of jubilee has come. Return, you exiles home.' "

The Harding brothers conferred. "Do you think Britain will come in on either side now that we're almost into a war?"

"My guess," said Alfred, "is that Britain needs Northern lumber just as much as she needs Southern cotton. I think she'll remain neutral and we won't be affected. I intend to pass my examinations in June, so look on the drilling as good exercise and don't forget your books."

In the midst of this came a letter from Roseltha who was not yet aware of the ferment in her brothers' lives.

My dear brother
I intended answering your letter sooner but we have all been sick with colds; and I have not felt like writing. I have not much time to spare to-day; but I will write a little while. I received a paper from you last mail and one previously for which I am much obliged. I would like to know what you are all doing and how you are getting along . . . comfortably and agreeably, I hope. You must write me all the particulars next time. Do not fear that I shall not be interested, triffles are interesting when they regard those we **love***. . . . I do hope you* **all** *get along agreeably together. "Be kind to one another" and bear with each others faults. We all have need to forgive and be forgiven. Go to the* **Bible** *for guidance and counsel. Read the 10 and 11 verses of the 12 chapter of Romans. Paul teaches us great and good lessons. How do you spend the Sabbath? "Remember the Sabbath day to keep it holy." I think of you every Sunday and pray the "Great Giver" of every good thing to enable you all to withstand temptations. How do Jasper and Newton get on with studies. I want them to write some next time you do. I have not seen or heard from father . . . but I do not think we will go to Walsingham . . . it will not seem like home now you are away. . . . Our little baby is growing finely. She is a fine healthy child, and looks like Jasper. . . . James has charge of Uncle Asa's lumber yard in Stratford and Rachel is keeping house for them. Harriet is with them going to school. . . . I had a letter from Uncle Silas not long since . . . my paper is nearly filled, and I must conclude with best wishes and a sister's love to you all. Good night.*

Sister Rose

Even as Rose was writing so tranquilly Newton was again noting in his diary: *"Drilled with the Home Guard. Drilled with Union Cadets."*

Alfred was not drilling. "War is evil," he said to his brothers. "Surely this can be settled without bloodshed, brother against brother. And we're Canadians."

"I don't care," retorted Newton. "All the fellows in my class are drilling."

Alfred turned to the Psalms for reassurance in the midst of the turmoil. "For in the time of trouble he shall hide me in his pavilion: in the secret of his tabernacle shall he hide me: he shall set me up upon a rock." Or he turned to *Walden,* or attended to details about the house that might still bring a sale price of $3,000 provided war talk did not depress the market. He could not help wishing that Cleveland could be as peaceful as Canada West had been on May 24th when his sister had described how she spent the holiday there.

In Canada West, on Queen Victoria's birthday, Roseltha and Will with little Eva Rose in her carriage, attended a picnic in nearby Woodstock. The day before the children, their hands full of hepaticas and trilliums from a day in the spring woods, had chanted as usual:

"The Twenty-fourth of May
The Queen's Birthday
If you don't give us a holiday
We'll all run away."

There were fireworks at night. All was well in Canada.

On June 15 Jasper was writing to his sister.

Dear Rose

I will not attempt to apologize for not writing to you sooner for the reason that it would be a useless waste of time and paper but will ask our pardon for past negligence and promise to do better in future. . . . I hope you spent the Queen's birthday pleasantly. In Cleveland that day is the same as others and nothing more. We have not gone off to fight the rebels as yet though Newton and I both belong to a military company and perhaps will soon go. The military excitement in this city is very great, though not so much as it has been. Camp Taylor which was located here has been vacated and the barracks are being pulled down. Very little business is going on in the city, and it is yet in mourning for Ellsworth and Douglas. We are attending the schools regularly, Alfred and I in the High School and Newton the Grammar, and are getting along very well. Of a class of about 27 in the High School Alfred and I passed in all the studies, last examination. We are now studying Algebra, Grammar and Ancient History. Next term we will drop

*Grammar, and take up English Composition. . . . Because you have not
heard from me regularly, do not think you are forgotten by*
your brother
Jasper [Harding]

Roseltha knew who Douglas was. He was the Democrat whom
Lincoln had defeated for the presidency, but who was Ellsworth?

The garrison in Fort Sumter had been surrendered without loss of
blood. Twenty-three year old Colonel Elmer Ellsworth was the first man
to fall in what was already a War between the States.

On May 23 Virginia had joined the seceding states. The secessionists
were now on Washington's doorstep, for Virginia's green hills could be
seen from the windows of the White House. In Virginia Colonel Robert
E. Lee was already organizing southern troops. Lincoln had offered Lee
the post of commander-in-chief of the federal forces. Lee refused. He
did not condone slavery but he could not countenance eradicating it by
force. He left Washington for Richmond where he offered his services
to Jefferson Davis. Uncertain who of those walking the streets of
Washington were friend or foe, or who in the army or in Congress itself
could be trusted, Lincoln had to act fast.

The immediate plan of the government was to protect the capital.
The army sent detachments of ninety-day militia across the Potomac to
occupy Arlington. Another detachment was sent in two steamers farther
down the river to Alexandria to ensure its loyalty. This detachment was
part of the 11th New York, a flamboyant crew recruited from New York
firemen who for the past two years had careered around the country led
by their young colonel, Elmer Ellsworth. The Fire Zouaves loved to
swagger around in their uniform of baggy gray pants, blue jackets and
scarlet turbans. When their country called, the Zouaves immediately
moved to Washington, spoiling for action.

On May 25, 1861, they marched out of Washington across the mile
and a quarter Long Bridge to embark for Alexandria, young and eager
to win glory. There, in the name of the United States of America they
seized the Orange and Alexandria railway depot. Then Ellsworth spied
the Stars and Bars flying from the roof of the Marshall House Hotel.
"Follow me," he cried and dashed through the front doors and up the
stairs to pull it down.

The proprietor of the Marshall House was a man so ardently pro-
slavery that he had cut off a piece of John Brown's ear with his clasp-
knife and displayed it in a bottle of alcohol in his bar. The flag flying on
the hotel roof was the visible sign of which side he supported and no
one, in uniform or out, was going to pull it down.

As Ellsworth and his men came clattering down the stairs with the flag, the secessionist met them with a gun. One shot and Ellsworth fell dead. Private Brownell, just behind him, shot and bayoneted the proprietor.

Ellsworth's body was taken to Washington where it lay in state. The whole North mourned the death of its hero, the first man to fall in the war. West High School in Cleveland draped its walls in black mourning crepe in deference to him and his companion in death, Stephen A. Douglas, abolitionist.

When the school term ended, all three lads were promoted, Newton from Eagle Street Grammar School into West High School. Newton was accorded the honour of giving the valedictory address for his class. He was quite equal to the occasion:

"In looking forward to the future," he said to the assembled school, *"it is natural for the youthful mind to indulge in bright hopes and pleasant anticipation. The world around us is fair and gay; all nature, dressed in robes of resplendent beauty, seems replete with joy;—and as we go forth from the close of this term, many of us probably without the expectation of again returning, we indulge in fond dreams of future usefulness and happiness.*

"Our lot has been cast in a republican land, where all have opportunities for distinguishing themselves; where the mind, the noblest work of omnipotence, is neither fettered, nor trammeled by petty tyranny, but where it is left with all its native energy, free to soar aloft into the bright realms of immensity;—to grasp the hidden mysteries of the universe; to explore the vast regions of mental illumination, and to revel in the glories of intellectual splendor . . . "

Borne on the wings of his eloquence he continued: *"To-day, five hundred millions of our fellow men are envelloped in pagan darkness. . . . The youth of America, the offspring of the nineteenth century, the children of liberty, reared in the cradle of freedom, watched over by admiring millions, and looked to by the oppressed of every clime as the hope of the world, on **them** devolves the great work of the world's regeneration. . . .*

We are now about to separate. We shall never all meet again on earth; but the earnest desire of one, who will ever remember Eagle Street School with pleasureable emotions, is that Parents and Friends, Teachers and Scholars, may at last meet in the better land, where the vicissitudes of life can never affect us, and where the parting word is never spoken. Farewell."

77

The Harding boys had lived up to their determination to do well. School was out, and now that they were no longer under the discipline of studying, they were surrounded more than ever by the war fever that filled the air and the streets. Besides, there was the thought of army pay and the knowledge that their father's business in Walsingham was not proving to be the gold mine he had expected.

Enos wrote, the business man in him expedient: The army will need lumber for barracks. See if you can collect our money. The house ought to be ready to sell by now. See about that too. Mind your words about secession and slavery. Keep your opinions to yourself. The Hopkins boys who live near Venison Creek were sounding off about supporting the South because they say Britain needs the cotton and they have some relatives in England who work in the factories in Manchester. Not everyone jeered at them. If that can happen here the same can happen in Cleveland though you say more of the people there, like Stephen Douglas, are abolitionists. They may be against slavery but not for the war.

Your father
Enos (Harding)

Yes, there was army pay and like every one their age, the boys needed money. There was also the real pressure of the comments: "Of course you're going to help, along with your classmates." Jasper and Newton talked of enlisting as either ninety-day or three-year volunteers. Alfred was perplexed how to advise them. He did not feel that he had the temperament of a soldier but he too was feeling the pull of events. He sought advice from the principal of the high school who had taken a strong interest in the four students from one family.

"We need more money to continue our education and every day we pass the recruiting station."

"Why don't you try the 50th New York? They're here recruiting teamsters."

"Teamsters! My brothers want to go as soldiers."

"A soldier gets only $13 a month and a teamster with a supply train gets $25. A wagonmaster gets $40 a month and as the oldest you would qualify for that. You won't have to carry a gun, the war will be over in a few months, and you can return to school in the fall with money in your pockets."

Daily the situation was becoming more serious. The 75,000 volunteers that the president had called for only a short time ago were no longer enough. On July 4th, he called for 500,000 to enlist for ninety days or longer. Already Union troops had occupied Baltimore when that city had tried to prevent troop trains from reaching the capital. General McDowell was in command of northeastern Virginia; Harper's Ferry had been abandoned to the Confederates; General McClellan had won engagements in Western Virginia; and by July 16, when the Harding boys were still wondering what to do, the Federals under McDowell were advancing against the Confederates who were assembling near the town of Manassas by a little creek called Bull Run. The Confederate South was preparing to capture the government in Washington.

It was too much for the Canadian lads who had crossed the border only to complete their education. On July 18, 1861, Jasper Harding recorded in his diary, *"Visited Carey & Co., to see about enlisting as teamster."*

On July 20, Alfred, Jasper and Newton Harding signed on as teamsters with the 50th New York. Alfred would be a wagonmaster with about twenty wagons under his jurisdiction. Their combined pay would be ninety dollars a month.

Hastily they rented the house, rushed out to have their pictures taken, grabbed a sheet of paper and scribbled a letter to their sister.

Cleveland, July 21

Dear Sister

I write to you for, it may be, the last that I shall have that privilege. Day after to-morrow we start for the wars. I do not go as a common soldier but as a teamster with the baggage waggons however I think we shall be with the army about all the time. We go from here on the cars to Harrisburg and thence to Hagerstown, Maryland, and I do not know where next but probably farther south. We go for three years unless "Uncle Sam" is through quarreling before then. I do not know as the post arrangements are so as to secure regular communication or not but we will write as often as possible and you must write often as you find out where we are but we will know as soon as we reach Hagerstown. Dear sister, you must not forget your poor soldier brothers I have not time to write any more as I want to write several letters and my time is limited.

I remain your affectionate brother
Newton

Newton, so recently valedictorian for his class, so concerned about the faraway hypothetical heathen, was now catapulted into the reality of war. He was fifteen years old.

Alfred's contribution came next.

Dear Rose

We are just starting and are in a great hurry. I would like to have seen you very much before we go but that cannot be. We are in good health and hopeful of success. The news of a terrible defeat has just arrived. Do not feel anxious for us. We hope to return if possible in a year. We have made many friends in Cleveland—many earnest sympathizers. We have been assured of their prayers in our behalf. We know that we are sure of yours. I have not time to add more. I leave my likeness with Mr. Hopkinson our teacher for father to get for you.

From your loving brother
Alfred

Jasper's addition followed:

Dear Rose

*You will no doubt think it strange that we should all go off south but we think it the best we can do at present. If we should remain here we could not go to school only a few months at the farthest and after that it is probable that we could not get into any business here until times get better and by going now we can, if not unfortunate, clear $500 or $600 a year and be enabled to go to school on our return. Where we are going we shall in all probability be in **no danger at all;** and certainly in a very little while as we do not go with the advance troops. It will not be long before you again hear from your affectionate brother.*

Jasper

No danger at all? The terrible defeat that Alfred had mentioned was the first battle of Bull Run.

Roseltha sank to her knees beside her baby's cradle. Dear God, keep my brothers safe from harm.

Chapter 8

Yankee Doodle

No one could say that the situation that had exploded into war had come upon the United States suddenly. It had been gathering since an August day in 1619 when a certain Master John Rolfe of Virginia recorded the coming of a "Dutch man of Warre that sold us twenty Negars." Thus the traffic in human flesh was brought to the New World; and the commerce was too lucrative to die in spite of the rising protests that were beginning irrevocably to set wage-paying North against slave-owning South.

For a decade now the tide had run swiftly in favour of the latter. In 1850 Congress passed the Fugitive Slave Act. In 1854 the Missouri Compromise of 1820 was repealed when Kansas and Nebraska, north of the Compromise line, were admitted either slave or free according to their choice. No challenge to the Fugitive Slave Act could seem to win. In 1857 came the Dred Scott decision that enslaved a negro again in a slave state even after he had lived free in a free state. In 1859 the Supreme Court upheld the Fugitive Slave Act again. No, the situation had not come suddenly to the country, but these hammer blows to anti-slave sentiment were coming too frequently now for those who hoped for a peaceful settlement—a settlement that was now being resolved by blood. That red blood might now come from the bodies of three Canadian brothers on their way to share as non-combatants in the defence of Washington.

If their sister, six hundred miles away in Goble's Corners, could have known the variety of opinions that reigned in Washington when the news of the firing on Fort Sumter reached it, she might have prayed even more intensely. As the commander-in-chief of the army, old General Winfield Scott, contemplated the question of the seceding states from his wheelchair, he meditated that a lot of nastiness could be avoided if they just let the secessionists go. His private opinions had to be secondary to the demands of his public position, but as he awoke from his afternoon nap it was hard for him to believe that Confederate soldiers were actually on the march.

The man who would soon be his successor was George McClellan, a former official observer for the War Department in the Crimean War, sent there to keep up-to-date on the latest ways to kill. As major-general of thirteen regiments of militia, McClellan did not feel as mildly on the subject as General Scott, but his convictions were a mixed bag. He was anti-secessionist but pro-slavery.

The chairman of the Foreign Relations Committee, Senator Charles Sumner, was both anti-secessionist and anti-slavery, but if secession remained in force, he was known to favour annexing Canada to compensate the North if it should lose the South. This would certainly embroil Great Britain and make a national conflict international. He orated, he gesticulated, he repeated himself. He did everything but reason, some said.

These were only jots and tittles in the total situation. Who could divine the opinions of subtle smiling Secretary of State William H. Seward, a thin sallow man smoking an ever-present cigar? Or of Secretary of War, Senator Simon Cameron of Pennsylvania with his reputation for unscrupulous political practices? Who actually was leading this country, the army commanders or the members of the cabinet who were being bombarded with demands for money for military purposes? Would the civilian president, the man in the rumpled black suit and a head full of tall tales, be equal to the situation? How single-minded ought the government of the North be in pursuing a war that had begun with just a few shots on Fort Sumter? Was that only a gesture designed to test the foe, like a chicken flapping its wings? How determined was the new president of the Confederacy, Jefferson Davis? Davis, as former military leader in the Mexican War and former member of both the House of Representatives and the Senate, was experienced in both military and political fields. Could any general in Washington equal Robert E. Lee who as military leader of the "Secesh" already seemed to know what the Feds would do before they knew it themselves? Who knew any of the answers in this improbable confrontation that was called a rebellion but was swiftly escalating into an ugly civil war?

Certainly not three Canadian youths who were slinging together a few belongings in Cleveland preparatory to moving off to Washington as teamsters, excited as if they were soldiers, and included in the general fanfare that was speeding the troops on their way.

As they closed the door of their house and started for the station, a detachment of soldiers went marching ahead of them. The drummer boy was only twelve. With his hat set saucily on the side of his head, he was nearly cracking his crotch as he tried to equal the strides of the older men. How happy he was in his attempt to be manful as he banged out on his drums:

> Yankee Doodle is the tune
> Americans delight in.

The men sang lustily and fifes tootled brightly:

> 'Twill do to whistle, sing, or play
> And just the thing for fightin'.

And the cornets came in:

> Yankee Doodle, keep it up,
> Yankee Doodle dandy,
> Mind the music and the step
> And with the girls be handy.

Ah—the girls, in their long dresses with their brooches centred in the fold of the fichus. Some of the more daring pinned little Stars and Stripes on their "breastworks" and joked, "How would you like to fight under these colours?" Some swore they would not give another kiss unless their sweethearts went off to war. They mobbed the departing soldiers and grabbed the buttons off their uniforms for souvenirs. Some departed with no buttons at all on their jackets.

"If we lose the war, don't blame me," called out one cocky fellow.

"If you lose, don't come back to me," was the saucy retort.

"The teamsters," remarked Newton who had not been too interested in girls until this moment, "don't get as much attention as the soldiers." He began to bellow out the version of Yankee Doodle he had learned on the Canadian side of the border:

> Yankee Doodle went to town
> Upon a load of switches,
> He pulled and I pulled
> And down came his britches.

They followed the soldiers till they reached the station platform where they kept close together as departure time loomed near. Alfred was his usual handsome composed self. Jasper tried not to look apprehensive, but excitement was making him pale. Newton tried his best to look grown-up, but being valedictorian for his class had not quite prepared him for anything like this.

There was a flurry of goodbyes, then they were all in their seats in the train and moving off. Suddenly it struck them that they had no conception of what was ahead of them. Away from friends and well-wishers in Cleveland, they were moving into the unknown towards a capital that only a few days before, July 21, had nearly succumbed to the enemy at Bull Run.

Bull Run, a little country creek in Virginia a few miles outside Washington. There the enemy had massed. If anyone had speculated before on the tenacity of Jefferson Davis' intentions, his doubts were now dispelled. Davis was striking immediately for Washington, capital of the Union that was seeking to impose its will on seven seceding states; Washington, only one hundred and twenty miles from the new Confederate capital in Richmond.

When the news spread over Washington that a battle was going to be fought that would end the rebellion in a few hours, the Northerners found it hard to take the situation seriously. "One Yankee is worth five soft Southerners," the Feds in the capital boasted, scarcely realizing that the Secesh in the capital who still comprised half the population of the city were boasting: "One Southern gentleman can whup five Northern scum."

Thinking that the fight would be little more than a football game, the Washingtonians piled into carriages and buggies or walked or rode across the Long Bridge behind the marching troops. They took picnic baskets, champagne, and field glasses so they could watch their boys send the Southerners scuttling back home. Senator Ely paid twenty-five dollars for a carriage to take him in style to see the inevitable rout of the foolhardy rebels who dared to give states' rights priority over those of the nation.

When they realized that the lines they saw drawn up on the other side of the plain were no fake drillers but men preparing to shoot to kill, some of the boys were not so hearty.

"I don't think I know how to fight," quavered one.

"You'd better learn fast."

> Yankee Doodle, fa so la,
> Yankee Doodle dandy,
> And so to keep his spirits up,
> He took a drink of brandy.

"Advance firing," rang out the order. "On to Richmond," rose the shout. "We'll hang Jeff Davis to a sour apple tree."

"Advance firing," rang out the order. "On to Washington," rose the shout. "Whip the craven Yanks."

"Watch out. Here they come."

This was no parade ground. It was brambles, bushes, bullets, swampy patches around the little wandering creek, trees, cannonballs, open meadow with nothing between you and the enemy, bodies to stumble over, cries of pain, cries for help, bayonets, smoke, roaring, losing your column, losing yourself, fighting with rifle butts as clubs, not knowing finally which was forward, sideward or backward, who was friend or foe, if the man in gray was on your side or the other, if you were alive or dying, if you were losing or winning.

The Confederates were on higher ground on the other side of Bull Run, placed there by General Beauregard, the man who had besieged Fort Sumter into surrender. It was a good position. To dislodge them, federal general Irvin McDowell ordered twelve infantry regiments with some cavalry and artillery to march two miles upstream to flank them. That was fine military strategy, but what McDowell could not know was that old General Patterson (veteran of the War of 1812), who had been sent forty miles away to Harper's ferry to keep 15,000 Confederate troops bottled up, had been given the slip. Southern General Joseph E. Johnston (given the intelligence by a lovely lady spy) quickly loaded his troops onto the Manassas Gap railroad. They arrived at Manassas station just in time to burst upon McDowell's flanking troops and scatter them.

The outcome of the battle depended on more than strategy. It depended on which generals were most ruthless, for war was not a game, and in spite of people's astonishment, this was war. This was the battle in which Southern General Thomas J. Jackson received his nickname. When the Federals were concentrating against Johnston and Beauregard, who were just behind the Henry farm house, General Bee rode over to Jackson's stand to report that his men were being beaten back. Jackson said, "Give the Yanks the bayonet." Bee galloped back to his brigade. "Look at Jackson standing there like a stone wall. Fix your bayonets and charge." It was now hand to hand combat, face to face with the man you were going to stab.

When the day was over, when the sun was setting on the carnage, the picnickers in their hoop skirts, bonnets, their subdued mouse trousers and their tall hats panicked back to Washington, breaking down the little bridge over Cub Run so that the troops were hampered in their own retreat towards Washington. The Cleveland Grays, who had been first on the field, were the last to leave.

That day a new verse was added to Yankee Doodle:

> Yankee Doodle, fa so la,
> Yankee Doodle dandy,
> When he got to Manassas plain,
> He never drank his brandy.

As the night came on, Johnny Reb, who had rejoiced that morning for the chance to flesh his maiden sword, lay on the darkening field 387 dead and 1,582 wounded. And Billy Yank, untried, untrained, hardly able to ride a horse if he had been put in the cavalry, lay 481 dead, 1,011 wounded beside him. The sacred red soil of Virginia sucked up both their bloods with a fine lack of discrimination.

Neither Washington nor Richmond had been entered, but now both sides knew that the war would not be over in a day, or in a month, maybe not even that year.

Three young teamsters from Canada, one of whom had not yet run a razor along his cheek, and none of whom had much notion of what "Fix your bayonets" meant, slept the night of Bull Run just outside Pittsburgh on the cold hard ground. Later, in spite of their untoward surroundings, Jasper took out his diary:

July 23. Started south at 1:15 a.m. R.R. bridge broke down in Alleghany. Crossed over to Pittsburgh and took the midnight train. Arrived in Harrisburg.

July 25. Staid in camp.

July 26. Staid in camp and got my team.

July 27. Teams on parade one hour.

July 28. In camp. Fair in a.m. Rain in p.m.

July 29. On parade in p.m.

If they had neglected at times to write home when they were safe at school in Cleveland, they did not forget now. They clung to their sister as to an anchor, for their father was travelling hither and thither on business, trying to meet his obligations. The money from Thatcher & Burt in Cleveland that he had been soliciting in vain arrived a week too late to save his good name from the judgment that went against him.

Camp Crossman, July 28, 61

Dear Rose

We arrived here a little before dark on the evening of the 24th and at once went into camp. The place is not altogether as I expected to find it, some parts of it being better, some worse. The camp looked rather gloomy the first night but since then I have concluded that it is only about as bad as Walsingham. I have got my team which is one of the best in camp, and am expecting soon to be ordered out, probably to Harper's Ferry. Alfred has succeeded in getting a situation a little above the teamsters and gets $40 pr month. Today is Sunday but there is little

86

*difference here the work goes on the same as on any other day. I have
had little experience in the business here as yet but I think I shall like it
better when I get more acquainted with it. We are 6 miles from Virginia,
and 11 from Pennsylvania and about 77 from Washington. There are
many secessionists here, I should think almost as many as there are
loyalists. This is a very hilly country here and very rocky. It is not as
warm as I expected nor are the nights as cold or damp. July 29th.
Alfred and I went all over the town last evening to find a church. We
found 3. Two of them were shut and the 3rd was dutch.*

    My address at present is

Hagerston
Maryland
Camp Crossman
    Your aff. brother
      J. [Harding]

Newton enclosed a note:

Camp Crossman, July 29, '61

Dear Sister,
    *It is very warm here now but the nights are cold and damp. The
change of climate and watter makes a good many sick. I have been
quite ill for a day or two past but I am much better now. The boys are
well. I am in pretty good spirits now but the day I came here I felt a little
down after my experience of Rail Road accidents the day before and I
tell you I did not like my reception at Pittsburg much. Hard times, hard
fare and hard work in camp! We have orders to prepare to go some
where and I do not know where in two hours. I am short of time to write
much and I remain*

Your affectionate Brother
Newton

Alfred wrote at greater length:

Hagerstown, July, Monday 29th, 1861

Dear Rose,
    *We have had six days experience in camp life. We left Cleveland on
the morning of the 23 of July and slept that night on the downy side of a
plank at Pittsburgh. We had a dreadful accident at Pittsburgh. The
railroad bridge at that place broke down entirely destroying several
passenger cars. There was 52 persons in our car en route for the army,
two of them were killed two jarred so bad that they will probably die—*

87

one man got his back broken and several others badly injured. We very fortunately escaped injury. Several of our company have been taken sick since our arrival and are now in hospital. Jasper had been well most of the time. Newton and I have been sick about half the time. We will probably be sworn in for one year this week. There is a report that the pay is to be raised to $25 per month. I have secured, through the influence of Cleveland friends, the position of captain of a supply train and will probably go to the seat of the war before long. I get $40 per month. The danger is nearly as great as it is in the ranks. A great many of those who came with us have got very homesick. Some of them intend returning immediately. We intend to leave when we can't stand it any longer. I get up between three & four o'clock and go to bed at 10 or 11 o'clock. It is the severest place I ever was in. Jasper has got a four horse team in my train and Newton will probably have to take one soon. We expect to draw pay this week for the time we have been here. I would like to hear from you very much. We do not hear the least bit of news from the war quarters although we are within 30 or 40 miles of the fighting. I would like to have visited Canada before coming here but could not. We hope to return in a year. I have no time to write further. Write soon Direct to Hagerstown P.O. care of Capt. McCullough camp Crossman.

From your brother
Alfred

P.S. I have not got any ink.

It was difficult writing when no answers had been received, but it eased Alfred's mind to do so. Besides, he was young, he liked to write, and he was travelling, whereas a week before he had never expected to be outside Cleveland. If he had been back in Cleveland he would have seen 90-day veterans, their term of service expired, parade down Euclid Avenue with a rebel battle flag and a captured cannon drawn by four captured southern mules. Instead, he was writing:

Camp Crossman Aug. 7th, 61

Dear Rose,
    It is now more than two weeks since we left Clevelend and we have not heard from there or Canada since. We wrote to you some time ago—[more than a week] but have as yet received no answer. We are all well at present. Our fare is very hard and we have to sleep on the ground or in the waggons. We expect to endure many hardships and dangers, but we will endeavour to meet them cheerfully—believing it to be for the best. This is a glorious country. Never before have I beheld

*nature dressed in such buteous robes. The lofty mountains, envelloped
in a mantle of dense foliage, appear to reach the clouds. Surely the iron
heel of the war-horse should never desecrate so lovely a portion of the
world of nature. But amid all her loveliness, the noble Maryland, one of
the earliest homes of religious liberty throughout the world, is struggling
within the grasp of a giant monster, that will, until discarded, cripple all
her noblest energies and loftiest aspirations. Slavery **will** fetter the
energies of any people. No sooner do we come within its precincts than
its influence is seen and felt. We expect to leave here to-day or tomorrow but do not know where we will go—probably nearer the seat of
war.*

    *Aug. 8 I had not time to finish my letter yesterday so I will try to
complete it to-day. We drew pay yesterday for the time we were
engaged last month. Jasper and Newton each received eight dollars for
12 days and I received sixteen making a total of $32. That is better than
doing nothing. We are going to send $25 to Cleveland to pay some
small debts there. Where is father. Is he going to be in Cleveland soon?
We would like to know what he intends to do about the Cleveland
property. There is a payment to be made on the lot yet. If we could
manage to get a few months time we could liquidate all claims, that is if
we are fortunate enough to retain our life and health. Write soon and
very often. We cannot always find time and paper to write as we expect
to be on the road the most of the time. Direct your letters for the
present, to Hagerstown, Maryland, care of Capt. McCullough wagon
master, Camp Crossman.*

*From your brother
Alfred*

On the back of the sheet the other brothers wrote:

Camp Crossman, Aug. 7th

Dear Rose
    *As Alfred has written and I have not written to you since I left home I
shall take this opportunity of doing so. You have I expect heard all about
the railroad smashup long before this and it would be needless for me to
give an account of it. Camp life is very hard yet I could stand it if it were
not so hot some days. The heat exhausts me soon. Hagerstown is not as
pretty as Cleveland. The houses are all built up eaven with the street
which makes it look cold the houses in Cleveland being built back from
the street with a small yard in front. The country around here is very old.
As I was out with the team I saw an old barn with the date of being built
as sixteen hundred and forty six [1646] and I have seen others which look*

older than that one. They are all built of stone. This place is situated seventy-five miles from the Potomac beyond which lies the "sacred soil of Virginia." You must write us as soon as possible for you do not know how anxious we are to hear from home. We do not have time to write much and when you write do not wait for an answer to it before you write again, for it is just at odd times when we can write at all. I have not time to write more.

I remain your affectionate brother
Newton

P.S. We start for Frederick, twenty six miles distant, tomorrow or next day morning. A.P.[H]. Aug. 8. 1861

At the bottom of the same page Jasper excused himself:

Dear Sister
Alfred and Newton between them have used up the paper and I must wait till next time much as I regret it.

Your brother
J. [Harding]

Rose answered,

I was so glad to receive your letters and to know that you are still safe. . . . You must excuse my miserable writing, for I have to hold Eva Rose and write both at once and she is what you might call "Perpetual Motion" demonstrated. She is generally very good; but she has taken cold and is quite troublesome to-day. So you must kindly overlook crooked letters and unconnected words. . . .

They received her letter in Frederick and Alfred answered Aug. 13th, 61.

Dear Sister Rose
As I have a few spare moments I will employ them in writing to you. We left Hagarstown on Friday evening last, for Frederick, twenty miles distant. We encamped a short distance from our starting place, for the night, and in the morning took an early start for our place of destination. Our route lay through the most beautiful country that I ever beheld. At eleven o'clock we halted for dinner on a level spot near the summit of the Blue Ridge Mountains. At two o'clock we stood upon the summit and gazed upon the most enchanting scene within this state. I wish you could have gazed upon it as we did. The beautiful valley, through which we had just come, extending to the North West ten or twelve miles, and

*nearly surrounded by the lofty range of the mountains seemed dressed
in a fairer robe than nature generally bestows. Light fleecy clouds,
silvered by the bright rays of a southern sun, floated between us and
the opposite hills. Farm houses, situated on well cultivated farms,
resembled the most costly city structures; and villages, whose lofty
spires glittered in the rays of the sun, combined to render it unequalled
in beauty and to fill the beholder, if a "lover of nature", with the most
pleasing emotions. That night we encamped within six miles of Fredrick,
and the next morning [Sunday] got into town about eight o'clock. In the
evening all three of us and one of the teamsters went to church. Our
dress, for church, consisted of gray pants and shirt, felt hat and red
blankets. We attracted some attention. Fredrick is a very pleasant city of
about nine thousand inhabitants. The legislature adjourned a few days
before our arrival. We are about forty-seven miles from Washington,
forty from Baltimore and nineteen from Harper's Ferry. We do not know
how long we will remain here. We are liable to be ordered out at any
time. We have a very pleasant time now, considering it is camp life. We
go to some farm house and buy some bread and milk every day and by
that means get along very well with our "rations". I have been furnished
with a tent where I sleep in rainy weather. When it is fair I sleep out on
the ground with my saddle for a pillow and my blanket for a covering.
The teamsters sleep with their wagons. Jasper drives a four horse team
and Newton is a kind of an assistant whose duty it is to drive if any of
the teamsters are sick and to help wherever he is wanted. He does not
have much to do. Our wagons are very large and covered. We use four
horses to each wagon and the driver rides one of them. I have a horse
to ride and Newton rides in the wagon. I have only eleven teams under
my charge at present but expect to have it increased to twenty-five. We
intend, if possible, to visit Washington before we return home. I intend to
try and get a furlough this fall long enough to visit home. I have not time
to add more. . . .*

From your brother
Alfred

*You may think it strange that I should not sooner mail my letter after
writing it. The reason is I could not get to the office to get a stamp
before it was closed at night. We are out on the road every day foraging
& I have received two letters from you within a few days dated Aug. 7th
and 16th and one from Melissa. We would like to hear from father. If it
will assist in clearing the Cleveland property with a prospect of its
ultimate redemption we could send $75 about the 10th of next month.
We are all in good health and the weather is very cool and refreshing.*

We will probably leave camp for Baltimore or Washington within a few days. Jasper is agoing to write. I will write when we start.

Alfred P. [H].

Since writing the within we received orders to go to Washington. We start at four o'clock in the morning. We will probably be transferred to a regiment soon and to the seat of war. I fear we shall not hear from you very soon. We will write in a few days and let you know where we are and how we are and probably will be able to give you a description of the fedral Capital. Good-by.

A.P. [H].

Before they broke camp Jasper seized time to write:

Fredrick Aug. 21, 61

Dear Sister

    It is just one month yesterday since I entered the service of the United States. As yet I have seen but little of the war except camp life. We have quite easy times now, with scarcely anything to do. We generally have enough to eat such as it is though we do sometimes get out of provisions. I generally buy milk once or twice a day and manage to get along quite well. We have no uniforms and buy our own clothes which can be got here as cheap as in Cleveland. You inquired about the RailRoad smash up. We had arrived at Alleghany city and were passing over to Pittsburgh when a large bridge which we were passing over gave way beneath the weight of our train and another engine which was coming from an opposite direction was on the other track. Two cars of our train and the engine tender of one passenger car of the other train were thrown down a distance of eighteen feet. The car which our company was in was stopped on the brink of the break. One man was killed instantly and three or four more were injured so badly that they died of their wounds. There are many slaves here, and also many free coloured people. The secessionists are quite numerous. We have received orders to go to Washington and I have no more time to write at present.

Your aff. brother,
Jasper [Harding]

It was just one month since the rout at Bull Run. Washington's prime task was to keep itself from falling into the hands of the Confederates, but it was not the only theatre of war. There was fighting in Missouri whose allegiance was divided, but the South was determined to hold it, for the Mississippi valley was one of the granaries of the nation. There was fighting in Cairo, vital because there the Ohio joined the Mississippi, both highways for supplies. There was fighting in newly declared Western Virginia, where the Feds were trying to hold strategic Harper's Ferry, the gateway to the rich Susquehanna Valley. But any troops that were in the vicinity were being drawn towards the capital, either to guard it against attack or to be deployed where needed most.

On August 22 the 50th New York with the Harding lads left Frederick and moved steadily towards Washington. They travelled all day and encamped that night in a miserable rain. The pickets were edgy. They were close enough to Washington for marauding Rebel bands to be about and too close for comfort to the railroad between Harper's Ferry and Baltimore. Maryland's loyalty was a moot question. When the first volunteers had been sent from New York to Washington, a mob of angry Baltimore secessionists tried to prevent troops from passing through. The railroad centre at Harper's Ferry was a continuing hot spot. In the camp of the 50th New York that night the pickets had orders to shoot anything moving in the darkness. One picket heard a rustling in a thicket, aimed and shot. The drums sounded the long roll that was the call to arms. The whole camp tumbled out, guns at ready. No Confederates were found, but the pig was dead and the next morning they had fresh pork for breakfast. That night the Hardings discovered that being a teamster with an army meant more than being able to harness a horse and buy hay from a reluctant farmer. Alfred was summoned to company headquarters.

"Here is a dispatch that you are to take to the colonel in the other camp. The password is "Scramble." Take your best horse. Now let's look at the map."

"Captain McCullough, I'm a teamster, not a soldier. I didn't sign on for carrying despatches."

"You're a good man for this job. Do as you are ordered. Here's a pistol and a rifle. Be careful, but go as fast as you can and report to me as soon as you return."

Alfred went to Jasper's wagon for a blanket and a horse. "Wish me well. Good thing I learned to shoot frogs in the frog pond when we were kids. But I never counted on this when I left Cleveland." He rode somewhat morosely into the darkness.

It was more a path than a road that he took at first. The rain and intermittent wind tossed the trees about him, making it hard to listen for alien sounds as he stopped at a crossroad before walking the horse across, fearful of making his presence known if he made a noisy dash for cover on the other side. It was difficult to gauge how far he had gone. Just as he was wondering if he had taken a wrong turn a figure rose from the bushes ahead and pointed a gun barrel at him.

"Halt," said a low voice.

"Scramble," Alfred blurted out. "I've a despatch for the colonel from Captain McCullough."

"Thank God you're not a Reb," said the picket. "I was just as scared as you."

He made his way back a little faster and arrived at the wagon at two thirty. He nudged Jasper. "I'm back safe."

Newton woke up. "Lucky dog. Wish I could have gone. Rather be a scout than a teamster's helper."

Alfred shed his wet blanket, crawled in beside his brothers and slept, exhausted.

Chapter 9

Wagon Park

Two days after Alfred's midnight ride they arrived in the legendary capital itself and made their way through the city.

Washington was one vast armed camp, filled with uniforms of every description, because it took time and contracts to dress an army in regulation uniform. Till then, the 7th New York was outfitted in gray with pipe-clayed crossbelts on their breasts, as trim as West Pointers. The 8th Wisconsin, in the gray of their native state, carried as a mascot a live eagle named Old Abe. The Fire Zouaves of the 11th New York, now minus Ellsworth who lay in Navy Yard, were still the most spectacular in their scarlet, blue and gray. They bounded about boasting that if they were given another chance they could go through the enemy lines like a dose of salts. When a fire broke out one day they rushed to fight it with all the unleashed spirits of men spoiling for action. They hung one man by the heels from the roof so he could direct a hose into the flames. Staid Washington was rather startled by its population explosion to 100,000 people and its new role as headquarters for a practising army. After the grief of Bull Run, General George McClellan had been summoned to the capital from his successes on the Ohio to organize the confusion into what would soon be called the Army of the Potomac.

Weary and excited, with eyes bulging but trying to look nonchalant, the teamsters of the 50th New York spread out on Monument Lot at the foot of the marble obelisk in memory of George Washington, as yet only about 175 feet high.

"So it's going to be 500 feet high when it's finished. Right now I'm not impressed," said Newton. "I'm too hungry to care. Wish they'd hurry up with the chow."

"I'm just as glad we're here at the end of August, not in June, or we'd be eaten alive by mosquitoes in this swamp," remarked Jasper. "I imagine American mosquitoes bite as hard Canadian."

"Don't feel too happy about no mosquitoes. Look at the flies around the offal from that slaughter-house and that cattle pen." Alfred aimed a kick at a pig roaming loose. "Get out of here, you dirty rascal."

He saw a goat chewing some rubbish, its beard waggling. "Newton, don't leave your pants hanging over the side of the wagon when you go to bed or that goat'll get them."

Next morning, before they had time to satisfy much of their curiosity about the capital, they were moved out of the city to a permanent camp, for how long no one knew. Rumours were rife. They heard they were to move. They heard they were to stay. No one was certain. It all seemed to depend on General McClellan, "Little Mac," whose task was to bring order out of chaos.

General McClellan himself hardly knew what was going to happen next. After Bull Run, he did not want to waste untrained men again before he knew the strength of the enemy. His scouts were not well trained enough to estimate the size of a camp or an army even if they did succeed in getting through enemy lines. He feared another inclusive encounter.

They were still trying to analyze Bull Run. "They say that old General Winfield Scott took his afternoon nap as usual the day of the battle."

"They say our boys panicked and ran."

"They say the ninety-day volunteers refused to fight."

"That isn't true. Their time was up the day before the battle and they were packed up ready to head for home when they got up that morning. They set off for Alexandria and just kept going the way they'd planned. They'd heard guns before. How did they know it was going to be a big battle?"

Alfred wrote to his father: "The danger for the teamsters could be nearly as great as it is in the ranks, because if a battle is a surprise and the men run out of ammunition, the teamsters have to haul it up to them in a double quick hurry. But there is no need to tell Roseltha that or she will worry. We still feel the war will be over by Christmas and we can return to school. When you get your affairs settled, can we lift the mortgage on the house?"

In spite of advising secrecy to his father, Alfred could not help giving a few exciting details to his sister about the despatch ride he had had to undertake.

Camp Ross, on Aug. 31st, 61

Dear Rose
As I am idle this morning I will employ my time in writing to you. My last letter to you was mailed on the road from Fredrick to Washington. We left Fredrick on the 22nd inst. for this place. It was a very disagreeable journey. During the first day it rained very hard. At night I was dispatched through the mud and rain six miles to carry dispatches to another company. The road was very dangerous and I was heavily armed. But a few nights afterwards nearly a whole regiment was cut to pieces on the very same road. We reached Washington on the 24th, encamped on Monument lot. The Washington monument is erected on this lot. . . . I did not have time to see much of Washington but what I did see of it did not near reach my expectations. . . . about sixty thousand inhabitants and if it was not for the Government buildings, would be numbered among the inferior second class American cities. I do not think that it is near as pleasant a place as Cleveland. The White House looks very pretty, but I had not time to call on "Old Abe". We left Washington on Monday the 26th for this camp. We are now located about five miles from Washington on the Bladensburg road, where we will probably remain for several weeks. Newton and I are in good health, but Jasper has not been very well since we left Fredrick. I am going to try to get a better position for him if possible. Since we came here we have been transferred to a larger train—numbering one hundred and ten horses and thirty-two men. I hold nearly the same position that I did before and get the same pay. As orders have just come for me to report to headquarters I will have to close. Write very often.

From your brother
Alfred

P.S. Excuse my poor writing. I have to write on a horse bucket.

Jasper added a note:

Dear Rose,
We are now encamped about five miles from Washington. We were encamped in that city a day and a half but did not have much chance to see the places of interest. I went through the Capitol and found it to be a very splendid building. I was also in the Treasury . . . We have many rumours here. First G. McClellan had driven the enemy out of Manassas, then one of our regiments had been attacked and cut to pieces by the secessionists, and again the enemy were attacking Washington. We have

heard some cannonading during the last few days. Direct your letters to Wagon Park, Washington D.C., Care of Capt. Putnam, Asst. Q.M.

Your aff. brother

Jasper [Harding]

Wagon Park was assuming a permanent look, the tents in neat rows and the routine well established. The multitudinous life of the camp ebbed and flowed around the brothers.

"The army beats clerking a lot," they heard one man say. "I like it fine."

They saw one fellow beating up an officer. "Who does he think he is?" the man shouted when restrained. "I called him Sam at home. Why can't I here? I'm a volunteer. He can't push me around."

They heard orders in all kinds of accents. A German drill sergeant shouted: "Eyes vront! Toes oudt! Little finger mit de seam de bantaloons. Vy shtand like a hayshtack."

As they hauled supplies, they saw drilling, drilling, drilling, so that a regiment could move to the beat of the drums instead of spoken orders, so that a regiment would not get itself separated in battle, so that it could move like a unit even under fire, so that no one would fire on their own men as they had at Bull Run. There was drilling everywhere. Some new sergeants forgot what they had swatted up in the drill book the night before. "Git up and git," one roared at the raw, bewildered ranks. Another, just off the farm, who wanted his men to wheel, yelled, "Gee, God dammit, gee!"

Nevertheless, when McClellan ordered a general review and galloped onto the field on his black horse, the great hurrah that ensued came from the throats of what would now be called the Army of the Potomac. They had all been gathered in to defend the capitol, to fight for the Union, to fight to free the slaves, to fight because it was better than clerking, or to fight because a new verse had been made to fit an old tune:

> "Yankee Doodle had a mind
> To whip the Southern traitors,
> Just because they wouldn't live
> On codfish and pertaters."

Soon the brothers had leave to visit the city and join the rubber-neckers milling through the streets. Into the city they drove, past the Soldiers' Home and Lincoln's summer residence, on to New York Avenue, past Stuntz Toy Store where Lincoln shopped for his boys, past 14th Street,—"Look, there's a horse trolley. Let's have a ride." But it was not headed into the centre of the city and they were. Leaving the horse and wagon hitched outside Riggs Bank at the corner of 15th and Pennsylvania Avenue, they jumped out to continue their sight-seeing on foot.

Opposite the bank was the Treasury Building. "They say the money is printed in the attic. Let's get some samples."

"That's the State Department building on the opposite corner. Look at the big addition they're building. They say there's room for 2,000 female clerks. Too bad Roseltha's married or she could get a job there."

"Look. That's Jefferson's statue. He was one of the signers of the Declaration of Independence. Wonder what he'd think of his country now?"

"Maybe he'd say that the state of the Union just matches the pig stys at the foot of Washington's monument."

Then, in front of them, was the White House itself, the palatial dwelling that housed the man on whom all decisions depended. "There's the window, that one on the second floor, where he gives his speeches."

"His office is on the second floor, there on the south side. Maybe we'll see him at the window."

"That's the War Department building over there on the right. Let's ask Stanton when McClellan is going to start to fight."

"Let's find the Quartermaster's Department and ask for chicken every Sunday."

"Come on around behind to the park where they say the band plays every Saturday afternoon."

They looked at the bandstand, vaulted over the low stone fence that separated the White House grounds from the President's Park and walked along the driveway onto Pennsylvania Avenue that led to the Capitol.

"Here's another horse trolley. Let's ride up in state." They paid 5¢, expecting a smoother ride than their wagons gave them, but Pennsylvania Avenue, the only paved street in the city of mud and dust, was only broken cobblestones that jounced them around as they joked and laughed.

"That's Willard's Hotel where the bigwigs pow-wow and Lincoln speaks from the balcony."

"They say the bar is the biggest room in the place."

"Bet the politicians haven't taken the pledge of no liquor till the war is over, as the 11th Massachusetts did before they left."

"Look at the gas lights along the street and the fancy restaurants."

"They're fancy on the north side, but look at those cheap ones on the south side. Saloons. Watch your money, boys. Likely to be pickpockets around."

"Brick sidewalks, no less, and awnings on the stores. Quite a posh promenade."

"Brick row houses. They say they're boarding houses for Congressmen. They look better than Wagon Park."

Over the bridge across Tiber Creek they went (seventy separate stinks, sniffed Newton), over the tracks of the Baltimore & Ohio railway (only twenty-six hours to New York, let's go, said Jasper), and there was the capitol itself, imposing even with construction scaffolding around the half-finished dome.

"So this is where they make or break the country," thought Alfred.

"Hurry up, Fred. Don't stand there staring." The others were racing up the steps.

They swarmed through the chambers of the Senate and House of Representatives, took turns delivering mock speeches, went down to the basement where the bakery was situated and where the first ninety-day volunteers had been quartered, wished they could see the newly installed water-closets and showers for the members—not even the White House had flush toilets.

"Bet the British wouldn't have burned the capitol in 1813 if it had had flush toilets then!"

They walked around behind the capitol, dodging the horses ridden by new recruits as they bounced crazily through the streets on the new government issue saddles built high in front and back. They wandered onto Ohio Street where painted Jezebels lolled at the windows. One called lewdly at the good-looking threesome. "Let's get out of here," said Alfred. They broke into a run, but they all took a good second look as they picked up speed.

Then they returned to camp where they pulled out the tin pail in which they ground coffee beans with a borrowed musket butt, listened to the drums beat out the signal for the 8:30 roll call, then taps that sounded like "Go to bed, Tom, go to bed, Tom, go to bed."

Newton did not fall immediately to sleep. He was reviewing the day's events in his mind. "Jas," he nudged, "if you call a woman a whore, what do you call a man who goes with her—a horror?"

"Shut up. What would father or Roseltha say if they heard you?"

"I've got another one too. If you call a woman a tart, would you call the man a Tartar?"

Jasper shook silently with laughter. "Alfred would call him a sinner. Go to sleep."

"I can't. I don't feel like it." But before he knew it Newton drifted off to dream of White Houses, admiring audiences and girls with long brown hair.

Wagon Park, Sept 15th 61

Dear Rose

We have received two letters from you since we last wrote to you. We received your last letter yesterday and we were very glad to hear from you. On Monday the 9th we drew our pay amounting to $90. Yesterday we sent $80 to Cleveland to A.L. Beswick who is going to apply it on the Cleveland debts. We have sent $105 altogether to Cleveland. . . . We are all in good health at present and are having easy times. We will pay for these "easy times" before next spring. Last Sunday I went about two miles to hear a Rhode Islander preach in the soldiers camp. It was a beautiful morning and I enjoyed myself very much. There were two bands present and a large number of Ladies and gentlemen from the city. We were in the city on the 13th and spent about three hours in the Capitol. It is one of the most magnificent structures I have ever beheld. I would describe it if I could. We visited the Senate chamber and the Hall of the House of Representatives; sat in the speaker's chair and declaimed to an immaginary audiance of legislative dignitaries. Sept. 16. Jasper and I went to church yesterday on horse-back. We have been out in the country after forage today. We are about ten miles from the enemies pickets, and within hearing of their cannonading. There will probably be a big battle soon. Jasper & Newton are going to write. I have not time to add more.

From your Brother
Fred

Newton has not time to write before the mail goes out.

Wagon Park Sep. 17

Dear Sister

It is but a few minutes until the mail leaves the Camp . . . We have very little to do now. We only go out about once or twice a week after hay or such like. We very often hear the booming of cannon and musketry. Sometimes it is skirmishing and at other times target shooting. There is not much prospect of our leaving this camp at present. We were paid off a few days ago. Newton and I received $25 each and Alfred $40. We sent $80 to Cleveland. Write where father is and what he is doing.

Your aff. brother
Jasper [H]

P.S. We have just mailed a letter to Lissa

A.P. [H].

As Roseltha in Canada West tried to follow the progress of the war through her brothers' letters and the papers, the war between the states wove its uncertain course. General George McClellan (Little Napoleon), still busy organizing the army of the Potomac in Washington, wrote to his wife of one year: "I find myself in a new strange position here: President, cabinet, Gen. Scott and all deferring to me. . . . I seem to have become the power of the land. . . . It seems to strike everybody that I am very young. . . . Who would have thought, when we were married, that I should so soon be called to save my country?"

McClellan's army was now able to parade acceptably, but on October 21 the Federal forces were defeated at Ball's Bluff, Virginia, twenty miles from Washington, where the Confederates were said to be massing. This was not called an actual battle, merely a "reconnaissance in force," but nevertheless the count of nine hundred dead was daunting. A defeat so near the capital was bad enough, but that was not the only shame. The general in charge was sent to prison afterwards, accused of not directing all his energies in the fray because he was pro-slavery. In addition, defiant Rebel batteries in the Bull Run region had closed the Potomac River to traffic.

There were other reverses too on the vast battlefield that stretched from Washington to New Orleans, and from the Atlantic seaboard to the far reaches of Kansas. Already the Confederates had captured the federal naval base at Norfolk, Virginia, because it guarded access to their capital at Richmond, farther up the James River. This gave the South enough guns to enable it to laugh at the proclaimed Northern blockade of the seacoast. It also gave them the scuttled ironclad battleship *Merrimac* that soon appeared on the Atlantic reconditioned and flying the Stars and Bars. The federal capture of Fort Hatteras farther down the North Carolina coast and an uncertain footing in the Gulf of Mexico on a sand bar offshore from Mobile Bay that guarded the way to New Orleans offset this somewhat. McClellan demurred at sending any troops to facilitate these naval sorties for they deprived Washington of soldiers and Washington was his main concern.

There was a certain rivalry between McClellan and General Fremont who had been placed in charge of the newly created Western Department. Fremont had campaigned in 1856 for the Republican presidency to the cries of Free Soil, Free Men, Fremont. He appealed to Washington for tents, tugboats, hardtack, artillery and mules but the War Department told him to find them himself. McClellan, with his Army of the Potomac, was closer than the outer reaches of the country. However, when Fremont declared martial law and the emancipation of the slaves in his territory, Washington could act fast enough, and speedily cancelled Fremont's freedom proclamation.

The three Canadian brothers were attached to the Army of the

Potomac. Newton wrote: Still hard times, hard work, hard fare in camp, but we are getting used to it. I was talking to a soldier who told me that when a man shoots he can see the bullet from the time it leaves the gun till it reaches the target. He was laughing, but when I told him so could the fellow he was trying to hit, and he could dodge and take a shot himself, he looked a little down in the mouth. But have no fear for us. They will never get past our boys in Washington. McClellan is too good for that. We do not forage in the country for hay as much as we used to but take wagons to the depot to haul back hay shipped in by the cars. We call the baggage-master Old Dad. He is about as fast as Old Jake in Harding. He's hardly caught on to the fact that he's in the middle of a war and not shipping horehound candy.

A few days later Jasper came back from hauling. It had been a long day. His face was flushed. He looked weary. Newton was not one to do someone else's work, but this time he offered to rub down Jasper's team and feed and water them. "Why don't you go to the tent and lie down? I'll finish your chores."

"Thanks, Newtie, I think I will." The baby name the brothers had used at home had been discarded long ago but it slipped past Jasper now. He curled up in the tent with his scarlet blanket around him. His cheeks matched it in colour. He felt restless and irritable, his tongue was sore, but he slept and next morning felt better. His abdomen was tender and he ran hastily for the latrine, but diarrhea was so common in camp that he thought nothing about it. He harnessed his team as usual and went out, driving past the new stables that were being built to house hundreds of horses, champing and neighing, bought by the government for the new cavalry units. Again he felt flushed and irritable when he returned to camp, but this time had to finish his chores himself for Newton was busy elsewhere and Alfred was at headquarters. He thought of going to the doctor but lay on his bed till roll call, hot and uncomfortable.

Next day as he dressed, Jasper saw some red spots on his chest. He looked at them but thought, "I've had chicken pox and measles. Guess it's just some bites." His nose started to bleed and in the fuss over stopping it he forgot about the spots.

Again he came back tired. "I wish you'd see the doctor," said Alfred. "There are typhoid cases in the hospital."

"It's nothing. Did a letter come from our sister today?"

"No, there wasn't any mail."

"Let me read the last letter then." Jasper lit the candle. Shadows flickered on the walls of the tent and over his boyish face. He read the letter, put it under his pillow. "Wonder if father and Alonzo are still in Walsingham? And Rose. She said the baby looks like me. Poor little girl, she should have looked like Alfred." He felt close to tears but dropped into a fitful sleep.

Almost at the same time Roseltha was writing to Alonzo:

Goble's Corners, Oct. 1, 1861

My dear Brother,

Why in the world don't you write to me. What has become of you all. You know you promised to write to me sometimes. . . . does Walsingham and the things of Walsingham so take up your time and attention that you cannot spare time to write even a few lines to me who thinks of you very often and feels very anxious for your welfare. When you get this letter just sit down and tell me all about yourself and father. I have not heard a word from you since you were here. Heman Fitch [sister Melissa's husband] is here . . . and intended to take the cars at five o'clock for Paris. I took him to Princeton we got there just in time to see the cars leave so he came back with me and will go down . . . in the morning. He has been attending the Institute at the Baptist Convention at Woodstock. . . . Granma has chills almost every day. She calls it Ague but I think it is worn out nature refusing its office. She wants very much to see you. . . . Tell father that man in Brantford is doing nothing about the monument. . . . Uncle Asa wished he would see something about it but he is not able to . . . Little [Eva Rose] is well and grows finely. . . . I have not time to write more tonight. Apple paring is the order of the evening. . . . Write all the news. Good Bye.

From your own dear sister
Rose

Even as Roseltha was scolding Alonzo for not writing, Jasper was being taken to the hospital in Washington. That morning he had wakened with a virulent rash all over him. He was beginning to mutter deliriously. His temperature was 103. It was typhoid fever. Who knew what was the cause—milk, water, an unknown carrier, a careless companion away from home for the first time, rarely changing his underwear. Some recruits had been told to bring nothing with them, for Uncle Sam would provide everything. Conditions in the hastily set up camps were still bad. The Board of Health had protested, the Surgeon-General of the army had inquired, the War Department had investigated.

104

It was now too late. Typhoid in Washington was already reaching epidemic proportions.

Now that he knew that Jasper had typhoid, Alfred had no choice but to write his family.

Washington, Oct. 4th

Dear Rose

*. . . I have very bad news to communicate to you. Jasper is sick. He has been in the hospital three days and is continually growing worse. He has the **Typhoid fever.** I fear he will have to suffer much and lay many weeks before he will be able to be out. The Doctors say he will be sick a month. I will probably have to throw up my position to attend to him. They are very kind and attentive at the hospital. If I thought he would be any better off I would procure a place for him in some private house and get the city doctors to attend to him; but I think he is better off where he is. Rest assured all that **money** and **attention** can effect will be accomplished. I have been in Virginia twice with a supply train of one hundred and ninety-two horses. I have it very hard while on the road with so large a train. Newton is well and hearty. Jasper's sickness makes me feel very depressed. The doctors will not let me be with him much; they fear excitement. He has been out of his head the most of the time for the last two days. He knows me when I go there; but soon commences talking about some fight or about his team. I shall not leave him until he is better. We are now encamped in the city. We saw the smoke of battle and heard the "deep-mouthed cannon's roar" this afternoon. A large balloon was descried hovering over the field of strife. It is late and I must conclude. Write soon. Jasper frequently speaks of you and father. If it was not so far I would like to have you come and see him.*

From your Brother
Alfred

Alfred posted the letter, then went with Newton to the hospital. This time Jasper frightened them with his delirium. "Get the hay for the horses. Thirsty aren't you? Whoa, boy, steady now, Yes, Mr. Hopkinson, I'll soon have the right answer to the question. Tired, tired, have to study. Can't get the right answer." He lapsed into confused utterances, became quiet, then his eyes cleared. He saw his brothers.

"Hello, Alfred, good to see you. I think I'm getting better. Newton, old sock, what mischief have you been up to without me?"

The effort was too much for him. The fever and incoherence rose again. "Church on Sunday. Have to shine my shoes. Here's your broad-axe, Daniel. Finish that log." Then he sang in a ragged voice, "O Beulah

Land, O Beulah Land. I like to hear you sing, mother. You've a voice like an angel." He thrashed on the narrow cot. "I think I see angels. There's a golden light somewhere. It's around you, mother. Or is it you, Rose? Here, Sadie, here's the chicken for dinner. Mind the blood."

Anxious and bewildered, the brothers left him. Hope in their hearts was low. Not everyone died of typhoid. Some did recover. Next day Jasper was weaker, too ill to toss. He lay quiet and thin. In the lamplight his teeth showed like a skull's under the drawn skin of his face. Again the fever cleared briefly. He looked at them with sudden knowledge in his eyes and cried, "Don't forget me. Don't forget me." Then he lapsed into stillness again.

Alfred and Newton looked at each other unbelievingly. It couldn't mean that Jasper had given up hope. Once more he rallied. "Goodbye. Come tomorrow," he whispered weakly as his brothers left.

In the wee hours that night a nurse drew a sheet over the lad's face and a message was sent to Captain Putnam that another of the teamsters was dead of typhoid. Jasper Harding had died at the age of seventeen years, three months and four days. No danger at all where they were going?

Chapter 10

Gather At The River

"What shall we do, Alfred?" asked Newton who was only fifteen and a half himself.

"We can't bury him here far away from home among strangers. We'll have his body embalmed and I'll take him back to Harding to lie beside mother and Daniel. You had better stay here and drive his team. Carter can take my place till I return."

So Alfred travelled the sad miles back to Canada West. His father and Alonzo met him at Princeton. "We'll have the service day after tomorrow in the Baptist church here and the burial in Harding," said Enos. "Maybe if we had stayed in Harding and not gone to Walsingham there would have been a finished church there as your mother wanted. Come, Roseltha and Will are waiting dinner for us."

Silently they climbed into the red velvet lined carriage to drive from the station to Goble's Corners. With tears in her eyes Rose kissed her brother, then handed little Eva Rose to him who gurgled and pulled his curly hair. Roseltha might had said—Why did you go to Washington?—but she refrained. This was no time for recrimination.

Silently, slowly, speaking in monosyllables, they ate, almost ashamed of having appetites, but grief as well as happiness requires strength for bearing it. There was little joy in the thought that they were together again for a brief period. Pushing their chairs back from the table, they knelt beside them. "Oh Lord, give us the strength to withstand this burden."

Two days later, after the church service, they followed the hearse through the sunshine to Harding. Past the cheese factory, past the flax mill, past the road that led to the sawmill that was quiet for the day of its owner's grief; around the corner where the four-storey house, empty of its

107

master's presence, seemed a mockery of his dreams, along the river shadowed with willows they rolled to the cemetery hill and formed a little cluster around the grave with the friends who had gathered from the countryside.

"The days of our age are threescore years and ten or, if men be so strong, they may come to fourscore years. It has pleased the Lord to take away our brother in the flower of his youth, we know not why, but His will be done."

The boy's father thought, "Why did He have to take away my son so young?"

"Fight the good fight, lay hold on Eternal Life," the voice continued. A great lump came to Alfred's throat. "No one here has seen what a fight, what a battle is like. No one here has seen the broken bodies being borne to the hospitals as I have. Is a Union worth it? Slavery maybe, but a country—a geographical division?" Then he felt guilty about having any thoughts at all as his brother was being lowered into the grave.

The voices rose in Jasper's favourite hymn, for he loved the river Nith.

> Shall we gather at the river,
> The beautiful, the beautiful ri-i-ver,
> Gather with the saints at the river
> That flows by the throne of God.

Alonzo thought, "He'll never hunt crabs again or fish for pike or climb the old buttonwood tree at the bend and dive naked off the bottom limb."

"At least he's gone to eternal life," thought Roseltha, "for he did nothing evil in all his life."

They left Jasper in the hilltop cemetery under the warm October sunshine with a breeze as sweet as those in Paradise ruffling the goldenrod, the purple asters and the teazels. A late bluebird peered from a knothole in a fence post.

Once again old Jake creaked his way over the fence with his shovel in his hand. "Didn't have too many rides in that red velvet carriage. He never even fought in a battle and he had to die. I wonder why?"

He leaned on his shovel as he watched the long procession wind down the cemetery road and separate into its several ways. The hearse turned right to follow the eighth concession up to the ninth and back by the Drumbo Road to Princeton. The Harding carriage turned left along the river to the village, passing the big house with alien families in it and no woman singing. On it went to the bridge over the winding river, its boards sounding as hollow under the horse's hooves as the thoughts of the family in the carriage. They took tea with their Aunt Eliza and friends in the house above the valley, then gathered outside to drive back to Goble's Corners before dark should fall.

Neridia Cline and her father had come from Walsingham. "Thank you for coming, Miss Cline," said Enos, holding her hand briefly. He turned to her father. "Thank you for coming. This was a heavy blow." He made no attempt to hide his tears.

Neridia kissed Roseltha, shook Alfred's and Alonzo's hands. "We're staying here for the night. Safe journey to you." As the carriage pulled away, the sun was already dropping behind the hill and the shadows in the valley stretched their long lengths across it. A cow lowed softly to her calf and her bell tinkled softly as she cropped.

Then Roseltha burst out. "He said there was no danger where you were going. Don't go back to Washington, Alfred. Stay here and tell Newtie to come home."

Alfred's thoughts froze as he tried to sort them out. Stay—what for? Go—what for? What *was* the best thing to do?

Aloud he said, "I have to go back for a time. I'll go by way of Cleveland to see about things there and visit our friends. Then I'll decide."

"It will have to be your decision, son," said Enos as he stopped the horses to light the side lantern and then drove with loosened reins so that the horses could pick their way along the dark road.

"What are you going to do, father?"

"I'll finish in Walsingham by spring. Your Uncle Asa needs help in the lumber mill in Stratford. I might go there. If it weren't for the war I might go to Kentucky to help Silas with his stage routes, but things are too uncertain there. Or I might return to Harding and take over the mill again. I've been studying some astronomy lately, and I can mount a telescope on the balcony off the cupola to watch the movements of the planets. I'll decide soon." For once there was little enthusiasm in Enos' voice.

"Alonzo, what are you going to do?"

Roseltha trembled when she heard the answer. "I'm going with Alfred."

The sympathy of the Cleveland friends warmed the brothers' grief. The members of the Philomathian Society of West High School passed Resolutions on the Death of J. (Harding):

Whereas, it has pleased the Almighty in His mysterious providence to remove from this world our much esteemed school mate and friend . . .

Be it resolved, that in this afflicting dispensation we have been bereft of a true and faithful friend and member, who while he was with us, was greatly endeared to us by his kind, modest and gentlemanly deportment towards all. . . .

Resolved, that in token of our respect and sorrow for our fellow member we cause our hall to be draped in black, and that we exhibit the usual sign of mourning for ten days. . . .

The Cleveland *Daily Herald,* October 23rd, 1861, noted:

Died—In the City of Washington, D.C., on the 12th day of Oct. 1861 of Typhoid fever, Jasper [Harding], aged 17 years. The deceased was formerly a member of West High School, which he entered from Eagle Street Grammar School in the fall of 1860, the best scholar in the city. He with his two brothers, one older and the other younger than himself, left his home in July, to serve their country, in which service he was stricken down by disease. He was kind and affectionate to his friends, modest in nature, and was respected by all who knew him as a model young man.

At home Roseltha was turning the pages of the boyish diary that Jasper had kept and which was virtually all she had now as a remembrance of her young brother. The sketchy record told not much more than the days he was in camp or went after hay. It ended on September 26, 1861. Sadly she took up her pen to conclude in her own copper-plate handwriting the record of the last days of her brother's sojourn on earth.

Sept. 29 and 30th. Sick.

Oct. 1 - Taken to the hospital, continued to grow worse.

Oct. 12. Died among strangers and far from home but not alone. A dear generous-hearted brother resigned his position, watched by him and ministered to his wants till he breathed his last, embalmed his body and brought him 600 miles amid difficulties and danger to the home of his childhood, that surrounded by loved ones and friends he might be laid in the tomb with his sainted mother and young brother.

Oct. 18. His remains arrived home.

Oct. 20. He was laid in his grave.

The tears that had not come when they stood on the hill around the gaping grave now coursed down her cheeks. She seized her pen to write to Washington. *"Come, home, come home,"* she pleaded, *"Surely Canada can shelter her sons."*

But Alfred and Alonzo along with Newton were already caught up in the camaraderie of camp life with its hardships and with its payday.

Dec. 15th, 1861

Dear Rose,

Have you come to the conclusion that we are all dead? If so, you are mistaken. But we have been very neglectful. I am well at present but Newton . . . has been in the hospital since last Tuesday. He will, probably, be out tomorrow or the next day. . . . I have had four teeth

filled, and am in hopes that I will not be bothered any more with them.
We have had delightful weather this month so far only the nights are very
cold. November was very disagreeable. We had ice one and a half inches
thick and a little snow. . . . We did not get in Cleveland until the Sunday
after we left your place. We staid in Cleveland over a week. I could
hardly get away from Mr. Hopkinson. He said he had lost two of his best
scholars and he was afraid I would never come back. One of the scholars
he referred to was lost on the lake the same day and hour that Jasper
died. The folks in Cleveland were very kind . . . They gave us everything
we could carry that we were likely to need and offered a good deal more
than we could take with us. . . . I think that I will come home next
summer if I do not like it any better than I do now. I am getting tired of
camp life. It is almost as bad as living in Walsingham. I would like to be
with you during the holidays but that cannot be. One of the teamsters in
the train I used to be in died a few days ago. He was only sixteen and
had no friends here. I telegraphed to his folks in Ohio but have not
received an answer. I am going to church to-day and must get ready so
Good-by.

Yours fraternally
A.P. [Harding]

Direct your letters to Washington Railroad Park, care of Capt. J.J. Dana.

If there were days when Alfred felt like flotsam and jetsam, his situation
was only parallelling that of the ship of state. Early in November old
General Winfield Scott had resigned and been replaced as commander-in-
chief of the army by dashing George McClellan. Watching one of
McClellan's grand reviews was better than a day at the races. The grand
reviews were not effective in dislodging the Confederates from their
proximity to the capital, but one of them resulted in a song that would
never be forgotten:

> "Mine eyes have seen the glory of the coming of the Lord:
> He is trampling out the vintage where the grapes of wrath
> are stored."

It was composed by Julia Ward Howe, abolitionist and wife of one of
John Brown's "Secret Six." One day, coming back from one of
McClellan's grand reviews, she and her party beguiled the tedium of the
drive by singing *John Brown's Body*. Its words did not impress Mrs.
Howe's pastor who was riding in her carriage. He suggested that she write
better words and on her return to Willard's Hotel Julia Howe wrote "The
Battle Hymn of the Republic."

"As He died to make men holy, let us live to make men free
    While God is marching on."
If Mrs. Howe seemed certain that the war was being fought to make
men free, the Government was not so sure and it resisted all demands to
declare slavery at an end.

There was no hesitation in another area. Because of her need for
cotton, and in spite of her humanity in abolishing the slave trade in her
dominions in 1833, Britain was inclined to favour the South. In
November the Confederacy dispatched two senators on a British ship
named the *Trent* to ascertain Britain's stand and obtain a promise of
money and materiel. When the North received intelligence of this errand,
it sent out a ship and on the high seas removed the emissaries from the
British ship. How would Britain react to this affront to her sovereignty?
Would there be war over the *Trent* affair?

Canada was fearful. There were rumours that the government was
going to fortify Toronto and that Governor-General Monck was going to
ask for an emergency Militia Act. They sent Alexander Galt to
Washington to confer, and with the mediation of Albert Edward, the
Prince Consort, war was averted.

Roseltha wrote from Goble's Corners. "Little Eva Rose made our
Christmas merry. I had placed an angel on our tree. "Anga, anga," she
said whenever she toddled into the parlour. I thought of my brothers
when we sang "O Little Town of Bethlehem" around the melodeon. This
is the season of Peace on Earth, goodwill towards men but you are within
the sound of guns that contravene all Christian principles. We miss you
sorely."

Washington, Jan. 23rd, 1862

Dear Rose,

*I received your letter . . . We are getting along very well at present.
Newton and I have very bad colds caught by exposure to mud and rain.
. . . For the last ten days it has rained almost incessantly and the mud
had reached an almost fabulous depth. We are frequently out in the rain
long after night and are thoroughly coated with ice by the time we reach
camp. If we had a comfortable place for to go to after we get in it would
not be so bad. Newton was in the Hospital about three weeks with a sore
neck. He had been out for some time. We have not received any money
for the last two months but expect to soon. I received a letter from
Thatcher Burt and Co. a few days since. They had taken up one of the
notes due on the lot in Cleveland which leaves a balance due them of
$17.50. There remains another note of $145 which is due. We will be able
to pay it in two or three weeks. Father expected to get some money from*

112

*the last shingles but we could not have taken up the note without using
the whole amount. If he wishes it we can send him some money after
next pay-day. Where is he now, and what is he doing? I suppose you
have plenty of sleighing now in Canada. It is quite probable that we will
go south soon as we are under marching orders. I would like very much
to be with you for a few days but that cannot be. I do not think I will
stay in the service longer than till next fall. So much exposure will
certainly break down a person's health after a while. I have not time to
write more as my candle is just out and I am nearly frozen. Write soon or
I may not get your letter. Remember me to all the folks and tell me how
you are getting along. I was just agoing to write to Uncle Asa as I
received your letter. I was very much surprised to hear of his death. Poor
man! I hope he is better off.*

From your affectionate brother
Alfred P. [Harding]

Their Uncle Asa was only fifty-seven years old, five years older than
their own father.

Feb. 20, 1862

Dear Rose,
*I received your last letter . . . the same day I mailed your last letter.
The news from home quite surprised me. I was very much surprised to
learn of the death of Uncle Asa. I little thought when I bid him good-by
that I should never see him again. I am glad he was willing to die. I
should like to have seen him e'er he died. I sent $35 to Cleveland about a
month ago but have not heard from it yet. Alonzo is going to send some
money to Father soon. We expect to send more money to Cleveland
soon. The most gigantic preparations are being made to crush out this
great rebellion and to meet any new danger that may arise. There are
great preparations agoing on to start out several new expeditions for
different parts of the South. I think that this season will finish the war. I
think I wrote you that it had been raining almost all the time since the
first of January. It has rained nearly every day since and the roads are
almost impassible. In some streets the mud and water has accumulated so
much that it has overflowed the pavements. I think that the war will be
over and we will all be home by next fall. I attended church last Sunday
evening and heard a very good sermon by a Lieutenant from Wisconsin.
He left another appointment although not in the church. He promised to
preach to the congregation in a **thousand years** to come. The place of
meeting to be on the plains of Glory where blooms the verdure of
immortality, the light to emanate from the unsurpassing radiance of the*

Great God. A singular appointment! Will the congregation keep it? I
have received several papers from you lately and am always glad to get
them. I am getting tired of camp life and shall be very glad when the war
is over. I think about home every day. How different it must be from the
days of yore! How widely separated are they who, but a few years ago
"clustered around one family tree." It is getting late and I am very cold so
I will have to say good-by.

From your brother
Fred

P.S. Alonzo is well. Newton is going to hospital tomorrow. He has got a
bad cold.

Soon after this letter Alfred was called to see his captain and told that, because of his good record, he would no longer be wagonmaster in the camp. He was being promoted to the Quartermaster's Department in Washington. He would not, of course, be in the head office of the Quartermaster General based in Corcoran's Art Building, corner of 17th and New York, but he would be in the midst of the city itself.

Chapter 11

Washington At War

Alfred Harding was only a minion in the melée of wartime Washington, but he could not live in the city without learning much of the enormous activity seething around him. The duty of the quartermaster's department was to feed, clothe, shelter, horse, wagon and arm a fast-growing body of men. The calls for men that had started at 75,000 ninety-day volunteers had escalated to 300,000 three-year volunteers. The quartermaster's department did not need to go back to Napoleon to know that an army marches on its stomach. Its maw seemed insatiable.

The quartermaster's department had had to recover quickly from its first great blow at the beginning of the war. Quartermaster-General Joseph Johnston was one of the first Washingtonians to defect to the South, leaving his important post vacant. His place was filled by Montgomery Meigs whose office was located in Winder's Building on Seventh Street opposite the War Department. Organization for war had improved immensely by the winter of 1862 but the mood of exuberant patriotism that had pervaded the capital before Bull Run had sobered. The insouciance with which Alfred himself had reconnoitred the city with his brothers only a few months before had settled into a ten-hour daily routine of work.

As he sloshed through the streets in the muddy Washington winter, he observed that the work on the Sisiphytic white marble monument to the Father of the Country was temporarily at a standstill, but workmen chipped daily at fluting the columns and carving cornices for the Capitol building. The sections for the statue of the bronze Freedom that would crown the dome lay separately on the ground in front. When he examined them, Alfred saw that this Freedom carried no torch to light the way for a weary world, but looked very martial with her protective shield.

As spring approached, the main question on every one's mind was when McClellan was going to initiate large scale action. McClellan was hesitant. Grand reviews were heartening but he was trying to size up the enemy's numbers. The reconnaissance balloon Alfred had seen the previous summer had ridden impressively over the Virginia hills but provided no significant information. It had not even discovered that the great guns that the Rebels were pointing ominously towards Washington this side of Fairfax were "Quaker guns," fabricated out of logs and pasteboard. McClellan feared to pit his 120,000 men against what he was told was a force of 200,000. Some prisoners who had "accidentally" ridden into federal lines had provided him with the information. He himself had not learned to use cavalry for reconnaissance but the Southerners who had been riding since they could sit on ponies were more adept at finding out his numbers.

The South had other means of intelligence-finding denied to the general. As he passed the A Street wing of the Old Capitol prison, Alfred sometimes heard Mrs. Rose Greenhow annoying her guards by belting out:

> I wish I was in Dixie, hurray, hurray,
> In Dixie Land I'll take my stand . . ."

Before the war the beauteous Mrs. Greenhow had been accustomed to entertain political dignitaries at supper. After war was declared it was difficult for Secretary of State William H. Seward and Senator Henry Wilson to change their ways suddenly and refuse the invitations of the elegant widow to sup with her even though she was open in her declaration of sympathy for the South. When they waxed loquacious from the wine, she turned into code the information she gained. Southern General Beauregard received a coded message from Mrs. Greenhow hidden in a packet in the long black hair of a Washington belle who crossed the Chain Bridge disguised in lowly dress. This was the reason why the Rebels were able to detrain ten days later at the critical point in the battle of Bull Run. Rosie Greenhow was behind bars now but she could still lean out of the prison window singing lustily:

> To live and die in Dixie,
> Away, away, away down south in Dixie.

Mrs. Greenhow was not the only lady to relay information gleaned in Washington. Fragile Mrs. Augusta Morris boasted that she had been apprehended too late by Pinkerton's men for she had already sent away intelligence gained from another prominent military man. The number of Secessionists in Washington with their ears to the ground overbalanced

116

lone Northern spies like La Fayette Baker who succeeded in getting in and out of Richmond without being caught. In addition, both sides were floating rumours back and forth with intent to deceive till neither really knew what to believe.

It was a restless scheming capital in which Alfred was now living. Secretary of War Stanton was contemptuous of General McClellan's reluctance to launch an all-out offensive. Victories were being won in the western sector. Why couldn't McClellan do the same? The roads would soon be dry enough so that transport wagons, men and horses would not disappear in the mire of muddy roads. His army was uniformed now in light blue trousers with dark blue tunics. The officers sparkled about the streets in white gloves and gaiters. There were 100,000 men in the Army of the Potomac now but still McClellan did not move.

McClellan did not live in camp with his men but in an elegant mansion not far from the White House where he gave champagne and oyster dinners while the snow around Fort Donelson in Tennessee was red with the blood of the dying. Lincoln, still numb with grief over the death of his beloved twelve year old Willie, taken by typhoid in the same epidemic that had cost Jasper Harding his life, tried to discover McClellan's plans. One night McClellan, in what was termed the "insolence of the epaulettes" left Lincoln waiting in his drawing room and went to bed. The civilian president endured the snubs for so long, then called McClellan a traitor for his lack of aggressiveness. It did not work. He had to leave McClellan in command, for McClellan dashing about on his big black horse gave his men confidence, and confidence in a commander could win a war.

Naturally Washington was intent on preserving its own skin but as Alfred observed the bills of lading for goods coming in and going out, he saw that their destinations were rarely as far afield as Missouri, for McClellan was on the spot to corner what he needed.

There was still grave discrepancy of opinion in the capital about how long the war was likely to last and how much effort ought to be put in it. In the midst of the indecision, crochety Adjutant-General Lorenzo Thomas shuffled his papers and looked doleful. He had his own opinion of the difficulty of ending the rebellion. He favoured what was called the Anadonda Plan. Strangle the South, step by step, breath by breath, kill, starve, crush. Down to New Orleans, in from the Mississippi eastward, in from the seacoast westward, up the Rappahannock, down the Potomac, up the Susquehanna, with sword, bayonet, musket, Sharpe's rifles, Minié bullets, bare hands, with 30-pound Parrott guns and great Dahlgren cannon, with ironclads, submergibles and ships brought in from the high seas to blockade the South. The ordinary Joe like Alfred could only surmise about policy but even he could not ignore the fact that a number of ships that used to bring supplies up the Potomac had ceased to come, prevented by the growing effectiveness of a Confederate blockade.

If no one in the North was yet committed to all-out war, the South was. The terrible determination that Jefferson Davis and Robert E. Lee were already displaying rested on an ideology deeper than the preservation of slavery. They said that the South was now standing just where their fathers had stood with Britain in 1776. The North was an outside power trying to coerce them. They said that all the presidents till Lincoln had been pro-South. One man who fanatically named his son "States Rights" was indicative of Southern passion.

At night, as Alfred walked out after dinner in his boarding-house to refresh his brain, he sometimes saw President Lincoln crossing the White House lawn to the War Department to learn what news had come by telegraph from the fighting that, because of winter and McClellan, was not being pressed too hard.

Though attacked on all sides by abolitionists, Lincoln was holding firm to his decision not to abolish slavery where it existed, just to prevent its spread. If he could hold the Union together this way, he would, and encouraged Congress to vote supplies for the army in preparation for what might come. Congress responded with fifty million in cash and two hundred and fifty million in a floated loan.

From his routine position in the quartermaster's department checking shipments of flour, beans, pork and uniforms, Alfred sensed the immensity of the task ahead. He was learning another side of it too. There was no hesitation in the actions of those who had seized on the war as a chance to get rich quick. Corruption was already rife. For instance, the government had paid $167,750 for 25,000 infantry coats that fell apart after a few wearings.

Then in March a man from Maryland walked into Alfred's office, said he had a carload of flour at the station that he wanted to sell. "You don't need to check it. It's all like this," he said, holding out a handful he took from a small bag. Then with his thumb he pushed away some of the flour from a folded greenback with a "50" in the corner. Quickly there flashed through Alfred's mind, "A month's wages clear, to save for going back to school." The impulse was only momentary. He looked at the man, said "Come," and set off for the B & O station where the car was drawn up on the siding.

"Hello, Dad, unlock the doors of this car for me." Then to one of the station hands, "Take out a dozen barrels."

The front barrels were good. The back barrels were filled with mouldy grey flour. "Seal the door and send it back where it came from," he ordered. "Charge demurrage too." And he marked "Rejected" on the bill of lading.

A week later Captain McCullough stormed in. "What do you mean by passing that carload of dirty flour? How big was the bribe? I'll have you dismissed."

"What flour?"

"A carload from Maryland shipped by Sloan's Mills."

"I turned that back. I remember it now. It wasn't fit for pigs."

There was no use protesting his incorruptibility. Who, in this strange city, even the captain who had recommended him, knew that Alfred Harding of Harding Hall, Harding, Canada West, could not be bribed. The quiet strength behind the hazel eyes might be only the practised simulation of a liar. Frantically he riffled through his desk but found no proof of his refusal.

Early next morning he went to the station. Maybe Old Dad for once would have his records in shape. There, crumpled in the back of a drawer, he found the bill of lading for Sloan's Mills marked "Refused, A. Harding." His name was cleared but the accusation had shaken him. Almost he wished he was back in the camp with Newton and Alonzo.

Newton and Alonzo brought in their sister's latest letter for Alfred to read. Along with family news she related an event that was at once startling and comforting—startling to think that there had been real danger of war over the Trent affair and comforting to think that the Mother Country was sending aid. On Feb. 1 she wrote: In Hamilton a great crowd of cheering citizens went to the Great Western railway station to hail the arrival of 450 British officers and men of the Prince Consorts Own Rifle Brigade. Five more companies followed in a few days. The men had marched on foot through bitter winter weather from New Brunswick to Montreal because the St. Lawrence River was ice-bound.

"We think it's cold when we go out foraging," said Alonzo, "but that must have been murder in below zero weather."

Alfred continued reading: Little Eva is playing with one of my gloves. You would think it had a hundred fingers she tries so hard to get her five inside. . . . The government here is talking of passing a Militia Bill to train an active force of 50,000 men with a reserve of the same number and they propose to place a gunboat flotilla on the Great Lakes. Canada

119

and the United States have not had gunboats on the lakes since the War of 1812 and God forbid that it should happen again. The paper says that even a month's training for that number of men will cost a million dollars, one-tenth of the provincial revenue, and a special tax will have to be levied to pay for it. Canada East is opposed to this and Canada West is not too happy either. Some say that Great Britain should pay the cost of our defense but a report from the London *Observer* says that Britons feel that it would be as difficult to guard Yorkshire against the rest of Britain as for Britain to guard Canada if the United States should invade it. The Macdonald government is facing severe opposition over this matter and may be defeated on it. Write often for I need to know you are safe.

"I wonder if things are as bad as they look," said Alonzo.

"I know I'm only a teamster," Newton interrupted, "but I'm doing target practice whenever I can. If we have to rush ammunition to the front when a push comes, I may need to know how to shoot better than I can now. It'll be different from shooting rabbits in the wintertime at home."

"Yes," spoke Alfred grimly, "it won't be rabbits now. It'll be other living human beings, God's creatures just like us. Stick to your hauling, Newton, we didn't sign up to kill. Only to drive horses."

"I don't want to kill either, just be ready for whatever might surprise me." Newton paced the floor. "I wish I had a better gun than the old musket I have in camp. Some of the boys are getting Springfield rifles." He grinned. "I guess I'll go to the White House and ask Old Abe for one like his. He has a beauty."

"Who told you what kind of gun Lincoln has? Why would he need one? He has guards. Maybe he only has a pistol in case he finds a Reb at his bedside some morning, all the way from Richmond. Pretty unlikely." Alonzo was scornful.

"You think the President wouldn't have the best there is even if he's guarded part of the time? He must be able to shoot. He'd have gone after coons when he was a boy, nice fat Kentucky coons. I hear he has a repeater that loads with bullets. No stopping to ram powder down the barrel, or three bucks and a ball while the other fellow comes at you with a bayonet. I listen to what the soldiers say when they come back after a skirmish. And Lincoln's gun fires seven rounds in twenty-eight seconds and the barrel is still cool. Now that's a gun." Newton sighed with longing.

"We may be shooting sooner than we expect if Uncle Sam seizes more than Mason and Slidell off British ships," Alonzo said. "And I hear that factory workers in Britain are refusing to spin cotton goods made with cotton from the slave-owning South. It's a complicated situation. If war does come with Britain, we'd be enemy aliens and end up in Navy Yard with Rebel prisoners. A little target practice might come in handy if we want to get away quick."

"Maybe you both want to go home?" Alfred asked.

"No, I don't want to go home and work for 25¢ a day. Here I get nearly a dollar. Or sit in Walsingham watching father trying to be an astronomer. But I won't help in any war against Britain either, would you?"

"Certainly not," Alfred and Alonzo said almost simultaneously.

"Well, let's ask him then. No sense being in the dark if we don't have to." Newton astonished himself at his daring statement. Go to the President himself? He rolled the idea over quickly in his mind.

"Go to the President?" scoffed Alfred. "Who would dare?"

"Ask to borrow his gun while you're at it." Alonzo shook with laughter at the thought of his young brother going to the President.

"You think I'm afraid to do it. I've been thinking about it for a number of days already. Some of the other Canadians in camp were talking about getting up a delegation to ask Abe where he stands. If it's war with Britain, then sure as guns we will go home, 25¢ a day or no 25¢." Newton was beginning to be tired of being laughed at. Maybe he would show his brothers what he could dare to do.

"You're aiming pretty high, aren't you, going to the President?" Alfred was joining what he thought was a game. "Wouldn't the secretary of war be high enough?"

"Father always said that if you want to find out anything you don't commence at the bottom, you go to the top." Newton stuck out his chin defensively.

Alfred chucked his brother on the shoulder. "You're some scallawag," he said affectionately. "Well, I have to check some shipments and you two have to go back to camp. Bye."

Newton and Alonzo set off for camp. "You know, Lon, Lincoln goes to church every Sunday. We could see him there faster than by lining up in the White House corridors." Details of a plan were beginning to form in Newton's head.

"I didn't think you were really serious, Newtie. You mean, go to the President of the United States, us Canadians, us teamsters?"

"Everyone says he is approachable and can fix things up like getting a widow her pension when no one else will hunt for the right papers. Why not?" Half of Newton was certain he could do it, but the other half couldn't believe what he heard himself saying.

Alfred set off for the station where, with the help of some contrabands, he checked incoming stores. "Contrabands," he thought, "what a name to give to human beings because they are negroes. Contrabands, prizes of war, just like guns. Why doesn't Lincoln declare general emancipation now? Well, what I think won't do much good."

The contrabands were slinging bags of oats into a wagon, chanting in time to their movements.

> God made bees, bees made honey
> God made man, man made money.
> God made a nigger, made him in the night,
> Made him in a hurry, forgot to paint him white.
> Singin' high-stepper, you shall be free
> When the good Lord comes to set you free.

They were still not free. They were still shackled till Lincoln should act.

Sometimes Alfred took a few minutes to talk to the station hands. One had been a foreman on a Virginia plantation. He bore the marks of his escape, the skin pocked where the chiggers had burrowed into his skin as he hid in the brush during the day. He said that parts of the South, even in Virginia, could grow no more cotton anyway for tobacco had drained the soil. "Some places now a bluejay flyin' ober has to tote his own food."

"Is that why you left?"

"Oder reasons too. Ain't no use me workin' hard, w'en I slave. And my gal work for diff'rent white folks. Dere's a bulldog in de yard. I try see her, bulldog dere. Bulldog won't bite me w'en de good Lord sets her free."

"Where's your gal now?"

"Back dere. They sell our two boys down ribber. That's all some of dem keeps us for now—make pickaninnies to sell South."

"I come from Canada."

"Sure nuff? I'se headin' dere if Marse Lincum don' ac' soon."

"Was it worse working for a master than working here?"

"'Tweren't some massas sometimes—was nebber knowin' what could come. 'Tweren't the massa but dem who sells human bein's." His voice turned hard. "Dealers in human blood. And w'en I free, want my gal wid me. I'll fine her." And again he sang:

> Oh I heard Queen Victoria say
> Dat she was standin' on de shore
> Wid arms extended wide
> To gib us all a peaceful home
> Beyond de rollin' tide.

The bright eyes rolled in anticipation. "Dad-burned if I'll wait longer case de Rebs git to Washington. Think I'll git to Canada."

Alfred returned to his office. He did not have the heart to tell the black man that there would be hardships in Canada too.

Newton lost no time. He gathered the Canadians in Wagon Park into a little meeting. He did not bother to remind himself that he was only sixteen years old, too young, some would say, to be a leader. Alonzo was older, but it was Newton's idea so he kept quiet. Newton collected Canadians from nearby camps too for Norman Goble, Roseltha's cousin-in-law, and half a dozen others from their township were serving as teamsters. Newton was appointed spokesman for approaching Lincoln the following Sunday.

"Mr. Lincoln," he said politely, "my name is Newton Harding. We here are all Canadians. We are here to help in the war against slavery, but not to fight against either Canada or Britain. How serious is the danger of war with Britain, which would mean war with Canada?"

Lincoln looked down from his great height, and that topped by a stovepipe hat, at young Harding, five foot eight.

"Mr. Harding," he replied with equal courtesy, "we are happy to have you Canadians helping the Northern cause and want you to stay. I am not in favour of war with either Britain or Canada. As long as I am president, there will be no such war, you may be sure of that. Good day, sir, and thank you for speaking up." Lincoln tipped his hat and proceeded to his carriage.

The little group of young Canadians gathered jubilantly around Newton. "You see, fellows," crowed Newton, "what you can do if you try." He turned to Alfred. "Now we know there's no danger of war with Canada."

Alfred was pleased but still cautious. "Lincoln may not be in favour of war with Britain, but who knows what Stanton and Sumner think?"

"Aw, you're just a born pessimist. You'll see. Uncle Sam will eat crow rather than fight over the Trent affair. We know that now." The group went off rejoicing.

"I hope your tent feels warmer now that you've spoken up," were Alfred's parting words as he returned to his boardinghouse, mansion-like in comparison with the tents in camp. He took out paper and pen to write to his sister:

Washington, April 11, 62

Dear Sister Rose,

. . . I never get homesick only when I hear from home but nevertheless I am heartily tired of this kind of life, and shall hail the approach of peace with unbounded delight. . . . We have had very bad weather the last few days. More snow has fallen within the last two days than we have had before this winter. Newton Goble is stationed about one hundred rods from Wagon Park and [the boys] see him daily. He looks very well

and seems contented but I think that he would be glad to be home. Uncle Silas has come and gone. He came here the same day that I received your letter and went home on the 31st of last month. I received a letter from him this morning. He put in some eighteen or twenty bids for mail routes in Kentucky and Missouri. If he succeeds in getting those in Missouri he wishes Alonzo and me to go out there and take charge of some of them. I must conclude as I have business to attend to. . . .
P.S. Excuse my bad penmanship as I am in a great hurry.

His brothers came in to visit him.

"We went visiting around the camps a few nights ago. Learned a lot too."

"Gossip, my boys, gossip."

"Gossip nothing. We found out that there were three women spies in Old Capitol prison, last summer, not just one."

"Greenhow and Morris and who else?"

"Belle Boyd. She'd sing "Maryland, my Maryland" to annoy the guards and when they told her to hush up she'd holler, "Huzza! she spurns the northern scum!""

"That must've been the woman I saw leaning out of the window one day. She was wearing a dress with a neck down to here and was shouting at passing soldiers."

"She must be quite a gal, Freddie. You should have gone closer," Newton suggested.

Alonzo wasn't to be left out. "Have you heard the story about the quinine lady?"

"Who was she?"

"She was the niece of Postmaster-General Montgomery Blair. He sent passes to her and her mother so that they could come from Virginia to shop. La Fayette Baker, one of Pinkerton's men, heard that they'd visited a number of drug stores and then a negro maid reported that Miss Buckner was having her make a special skirt with pockets in it. They had bought six hundred ounces of quinine to take back behind the Confederate lines. That quinine would have saved the lives of a good many Southern officers sick with fever."

Alfred replied, "The Bible forgot to say 'Thou shalt not kill by seizing quinine.' Good old Secretary of War Stanton, always on the watch."

"Why don't you come out to camp next Saturday? We're going to have a stunt night. They say a couple of fellows are going to trim moustaches with pistols at twenty paces."

"See that you don't grow moustaches before then! Did you go to church on Sunday?"

124

"Sure did. The minister was preaching about morals. When he said part of his job was to save fallen women, a joker behind me whispered, 'Save one for me.' Are you coming Saturday night?"

"I will if I get back from Georgetown in time. I've a job there that day."

There were many fine homes in Georgetown, not as palatial as those clustered around the White House, certainly, but very genteel. There was boating on the river and as Alfred wandered down to the wharf when his task was finished, he looked across Froggy Bottom marsh to the vast expanse of stables, wagon sheds and corrals that would house as many as 30,000 horses at a time. There were bookstores in Georgetown as well so he decided to finish the afternoon with a bit of browsing.

The bookstore was dim on this dull day. There was no one at the front as he entered but he heard a rustling toward the back of the aisles of shelves that let him know there was an attendant somewhere. He turned to a row beside the window, and there he saw her, her face half in light and half in shadow like a picture by Rembrandt. Bright colour graced her cheeks and burnished her hair. She spoke with a southern lilt.

"May I help you, suh?" she said and flirted with her eyes at the young man who was as good-looking as she.

Alfred stammered, for since coming to Washington he had made few female acquaintances. "I'm fond of poetry."

"Come this way, please." Like an angel in silk she moved in front of him, her skirts gently swaying, her little feet tapping on the wooden floor.

"The poetry books are here. We're up-to-date." She moved out of range of his vision.

Alfred lingered up and down the shelves, then pulled out a wide, thin book with a dark green cover. He leafed over it. "It must be poetry," he said to himself, "but it's mighty strange with those long, ragged lines. No rhymes either." He read a bit.

> I celebrate myself,
> And what I assume, you shall assume,
> For every atom belonging to me as good belongs to you.
> I loafe and invite my soul
> I lean and loafe at my ease observing a spear of summer
>   grass. . . .
> Creeds and schools in abeyance . . .

His eye raced on:

> Houses and rooms are full of perfumes . . .
>> the shelves are crowded with perfumes,
> I breathe the fragrance myself and know it and like it,
> The distillation would intoxicate me also,
>> but I shall not let it.

He turned the pages, devouring the lines though they were unlike anything he had ever read or felt. Here was a poet who seemed to trumpet out his words, his thoughts, his feelings.

> There was never any more inception than there is now,
> Nor any more youth or age than there is now,
> And will never be any more perfection than there is now,
> Nor any more heaven or hell than there is now.

"What does he mean—no more heaven or hell than there is now?" He leafed over:

> It is no small matter, this round and delicious globe,
>> moving so exactly in its orbit for ever and ever,
>> without one jolt or untruth of a single second;
> I do not think it was made in six days, nor in ten years,
>> nor in ten decillions of years, . . .

"Who is he to say that about the world? The world was created in six days and on the seventh God rested." He continued turning the pages as if entranced.

> A show of the summer softness—a contact of
>> something unseen, an amour of the light and air,
> I am jealous and overwhelm'd with friendliness,
> And will go gallivant with the light and air myself.

"Gallivant with light and air! How free this person sounds!" He looked for the author's name. Walt Whitman, *Leaves of Grass,* 1855.

"I must have this book," he thought greedily. "I'll buy it. I can save for my education some other day. Maybe this is part of it," he excused himself.

The young lady took his money, discomposing him as her fingers brushed his hand. He lingered. "Do you know anything about this poet?"

"I think he was editor of a Brooklyn paper but he is working for the government now. His poetry is so different that it is eccentric. I'm glad you like it. It's the only copy we have." Again she flirted with her eyes. "You-all come back again. Mind you do," she said sweetly. As she lifted her arm to pat her hair, the red frill on the sleeve of her blouse framed the white skin.

Alfred walked joyously out of the store. "How beautiful and good she is. I wish I could get to know her." He read the strange poetry till he fell asleep and woke in the morning with the words sounding through his mind and happiness swelling within him. War-time Washington seemed far away and cleanliness filled the air.

Every hour, every page of the poems brought back the memory of that winsome face. "Next time I'm in Georgetown I'll see her again."

A few weeks later as he was going down Pennsylvania Avenue he encountered a crowd gathered in front of a store.

"What's happening?" he asked a bystander.

"Some secessionists are trying to nab a fugitive slave. Some woman recognized him as belonging to her uncle in Virginia."

"The crowd looks angry," said Alfred to himself as he glanced around. Then he saw her, his lady of the bookstore. She was seated on a sleek bay, her slender form rising like a flower from the riding skirt spread over its flanks. Her face was contorted with rage. "Get him, get him, he's a runaway," she shrieked, half rearing her horse in her passion. The black man cringed.

A man elbowed his way through the crowd. He took the black man's arm and pulled him into an alley between two stores before the crowd realized what was happening.

A woman beside Alfred said excitedly, "That's William Ellery Channing, minister of All Souls Unitarian church. He's only been here a short time but he's lost a large number of wealthy families from his church because he's an abolitionist, and he's not afraid to let people know it."

The lady in the riding habit jerked her horse around as if to search for the minister and the man, changed her mind and rode away. "We'll get him yet," she shouted.

Alfred watched her go. "And I thought her good because she was beautiful. How little I know about women."

As he continued on his errand, he met a gaggle of Rebel prisoners being taken to jail. A woman and her little boy stood aside to let them pass.

"Who are they, ma? Whose side are they on?"

"They're Rebels, they're fighting against us, the fiends."

"But ma, they look just like us."

"Hush, child, they're Southerners. They keep slaves. They're Secessionists. They want to break the Union."

"But ma, that man's bleeding . . ."

Chapter 12

Summer Of '62

It was a perplexed, equivocating, discombobulated country that the war was zig-zagging across.

Kentucky, January, federal victory at Mill Springs under General Thomas.

Tennessee, February, federal victories at Fort Henry, Fort Donelson and Nashville under General Grant.

North Carolina, February, federal victory at Roanoke Island under General Burnside.

Arkansas, March, federal victory at Pea Ridge under General Halleck.

Mississippi, April, General Sherman reached Shiloh, twenty miles away from the main Confederate army, ready to advance on the railway junction at Corinth which provided the Confederates with supplies and reinforcements.

But Jeff Davis was still in Richmond and the Army of the Potomac was just preparing to go into action.

McClellan, still torn with doubt, sent a detachment down the Potomac to rout out a Rebel battery that was blockading the river, but the boats were six inches too wide to go through the locks. The Rebels remained. Finally, another decision was made. General McDowell with 35,000 men would stay in the capital and McClellan would take the rest of the army down the Potomac into Chesapeake Bay and advance up the peninsula between the James and York rivers, lay siege to and take Richmond and the war would be over. On paper the Peninsular campaign would take a month—if nothing crimped the plans.

Alonzo and Newton were too busy now in camp to learn much except rumours, but Alfred followed the Washington papers avidly. On March 17 the Army of the Potomac began to embark and by April 2 the vast assemblage had reached Fort Munroe. Seventy-five miles to Richmond, only a few weeks away, if nothing crimped the plans.

The war will be over soon, thought Alfred cheerfully, and read with great satisfaction in the paper that Congress was so certain of the outcome of the Peninsular Campaign that Secretary of War Stanton had ordered recruiting to be discontinued in every state.

He turned the pages of the paper and was struck by an account of the woes of women working in wartime Washington.

"If she is young and pretty, she is surrounded by men who seek her moral destruction. . . . She has need of all her purity, all her firmness, for those who would injure her ply every art known to men. They surround her with flattery, with temptations of every description, and when these fail, threaten her with a dismissal from the place where she earns her bread, if she does not yield."

"There aren't any women where I work," thought Alfred, "so how could I know this is going on. Whew, and I thought it would be nice for Roseltha to work here if she weren't married!"

The account continued: *"There are about 600 female clerks in the service of the government, most of them in the Treasury Department, others in the Post Office and Interior Departments, earning between $600 and $900 a year, sums notoriously insufficient to support a woman decently. . . . A father of a girl who had been propositioned swore that the superintendent of the division of the Printing Bureau and Engraving deliberately told the said girl that if she would go with him to a certain hotel and submit to his wishes, he would raise her salary to $75 per month."*

"Well," thought Alfred, "it's one thing for Jezebels to hang around hotels but it's going too far to try to trap innocent ones. This is an unexpected side of the war."

Yes, the war, and the army that had been sent to end it by capturing Richmond. McClellan was proceeding slowly and carefully, planning, figuring, digging, building bridges, listening to reports from Pinkerton's spies about the numbers of the enemy. They were inflated as usual, but how could a spy in danger of his life ascertain that Southern General Magruder was marching the same men up and down and around and about so that he seemed to have a limitless force? When Quartermaster-general Meigs in Washington read the papers he had spirited in from Richmond, he could tell fairly well the size of the southern army but McClellan was still cautious.

Lee gambled on McClellan's caution, for he had been cautious when both had been classmates at West Point. The South had to gamble for, unlike the North, its resources were limited. McClellan's caution gave

Southern General Joe Johnston time to bring his army from the Rappahannock River to Magruder's aid. Because of his caution McClellan was now facing two armies instead of one. Quite a crimp in his plan.

Alonzo and Newton came in from camp to see their brother. "What do the papers say?"

"If it weren't tragic it would be funny. Everyone's blaming McClellan for being so slow but part of it isn't his fault. He counted on the quartermaster to get supplies to him by sea but he can't because of the *Merrimac*."

"Stop laughing and let us in on the joke," said Newton.

"You know the *Merrimac*, the ironclad that the North sank in Norfolk Navy Yard so the South couldn't get it. Well, the South raised it just in time to use it against McClellan. They steamed it out of Hampton Roads and sank two of our wooden warships in one day. When we trained our cannon against it, it bounced back the cannonballs as if they were marbles. I'd like to have seen it."

"Ha, ha," said Alonzo. "I suppose you'd laugh if it came up the Potomac and bombarded Washington. What's to stop it?"

"It can't now. They say Lincoln is no soldier, but he was wise enough when the *Merrimac* was sunk to order the building of another ironclad called the *Monitor*. It went staggering down the coast from New York in time to battle against the *Merrimac* that the South has re-christened the *Virginia*. The papers say that they blazed away at each other for a whole day and neither could dent the other."

"All right, what are they doing now?"

"They're both sitting there glaring at each other from opposite sides of the James, and without moving an inch the *Virginia* keeps us from getting supplies to McClellan up the easy water route. They have to go by land."

"I don't think that's so funny. Makes a lot of work for the teamsters who were sent in with the army. Alonzo and I were lucky we weren't sent there."

"I wouldn't have minded. I'm getting tired of Washington," said Alonzo. "I'm thinking of heading for Missouri so I can see the West. Come on, Newton, or we'll be late getting back to camp and catch hell."

"Watch your language, brother," Alfred was quick to interject. "You're stuck in camp too much. And now that I remember, I think I smelled tobacco on your breath when you came in. Don't tell me, Lon, that you've begun to smoke."

"Just a bit." Alonzo looked a little shame-faced for his Baptist upbringing regarded smoking as a thing of the devil. "It helps pass the time when I'm out with the wagon."

"Better think it over, Lon. It'll do you no good. Good night."
"See you soon. I hope it doesn't rain tomorrow if we have to go out."

Far from the imponderable situation in Washington, Enos Harding had left Walsingham and returned to live once more in Harding Hall. Ever resourceful, he occupied his days with business details but when dusk fell he climbed to the cupola with a lamp, some astronomy books and a newly constructed telescope. Leaving the lamp inside, he took his chair onto the balcony, feasted his eyes on the myriad stars and teased his mind with speculation about the order of the universe. What were the principles that governed the planets on their wandering way through the heavens? Copernicus, he knew, had established that the earth rotates daily on its axis and that the planets revolve around the sun. He knew that Galileo had tried to find confirmation in the scriptures for the heretical theory that the earth was not the centre of the universe because the earth too revolved around the sun. Maybe I can find proof in the Bible that the sun as the centre of the universe is immoveable and that God created it that way.

The night breeze ruffled his hair as he guided the telescope from its focus on Venus, now too low for observation, to Mars, higher in the sky. His imagination carried him back to the creation of Adam and, fired with the thought of what might have been in Adam's mind, he went in and began to write:

Oft have I swept backwards in imagination six thousand years and stood beside our great ancestor as he gazed for the first time upon the going down of the sun. What strange sensations must have swept through his bewildered mind as he wacht the last departing rays of the sinking orb, unconscious whether he would ever behold its return. Wrapt in a maze of thought strange and startling his eye long lingered about the place at which the sun had sloly falen from his vision. A misterious darkness hitherto inexperienced creeps over the face of nature. The beautiful scenes of earth which through the swift hour of the first wonderful day of his existence had so charmed his sences are sloly fadeing one by one from his dimed vision. A gloom deeper than that which covers the earth steels across the mind of earth's solitary inhabitant. He raises his enquiring gaze towards heaven and lo a silver cresent of light clear and beautiful hanging in the western sky meets his astonisht eye. The yong moon charms his untutored vision and leads him upward to her bright attendants which are now steeling one by one from out of the deep blue sky. The solitary gazer bows and wonders and adores. The hours glide by, the silver moon is gone, the stars are rising sloly assending the heighths of heaven, and slowly sweeping downward in the stillness of the night. The first grand revolution to mortal vision is nearly completed. A faint streak of rosy light is seen in the east. It britens the stars fade, there lights are extinguisht, the eye is fixt in mute astonishment on the growing splender till the first rays of the returning sun dart there radiance on the yong earth and its sollitary inhabitant. To him the evening and the morning are the first day. . . .

He set down his pen, exhausted from the wonder. "How am I ever going to master the incomprehensibility of it all? Maybe I should begin with just the planets and their movements." He picked up the lamp to light his way through the empty house down to the second floor.

Then a thought struck him. "I said Adam was a solitary observer! I forgot about Eve." His thoughts returned to Walsingham and little Miss Neridia Cline. "She's much younger than I—but I think she might be willing. I wonder what my sons will say?"

As the two great lumbering armoured engined rafts called ironclads floated opposite each other like half-submerged barns, McClellan wired Washington to send General McDowell and the corps of 35,000 men still in Washington. The military governor of the military district of Washington who had advised an advance through Virginia instead of up the peninsula, convinced the secretary of war that McClellan's army was large enough for its purpose. Adjutant-General Lorenzo Thomas disagreed but some Democrats spread the rumour that McClellan wanted to leave the capital unprotected because he secretly sympathized with the South. They contrasted the Peninsular Campaign to the victories being won in the western sector.

Again McClellan pleaded for aid. He wired that without more men he would have to lay siege to Yorktown instead of ploughing through it. He drew up his heavy guns and settled in. This was a second crimp in his grand plan to reach Richmond.

The Washington papers were fairly laconic about the progress in the peninsula but Alfred could read between the lines for he saw the war wounded being transported daily through the streets. What he surmised was nothing compared to actuality when he read a copy of a letter one of Newton's teamster acquaintances had received from his mother in the Niagara district of Canada West. The teamster's brother, the young scamp, had run away to join the American army. Now he was part of the siege of Yorktown.

"Read this," he said to Newton, "the papers don't tell this story."

It rained awful hard last night . . . and they say it will be twice as hot . . . .

We are about 19 miles from Richmond by land & about forty by water, the river is so crooked. . . . We get some good water here since we have dug wells & found springs but first the water was very bad but the boys said that we could like to drink it if we had been where they had—some of them said that they drank out of swamps and mud holes along the road & one said that he drove a hog out of a hole & drank the water. In the battle . . . one of the officers told his men if they attempted to carry a wounded man off the field he would shoot them & he was the first man that was wounded and called for help . . . .I am quite shure that if I was home now I would let the south whip the north or vice versa or any other way for all I care, soldiering is very nice in peace & it is all very nice to fight for one's country but when you are treated as slaves & that too worse than the slaves at the south who get vegetables & soft bread & everything comfortable & eatable provided for them not so the Soldiers who get hard crackers & some nasty coffee for breakfast, the same for supper . . . but the officers have everything good for themselves, lots of vegetables, etc.—nuff sed. . . . There is no Church here, how I wish I was home with you today to hear Mr. Carey preach . . . ask how much Willie would take for a share in the store when I get home. I think that I shall settle down & keep cool for the rest of my life if God spares me & everything goes on well. I hope to meet you all & live a long while yet but if it is willed otherwise may God in his mercy have us all meet in heaven never more to part. . . .

Alfred shuddered, "I think we'd better not complain about anything in Washington now."

As McClellan trained his big guns on Yorktown, the question of freeing the negroes was being debated once more in Washington. The abolitionists were working steadily but so were their opponents high and low. As Alfred waited at the station for a shipment, he heard a man say:

"I ain't gwine to shoot a white man I don't know nothin' at all of all along of a cuss of a stinkin' nigger. It's these here roasted Black Republicans is at the bottom of it all. But let me tell you, Sir, before another month that party'll be clean dead in the States. You'll never hear on them agin. they're dyin' fast, Sir, dying of nigger on the brain. Talk of the United States! A man had better be under that darned old British flag nor our'n. If I had my way I'd soon fix the war. I'd hang up old Abe Lincoln and all his Secretaries and half a dozen ginerals on a gallus, ten times higher nor Haman's was."

Again Alfred read the unrevealing battle reports in his paper but passed over them to look at what was being played in the theatres.

Donizetti's *Lucretia Borgia* was being produced at the Washington Theatre. "As entertainment, that's too bloody for these times," he thought, dismissing it from his mind. Much as he would have liked to attend something else he decided not to for there were still some payments to be made in Cleveland. "I guess I'll just go to the free band concert at the White House," he decided and looked down the page for a moment.

On the same page as the advertisements for the theatres one-third of a column was devoted to the standard advertisement of Dr. Johnson of Baltimore: *"Young men and others who have injured themselves by a certain practice indulged in when alone . . . destroys both mind and body . . . causes palpitations, debility, loss of memory . . . all impediments to marriage . . . trembling, nervous exhaustion . . . cured . . . 17 years' experience."*

The Washington *Evening Post* would carry this advertisement but it would never mention that a certain section of Washington's populace who dwelt on certain streets was known as Hooker's Division because of the visits they received from General Hooker's men.

Alfred threw the paper down and went to the band concert in the fresh air.

On April 6 came reports of a federal victory at Pittsburg Landing on the Tennessee River. Generals Grant, Sherman and Buell were winning victories all right but no one was prepared for the casualty lists. The new name for Pittsburg Landing was Bloody Shiloh. Grant was not losing a minute in his steady advance. The dead at Shiloh were buried so hastily that from one mound of earth there reached an outstretched hand. With grim humour a soldier broke rank, took a hardtack from his haversack, stuck it in the hand and marched on. The wounded lay among fallen peach blossoms waiting for help. Reports came to Washington that Grant was drinking, that he was insubordinate. Remove him, urged the papers. Lincoln, with his feet to the fire in his White House office, said to the Congressman who was urging it too, "I can't spare this man. He fights."

In the middle of April, flushed with western successes, Congress passed an Act abolishing slavery in the District of Columbia. Big deal, some scoffed. Big gain, said the abolitionists. But the situation was paradoxical for one black man might be free and one a mile away be a slave.

"Well, Jonah," said Alfred as he supervised loading at the B&O station next day. "How does it feel to be free? Still heading for Canada?"

"No suh, stayin' right here. On to Richmond and we's all be free. North Star can git 'long widout me. And I'll soon git my gal when we's all be free."

"If I were a drinker, I'd drink to that! Maybe you'll even get a raise in pay."

"I ain't contraband no more. Maybe I will. Boss, I'll say, I'se free. Want more money."

"All right, maybe I'll ask for more too. I could use it. But right now if we don't get these supplies away, the boys'll be too hungry to fight old Jeff Davis. Get going, everyone."

Then they sang as they worked because a gain had been made in the cause.

> Tramp, tramp, tramp, the boys are marching
> Cheer, brave comrades, they will come,
> Every heart is in the sight
> Of the cause of truth and right
> And the freedom of our own beloved land.

McClellan's men suffered in the humid swamps and torrid heat around Yorktown as the siege continued. Again the Canadian lad from Niagara wrote his kin, and again his mother sent a copy of the letter to his brother in Washington:

"You may write to Lord Lyons (the British minister in Washington) & try to get me out if you can—try very hard if you please—I want to get out very bad—tell him that I enlisted under eighteen & that I am only five months over it now. Tell him that I am a British subject . . . We got half a lemmon & four potatoes one day & that was all. . . . we are full of lice . . . I am broke out all over except the face in mattery sores so that I can hardly set or lay down . . . the bones stick out all over me . . . I saw the Rebels on the other side of the river . . . on picket but I did not fire at them—it seemed too much like murder & I thought of the Golden Rule—do unto others as you would they should do unto you . . . I have got the dioreha awful bad & it makes me feel weak as a cat . . . I have got the same shirt on now that I had on when we left Harrison's Landing . . . you must send a sheet of paper & an envelope in your next letter if you want me to answer it, so remember. . . . the men gamble awful down here. They all laugh at me for not doing as they do . . . I hope I may soon be buried with Christ in baptism to rise and walk in newness of life that when I am called from this world I may be found at his right hand . . . Where is the Merrimac . . . the food didn't come . . . I am growing a little hair on my upper lip . . ."

Again McClellan asked for reinforcements and again he was refused. Why would not Washington send reinforcements to the crucial siege of

Yorktown, so close to Richmond? Stonewall Jackson was coming down the Shenandoah to a Union outpost at Kernstown. After Kernstown where would he head—to Richmond or Washington? A killer's eyes looked out from under Jackson's old peak cap and his men travelled with the handles of their frying pans stuck in the barrells of their muskets. Jackson had no miles-long supply trains like the ones that lumbered behind McClellan with the teamsters fighting to be first in the line for the last ones got the worst places along the overworked roads. Jackson's men were coming as fast and light as wolves. Washington was shaking in its shoes as Jackson sped along.

May came. At last Yorktown was abandoned by the Confederates. McClellan moved on to Williamsburg. The Rebels abandoned Norfolk and blew up the ironclad *Virginia* for it was too hard to hold and too clumsy to move to deep water. Confederate General Joe Johnston was backed up to the suburbs of Richmond but McClellan snailed along behind his heavy guns. Jackson defeated the Feds again in the valley of the Shenandoah and finally slipped out of their grasp to join Johnston at Richmond. It was more important for him to help save Richmond than to advance single-armied against Washington.

June. McClellan was now six miles from Richmond on the banks of a little stream called Chickahominy. McClellan bridged it and spread his men on either side for he expected his northern flank to be joined by McDowell. McDowell did not come. They fought around a farm called Fair Oaks and a railway station called Seven Pines. Bloodshed belied the beautiful names. Only six miles from Richmond but the Southern lines held.

The stench of bodies waiting to be buried filled the steamy air. Nevertheless morale in McClellan's army remained high for they believed that the general's plan to advance slowly behind the great siege guns spelled protection for them.

It rained. The guns were immobilized. The general waited for the ground to dry before advancing. This was the time when Stonewall Jackson joined the forces protecting Richmond. Southern General Joe Johnston was wounded and Davis sent Robert E. Lee to replace him. Quick-thinking, decisive Lee.

Both sides were edgy as they tried to estimate each other's strength. Lee sent his jaunty cavalier, Jeb Stuart, to ride all around McClellan's army and estimate its numbers. McClellan believed Pinkerton's unreliable reports and Stonewall Jackson's presence unnerved him so much that he abandoned the offensive and took the defensive.

Mechanicsville. Lee took the initiative.

Beaver Dam Creek. A stalemate.

Gaines Mill. A Southern victory sent the Northern troops south of the Chickahominy again. Twice McClellan had been so close to Richmond that he could see the church spires and twice he had withdrawn.

Savage Station, White Oak Swamp. Lee was trying to get between McClellan and the sea, a pincer move. As the telegrams clicked back and forth between the army and the War Department, Stanton ordered recruiting resumed and Lincoln agonized. What was McClellan doing, advancing or retreating?

Four miles from Richmond. Why didn't he take it?

The wounded from the Peninsular Campaign poured into Washington. They lay half dead and neglected on decks or docks or limped and wavered ashore with the help of comrades. The hospitals could not contain them all, even considering the beds emptied through death. After one year of war the antiquated machinery of the Medical Bureau had barely begun to creak. The Medical Bill prepared by Dr. Henry Bellows, president of the newly formed civilian Sanitary Commission, had not yet been passed by Congress. Bellows turned to All Souls Unitarian church for help. Pews were removed and beds moved in. Other churches followed suit.

All Souls was at the corner of Sixth and E Streets not far from Alfred's boarding house. He went in on his way home one day. Some ladies in hoops and hats and violet kid gloves stood around like bonbons in a box. They pitied, gagged, and then disappeared. Others in narrow serviceable skirts began quietly to minister. A doctor oiled a silk rag into a twist, drew it through a bullet hole that went in one side and out the other of a lad's head, talked soothingly to him, drew out the maggots that had finished their job of cleaning the wound, dressed it and went on to the next. A stench arose from a pile of amputated gangrenous legs, hands and arms outside the open window.

"So this is the war to save the Union, or the war of liberation of the South from the North," thought Alfred with his insides churning. "What a terrible, stupid way to solve a difference of opinion." It was not the first time he had thought of the war that way, but the sight of the wrecked and suffering bodies jolted him now beyond measure. "And I, in my way, am part of it though I say I am only on the side lines. I'm in it so the least I can do is help." Taking off his coat he asked what he could do and worked till midnight and exhaustion.

He began to go regularly.

Dear Roseltha,

The churches and hospitals are filled with wounded coming in from the Peninsular Campaign. I have volunteered to help two nights a week and sometimes Sunday afternoon. Yesterday I stayed beside the bed of a

138

young man who was dying. He begged me not to leave him. I wrote a letter home for him but did not post it till after I added a postscript telling his family that he died hoping for a better life in heaven. I thought of Jasper as I stayed there. I am visiting the E Street hospital now instead of working in the church I was going to. The War Department has jockeyed the generals around again. Don't know how much difference it will make. Uncle Silas writes that a Colonel Morgan has been conducting cavalry raids into Kentucky. The Union army can never compete with those Southern riders. The raiders can capture pickets and videttes and gain information as well as disrupt communications. Some women are helping in the hospital though there is opposition from those who think it not a proper place for them. One is a doctor's daughter. She said her father is so busy now that she is lonesome at home. Her mother is dead. Besides she wants to help the poor men who have been fighting so well. I wonder how she stands the work and how the men who arrive could survive the hard trip from the peninsula to here. Remember me to everyone. How is little Eva? I suppose you are putting down fruit for the winter. Did the robins get all the cherries this year or leave some for you? How much do you learn from the Canadian papers. McClellan seems to be at a stalemate but at least he has not given up. On June 20 Congress passed a law prohibiting slavery in the territories. That is another significant gain for the abolitionists but there is a long way to go yet. Alonzo and Newton are well but Newton does not like the heat. Has father returned to Harding yet?

His sister answered:
It does my heart good to know that you are safe. I put down twenty-five jars of cherries for the winter and made two pies yesterday. You ask about your father. He has done fairly well selling the last of the shingles and the machinery in Walsingham. I have a feeling that he is considering marrying again and it will likely be Neridia Cline. I don't quite know what to think of it when I remember our dear mother but he is very much alone now. Neridia is a pleasant pretty person but is not too strong. Time will tell.

July in the Peninsula. Lee was never quite able to get between McClellan and the sea. Sickened by the slaughter of the battles of the Seven Days, June 26 to July 2, McClellan retreated to Harrison's Landing where there was dry land for his army, deep water for supply vessels, and comfortable mansions for headquarters.

The road to Harrison's Landing led over a height called Malvern Hill.

There McClellan ordered General Porter to take a stand against Lee's inexorable advance. Backed by artillery and naval guns, Porter engaged Lee's exhausted men. Worn out as they were, they fought yet another day. By nightfall the Northern army was still in possession of the hill but McClellan refused to consider it a victory and press on. A one-armed feisty commander named Phil Kearny stormed and swore when McClellan ordered the men off the hill instead of driving through Lee's shattered ranks. On the morning of July 2 the Rebels had the field to themselves.

The great, confident, much-paraded Army of the Potomac was safe at Harrison's Landing but Richmond was safe too. When the news reached Washington that McClellan was staying at the Landing, they divined that the great push was over. The campaign that was to have ended the war had failed. The successes in the western sector were not nullified by this failure, but now they would all have to keep on and on. The Anaconda Plan to strangle the South bit by bit was the only way.

As McClellan was embarking his troops for the return to Washington, Alfred received a letter from his father. . . . I have sold all the shingles and lumber to Cleveland and am giving up the business in Walsingham. I am back in Harding where I am taking over the operation of the mill myself. My astronomy is going well. We have had many clear nights. It is good to be back with our friends and relatives again. You may be surprised to learn that I am not alone. Miss Cline and I were married a few weeks ago. She looked very pretty in her white dress with a bouquet of roses. We drove in the carriage to Harding Hall where we are living now. Do not fear that because I am married again that I shall forget your mother. What the heart has once known is never forgotten.

Alfred sat back stunned. Someone else in Harding Hall. Someone else playing his mother's melodeon. Someone else in the red velvet lined carriage.

He went to the camp to show the letter to his brothers. "Jumping Jehosophat," said Newton, "I'm flabbergasted."

Alonzo was quiet for a moment, then he said, "Let's write and wish them well. That's all we can do from here."

Alfred returned to his boarding-house to write:
"I shall be happy to meet Mrs. Harding and present her with my compliments. Please give her my filial respects and tell her that I shall be happy to call on her at my earliest convenience."

I wonder when that will be, now that McClellan has failed to take Richmond? I wonder what Lee will do next?

Chapter 13

The Sharpshooter

As McClellan bivouacked his army at Harrison's Landing and the forts ringing Washington dreamed in the hot sun, Lee was not resting. As soon as the pressure on his capital was relieved, he was ready to strike at the capital of the enemy before McClellan could quite recover. Lee could not husband his resources for they were far from being inexhaustible. To answer the threat Lincoln issued another call for volunteers to sign up for three years, and Congress passed an Act authorizing the acceptance of negroes for military duty.

Forty young black men from the Canadian negro community at Elgin and seventeen from Buxton crossed the border at Detroit to join the fight for the liberty of their black brothers.

Early in August 1862 Alonzo wrote one of his brief notes to his sister. He knew she did not like her name to be tampered with but he was in a teasing mood.

Dear Rosie,

McClellan has been ordered to bring his army back from the peninsula. There are many rumours about Lee's intentions but all of them say he is moving north. There was a big fight at Cedar Mountain two days ago. It is forty miles south of Manassas Junction near Culpepper. You know that is where the Bull Run battle was fought about this time last year. They have a new name for Cedar Mountain, Slaughter Mountain, so you may guess it was quite a rumpus. It looks as if Lee is trying to separate our General Pope from his supply base at Manassas station and if he does there will be a merry time in the old town, as they say, and the old town might be right here in Washington. But don't worry, they won't take Washington. Some of McClellan's army have already arrived. Alfred is still going to the hospital to help out. I'm glad

I'm in camp. I'd rather see nothing but hay and horses than all those wounded. Newton has a different wagonmaster from me. Sometimes he has to bring in wounded from the docks. He wants to transfer to different work if he can. Congress has just passed a law authorizing the president to accept negroes for military duty. Many white soldiers are not too pleased to think they might be fighting next to niggers but there is no doubt now there'll be all black regiments. We are all well.

Your aff. brother
Alonzo

Dear Roseltha

I came in from the camp tonight to visit Alfred but he is at the hospital. I am sure he does a great deal of good but I couldn't do it myself. I see enough of the wounded. There are never enough ambulances. Some of them are two-wheeled carts and they jolt the poor fellows unmercifully. One is a converted Ginger Pop wagon. You can still see the printing under the paint. Yesterday I had two men in my wagon who were not in too much pain to talk. They were talking about death because both had had a close shave. One was scoffing at the Bible for saying that we will go to heaven when we die. The other believed in heaven and found it comforting to think he would go there if killed in battle. He said to the scoffer, How would you feel if you were lying dead in your coffin without the hope of eternal life? The other one just laughed and said, I'd be all dressed up and nowhere to go. I burst out laughing. Being so close to the war makes you wonder about things.

There is a woman here called Clara Barton who has coaxed the quartermaster's department to give her a wagon drawn by mules to take supplies and medicine to soldiers after the battles. She is a nervous little woman about forty who looks as if she would be afraid of her shadow but she loads her wagon and takes off into the thick of anything. They said that at Slaughter Mountain she used up everything she had in the wagon till she was down to crumbs mixed with whiskey, brown sugar and water. Maybe some of the men she spooned it into had never tasted liquor before but they were too far gone to ask questions. One of our drivers who was assigned to her swears even more than most mule-skinners but he turned into a gentleman for her. Her six mules were pretty frisky when they left but I imagine their ears will be down by the time she gets back. The lot in Cleveland is paid for now. Write soon as we may be posted out, we never know.

Your brother
N. (Harding) Esq.

When he returned to the camp he drew out his little diary:
Hauled hay from railroad hayyard on requisition. Hauled hay from 7th St. wharf and railroad hayyard to Captain J.J. Dana's hayyard. [Not much excitement these days.]

Goble's Corners, July 24, 62

Dear Brothers

You cannot write too often to please me. We had quite a scare two days ago. The air had been heavy and oppressive for nearly two days when suddenly a storm broke and the rain came down in sheets chased by high winds. We were lucky here but it was a tornado by the time it reached Galt. It tore the roofs off buildings and threw some completely off their foundations. When it crossed the Grand River the paper said it forcibly threw the water up. A wagon standing on a street was picked up and thrown to the other side where it landed on the verandah of a house. In one field, potatoes were torn out of the ground. One limb of an old apple tree fell down at the back of our garden but otherwise we suffered no damage and I must say the rain has done a great deal of good. The raspberries are ripe and I make pies every day. I love the colour of the raspberry juice when I make jelly—so red and shining. Will and little Eva are well. We intend to drive in to Woodstock on Saturday. It is only twelve miles and makes a pleasant change.

After Slaughter Mountain Lee moved steadily northward, preparing to pit his Army of Northern Virginia against General Pope's Army of Virginia, before McClellan's men all reached Washington. His objective was undoubtedly the capital itself. Newton Goble, the Hardings' cousin-in-law, was a soldier, not a teamster. He was out with General King's division writing in his diary between engagements:

Aug. 11, Culpepper, Va.
Aug. 22, White Sulphur Springs
Aug. 28, Fought against 5000 rebels under Jackson at Gainesville.

Lee was coming fast. General Pope rested his army as he waited for McClellan. Lee would not wait for that. He divided his army and sent half under Stonewall Jackson to sweep around Pope to get at the federal supply base at Manassas Junction. Jackson made no allowance for rest for his men, and they would have followed him barefoot. They made a forced march of fifty-eight killing hours around and through Bull Run Mountains destroying Pope's supply base as they went. Thrown into confusion by Lee's swiftness, Pope fumbled. Jackson lost no time in taking a stand on the high ground overlooking the old Bull Run battlefield and Lee brought his men to join him there. This time no ladies in crinolines or congressmen in tall silk hats came crowding to see. All Washington tensed as it waited for news.

On August 29 Newton Goble wrote in his diary: *Repulsed at Bull Run. August 30: Terrible battle at Bull Run.*

Twice beaten at Bull Run. What next?

Alfred had returned to his boarding-house after visiting the hospital. In spite of the debilitating nature of his work, for compassion drained him of strength, he was elated this evening for he had spoken to Miss Melinda Hamilton, the doctor's daughter whom he had observed many times as they went about their work. There was little time for idle chatting in the hospitals and now there would be another influx from Bull Run. Every one was overworked and edgy but Alfred was happy, because at last he had been able to speak to her as Melinda brought a tea tray to a wounded man. Alfred lifted the man up so that he could drink a little. Even that slight movement reddened the bandages.

Melinda held the cup and Alfred the man's head. "There, there," she said, "try a little harder. This will do you good and you'll feel better."

"Thank you, ma'am," the man murmured as he sank back on the pillow. "I think I can sleep now. I wonder where my buddy is."

"Don't worry. Tell us about him tomorrow and we'll find him."

Melinda and Alfred left the bedside together. "Do you think he'll pull through?" she said.

"It will be a tight squeeze," Alfred answered, taking the tray that by now was laden with dishes from other trays. "You come often, don't you?"

"Yes, and so do you. I've seen you many times. I'm coming again tomorrow but may not stay till evening. My father, Dr. Hamilton, won't allow me to get too tired."

"My name is Alfred Harding. I'm a Canadian but I'm with the quartermaster's department."

"Thank you for helping, Mr. Harding. We need it. Good night, my father is waiting for me."

Alfred went home soon after. As he reviewed his conversation with the young woman he had been admiring from afar, Alfred took up his newspaper to read what was reported about the armies fighting so desperately at Bull Run. He heard boots clumping up the stairs and Newton came into his room, his face white and his clothes heavy with dust.

"Get me some coffee, please. I feel bad."

He gulped the hot drink and lay back in the chair, breathing heavily. "What's wrong, Newtie?"

"I killed two men." He began to cry. The tears streaked the dust on his sixteen year old face.

"You've been out to Bull Run then. I was hoping you wouldn't be sent there."

"The fighting's over. They beat us again."

"Not again? A second time at Bull Run? But what about you? You were only driving."

"I had a six horse team, for we were told to rush up ammunition. When we got near the fighting one of the horses was creased with a bullet and they all bolted. I tried to stop them but it was like trying to hold a juggernaut. They ran off the road into a field. I was riding the lead horse and Virgil was on the seat. We halted them before they reached the trees on the far side of the field or we'd have all gone up in smoke."

Newton paused to blow his nose and wipe his face. "There was fighting a quarter of a mile away. Suddenly a Reb came in front of us and raised his gun. I ducked as he fired. The bullet hit Virgil. He fell over. I ran back to grab the reins so the horses wouldn't take off again. I held the horses but when I looked at Virgil I knew he was finished. The Reb had got him in the heart. If I hadn't ducked, he wouldn't have been killed."

"You didn't kill him. It was fate. It wasn't your fault, Newtie. Pull yourself together."

"That's not all. It made me fighting mad. When I looked for the Reb he was gone, then a bullet whistled past my ear. I thought it came from a tree over to the left. I grabbed a gun we had in the wagon, ducked behind the wagon, and then I saw a puff like a cotton ball coming from up in a tree. I drew a bead on the place where the puff came from and fired. A man tumbled down and when I ran to see how he was, he was dead too."

Newton's voice rose to a wail. "He wasn't any older than me. I didn't sign up to kill, Freddie. I just signed up to be a teamster. Now I've killed two men. It's like being a murderer. I want to go home."

"Calm down. It wasn't your fault. You'll feel better soon. Stay the night with me."

"I can't. I have to get back. I'll be needed to bring in more wounded. They've left the dead ones there."

August 30, 1862. The northern forces retreated behind Washington's ring of forts or travelled north of the city in case Lee would attack where the Potomac was shallow enough so that an army could be forded across.

Dear Rose,

We are all well. They routed us again at Bull Run and the city is gloomy. Horace Greeley in the New York Tribune has said that the Union cause is suffering because Lincoln fails to free the slaves. Last week Lincoln published an answer to Greeley in the Washington *Intelligencer* and I will copy it out for you because I know your great interest in the matter: "My paramount object in this struggle is to save the Union, and is not either to save or destroy slavery. If I could save it by freeing some and leaving others alone, I would also do that." This seemed to satisfy a good many people and his popularity has not suffered. The volunteers are coming in and they are singing a new song: We are coming, Father Abraham, three hundred thousand more. But some of them are not real volunteers. They had to be paid bounties to join up. The blacks are joining up too. Newton says that some owners are trying to get their slaves back from the camps for the Fugitive Slave Law is still law. I hear that Lincoln has offered slave owners $400 compensation for each slave. Four million slaves! But it would be cheaper than continuing the war. As if money were the only thing involved. I have seen enough of war in the hospitals. I cannot imagine what a battlefield would look like. Newton was close to Bull Run last week. His horses bolted but he was able to stop them before they were blown to bits. We had a letter from father telling us about his marriage to Miss Cline. I hope the house was in good condition after the tenants left.

Your Affectionate Brother
Alfred

Alfred sat once more at the side of a dying soldier. "I prayed to God before we went into battle that our side would win, but it didn't do much good."

The blue eyes closed and the hand lying on his chest dropped to his side. The breathing was heavy and laboured. He spoke again with difficulty. "I guess the men on the other side prayed too."

After he had drawn the sheet over the sightless eyes, Alfred went home and took down his book of Whitman's poetry.

> You shall possess the origin of all poems,
> You shall possess the good of the earth and sun-
>   there are millions of suns left-
> You shall no longer take things at second or third hand,
>   nor look through the eyes of the dead,
>   nor feed on specters in books,
> You shall not look through my eyes either,
>   nor take things from me,
> You shall listen to all sides and filter them for yourself.

How is it possible to listen to all sides? Will Lincoln free the slaves?

Relieved of some of his household cares by his young wife and spurred on by her adoring and uncritical presence, Enos continued his obsessive study of the stars. Sometimes, when bewildered with the complexity of his research, he took up his pen again, partly to clarify his thinking and partly with the half-formed intention of giving lectures on his findings. He alternated between an assiduous reading of his Bible and the few books he had been able to purchase in Woodstock and Hamilton.

The astronomer comenses his investigations on the hill tops of Eden. He studies the stars through the long centuries of antediluvian life. the deluge sweeps from the earth its inhabitants the citys and thare monuments but when the storm is past and the heavens shine forth in thare original beauty from the summit of mount arrarat, the astronomer resumes his endless vigils. in Babilon he keeps his watch, and among the Egyptian priests he inspires a desire for the sacred misteries of the stars. the planes of shinar the temples of india, the pirrimids of egypt are equally his watching places. when science fled to Greece his home was in the schools of the philosophers and when darkness covered the earth for a thousand years he persued his never ending search from the midst of the burning deserts of arabia. When science dawned on Europe the astronomer was thare, toiling with Copernicus, watching with Tycho, suffering with Galileo, triumphing with Keppler.

He looked over what he had written. "Neridia," he called, "if I stop to correct my spelling, I can't go as fast as I like. Look over this, will you, please?"

As Neridia took up her pencil, he leaned back in his chair. "I don't think I can fathom the laws of the universe till I work on the motion of the planets and how they revolve around the sun. I shall have to build an orrery, Neridia. If I knew where to buy one fast, I would. Since I don't, I'll build one myself and learn as I go."

Then he noticed that his wife was looking pale. "Come here till I pinch some colour in your cheeks. I must buy you some port to drink before dinner to enrich your blood."

Abraham Lincoln paced the White House. Virginia was lost. Much of Tennessee was gone. Kentucky was falling to Bragg's victorious army. Richmond was still inviolate. The latest Northern recruits, in spite of their songs, were often half-hearted, but most of Davis' supporters were dedicated still to the cause of states' rights.

If any one had doubted it before, it was now becoming clear that the issue inevitably was slavery. Horace Greeley kept hammering the point.

On August 19 he had said it again: "Even if the war would be over, if slavery be left, another rebellion would break out in a year."

It was also now evident that the Union must mobilize every avenue of support, and the greatest untapped resource lay in those dedicated to emancipation. Hoping for their aid now, Lincoln drafted a proclamation of freedom for the slaves. If it passed Congress, four million black slaves would become persons and the rebellion would be turned into a social revolution.

Moving unobtrusively through the White House these days was an artist named Francis B. Carpenter. His commission was to paint the president. Daily he followed him, watching and sketching, probing his nature so that his portrait would be true. "Absorbed in his papers," wrote Carpenter, "he would often become unconscious of my presence while I studied each line and expression of that furrowed face, the saddest face in repose I ever knew. There were days when I could scarcely look at him without crying."

Secretary of State Seward advised Lincoln that his emancipation proclamation could not be issued in a time of defeat. A victory must precede it. Lincoln put the papers in a pigeon-hole.

John Brown, the time is not yet. The success of your cause is in the hands of the generals.

all My Dear Brothers and make you happy.

Your own dear Philip Pegg

To Newton   Sunday March 19th 1860.

My Dear Brother. I have been trying to find time this long while to write to you 'tis too bad I have not written to you this winter; and 'tis more than too bad you have not written to me. You know there is four of you boys to write too while I am only one unless I count Dora; and she is not much help in writing. She generally manages to raise some kind of a fuss about the time I get ready to write. I am so glad you are getting on well with your studies. Alonzo wrote you were head of your class; and Jassy of his. Father was much pleased when he was here that you & Jassy were doing so well. He is doing the best he can for you do all you can for yourselves. It will not be long before you will be twelve and have something else to do. Improve the present opportunity to the best of your ability— I think of you every day; and would like very much to see you.

I feel very anxious for my dear Motherless brothers. Be a good boy and do all you can. Be very careful of the boys you go with and try and not get any bad habits It is much easier to acquire bad vulgar habits than when they are once formed to get rid of them. You cannot be too careful Lessa says she wrote to you, but you do not answer her. She is anxious to hear from you. You must write to her and also to me as soon as you get this If you knew how often I think of you and much I want to hear from you & Jassy. You would both if you write me a long letter as soon as you get this. Tell me about your studies, troubles, hopes, aims and Pleasures. Do you ever get lonesome and want to come home? or are you quite satisfied where you are? Do you go to Meeting & Sunday School I got a nice little Paper from you some time ago. I am glad you read good Papers Among all your reading and studying do not forget your Bible. but read it often with careful earnestness. May God bless you

By Permission

Copy of original letter written by Roseltha to her brother Newton in Cleveland, Ohio.

Jasper you must Be a good Boy and work hard
to gain knowledge while you have an opertunity
it may not last long Beshure to obstain from
bad habits encourage Newton to be a good Boy
write to us and let us know al about the School
and how you get along atend Church and S. S.

Newton my son — you will remember you
are now forming your Caracter for the rest of
your life and that you have no mother to watch
you nor father to look after you but God sees you
mind what Alonzo tells you and try and make
your self respected Spend your time dilligent in
your studdies keep your self tidy and Clean and
be a good Boy atend Church and S. S. and
write and let me know all about your situation
we are all well in Canada So farewell

Enos Woliston
M. Woliston

to (Alonzo
Jasper and   ) Woliston
Newton

Cleaveland
Ohio

P. S
See if the shingly shiflt from Alwood
is sold or what became! then he
wants his pay

By Permission

Copy of letter written by Enos to his sons at school in Cleveland.

Camp Crossman Aug. 7th/61.

Dear Rose.

It is now more than two weeks since we left Cleveland and we have not heard from there or Canada since. We wrote to you some time ago (more than a week) but have as yet received no answer. We are all well at present. Our fare is very ha— and we have to sleep on the ground or in the wagons. We expect to endure many hardships and dangers, but we will endeavour to ——t them cheerfully—believing it to be for the best. This is a glorious country. Never before have I beheld nature dressed in such beauteous robes. The lofty mountains enveloped in a mantle of dense foliage, appear to reach the clouds. Surely the iron heel of the war-horse should never desecrate so lovely a portion of the world of nature. But amid all her loveliness, the noble Maryland, one of the earliest homes of religious liberty throughout the world, is struggling within the grasp of a grant monster, that will, until discarded, cripple all her noblest energies and loftiest aspirations. Slavery will fetter the energies of any people. No sooner do we come within its precincts, than its influence is seen and felt. We expect to leave here today or to morrow, but do not know where we will go—probably nearer the seat of war. Aug. 8th I had not time to finish this letter yesterday, so I will try and send it to day. We drew pay yesterday for the time we were engaged last month [in 11 days] Jasper & Newton each received eight dollars, and I received sixteen making a total of $32. That is better than doing nothing. We are going to send $25 to Cleveland to pay some small debts there. Where is father? Is he going to be in Cleveland soon? We would like to know what he intends doing about the —— and property. There is a payment to be made on the —— yet. If we could manage to get a few months time we could liquidate all claims, that is if we are fortunate enough to ——retain—— —— & health. Write soon & very often. We cannot always find time and paper to write as we expect to be on the road most of the time. Direct your letters for the present, to Hagerstown, Maryland, care Capt. McCullough wagon master, Camp Crossman. From Your Brother Alfred

By Permission

Copy of letter written by Alfred en route to Washington from Cleveland with the 50th New York—to his sister, Roseltha.

In camp two miles from Nashville
Dec. 4th 1864 –

My Dear Sister

I should have written ~~sooner~~ but
it has been impossible, we have been moving
from place to place and building breastworks as well
as fighting occasionally so that I have had no time
to do anything; I expected when I wrote you last that
I should soon be north, but the Government would
not recognize our Parol so we were ordered to report
for duty, in the mean time the Battery had left
Chattanooga and I started for the Battery on the 30th of
October and joined it at Pulaski on the 6th of
November where we remained till the 23rd when
Hood flanked us and our army had to evacuate
the town, We marched to Columbia where we
fought them three days, There was no very heavy
fighting chiefly artillery duelling, again Hood
forced us to move further north as far as Franklin
where we arrived on the 30th at noon and our
Generals determined to make a stand, and threw
up breastworks, at four oclock the Rebs came
on to us in full force and there ensued one
of the hardest fought battles for the time it
lasted there has bee since this war commenced

(cont'd)

*Copy of letter written by Alonzo in camp two miles from Nashville—at
the peak of the Nashville campaign—to Roseltha.*

the rebs seemed determined to conquer or die they made thirteen desperate charges, several times they planted their colors within ten feet of our cannon and our men would knock them down with their muskets or their artillerymen with their sponge staffs or handspikes

our Battery was in the centre the very hottest of the fight—we lost nearly half our men and came out of the battle commanded by a sargeant, I never dreamed that men would fight with such desperation. I never expected to come out alive but was fortunate, I was struck twice once in the cheek the ball just grazed my face and cut through the skin it bled freely but did not

amount to much, and once in the hip the ball cut through my pants drawers and shirt and made a slight wound but not enough but what I attend to my duty. About ten oclock the rebs withdrew and our army started for Nashville bringing the wounded along but the dead were left lying. I never realized before what a battle was. the roar of Musketry and thunder of artillery &c was deafning, it was full as dark ten minutes after the battle commenced as when it ceased. the only way we could tell when night come was by the stars. Hood is now within four miles of us but I do not think he will venture to attack this place he got whipped to bad at Franklin. I can form no Idea what our loss was but it was heavy, and the rebs must have lost four times as much as ours the ground was covered as far as I could see with their dead. I will write again in a few days when I have a better chance and give you full particulars Brother Alonzo

By Permission

153

Villanow 15 Oct 64

I, A. Wolverton   20th Ohio Baty

Regt   Brig

Divn   Corps USA

being a prisoner of war in the hands of the CSA do solemnly swear that I will not bear arms against the Confederate States, or aid, or assist, any one to doing until regularly exchanged.

A his + mark Walverton

Attest:
J. Jorman,
Cor. 44th NC I

Attest:

By Comd Genl Hood,
S. J. Harris
Col & Inspec Genl, AT.

By Permission

Alonzo's certificate of parole after his capture by the Southern Army at Villanow, Georgia.

By Permission

Copy of letter to Alonzo from Newton who was helping to defend Canada against the Fenians at Philipsburg, Canada East.

By Permission

Photo of the spiral staircase which rises to the cupola.

By Permission

Original family home built by Enos around 1855. Still standing to-day, in Wolverton, Ontario.

Ontario Archives S.11831

George Brown, anti-slavery editor of the Toronto **Globe.**

Ontario Archives S.18071

Sir John A. MacDonald, first Prime Minister of the Dominion of Canada.

Photo by Mathew B. Brady about October 2, 1862 at Antietam of President Abraham Lincoln speaking with General George B. McClellan.

Foraging Party slaughtering bull.

London Illustrated News Sep. 14, 1961

159

Battles of the Virginia Wilderness where General Grant refused defeat, May 5 - 12, 1864.

Burnside's bridge, at the battle of Antietam, September 17, 1862, where Alonzo was wounded.

ROBERT E. LEE
General-in-chief of the Confederate Army in 1865.

ULYSSES S. GRANT
General-in-chief of the Federal Army in 1865.

Copper engravings of Abraham Lincoln, President of the United States of America and Jefferson Davis, President of the Confederate States of America.

Public Archives Canada P.A.89325

By Permission

Newton in 1865 while a member of the 22nd Oxford Rifles, guarding the frontier at Prescott, Ontario with the 13th Royal Regiment.

Chapter 14

Bloody Lane

As Alfred and his colleagues tried to cope with the frenzied activity in the quartermaster's department and to throw off the dejection prevalent in Washington after second Bull Run, Robert E. Lee and his men forded the Potomac into Maryland singing "Maryland, my Maryland" as if the state were already theirs. On September 8, 1862, Lee issued a proclamation: "The people of the South have long wished to aid you in throwing off this foreign yoke, to enable you again to enjoy the inalienable rights of freemen, and to restore independence and sovereignty to your State." But Maryland did not rush to offer supplies to Lee as he deployed his army for what he considered would be a finish to Washington's power. In addition, a decisive victory might induce foreign countries to acknowledge the Confederacy as a sovereign state.

The place where Lee chose to take his stand was outside the town of Sharpsburg, fifty miles northwest of the capital, on Antietam Creek. The little stream would supply his army with water as he waited for Stonewall Jackson to rout the Federals once again from strategic Harper's Ferry, about eight miles away. Quickly Lee decided on his strategy and sent copies of his battle plans to three of his commanders in the field. One went to Stonewall Jackson at the railway junction at the Ferry.

The fighting at Harper's Ferry was back and forth, nip and tuck. On September 13 one of Jackson's generals, D.H. Hill, evacuated his headquarters in a double quick hurry as the Union men came pouring in. A Union private who entered the house picked up a fat envelope from the floor. Looked at it, turned it over. Might be money inside, good money, not Confederate stuff. No, there were only three cigars crudely hand-rolled in writing paper, but there was writing on one of the wrappers. He took it to his commanding officer. It was one of the three copies of Lee's battle orders.

165

With the battle plans in his hands that told him precisely what Lee's intention was, McClellan could have proceeded immediately and confidently but once again he hesitated, fearful that Lee's numbers might be greater than his. He might have guessed, but he could not know, that Lee, in addition to the 9,000 dead, wounded and missing at Bull Run, had lost some 15,000 more, some through desertion and some without shoes who dropped out through sheer inability to march a step further. The country roads of Virginia had been kinder to their feet than the macadam roads of Maryland.

Along those Maryland roads, intent on joining Lee, A.P. Hill, crueller than any slave driver, was urging his men. His red shirt and his flashing sword were the terror of any laggard. Finding an officer sitting exhausted by the roadside, he grabbed the officer's sword and broke it in two over his knee. "Now get on," he roared as he spurred his horse.

Cautious as usual, for Bull Run was only two weeks behind him, McClellan took three days to move his men twenty miles and then he dallied a day to think. This was all the time Jackson needed to oust the Union forces once again from Harper's Ferry, leave a defending garrison, and march his men all night to come to Lee's aid.

In the hasty remobilization following General Pope's retreat from Bull Run to the safety of Washington's fortifications, all of Washington's reserves were called into play. Before he had time to think, Alonzo Harding was detailed to drive a six-horse team to transport ammunition by the Porterstown road to the artillery in General Burnside's division.

As he woke in the misty dawn of September 17, Antietam Creek burbled over its stones on its way to join the Potomac a few miles above Harper's Ferry. The sun was beginning to glint over the tassels of a forty-acre cornfield and the white walls of a little Dunker church that gleamed against its background of green trees. Two miles farther south it shone on the cold stones of a Roman-arched bridge over the creek that was General Burnside's task to hold. If he allowed the Confederates to take it, they could turn and lash the rear of the whole Northern army.

Two armies, and a little stream between.

The tents dripped with dew and the ashes of the cooking-fires that had twinkled among them the night before were black and sodden. As the drums sounded wake-up, 87,000 Union men and 40,000 Confederates rose and stretched without grumbling for both sides had slept fitfully, tense with the knowledge that something would happen soon—and hard.

Alonzo watered his horses from buckets he had filled the night before and patted their warm necks. He spoke quietly to his helper, Moses McBain. "It's a long line of battle, nearly three miles. Where d'you think they'll commence?"

"They'll come for the bridge for sure but we can't see much from here. They say Hooker's at the woods on Red Hill and that the corn in the big field is higher than a man's head. Anyway, we're behind the lines."

"They say old Sideburns Burnside knows what he's doing."

"Yah, but does McClellan? He's in charge."

McClellan had placed Fighting Joe Hooker to face Stonewall Jackson who had ensconced himself on the rise in front of the Dunker Church of God, using the cornfield and woodlot for cover. At 5:30 a.m. Hooker opened fire on Jackson's men, sweeping the cornfield with three dozen cannon. Jackson's men rushed forward. For two hours the fighting surged back and forward across the field. When Hooker himself was wounded in the foot and his men were hard pressed, McClellan sent "Old Bull" Sumner to his aid.

Sumner hurled his men against another Confederate line drawn up south of the cornfield behind breastworks, or crouched in the trench of a sunken lane. In an hour this lane was filled so full of dead and wounded that the rush of opposing soldiers fought on a mass of yielding bodies. Advancing doggedly over this gruesome ground the Union soldiers forced the Rebels to retreat. Another concerted rush up the hill and the Rebels regained it. Bloody Lane, it was called by those who survived.

If McClellan had ordered a combined offensive against the whole line of Lee's men, victory could have been his and many lives would have been saved. Instead, attack was carried out piecemeal. At noon, when the offensive at the cornfield was halted, he ordered combat two and a half miles southwest at the arched stone bridge where Burnside's men waited, ready to prevent the Rebels from crossing the creek, or ready to cross it themselves to smash against the waiting enemy.

Behind Burnside's line the teamsters tried not to appear nervous. Since reveille they had heard the sounds of battle in the distance, ignorant of the outcome. Impatient at being harnessed so long, the horses stamped and neighed. Alonzo chewed on a hardtack from his haversack and took a small swig from his water-bottle for its level was going down fast as the sun grew hotter. Moses McBain whittled a stick in the diminishing shadow of the wagon. "If it gets any hotter this stuff will explode by itself," he grumbled. He got up and shifted a few of the boxes by their rope handles.

"What's wrong, Mose," twitted Alonzo. "Scared?"

"Kinda," grunted Mose, then he came out with the truth. "Hell," he said, "what's the use of sayin' I'm not skeered when I am skeered. It's the waitin'."

"Waiting's better than being in the thick of it. That fighting over there's been going on a long time. Glad I'm a teamster, not a soldier."

Alonzo climbed out from under the wagon, the only shelter there was from the sun, and squinted ahead through a grove of trees to where Burnside's battle line was drawn. "Sure looks pretty down in the valley into the creek. Sun's hot but it's better than rain and mud. Had plenty of that last spring."

He took a little magnifying glass from his pocket, focussed the sun on a blade of grass, watched it blacken, smoke, break into flame. Then he tramped it out after it had spread a couple of inches.

Moses looked at him. "Better not try that trick on our wagon load or we'll be in hell sooner than you expect."

There was a sound of rifle firing nearer than usual. Alonzo vaulted into the wagon, shaded his eyes and looked towards the sound. "Wish we knew what's happening."

"Listen," said Mose. "It's the rebel yell. Something's up."

Clean up from the valley came a high falsetto unnerving yell as the Rebels charged, then an uproar of firing as rifles and artillery on both sides of the creek cracked and boomed.

"This is it. They're attacking. Just hope they don't get across or we'll have to skedaddle."

Burnside had four divisions but he put them in action one by one. His aim was to secure all the crossings near him on Antietam Creek and get to the high ground overlooking Sharpsburg. His supporting artillery was situated on a rise behind him where it could rake the oncoming enemy without mowing down his own men. They grappled on the bridge, hand-to-hand combat. They won it, they lost it, the dead lay all around, they won it again and crossed the creek. By mid-afternoon the Union forces occupied the high ground and it looked as if they could flank Lee's army and win the day. But once again reinforcements arrived to turn the tide. Lee's general, A.P. Hill, the general who had whipped his Southerners unmercifully forward, arrived from Harper's Ferry in time to attack Burnside's flank. For a while confusion was everywhere.

The teamsters behind the lines jumped to their seats, not knowing what to do. The sun was no longer blazing overhead but was slanting downwards. The sounds of battle raged around.

"Won't that sun ever set?" thought Alonzo. "It seems like the day Joshua commanded the sun to stand still. I'd like to command it to fall like a plummet for when it sets the fighting has to stop."

A lieutenant strode briskly by. "Get ready to move up your load if things get tighter. They'll be getting low on ammunition."

Moses mounted the lead horse. The horse laid back its ears and pawed the grass, then bent its head to seize a mouthfull of grass. Moses jerked its head up. The horse bared its teeth and whinnied. "Shut up, you son-of-a-gun, or I'll cut off your head behind the ears."

168

Alonzo sat with the reins ready in his hands. A signaller ahead began to wave his flags. "Get your load up to the guns," shouted the lieutenant. "Just one wagon, you, Mose, move."

McBain dug his heels into the horse's flanks. Alonzo yelled "Giddup." The wagon lurched forward. "Not too fast down hill," shouted Mose as the wheels rattled over the uneven ground.

They were nearing the guns and Rebel bullets were whistling about them. "Hope none of our men fires backwards," muttered Alonzo as a couple of bullets hit the wagon.

"Sure gettin' hot," yelled McBain. "Get ready to unload and then we'll beat it back."

They moved in beside the sweating gunners. One was wounded and one was dead but the rest were ramming home charges.

"Turn the wagon around so the horses face the other way." The horses reared. "Hold them," shouted Alonzo and jumped out to unload. The last boxes were hard to reach. The near gun exploded its charge. It was too much for the team. They bolted. Alonzo leaped to grab the reins and missed. He couldn't catch the wagon. He was left there unarmed.

A little group of Rebs came yelling up the rise, bayonets fixed for close fighting. Alonzo had one glimpse of a grimy triumphant face and a bayonet ready to pierce him. Then he blacked out as the Rebel rammed his guts.

Slowly the void gave way to a golden light and Alonzo felt himself weightless in the glow. A soothing murmur rang in his ears and pulsating light surrounded him. His body seemed non-existent. His thoughts were only feeling. Peace and languour prevailed throughout him.

A figure floated into the glow. It came closer, bent over him. It did not menace. It was formless but beneficent. Another came and went away accompanied only by a movement of light and a lovely humming sound. "I must be in heaven," the thought formed in Alonzo's mind. "It's angels and harps and the golden gate."

He floated up again in the golden atmosphere, weightless and serene. He floated down again and seemed to hear a voice coming from somewhere. It said, "All these look pretty dead."

The glow receded a little as Alonzo tried to remember where he was. He couldn't quite figure things out but he felt he needed help. He couldn't speak but his thoughts called out to the two figures he felt were near him—Don't leave me, they said—but no sound issued from his mouth. The figures were going away. The glow receded still more. He tried again.

Still no sound but this time the golden glow turned momentarily into a clear heavenly blue above him.

"Wait. I think this one opened his eyes a bit."

Alonzo felt his wrist being lifted. "Come here, Mose, he's alive, but look at the blood he's lost."

"It's him. It's Lon. We've found him. Let's get him out of here," said Moses McBain.

Again the men turned into spirits, then blackness, as Alonzo lapsed into unconsciousness from the pain of being moved.

Alonzo Harding had joined the great army of the wounded. He had lain all night and into the next morning on the battlefield, and his fellow teamster had braved danger to go back to look for him for, though Lee's army was not moving, Lee had not yet retreated. Alonzo had been incredibly lucky for there were few trained stretcher-bearers even yet in the army. Sometimes the bandsmen were sent after the wounded, sometimes the slightly wounded did the work. Sometimes a buddy searched for his missing friend, using a blanket for a stretcher. Sometimes no one came in time.

After a day of silence broken only by sporadic sparring among the pickets, Lee marched his long gray columns back into Virginia to recuperate. His army had not been destroyed. It would fight again, but for the moment his offensive had been balked.

Once again Washington was safe for Lee had retreated. Antietam, with Bloody Lane, its Burnside Bridge, and more casualties than almost any other battle, had given Lincoln the victory that Secretary of War Stanton had said was necessary. Out from a pigeon-hole on September 22 came the preliminary emancipation proclamation. It would go into effect at midnight, January 1, 1863. Now the extirpation of slavery ranked equal with the preservation of the Union. Borderline opinion rallied to the side of the North, both at home and aboard. When Alfred went to the station to inspect incoming stores, Jonah the foreman was ecstatic. "Today the sun shine like gold," he exulted.

"I haven't heard from my brother since Antietam," said Alfred looking in the other direction.

"I sorry, Mr. Hardin'. Maybe I too fight 'cause now dey take negro sojers. All dey want us 'fore was cook and wash. White men funny. Fight for us but not fight 'side us."

And that was true. Only a few days before, Alfred had seen another racist clash in Washington streets for many Northern soldiers still could not tolerate the thought of having niggers fight on an equal footing with them.

Newton came in from camp. "Heard from Lonnie yet?"

"No, and I haven't written to Canada. Let's wait for some definite news before we worry them."

"Here's a letter that came for him today. Let's open it."

Dear Alonzo

I wish I could send you some of the apples from the orchard. The Sheepnoses are finished but the MacIntosh Reds are as bright as jewels and the Northern spies are plentiful. I journeyed on the cars to Woodstock last week to do some shopping. I was much amused when I came home with a lady on the cars. She was going through from the West to her home in Connecticut. She expressed a good deal of sorrow and pity for me because I lived in such a dreadful place, wanted to know if we had any gardens. I told her Canada was a glorious land and so it is with her great lakes, broad rivers, and beautiful forests. The lady seemed to feel a sort of disdainful pity that I was contented in such a dreary place. Canadians prize their country and institutions better than they did before the war. When will this terrible war end? . . . I have not been to [Harding] for a long time, it storms every time we make arrangements to go. . . . I have not seen father since I wrote you before. . . . It makes me very sad when I think of our old home circle broken, but God knoweth best. I would trust submissively to his decrees. . . . All send kind regards . . .

As ever, your affectionate sister
Roseltha

Alfred put the letter down. For a few minutes while reading he had been transported to another world, a normal one, but as soon as he stopped reading he remembered he was in war-menaced Washington, waiting to hear from Alonzo. They knew that Lee had gone back into Virginia but news of the terrible losses was pouring in. Alonzo had not returned nor sent word. Alfred prayed silently and Newton returned to camp where there was more hope of news than in the city.

Next night Alfred went to help at Armory Square Hospital. Heavy-hearted, he approached each newly filled bed with the fear that Alonzo's might be the face he would see on the pillow—and the fear that it wouldn't. He thought of searching other hospitals but it would have been a hopeless task. Washington was one vast infirmary, one enormous hospital base for the Army of the Potomac. Two thousand cots filled the halls of the House of Representatives and the Senate. The E Street

Infirmary that had been burned late in '61 had been replaced by Judiciary Square Hospital. There were Stanton, Douglas, Lincoln, Emory, Seventh, Fourteenth, Harewood, Columbian, Mount Pleasant hospitals. The wounded were in barracks, hotels, houses, schools, seminaries, lodges of fraternal orders, churches with floors laid over the backs of pews and whose bells could no longer be rung for they clashed like cracks of doom in the ears of the sick—all were now hospitals flying the flag of the Union. Outside them the naked dead were placed in rows waiting for undertakers to remove them for burial at the cut rate price of $4.99 per corpse. Inside, the surgeons moistened the sutures in their mouths and picked up sponges from the floor to plunge into another wound. Their ungloved hands went from one suppurating gash to another. The War Department could invite foreign ballistics experts to advise on what bullet would do the most damage when it entered the human body, but it had no correspondence with Lister and Pasteur who were coming to the climax of their work on bacteria.

The beds that were being emptied after Second Bull Run either from death or convalescence were now being refilled from Antietam. With no word from Alonzo, Alfred could not share the elation that filled Washington—outside the hospitals. This evening there was not even the comfort of a brief chat with Melinda Hamilton for she had not come this night.

On Sunday afternoon, for no friend seemed available as a companion and because his mood was sombre, Alfred took a horse-car to Georgetown for a quiet walk along the river. People were renting rowboats. The water dropping from their oars flashed gaily in the sunshine. Bonnets, summer dresses, and straw hats enlivened the scene. He stood idly watching, wishing he were on the river himself. He thought of the Nith river at home in Canada West where he and his brothers had caught pike from their own boat and learned to swim, splashing and diving naked around the Bend where girls could not see them. He thought of his mother and the sister who had sometimes been jealous of the freedom enjoyed by her brothers, for the only time she could bathe in the river was when Harriet watched from the bank. Girls, somehow, were suspected of being more susceptible to drowning than boys, and no wonder, for their bathing attire was usually just an old dress that clung around their legs.

Now it was the Potomac that was sliding by, catching up Alfred on its lazy rhythm, making him forget Alonzo who had been in every waking thought since the battle. A robin searched busily for worms. A mocking-bird trilled tirelessly in the tiptop of a tree. Red-wings teetered on reeds at the river's edge.

He sat down under a tree, sighing a little with the satisfaction of having some time to himself. He recalled the brightness of the young woman who had served him in the bookshop and wished she was not a Secessionist. He pulled a book from his pocket. He had been led recently from his reading of Thoreau's *Walden* to the essays of a friend of Thoreau's, Ralph Waldo Emerson. The two men shared a love of nature, but as Alfred was beginning to perceive, Emerson went so far as to say that the beauty of nature and God, the all-fair, were close kin. Quite a bit different from the God I learned about in the Old Testament, he thought.

The sunshine and the breeze were not conducive to steady reading and he leafed over the pages till a sentence caught his eye—"I know of no more encouraging fact than the unquestionable ability of man to elevate his life by conscious endeavour." It made him wish his own life was more purposeful. How disruptive war is, he almost said aloud.

A shadow fell over his book and he looked into the folds of a great flowered skirt. "How do you do, Mr. Harding," said a voice he recognized, but Miss Hamilton's appearance was so different from the helper he was accustomed to see in the hospital that he was startled. In the hospital she had been dressed plainly for work in what fashionable women sneered at as one of those "perpendicular skirts." Now in her wide hoop skirt she was gay and bright as one of Mistress Mary's flowers.

"Miss Hamilton," he said joyously, jumping to his feet and tipping his hat. "How good to see you. What brings you here?"

"I was supposed to come walking with a friend but she was too tired and father is at the hospital. I have to get away from the hospital sometimes, so I ventured out alone as it is Sunday afternoon. I live not far away. I love the Potomac. Watching it purifies me after the misery in the hospital."

The sun assumed an extra brilliance for Alfred and the very ground seemed to rise to meet him. "You need no added purity, Miss Hamilton. Come, let us walk along the path," he invited, taking her hand and placing it in the crook of his arm, astonished at his boldness with one he barely knew. "All the boats are rented out but maybe we could go for a row when one is disengaged."

"That would please me very much," the sweet voice replied from the depths of the flowered bonnet.

"Melinda Hamilton," said Alfred, "I think you have a beautiful name. And you are much too beautiful to work in a hospital. May I call you Miss Melinda instead of Miss Hamilton?"

"I would be delighted, and thank you for the compliment, Mr. Harding, but I feel I must help in this war. You know that Miss Dorothea Dix has persuaded the Sanitary Commission that women must come out of the seclusion of domestic life to help in the great emergency of the war. There was a woman called Florence Nightingale who helped a great deal with the wounded in the Crimean War. Surely I can do my part here."

"That is why I work in the hospital too. I hate the war for I think things could have been solved peacefully. But then, I make more money here than at home in Canada and I wish money to continue my education. I left school in Cleveland to come here."

Melinda looked up. "You are ambitious, Mr. Harding?"

"I don't seem to be right now, just working in the quartermaster's department, but when I am finished I read a good deal and maybe soon I'll know what I should be. Shall we sit here on this big rock?"

Alfred led Melinda to the shade. They sat watching the sun glinting on the river and the ants struggling through the grass.

"Look at that little ant carrying a crumb that is the size of this rock to it. I wonder how it does it," mused Melinda.

"I'd like to know how big its brain is in proportion to its body. Does an ant think, or does it operate solely on instinct?"

"I think insects are not like people who have to learn everything fresh from the cradle to the grave. Insects have instinct alone for they never vary the pattern of their existence. They waste no energy on decision-making as you and I do."

"You have a penetrating mind, Miss Melinda, but these are weighty matters to discuss on such a glorious day. Let's see if a boat has come back yet."

Alfred helped Melinda step into the bow and waited for her skirt to billow into place. Then he grasped the oars and manoeuvred onto the river.

The sun encapsulated them. Melinda removed her bonnet and let the sun shine through her hair.

"What colours there are today—the sky so blue, the sun so golden, the trees so green. Even the reeds are beautiful today." She settled back comfortably on the cushions piled against the thwart. "I wish I could live forever in a cocoon of colour," she said, lifting her face to the sun.

"I do not think you belong in a cocoon," replied Alfred with a gallantry he had not suspected was in him. "I think you are the butterfly that has emerged from the cocoon. Let this rowboat be the cocoon you have just emerged from."

"You have a poetic mind, sir," replied the maiden. "You have a book in your pocket. Will you tell me its name?"

"It is not poetry. It is a book of Emerson's essays, but I do read poetry. I like Whitman and Whittier."

"Those are two extremes, Mr. Harding. One is orthodox and the other unorthodox."

"How do you know that?" Alfred was so astonished that he shipped his oars to wait for her reply.

"Oh, we ladies are not so idle as you think. I read a great deal to my father who likes to relax after a day at the hospital."

"I find Whitman strong medicine at times. Whittier is comforting but Whitman is stimulating. He sees all sides of life, the good and the bad, the beautiful and the ugly. I'd like to think only of the beautiful but I cannot while this war goes on." Alfred did not mention that he had lost one brother and that another brother was missing, because the subject was too close to his heart.

"Do you think much of politics, Mr. Harding?"

"I am a Canadian, Miss Melinda, and therefore have no vote but since I am working here I feel a part of the country. I often wrestle in my mind with the right and wrong of this war. My mother, who is dead, hated slavery and so does my sister in Canada."

"My father is a Democrat, a Peace Democrat, a friend of Clement Vallandigham, a Congressman from Ohio. He is being called a traitor because he opposes a war that the Republicans began."

"I've heard of Vallandigham, but I don't quite know what to think of him. Is he just against the war because he wants his party to get into power or is he sincere? He believes in the constitution which he says allows slavery as a state right but he says that the war is a senseless and cruel way of solving differences."

"My father says he is sincere and he will vote against the Republicans in the next election. He favours peace at any cost and an end to the slaughter."

"It is time to go now. I have enjoyed the afternoon and I'll think of what you have said." As he helped Melinda to shore he broke out, "My brother Alonzo is missing after the battle at Antietam. He was not a soldier but a teamster and he's missing."

Melinda looked with concern into Alfred's eyes. "I'm so sorry. My father can sometimes help to trace people. If we can help we'll be glad to do what we can."

A week later Newton rushed in from camp. "Mose McBain is back. He found Lon. He's wounded bad but they'll bring him here as soon as they can." The two brothers hugged each other, then wiped their eyes.

They went to see Alonzo in the hospital. "Would have hid behind the horses if they hadn't bolted," he joked weakly. Then he blurted out. "We were behind Burnside at the bridge. It was bad enough there but they say four thousand died around Bloody Lane."

"Try to forget it. You're safe now. What kind of wound is it?"

"A bayonet and it came out clean. Lucky it wasn't a Minié bullet or it would have shattered a bone. I was just lucky I didn't bleed to death."

"You were lucky to be found."

"Mose came looking for me next morning. They'd left me for dead but when he came up he said I opened my eyes a bit."

"It was a miracle. How long before you get out?"

"Three weeks at least. Then two months to get my strength. I think I'll go back to Canada till I'm better."

"We brought you some eggs."

"Break one in a glass and I'll swallow it." The gentle nourishing egg slid down his throat. He closed his eyes, exhausted, and his brothers went quietly away.

Their cousin Newton Goble had also survived Antietam. His diary told simply of events leading up to the climax:

August 7	*Went for hay*
August 8	*Went for hay*
August 10	*Went for hay*
August 11	*Culpepper Valley*
August 29	*White Sulphur Springs*
September 14	*Middletown. General Lee's son killed.*
September 16	*Went for hay. Near Sharpsburg. Close to Lee.*

Lee's second big attempt to capture Washington had failed. How soon would he try again? Or could the North strangle the South before that would come about?

Elsewhere the Union armies were again making headway. Corinth, in northern Mississippi on the railway between Memphis and Chickamauga, had fallen but Vicksburg, in Mississippi near the junction of the Yazoo and the Mississippi rivers on the railroad leading towards Alabama, remained to be taken. In east Tennessee beleaguered Unionists were holding their own but before they would be victorious the railway centre at Chattanooga that brought supplies from the west would have to be captured. Before Chattanooga could be captured the Louisville railway would have to be repaired and two million rations stored at Nashville. Dynamited bridges would have to be rebuilt. General Rosecrans began to throw up bridges to replace the ones the South was destroying. Matchstick bridges, Lincoln called them flimsy-looking trestles when he viewed a similiar one north of Washington. In November General McClellan was replaced by General Burnside as commander of the Army of the Potomac.

"On to Richmond," said General Burnside. Determined to show up McClellan, he prepared to cross the Rappahannock river near Fredericksburg. The pontoon bridge that was to come from Washington so that the crossing would surprise the Rebels did not come soon enough. Lee had placed his men on the impregnable Fredericksburg heights. Rain, mud and December cold mired the Union men. When Burnside attacked, 12,000 Union men died or were wounded, and Lee remained undefeated.

Again the wounded poured into the capital. Dr. Hamilton answered the call to hurry to the unpleasant old Union Hotel in Georgetown that had been commandeered for still more beds. Forty wagonloads of wounded lined the dim December streets outside this one hospital. There they lay, smelling of dirty bodies, suppurating wounds, mud—and defeat.

Melinda went with her father. She made her way into the building, dodging coal hods, slop pails and dirty food trays. Then with basin, soap and towels she started in to clean up the damaged bodies and try not to hear the screams, for no ether was used for amputations.

So ended 1862. After a year and a half of war more bodies than John Brown's lay a-mouldering in the grave.

Chapter 15

Spring 1863

There was one silver lining for some as 1862 expired. January 1, 1863, was the day when Lincoln would sign the Emancipation Proclamation that he had promised four months ago after Antietam. On the stroke of twelve that New Year's Eve the negroes in the Contraband Camp far out on North Twelfth Street in Washington sang for joy. Those in the churches carrolled, "Jesus Christ has made me free." Others who gathered in muddy quadrangles rejoiced:

> De massa run, ha ha!
> De darky stay, ho ho!
> I think it must be Kingdom comin'
> And the year of Jubilo!

Their joy was soon tinged with bewilderment when Superintendent D.B. Nichols read out the text of the proclamation that Lincoln would sign later that day. Only those slaves were freed who were the slaves of rebel masters. Some from certain Virginia counties were free, some were not, and the Fugitive Slave Law remained. Was this emancipation? It was said that the main reason why even this much freedom had been granted was not altruism but the ploy of the War Department to drain the South of the working power of the field hands that left the white masters free to go to war.

When Lincoln took up his pen later that day to sign the Emancipation Proclamation with an arm numb from shaking hands at the New Year's Day reception, only a handful of his dwindling supporters climbed the stairs to the President's office to witness the historic act. What Lincoln was doing that day was alienating his cabinet, except for William Seward, and many of his moderate supporters. Yet he had done it.

When Alfred went to the railway station Jonah was jubilant. "I cry all night," he said, "but fo' joy. No mo' sell ma chil'un down ribber, nebber t' see till Judgmun Day. No mo' dat. When Philomena an' ma chil'un here, dey'll be free, free, free. Lincum good, gubbermun good."

"Yes, I'm glad you're free." Abolitionist though he was, Alfred had never touched a negro before. He put his hands on Jonah's shoulders and kissed him on the cheek. To his surprise the negro's skin was as soft as his own. For a moment they looked into each other's eyes, tears coming unbidden to both. Then each turned, wordless, to his separate task.

When the rush of wounded from Fredericksburg had died down, Melinda Hamilton invited Alfred to Sunday high tea. As he entered the hallway after the black maid answered the door, the atmosphere overwhelmed him with the thoughts of Harding Hall and the days when his mother was singing there. The gaslight glowed on the rich red rug, on Melinda's brown hair and her father's greying beard. His spoon tinkled against the most delicate cup he had held since leaving home.

Politics was contentious as a subject of conversation but as it and the war were intertwined and pervasive, talk drifted towards it.

"Yes, the fall elections went against the Republicans, much to the President's dismay. Miss Melinda tells me that you were pleased, Dr. Hamilton."

Dr. Hamilton looked over his glasses at the straightforward young man whom he was beginning to like in spite of his fatherly predetermination not to. "More votes would have been cast against the Republicans if fewer Democrats had been imprisoned on false charges beforehand. Mr. Lincoln allows his generals to play fast and loose with civil liberties."

"Sir?" Alfred was astonished at the allegation for he had read little of it in his newspaper.

"Men like Dr. Olds and James Wall were imprisoned for allegedly discouraging enlistments and therefore negating government policy. Republican government policy, naturally."

"Indeed," answered Alfred, for he was young enough to think that elections were free, not manipulated. "I did not know that, but Miss Melinda tells me that you favour the Peace Democrats headed by Congressman Clement Vallandigham."

"I do, for he is trying to get the government to force the military authorities to report to the courts all political imprisonments. He fears we will have no civil liberty if arbitrary imprisonments continue to escalate."

"Mr. Vallandigham," Melinda broke in, "is very definite in his views. He feels that slavery would have disappeared in time of its own accord and that emancipation by federal law has interfered with states' rights. Therefore he opposes the continuation of the war and is a leader of the Peace Democrats."

"You have heard, I suppose, Mr. Harding," continued Dr. Hamilton, "that General Burnside in Order no. 38 has imposed severe punishment on those who are guilty of even implied treason. General Burnside, who has failed so miserably in the military field, is now in charge of our civil liberties, it seems. Another of his orders, No. 9, prohibits criticism of the civil and military administration. Mr. Vallandigham claims that it is his democratic right to condemn any action of the administration which he considers is wrong. I fear measures may soon be taken to silence Mr. Vallandigham."

"Careful, father, or you too may be silenced under this order. They say the walls have ears these days. Do you sympathize with the Copperheads, Mr. Harding?"

"As a Canadian I do not take sides," answered Alfred cautiously. "I've seen the Copperheads wearing as a badge the head with the word Liberty under it that they've cut from coppers. They held a big rally recently in Dayton, Ohio, I understand. I read all the Ohio news. I have told Miss Melinda, sir, that I was at school in Cleveland when the war broke out."

"Ah, Mr. Harding, you did not finish your education?"

"No, I'm saving money to continue as soon as I can. We Canadians did not expect the war to last so long when we came."

"Neither did we Americans," said Dr. Hamilton grimly. "But to return to the question of civil liberty. Colonel Carrington in Indiana has prohibited people from carrying arms. We Democrats claim that infringes on our rights. In Indianapolis the Republicans destroyed some of the Democratic presses when they printed objections. The Democrats claim they have to carry arms to protect themselves against the party in power. It is a bad situation."

"Would you like a piece of cake, Mr. Harding, and may I fill your cup? Father becomes very serious about such matters as civil liberty. He does not approve either of the suspension of *habeas corpus* ordered recently by President Lincoln."

Alfred felt he might get into deep waters. "From my study of history, Miss Melinda, I remember that that is a measure often invoked in war time. Before this, it was only a subject I had read about in books, but I can see that it is a grave personal matter now."

January darkness had long fallen when Alfred said goodnight, elated because Melinda had invited him to her home, sorrowful because his visit had made him realize he was only a junior clerk in a vast quartermaster's department. Never mind, he told himself, at least I'm gaining experience and I've had one promotion.

His thoughts returned to Melinda. How lovely she looked pouring tea. She was not wearing any jewellry. Mother had a lovely necklace that Roseltha wears now. Melinda would look very well in one. He passed a jeweller's window and looked longingly at its display. I have money saved up. Dare I buy her a present? No, I must save to go back to school, he told himself sternly.

A group of rollicking soldiers, shouting, laughing and singing, passed him. A couple unsteady on their feet were being assisted by the others. Alfred caught the words of a song:

> "If de debble do not ketch
> Jeff Davis, that eternal wretch,
> An' roast and frigazee dat rebble
> What's de use of any debble?"

"Debble, debble, debble," roared one lustily at the end. With a start Alfred recognized Newton. What was he doing? Was he drinking as well as smoking? He's my young brother. He should be in bed at camp. Alfred raced after the rollicking bunch.

He caught up to Newton. "What are you doing here?"

Newton pulled away, exasperated. "I'm just having a bit of fun. I'm tired of carting bodies. Go away, you old stick-in-the-mud, and read your books."

Before he could think, Alfred grabbed him. "I'll bash your nose for saying that."

"I dare you to." Then Newton dropped his fists and started to laugh. "Aw forget it, Freddie. This war's getting us both down. Don't worry, I'm not going to Hooker's Division, if that's what you're thinking. We're on our way back to camp. Johnnie and Lige got into some liquor and we're looking after them. They were trying to forget Fredericksburg. De debble hasn't got me yet."

"Well, see that he doesn't. Remember you're a Harding."

Alonzo had recovered sufficiently from his wound to return home. Alfred and Newton accompanied him to the station, carrying his belongings. A little colour had returned to Alonzo's face but he was still stooped from the pull of the wound in his abdomen.

"Do you think I'll ever be able to walk straight again?" he asked, half bent over as they waited for the train to whistle down the track.

"I've seen men worse off than you walk straight again." said Alfred. "Give our best to father and the folks and don't forget to write."

"I almost wish we were going with you," said Newton, unusually downcast for him. His hope for a letter from his brother made him realize he should write his sister.

Washington, Feb. 13, 1863

Dear Sister Rose

I am driving again having left my place in the forage Dept. the ninth of January because I could not work under those put over me. I have hopes of obtaining a better situation before long. . . . I have to get up at four in the morning and generally get in with my teams about three in the afternoon, but by the time I see that they are all properly cared for it is after dark. So you see I have not too much leisure. Tell Alonzo that "old dad" is getting quite sociable . . . I have good health. When I seen Alonzo go I wished I was going with him. But it costs so much to go home and I wish to make as much money as possible to continue my education. Tell Alonzo to write as he promised as we are anxious to hear from him. If I do not get a better situation before July I think I shall visit home for a short time. The weather is beautiful now and today the sun is shining so warm that I am writing with the door open and no fire. There has been no rain of any account here this winter but one snowstorm which lasted two days at the end of which there was no snow on the ground. There is much talk here about raising Negro regiments which is approved by some and others speak ill of it. I remain your

affectionate Brother
Newton

Feb. 14, 63

Dear Roseltha

. . . I should have written sooner had I not expected a letter from Alonzo long ere this. He promised to write as soon as he got home but I have not heard a word from him since he left. I think he is very neglectfull. [Today is his birthday. I guess he is twenty-two, a ripe old age.] Newton . . . is tending to forage . . . and will do better than he did as clerk. I was very sorry to see Alonzo leave and would like very much to have him come back. . . . give Alonzo a terrible scolding if he is there, for not writing. . . . Remember me to all the "Old folks at home"—I mean old acquaintances of course. Write soon. Rest assured that, although I may seem neglectful, yet my heart's affection teaches me that the strongest—almost only—tie I have on earth is that which binds me to the loved ones at home.

Your loving brother
Alfred

Finally Alonzo wrote:

Dear Brothers

Glad you told me I would be walking straight again for this week I am almost myself. Before long I should be able to do a bit of work. The house seems strange with a woman here who is not my mother. I think I'll visit Rose for a while. The flour mills are running out of grain to mill for the farmers are using their grain for feed till the cows can get out onto the grass which will not be for some time. I would like to go to either Toronto or Hamilton for work. I hear the crimps are busy in the cities. President Lincoln's latest call for more volunteers has made business brisk for them. The crimps dazzle some poor boy's eyes with the promise of as much as a thousand dollars and before he knows it they have him across the lake and into the army. The crimp collects his share of the bounty the army pays for recruits now. I would never fall for the crimps nor would I ever be found in the taverns where they make some drunk and get them that way. There are stories too that the crimps in Windsor are not past slugging a fellow on the head and when he wakes up he is across the border at Detroit and into the army. There is another trick the crimps play too. They round up a few men, take them across Lake Ontario at night, land them in the morning. They enlist, collect the bounty, then they desert and meet the captain down shore who takes them back to Toronto next night. Of course the captain gets his share. If they are caught they are in danger of being shot but so far one man from Woodstock that Will Goble has heard of collected about one thousand dollars in a year and still has his head. The bounty is going up, I hear. Roseltha is afraid I will return to Washington and enlist but I don't think so. Father remains cheerful in spite of being temporarily at a standstill again.

Your Brother
Alonzo

Newton was looking at a lot on Maryland Street to spend his pay on. "Why don't you buy the one next to it, Alfred? They're both large and if we put them together we could divide the two into three and make good money. It's a sure-fire investment."

"If I tie my money up in land there won't be any for anything else when the war is over. You buy one if you're set on it and we'll see about the other one later."

"I'm buying mine this week. I'm tired of 'when this war is over' talk. You think because I'm only seventeen years old that I shouldn't take a flyer in business."

"Later, maybe." Alfred found it hard to resist Newton's persuasiveness but he was thinking of a necklace in the jeweller's window, one with fine gold scrollwork set with small pearls suspending a bird with amethyst eyes holding in its beak a little heart set with three more pearls. Did he dare? He hadn't even told Melinda how much he thought of her, but a gift would show her more than words.

That evening was one of Alfred's nights at the Armoury Hospital. As Alfred wrote a letter, sent a telegram, or brought fresh water, he saw often now a man with a long white beard, pink complexion and shirt open at the collar, Byronic fashion, who passed quietly from bed to bed through the wards. To one he gave an orange or apple, to another a ten cent piece to pay for fresh milk when it was sold in the wards, or he held a hand or kissed a brow. Alfred almost envied the way eyes lit up as he approached and followed him as he left.

"Who is that man?" he asked Melinda.

"That is your hero poet, Walt Whitman," she answered. "Father says he came to Washington to hunt for his brother who was wounded at Fredericksburg. Some people criticize him for they say his poetry is impossible but the good he does when he visits the wards is very great. I think he lives the compassion he puts into his poetry."

"I wonder that a man so gentle can write such vigorous poetry. He must be rich because he is always giving presents."

"He is not rich, but some people who could never visit a hospital themselves give him small sums so that he can continue his work."

"What a big heart he must have," replied Alfred. As he hurried home through the cold night he thought he would like to speak to Mr. Whitman as he seemed approachable if a little eccentric in his dress.

On all fronts the war continued.

Texas. The Confederates took Galveston.

Tennessee. The Federals claimed a victory at Murfreesboro but the list of dead and wounded made it hard to believe.

Mississippi. Grant failed to take Vicksburg.

Rappahannock River, Virginia. General Burnside prevaricated, fearful of moving after the débacle of the impossible mud-march he had ordered.

When Lincoln asked commander-in-chief Halleck to leave Washington and investigate, Halleck did not like the tone of the president's letter and threatened to resign. The civilian president withdrew his request.

Burnside was replaced as leader of the Army of the Potomac by

General "Fighting Joe" Hooker, the big blonde man who rode a milk-white steed through Washington. The army returned to winter quarters. Washington waited for spring to come, wrestling with other problems.

One was the mounting number of secret arrests. Finally through Vallindigham's efforts Congress decided that all political prisoners must be reported to the Secretary of War.

Another was the negro problem that had in no way been eliminated by the New Year declaration of partial freedom. When one Washington minister announced a text with the word Ethiopia in it, part of his congregation walked out. When Dr. Anderson Abbot, a Canadian black army physician with a major's oak leaves on his uniform, refused to ride outside on a street car on a rainy day, he walked to the court martial at which he was to be a witness, explaining his lateness to the hearing of all in the Senate chamber.

Far from Washington, ten miles of freed rejoicing negroes followed General Sherman after the sacking of the railway centre at Meridian, Mississippi, a headquarters for Southern guerilas. And Ulysses S. Grant wrote: "Slavery is dead and cannot be resurrected. It would take a standing army to maintain slavery in the South if we were to make peace today, guaranteeing to the South all their former constitutional privileges."

In April, Fort Sumter resisted re-capture and General Grant was forced to lay siege to Vicksburg. Movements in Lee's camp brought fear of another invasion of the North. Opposition doubled to a war that seemed endless and was solving nothing.

On May 1, Vallandigham addressed a great Democratic rally at Mount Vernon, Ohio. "This war is a wicked, cruel and unnecessary war," he thundered, "a war that is not being waged for the preservation of the Union but for the purpose of crushing out Liberty." He was arrested by order of General Burnside and taken to a military prison in Cincinnatti. When he was refused release on a writ of *habeas corpus*, a mob of Democrats burned the offices of the Republican *Journal*, tore up the railroad to Dayton and cut telegraph lines.

Alfred said to Melinda, "It looks as if there's a civil war within a civil war. What next?"

"Father says that General Burnside wanted Mr. Vallandigham shot but Mr. Lincoln has commuted his sentence to exile to the South."

"Now that's a switch! I think Jeff Davis would just as soon have a viper landed on him as Democrat Vallandigham."

Alfred was right. Davis expelled the congressman from his haven, using the Confederate Enemy Alien Act. Vallandigham made his way via Bermuda to Canada which gave him asylum. On June 11 Alfred read that Ohio had nominated him *in absentia* as governor of Ohio.

"I feel very confused," Alfred said to Melinda as they walked once again along the Potomac. Her wide skirt moved gently against Alfred's ankles as he held her hand in the crook of his arm. The June sun shone warm about them as they loitered in the shade. A squirrel poured itself down a tree and looped across the clearing. He stopped, flipping his tail and chattering as they approached, then raced up another tree and floated from branch to branch. "The more I see of this war and the hospitals, the less I like it. Maybe Vallandigham is right and there is another way. I'm beginning to feel trapped."

"You're not thinking of returning to Canada, are you?" asked Melinda softly, fearing the answer.

"No, not right now," he said, looking at her, unable any longer to conceal the love showing in his eyes. The sunlight danced around them.

A few days later Newton came in from camp. "I hear that Adjutant-General Lorenzo Thomas has been sent south to enlist freed slaves in the army."

"So he has, but we've been told that their pay is less than a white soldier's—just ten dollars a month with no clothing allowance and no bounty for enlisting. It doesn't seem fair."

"A lot of freed blacks are coming into Washington now. We have some coming to the camp looking for work."

"They'd better be careful. Soldiers stoned some in the streets last week. People are afraid of what they might do, like wanting vengeance for the way they've been treated."

"You said that you'd been out to the contraband camp on North Twelfth Street. Better be careful, Fred, I hear there's smallpox around. Remember the typhoid epidemic that took Jasper two years ago."

"I don't think I'll be going there again. I'm being detailed to the new Freedman's Village near Arlington. It's going to have shops, schools and a church. Poor Jasper, he was too young to die."

Alfred didn't say to Newton that he had seen the pockmarked faces of the lucky ones who had recovered from smallpox. He drew a hand over his fine clear skin. "Oh well," he joked to himself. "If it happens to me I can grow a beard."

On Sunday he was invited to Melinda's home for dinner. This time his happiness was tinged with uneasiness. If he continued his education he would not be earning. If he stayed where he was, what would his future be? He had saved over three hundred dollars by careful living but what had he to offer a lady like Melinda? He knew now he was hopelessly in love and that Melinda was not indifferent to him, but he could not with honour speak to her till he was better settled in life. As he returned to his boarding-house that night, his flesh cried out with the agony of denial.

To comfort himself somewhat he wrote to his sister:

"You ask if I am not often weary with such a treadmill round of duties. I try to take everything cheerful and to think that, perhaps, I am but performing my part in the vast machinery of the Universe. But still I have my moments of despondence; but I try to crown them with the garland of Hope, and soothe my hours of gloom with the balm of contentment. I should like very much to come home this summer but cannot without losing my place . . . Remember me to Father and all the folks at home. Write soon.

From your Brother
Alfred

He went disconsolately to bed, dreaming a mixture of mother, sister, Melinda.

Goble's Corners, June 25, 1863

My dear brothers

We are all well here. Little Eva loves to run outdoors. Sometimes I worry that she will run away as she follows butterflies and birds but so far she has not lost herself. I tire somewhat easily these days and cannot run after her very well.

I read in the paper that Peace Democrat Vallandigham is now in Windsor where he is directing his campaign as a candidate for governor of Ohio. He says that if he is elected 50,000 armed Ohioans will march to Windsor and lead him in triumph to the state house. I hope it does not mean trouble here. He has been introduced to our government by John A. Macdonald and D'Arcy McGee. He claims that Lincoln has made no effort to have Britain or any other country mediate between North and South to end this dreadful war. He is heading a secret society called Knights of the Golden Circle. They work to end the war. Alonzo is getting restless now that he has recovered from his wound. I do not want him to return to Washington but you know what you young men will do in search of adventure. I suppose that if President Lincoln is re-elected it means that the war will go on till either side is crushed. May God keep you safe from harm . . .

It was over a week before Roseltha could finish her letter. A message came from Harding that Neridia was very ill. Neridia Cline Harding was dead by the time Rose arrived. She had been Enos Harding's second wife for only a year. To get him away from Harding Hall that had seen him twice bereaved, Rose took him home with her. As she sat finishing the letter to her brothers, Enos was trying to respond to Eva's pleas to come outside and play with her. Roseltha finished her letter:

"You will not believe what I have to tell you now, my brothers. Alonzo has left, maybe for Washington, to find work in the States. But that is not all. Neridia is dead. Father cannot believe it yet. She was buried in her wedding dress wearing the necklace father gave her when they were married. She was buried in the Harding plot in the cemetery on the hill. I will write no more now."

"Poor father," said Alfred and Newton, too stunned to say more. Then second shock came when they received a letter from Alonzo postmarked Rolla, Missouri. Alfred wrote home.

Dear Father and Rose,

I am sorry to hear of Mrs. Harding's death. It is a difficult time for you, father, and for Mr. and Mrs. Cline. May Neridia sleep the good sleep in Paradise. We received a letter from Alonzo about ten days ago and were surprised to learn that he is in Rolla, Missouri. *It appears that he started for St. Louis and on the way fell in with the Q.M. of St. Louis who, when they arrived in that place, put him in charge of about forty men and sent him on to Rolla. When he got there they gave him a Wagon Train—pay $60 per mo.—and he was to start the next morning for Springfield about three hundred miles South-west of St. Louis....* Rolla may not be any more wild west than Washington for we have fights in the streets here. There is great opposition now to the new draft law that says that a man may buy his way out if he pays $300 for a substitute. The poor say the law is loaded against them for they have no money to buy their way out and why should the rich go free? The term of the three-year volunteers is coming to an end and they are being offered $250 to re-enlist. Lee is on the move again. I wish I could see Little Eva. Does she still look like Jasper? I'm glad she has curly hair like me.

Affectionately

Alfred

Alfred sealed the letter, addressing it in his best writing, curling the capitals with care, and putting all his manhood into the deep down strokes. He sorrowed for his father's loss but he thought of Melinda, how the sun shone on the curls that escaped from beneath her bonnet, how he loved her quick, bright step beside him and her intuitive grasp of his thoughts. If the war should end by winter, shall I go home or stay? He blew out the lamp and tossed until he slept.

Chapter 16

Smallpox

The late June heat lay heavy on Washington. In Melinda's home the heavy rugs were rolled away for they held the humidity, and the velvet portières were taken down for they nullified any breeze that might come in. The usual alacrity with which Alfred attacked his work, the alacrity that had earned him two promotions, turned to lassitude. In the early morning when he went to the station to supervise the dispersal of supplies it was already hot.

This morning Jonah looked tired. "Up all night?" joshed Alfred.

"Jus' about. I's at camp on Boun'ry Street lookin' if Philomena was come maybe. Maybe I wish she not come 'cuz smallpox there."

"There's smallpox among the soldiers, too. They've been moved to Kalorama Isolation Hospital on North Twelfth Street. One was taken out of the ward where I was last night. I hope it's not going to be an epidemic like the typhoid one that took my brother Jasper."

In the midst of the heat two armies jockeyed around the capital, each trying to discover the intentions of the other. On June 26 the Confederates, determined to make a third attempt to capture Washington, crossed the Potomac to Union soil. Lee did not consider this a suicidal move for he had been markedly successful for the last two months against the Federals and General Hooker on his white charger.

Mindful of Burnside's disastrous "mud-march", Hooker decided not to try to cross the Rappahannock at Fredericksburg. He would cross higher up over the Rapidan, concealing his movements to flank Lee's army by feinting. Nothing could equal the divining powers of Lee and Jackson. They separated their armies and proceeded to envelop the enveloppers. As all Hooker's planning went awry, he was bewildered beyond measure.

When he was knocked insensible by a cannonball that hit the verandah post he was leaning against, they said he was no more dazed after it than before. The result was the terrible Federal defeat at Chancellorsville. When Lincoln received the telegram with this news, his face turned as gray as the French-gray paper on the wall.

The only bright spot for the Federals in that May defeat was the mortal wounding of Stonewall Jackson. Jackson was shot by his own men as he rode forward in the dusk to organize the pursuit of the retreating North. Now Lee was bereft of the man who was like his right arm, the man who divined what Lee would do even if miles separated them, the man who could always seem to lead his ragged rebels to victory. Despite the loss of his brilliant strategist, Lee pushed onward to Washington.

Alfred met Melinda at the hospital. "I hear that General Hooker has been replaced by General Meade as head of the Army of the Potomac."

"Yes, I know," replied Melinda. "I don't know how the army keeps up any morale at all with this constant shift of commanders. It must be because the volunteers just refuse to give up."

Neither Alfred nor Melinda needed to read in the Washington *Intelligencer* that "Large numbers of sick soldiers from the Army of the Potomac continue to arrive in the city daily." They were in the midst of a non-stop deluge. There were black faces among the sick now. Though prejudice was still rife, the white soldiers were finding that the black men in their uniforms were just as steadfast fighters as they.

There was little time for the two friends to do more than smile as they passed in the wards or snatched a cup of tea together. Twice Alfred hired a hack to drive Melinda home after she had worked all day and the evening too.

"You must not tire yourself so or you will become ill," he said as they parted at her door.

"I could say the same to you as well," she anwered softly, laying a hand for a moment on his sleeve. "Take care, Mr. Harding. Good night." And she vanished through the door.

Not all of Washington followed their pattern of selfless living. After two years of war the capital was callous to the deaths of so many young men. The time had passed when the shooting of one young colonel named Elmer Ellsworth was regarded as a national disaster. As Alfred took a horse-car home from Melinda's house, the main streets were filled with barouches carrying fashionable women and gaudy officers. Ice cream and roasted chestnut vendors hawked their wares under flickering gas lights. Gay red bonnets bobbed saucily along the streets and their owners turned away when a one-armed or one-legged soldier came too near. So what if Lee had crossed the Potomac on June 26 and was raiding Pennsylvania and Maryland? Long live today!

Then the whole Army of the Potomac seemed to vanish into thin air. On June 21 as Alfred came out of church, he heard the sound of artillery fire in the direction of Bull Run. Was there going to be a third Bull Run? Would General George C. Meade do any better than his predecessors?

July 1, 1863, the two armies, searching for each other's vulnerability like giant inchworms, met at Gettysburg, Pennsylvania where Lee was beginning to concentrate a sixty-mile line of soldiers. The Federals marched into battle to the tune of fifes playing "The Campbells are coming, hurrah, hurrah." A day's fighting ended in a draw but neither side retreated.

July 2. The onslaught raged around Cemetery Hill, Seminary Ridge, Little Round Top, Big Round Top, Cemetery Ridge. General Meade held them all as up the inclines the Confederates charged again and again through the blue fog of cannon fire and the bright blaze of rifles. In a wheat field the two sides knelt thirty paces from each other and fired till one side was gone. In Devil's Den the wounded hid behind rocks to escape the murderous barrage. They fought till dark when only flashes from muzzles told where the battle line was. Neither side withdrew.

July 3. Both armies pulled their lines together and were ready by noon for the greatest bombardment of the war. Add grapeshot and Johnny Reb was mowed down.

July 4. Both sides tense but immobile. After three days' bombardment would either try again?

July 5. Lee gave way. He marched his army down the Hagerstown road, repelled but again not destroyed.

The toll on both sides at Gettysburg was over fifty thousand dead, wounded and missing. In Pickett's famous cavalry charge over three-quarters of his complement, 3,393 officers and men out of 4,800, were left on the field.

On July 5 Alfred Harding watched the fireworks explode for two victories, not one, as under Grant's persistent siege Vicksburg had fallen. On the Mississippi the North was winning, but Lee was back on Confederate soil and like a phoenix he would probably rise again.

Because of the continuing casualties—23,000 Federal dead and wounded lay in the rain after Gettysburg—the government continued its hated conscription policy that allowed a man to buy his way out for three hundred dollars. The poor cried that under a Republican government they were treated like slaves. Draft riots broke out in New York city. In the Irish section negroes were beaten and hunted. The Irish said they were not only the cause of the war but they were scabs and strike-breakers as well. Abolitionist Horace Greeley's New York *Tribune* office was attacked. Copperhead cries for peace were added to the melée. Troops sent from Washington used howitzers to disperse the crowds.

The Enrolment Act remained, since able-bodied men were still plentiful in the North. Three hundred dollars substitute money plus the Federal bounty looked like a bonanza. And you could trust to luck that you wouldn't be killed.

In Canada, Roseltha read about the riots in New York, the victory at Gettysburg and the fall of Vicksburg. She knew that Alfred and Newton were safe in Washington because of Lee's defeat, but where was Alonzo? In Missouri or farther south and closer to danger?

Newton came into the city to see Alfred. He was tired and dispirited from hauling wounded to the hospitals. He had a copy of the *Intelligencer* with him and as he slumped into a chair in Alfred's room he read the headlines about the riots.

"If New York opts out of the war, there'll be the dickens to pay because most of our supplies are routed through New York. The money's there too, in the banks, and money pays the army and the teamsters." Then he noticed that Alfred was pale and quiet.

"Anything wrong? What are you doing for recreation these days? Or maybe you're in love."

"Don't feel well. Just feel bad, Think I'll get into bed. You read the papers to me, but pick out some good news like the end of the war maybe."

Next day Alfred woke, too sick to go to work. He turned over and slept. At noon his landlady brought him some soup. He slept but woke feverish. Newton came in from the camp.

"You look sick. What's wrong?"

"Don't know. Feel bad."

"You need a doctor and I'm going to get one."

Newton went for Dr. Magruder. He was not in his office. He left a message for him to call as soon as possible at Alfred's address. He did what he could for his brother before leaving for roll-call at camp. Next day he went again for the doctor who had not yet come. The following night he found that the doctor had been there and said it was verriloid, a disease like smallpox and not too serious, but before Newton left, Alfred was slightly delirious. He was calling for his mother, Newton thought, but her name was Harriet, not Melinda. Wonder where he got that name? Newton returned to camp and when he came back next day Alfred was better and quite rational.

"Lucky it's only a mild case," he said cheerfully. "I feel as if I could get up and go to work."

"No, you stay in bed."

"Then take this book of *Rules and Regulations of the Quartermaster's Department* to Mr. Garner. I brought it home to study, but I know he'll be needing it. Better ask for a receipt."

Newton went whistling off on his errand, happy that Alfred was recovering. "It even feels cooler today."

Alfred dozed off, then began to toss as the fever mounted again after its brief respite. He called out, gabbled a little, slept. He awoke weak, but clear in his head. He opened his eyes, looked at the sunshine pouring in the window, warm and vital, with dust motes dancing in its beam. How beautiful the sunshine is and how refreshing the breeze is blowing through the curtains, he marvelled. Then suddenly he began to shake. He broke out into a sweat that was not fever. Suddenly he knew, he knew inevitably, his senses told him, that he was very ill and it was the last time he would see the sunshine.

For a few moments he lay uncertainly, then he mustered his strength. This was no time for grief, self pity or regret. There were three things he must do before his life would snuff itself out. He pulled out his strongbox from under the bed but could not open it and he could not remember where he kept the key. He washed his face and hands at the basin on the commode, dressed quickly, smoothed his hair, went down the back stairs quietly. No one was in the kitchen. He was looking for an axe. He found one in the woodshed and took it to his room.

With one blow he broke open the box and took out his money, all but thirty dollars. "Better leave a bit behind." He went down the front stairs and out into the tree-lined street.

He went first to Galt's jewellry store on Pennsylvania Avenue. "I'll take the gold and pearl lavaliere in the window. Please send it to Miss Melinda Hamilton, Georgetown." On the card he wrote, "Melinda, I love you. Alfred." He paid the price without hesitation.

The hospital was next. He put twenty-five dollars in an envelope and addressed it with a flourish—Mr. Walt Whitman. Then he inserted a note: From one who admires your poetry and your work in the hospital. Use it to allay suffering. Alfred Harding. "Give it to him when he comes tonight," he asked the receptionist.

Two more stops. He went to the post office. "There's some money still owing in Cleveland. I'll pay my share and that will help my brothers and father." He sealed the letter with a tongue coated with fur.

"Now I have to go to the White House to beg Mr. Lincoln to stop the war at once. He goes to see the wounded but it is usually to the Soldier's

Hospital and it's a show place compared with the others. He just doesn't see what I've seen."

He was beginning to feel faint. Better have something to eat. He was now in front of Willard's Hotel. He had looked at the dining-room on a couple of occasions when he and Newton had watched the Senators and Representatives chatting in the lobby. He had never treated himself to a meal there for it would have been an unnecessary extravagance taking away what he needed for his education. "I'm going to have dinner here, and wine in a crystal goblet." Drinking wine was against his family principles but now Alfred felt that the gesture of holding up a graceful glass and gazing into the ruby lights of a fine wine would satisfy an unidentified aesthetic longing.

Just as he reached the door and the head waiter approached him, his head began to whirl. He felt the fever beginning to rise again. He turned away. "I can't waste time eating. Better get to the White House. Must see the president. Must end the war."

Though the White House was not far away, he hailed a horse cab and sank onto the leather cushions. "To the White House," he ordered.

"Migod, sir," said the cabbie as he looked at Alfred, "you'd better get a doctor."

"No time now. Later."

The cab drew up in front of the White House portico. As the driver put on the horse's feed-bag, Alfred paid him impatiently, then walked into the White House. Lincoln was casual about security, resenting even a guard of one when he went riding, though some one had taken a shot at him recently as he was riding alone near his summer home past the Soldier's Rest Home. There was a distant murmur of voices from the second floor where Lincoln received visitors, personal or political. Alfred clung to the bannister as he walked up the stairs. The voices became louder and as he entered the upstairs hall he could see a dozen people waiting to see Lincoln, some seated, some standing as they talked.

Alfred muttered to himself, "My mission is urgent. I want the war stopped. Why should I wait in line till these others ask for some job or favour?" His innate courtesy won out over his acute desire to speak. He sat down on a chair next to the man at the end of the line.

The fever mounted again. His head weighed so heavy he could hardly hold it up. He wanted to lie down. He forgot why he was there. He rose, walked down the stairs hanging to the bannister for dear life, hailed another cab, gave his home address and collapsed on the seat.

When Newton returned from giving Garner the Rule Book, Alfred's bed was empty and the strong box, only half hidden under the bed, had been broken open. Where was Alfred?

"Did you see him?" he asked the landlady.

"No, I just heard him go out a few hours ago."

"I must find him," and he set off. He hired a horse. He rode to the depot. Old Dad was resting on a box.

"Have you seen Alfred?"

"Nope."

He went to the quartermaster's department. "Has Harding been here?"

"No. Anything wrong?"

He went to the hospital. Alfred had not been there for a week. He met a friend, Clarey Donaldson. They went up H Street to 7th, to Pennsylvania Avenue, then to 20th Street where they met another friend, R. Stanley.

"Have you seen Alfred? He's not home and he's sick."

"Yes, I saw him near the President's mansion a while ago."

"Come on, let's go." No sight of Alfred. They went to the hospitals, then to the Medical Directory's Office. When it was nearly sundown they returned to the boarding-house, done out and disappointed. There was Alfred in bed.

"Where have you been? How are you feeling? Your strong-box is broken open. Did someone rob you?"

"Don't know. Don't bother me. I think I'm real sick."

They took him to Kalorama Hospital, the Pest-House, for by now the tell-tale spots were breaking out all over Alfred's young handsome face. Newton was sent away for this was an isolation hospital.

Relieved that his brother was in competent hands at last but anxious because of the virulence of the disease that gripped him, Newton wrote in his diary each day:

Sunday. In camp most of the day as it was very dangerous to go to the hospital to see Alfred. Went in the evening. He semed some better but could not tell me anything about his money.

Monday. Did not see Alfred today but was very busy inquiring about his money. Could find no positive clue to it.

Tuesday. Saw Alfred in the evening. He did not know anything about his money. Thought he had given it to Germaine to keep for him. He looked worse than I had expected.

Wednesday. They would not let me see him.

Thursday. Same.

Friday. Saw Alfred in morning. He was very bad. Do not expect him to live. Came home, saw Clarey and Germaine about his money. Germaine denied receiving it. Went back to hospital, but Alfred not there—he was dead and buried.

Then Newton had to write the dread letter home.

Dear Sister

Alfred is dead. He died about 11 o'clock last night. I saw him in the afternoon yesterday he seemed some better but when I went this morning he was dead. I cannot get his body under circumstances whatever. He will be buried at the "Soldier's Home" tomorrow. He died very easy. I can write no more now.

Yours
Newton

When Newton wrote his sister he thought his brother would be buried at Soldier's Rest Cemetery near Silver Spring and Lincoln's summer retreat. This was now impossible because the order was given that all smallpox dead were to be put swiftly into rough wooden boxes and buried immediately to save the living from infection. When Newton sought to claim his brother he found that Alfred Harding of Harding, Canada West, had been buried in Glenwood Cemetery in the pauper's burying ground with only a small board for a marker.

"I can't leave my brother there. We're not paupers," cried the seventeen year old to himself, "but how can I move him without any one knowing?"

He went to an undertaker named Sands. Sands had in his employ four men who were immune to smallpox for they had recovered from it. He bribed the caretaker at Glenwood to forget to lock the gate that night. He bought a decent casket to replace the pauper's box. He pushed open the unlocked gate and his helpers, working by torchlight, performed their task. As Newton held the gate open for them to leave, one whistled softly, "Listen to the mocking-bird, listen to the mocking-bird." It was a tune fitting to mock the vanquished hopes of the twenty-four year old young man in the casket.

It was not the tune that came to Newton's mind as they lowered Alfred to his new resting-place in Columbia Harmony Cemetery. It was the song his mother loved, "There's a church in the valley by the wildwood." No wildwood this, but at least there was a cedar tree and a rosebush in bloom where they were burying him.

How could he leave his brother without some kind of service? As the last clod dropped into place on the mound and the four men went away with their shovels over their shoulders, Newton searched his mind for some of the Bible words Alfred had loved to memorize. Slowly part of Psalm 103 came to him and he said it softly as the night wind ruffled his hair: "that we are dust. As for man, his days are as grass: as a flower of the field, so he flourisheth. For the wind passeth over it, and it is gone; and the place thereof shall know it no more."

"No more," he repeated as tears blinded his eyes. Picking a red rose from the nearby bush, he laid it on the earth.

In Canada West Enos Harding said to his daughter, "Two sons are too much to give. I'm going to Washington to bring Newton home." Alonzo was in Missouri too far away to fetch. Roseltha wrote to him there.

Goble's Corners

My dear brother,

*I received a letter this morning from father at Washington and in it was tidings from you. I am truly thankful to the "God of Israel" that you are indeed alive. I have not received **a word from you since you left Canada** nor heard from you since you wrote to father from Rolla the 14th of last month . . . I have written several letters to you but I suppose you did not get them. I directed them all to Rolla as I knew of no where else to send them. My poor brother **you too** have been sick, alone, among strangers, but I hope you have recovered by this time; and now why will you go yet farther away. Do please come home **only two of you left**. I cannot bear to think of you going to Vicksburg or Texas. Canada is broad enough and free enough to shelter her sons. Father said he had written to you, so you have doubtless if you have received his letter, heard the sad, sad news from Washington. Poor, dear Alfred sleeps the last long sleep of death there. I cannot yet make it seem so. I hardly know how to write to you my heart is O! so sad. My precious brothers three are gone, and those left are far away exposed to like disease and death. The Saviour said that not even a Sparrow should fall to the ground without his notice. Will he not much more care for his creatures made in his own image. May he preserve you, for O! how vain is the help of man. This world is not our home. O! may we in truth have a clear title to that better land. "Eye hath not seen, ear hath not heard neither hath it entered into the heart of man to conceive the glories of that better land." But I must tell you of our lost brother. He had not been well for some time the last letter I had from him was the 9th . . . The 14th he was worse Newton went for the Dr. he did not come and the next day he went again for him he did not come till the next day Thursday the 16th. Alfred was then broken out. He pronounced the disease Veriloid and told Newton he had better keep him there instead of sending him to the Hospital. Friday he was delerious, but Saturday morning he seemed better and quite rational. He told Newton to take a book he had neglected to give to the new Waggon Master and get a receipt for it. Newton went and while he was gone Alfred got up dressed himself broke open his chest [Newton had the key of it] took his money $297 and when Newton came back he was gone. Newton went immediately in search of him traced him by*

199

inquiry as far as the President's house and then lost all trace of him. With several others he searched all day without finding him. About dark he came back but with only $20.60 and could not tell what he had done with the rest. He was then immediately sent to the hospital. A few days later the Dr. pronounced the disease smallpox and a very bad case. He seems to have continued to grow worse till Friday night at 11 o'clock . . . he died. Newton was not allowed to go into his room but he visited him secretly once every day at the window where he could see him and hear him speak. Friday afternoon he saw him and thought him better, when he went again the next morning he was **dead**. The Attendant said he died very easy. He could not under the circumstances get his body; and so on Sunday the 26th he was buried in Glenwood Cemetery with a weeping willow at his head and a blooming rose at his feet. Not only died among strangers; but he sleeps there too. I would love to see the spot where he lies but that may never be.— 'tis very sad, but we may submit to Him who knoweth better than we. "Man proposes and God disposes." He died at the Kanorama Hospital . . . aged 24 years 9 months and 8 days. Newton tried to find his money but without success. Do you know of any friend with whom Alfred would be likely to deposit it. Father has been hunting for it without success. Newton too has been very unfortunate he had $75 in money and 40 dollars worth of new clothes burned up in camp leaving him penniless with only the clothes on his back. He was not likely to get money or get home and so father concluded to go after him. He left Drumbo . . . 16th for Washington went to Suspension Bridge, bought his ticket for Baltimore had his money in bills in an envelope in his inside coat pocket went to Rochester intending to stay there all night after he went to his room thought of his money when lo! it was all gone $123 and **all he had**. The police searched for it arrested several men but could find no clue to it. His pocket must have been picked. He came back here the next evening [17th] staid all night went to Paris in the morning got money of Mr. Hill and started again Thursday noon, got in Washington Friday night 10 o'clock found Newton well. Jasper [Goble] wrote to Newton Goble to send immediately all the mony he owed you and Alfred to Newton at Washington. When father wrote the 25th Inst he had not got anything from him. If he fails in sending it and father cannot get what the Government owed the boys Newton can't come home even now but will have to work there again. I do hope that may not be the case he is very anxious to come home. He is only 17 too young to be left in such a place alone. How are you off for funds and have you been in the Hospital. O! how I do wish you were all at home again. Dear Alonzo come home if you can only make your board. Surely in Cleveland or here you can find something to do. I had a letter from Uncle Silas written

200

June 14th they have a great deal of trouble there. Will has moved from there to Indiana, 7 miles from Indianappolis on the Crawfordsville Road near what is called Holm Mills. He is farming and if the rest shall be obliged to leave Lexington they will go there too. If it should be in your way, go and see them. I do hope you may get this letter and that I may get yours. Uncle Silas has written several letters which we have not received. Lissa and family are well. She was down last week. Heman preached here Sunday. Maggie Dawson is very sick not expected to live; but she is not afraid to die. The Lord bless you my darling brother.

Ever your affectionate Sister
Rose

Melinda too was mourning for Alfred. When the package was delivered from the jeweller's, she was mystified to know who was sending her a gift. "It isn't my birthday, so it isn't from father." She opened it. Underneath the gold and pearl lavaliere was the card, "I love you, Alfred."

She clasped the chain around her neck, rushed to the mirror gasping with delight, thought, "Surely he'll come tonight to see me. I won't go to the hospital today at all."

She waited. Alfred did not come. For three days she waited, hesitating to be so forward as to search for the man she loved in return, hesitant to show the necklace to her father who might not approve. On the fourth day she could endure the suspense no longer.

"Father," she began, then as her voice broke she ran to lay her head on his shoulder. "Father, Alfred gave me this necklace and he says he loves me. He sent me this four days ago but he has not come to see me and he wasn't at the hospital when he usually comes. What shall I do?"

"I'll inquire for you. He may have been sent on some secret errand. I don't imagine there's much wrong." To himself he said, "This affair is getting too serious. Melinda is young but I was beginning to like the lad."

He inquired at the hospital. They knew nothing. He asked at the quartermaster's department, was given a boarding-house address, was told there that Alfred had been taken delirious to Kalorama. There he located a name on the register—Alfred Harding, died, smallpox. The date was two days previous. Because he was a doctor, he was accustomed to delivering verdicts. This was different. Melinda was his daughter.

"Put the necklace away till you feel better. Time will heal."

"He loved me, father, and I never had a chance to tell him that I loved him too."

When Enos and Newton studied the contents of Alfred's pockets in the clothes he was wearing before he was taken to the hospital, the receipt for

201

a necklace puzzled him. Where was the necklace now? Had Alfred intended it for his sister? The jeweller could not remember if the necklace had been taken or delivered. Still puzzled, they returned to Canada, leaving the war and their dead behind them.

The victories at Gettysburg and Vicksburg caused Canadians to regard the Union army in a new light. The war that many had cheered at first as heralding the end of slavery was now beginning to look like a war of conquest. What if that victorious army, after subduing the South, should turn its glaring eyes towards Canada? Since the days of the Loyalists a hard core of Canadians thought it their duty to hate the braggart, greedy, grasping Yankee symbolized by Lincoln, the incarnation of republicanism and Yankeedom. Many Canadians, except ardent abolitionists, favoured King Cotton and that Southern gentleman, Jefferson Davis.

To be sure William MacDougall, Commissioner of Crown Lands for Canada West and East, had been present at the dedication of the Gettysburg Cemetery and had been impressed with the obvious strength and sincerity of the American President. And that suave Torontonian, ex-Oxford professor Goldwin Smith, who earlier had said that the United States would annex Hell as a market if necessary, conceded when he met General Grant that he was "rather taken with the beast." But fear of possible rapacity was growing.

This fear was fed by the presence in Toronto, Hamilton and Montreal of pods of Confederate personnel who were plotting to use British Canada as a base for offensive operations against the North. Many lived in the St. Lawrence Hotel in Montreal and the American or Queen's Hotel in Toronto. Some of the younger Southerners enrolled in the University of Toronto when espionage did not occupy their time. If they became bored with provincial Canada West society or had real news to report, they travelled to Halifax, took ship for Nassau's sunny clime, then boarded a blockade runner for Georgia or North Carolina.

As the manpower of the South was being depleted, plotting to attack the North from Canada was stepped up. They tried to enlist aid from Clement Vallandigham in Windsor but he was too busy with his gubernatorial campaign to aid them.

They plotted to raid the Northern prison on Johnson Island in Lake Erie, just off Sandusky, to free a thousand Southern officers, some of whom had been with Morgan's famous band of cavalry raiders. With this force at their disposal, they intended to hijack a federal warship in the harbour, sack Detroit, Cleveland and Buffalo and cut a swath as far as

Kentucky. The plot was foiled by John Wilson Murray, the great Canadian detective.

They tried to destroy Canadian and British neutrality a few weeks later (December 1863) by seizing the *Chesapeake*, the fastest ship on the New England coast, to use as a Confederate privateer to prey on Northern shipping. Pro-Southern citizens in Liverpool, Nova Scotia, allowed the ship to re-fuel and the leader of the plot to escape ashore; but next day the North re-captured its ship in British waters. The situation was as tense as during the Trent affair two years previous. Lincoln refused to be trapped. He said one war at a time was enough and Governor-General Lord Monck in Canada breathed a sigh of relief. Britain and British North America were still neutral.

In Harding life was proceeding as much as usual. Enos was still winding up Walsingham affairs and Newton was writing to Alonzo.

[Harding] Nov. 5 1863

Dear Brother
*Father has gone to Port Burwell to try and get the money for the shingles. He started Tuesday. I recd [28.00] twenty-eight dollars from Mr. Honeyman this morning and according to Gatner's directions send you [25.00] twenty-five dollars of it. If father obtains that money **I think** he will forward some of it to you from there. When you go to Nashville if there is any site for me write and let me know. Father thinks of renting the farm. A man who works a farm above the "big hill" [I forget his name] wishes to rent it. . . . I went to Brantford today on excursion. Celebration "Gunpowder plott." Elder Haviland preached here last Sunday evening house was full. I have just got over the Quinsey. Dick Reed's house burned down tuesday. If you come back to Canada bring my school books.*

Your brother
Newton

Newton was at home safe, but why were they sending money to Alonzo? The news of Alfred's death had made Alonzo start for home from Rolla. That did not mean that he reached there as his sister was learning.

Goble's Corners, Nov. 17 1863

My Dear Brother

*I have only a little spare time before mail time and I have decided to devote it to you, and give you a good scolding; you naughty, naughty boy, why have you not written to me. When I came home from Toronto I supposed you were in Cleveland till one morning Newton popped in and surprised me by saying you were in Walsingham running Mr. Smith's mill. Then for some time I thought of you, pitied you, and felt much sympathy for you, in that dismal place. Till not long ago father happened here on his way to Walsingham and said you were in Cleveland but said you talked of going South again and now for aught I know you are away and may not receive this letter at all. I am so sorry you think of going so far away again, but if you think it best I suppose you e'en must go; but it would be better to make a little and run no risks; what a hundred years from now will avail all this buzz and trouble about the things of this life. Do not my dear Brother sacrifice one prospect of good to any hope of worldly gain for what will be the benefit at the last. I wish you would write me often and be not chary of your confidence. Newton is in [Harding] jobbing about not improving much I fear in either heart and manners. I hope he will be able to go to School before very long. . . . I wish you would get your Photograph taken and send it to me. I have an Album and want all the loved ones in it . . . there is one thing more I want to say if you go South and are much exposed as you will be, be sure and wear **all the time** flannel underwear clothes. I am sure it was exposure to cold and rain that caused both Jasper and Alfred to pass away; . . . With many earnest wishes and prayers for your safety and happiness I am*

> *Your affectionate*
> *Sister Rose*

It was just as well that Sister Rose could not see the photograph that was being taken about that time of the men who were directing the war. They were grouped at the foot of a falls near Washington as if they were on a picnic. These were the leaders of the great nations of the world who had come to confer with the real participants in this war that was sometimes called the war of the rebellion and sometimes a civil war. They stood against the background of falling water like ordinary trippers, faces pleasantly inscrutable, each wishing he had a crystal ball or resident mind-reader to divine what the others were thinking.

What was in Lord Lyons' mind, British Minister to Washington, about the cruisers that were being built in British shipyards for use by the South?

Was Mr. Mercier of France contemplating his correspondence with John Bigelow about the vessels France also was building for the South? Or was he thinking about what Emperor Napoleon III might do from the base of his pawn Maximilian in Mexico?

Baron de Stoekel of Russia had been authorized by Czar Alexander III to offer firm friendship to the North at this time, but could William H. Seward, Secretary of State, believe him?

Had M. Schlienen, Hanseatic Minister, come for a trading entente or to study new American methods of warfare for use in the next European conflict?

Signor Bertenatti of Italy, Count Piper of Sweden, Mr. Sheffield, attaché of the Polish delegation—their minds were assuredly not blank as the droplets from the falls were blown gently towards them.

What was in Abraham Lincoln's mind as he contemplated the results of the late anti-conscription riots in New York and the changes in army command he had just made? Surely Grant and Sherman in the South, if not Meade in the North, would be the ones to achieve an end to the war.

The war was not Lincoln's only sorrow. His wife still wept inconsolably for her dead son, little Willie, so much so that he feared for her mental stability. He himself had suffered a mild dose of smallpox. He could control his nerves better than his wife but in September, after the victories at Gettysburg and Vicksburg, came news of a Federal defeat at Chickamauga.

Chickamauga, was thirty miles south of Chattanooga. Chattanooga, on the Tennessee river, was at the junction of the railroads that brought supplies to the Southern forces from both west and north. It was the key to Federal entry into the Confederacy. It had been captured and became the Federal base of supplies. Determined to re-capture it, Southern General Bragg brought up his army to the valley of the little creek known as Chickamauga. The very name was ominous for long ago after some forgotten tragedy the Indians had given it the name of "River of Death." Two days of fighting confirmed the name. The two armies, fairly equal with 60,000 men, left 16,000 dead along the creek and in the heavy underbrush. But General George H. Thomas, now called the Rock of Chickamauga, had prevented Confederate General Bragg from reaching Chattanooga.

What would break the stalemate of the war? Lincoln was beginning to think that the only way to tighten the Anaconda Plan was to put one supreme commander in charge of all army operations. Would generals, as jealous of their rights as the states themselves, agree to the dictates of one man? More than one despatch was couched in green-eyed terms: "Major-General Granger to General W.S. Rosecrans—All quiet in front. No movement of enemy reported. The Eighteenth and Twenty-second Michigan, en route from Kentucky, have always belonged to me. I hope you assign them to my command again." It had taken nearly three years of war for one man to stand out as the one who was most likely to bring victory. Would Congress, due to convene in two months, accept Lincoln's recommendation? And who did Lincoln have in mind?

Chapter 17

The 20th Ohio Light Artillery

Newton was glad to be back in Harding but sometimes he missed the camp and Washington's hustle. The gaiety that had exploded after Lee's defeat at Gettysburg guaranteed its security had continued unabated. He missed Pennsylvania Avenue with its effervescent stream of bright people—ladies in velvet, moiré, ribbons, feathers and jewels, on their way to innumerable balls, so many that one evening would witness several functions. There were officers with their fancy women and madams in their resplendent carriages. Fine outfits did not mean fine manners. One madam called her rival a tub of guts as their carriages happened to pull alongside each other.

The madams rented the best houses, one of them next door to First Baptist Church on Thirteenth Street. One Sunday as Newton had joined Alfred for church there, they saw the saucy daughters of Eve leaning boldly out of the windows to shock church-going wives clinging to their husband's arms. Each brother pretended not to let the other see him watching, but it was obvious that both were gawking like country bumpkins.

Gin cocktails at eight cents a glass were a favourite drink in such establishments but liquor was forbidden in the camps. When Newton returned that day he saw the guards refusing to pass two "sisters" seeking to visit their "brothers." The guards were becoming adept at recognizing sisters with too prominent "lacteal fountains" in front or out-sized bustles behind.

Theatre-going was a passion. When Mr. Ford's remodelled Baptist church on Tenth Street called the Athenaeum was burned down, he had no difficulty in obtaining sufficient financial support to re-build. One of Newton's Washington friends sent him a paper describing the opening of

Ford's new theatre in August. Twenty-four hundred people entered in a blaze of gaslight. Tobacco spitting on the floor was prohibited and police at the door refused entrance to painted Jezebels.

He and Alfred had attended the theatre occasionally. When Newton read that Mr. Lincoln had gone to see John Wilkes Booth perform in *The Marble Heart*, he recalled that he had seen the handsome actor too.

There were some things about Washington that Newton did not miss. The cost of living was rising. It now took $1333 a year for a family of five to live modestly in the capital. Though Secretary of the Treasury Salmon P. Chase had blown four thousand dollars on his wedding reception, he threatened with dismissal the workers building the extension to the Treasury Building when they laid down their tools in protest against having their lunch hour cut from one hour to half an hour. The money the teamsters were being paid didn't stretch very far when Newton left for home. He also did not miss the early morning sounds of guns that signified a firing squad shooting deserters and bounty jumpers.

It was odd to be back in the placid village beside the deep-running Nith. There were new houses and a white clapboard church in the valley, his mother's dream. The big house was as imposing as ever but Harding Hall lifting over him felt strange after the confines of a tent. Newton's spirits alternately rose as high as the cupola or sank to the cellar as he longed for the sound of his mother's voice in the kitchen or parlour. He was freed from the pressures and privations, the heat and cold, the rain and dust of a teamster's life, but the demands of keeping house were different from casual chores around a campfire with a bunch of fellows. Nevertheless he was glad to be a personage again in the familiar country village.

He wasted no time in harnessing Phoenix to the buggy, keeping a weather eye open for whatever girl was walking. Then he took out the carriage, driving the frisky colts and sitting nonchalantly on the velvet cushions, now a little less than their original resplendent red. He had been away from Harding for nearly four years, and the girls he had played hide and seek with before they had moved to Walsingham were prim young things in long skirts with their pigtails transformed into coiffures and their bare feet encased in buttoned slippers.

He went to the meetings of the local Temple association. "Tell us about the war," they clamoured.

"All right, next week."

He launched into some of the stories that had filtered back to Washington from the battlefields. One-armed Phil Kearney would ride into battle holding the reins in his teeth. One colonel went into battle resting his wounded foot on a pillow. Another was thrown by his horse as they were climbing a ridge. He grabbed the horse's tail as it went by and at the top vaulted into the saddle again. At Shiloh a general's horse was struck by a shell and killed under him. The general was blown ten feet. He got up, roared for another horse, and went right on.

"That's what the generals did. What did you do?"

What did I do? Tell them I was just a teamster hauling hay or corpses? Fired by a sense of the occasion Newton embroidered a bit. Pointing an imaginary rifle with dramatic effect at the upturned faces of his audience, he proclaimed that he had been one of the best sharpshooters in the Union army. He did not tell how he had sobbed to his brother that he had killed two men. The conflict already seemed more legend than reality.

"Did you see any Rebs?"

"Saw them in the distance. Saw them as prisoners being taken through the streets of Washington. Saw some of them in the hospitals. Heard one man say that he and a Reb had fought face to face till both fell down wounded. When he came to, there was a dead Reb beside him and he was covered with a Rebel butternut coat."

The faces of some of those listening were envious and some were unbelieving and grave. War did mean death, didn't it, and not all glamour.

He attended Wednesday prayer meetings to please his father. Prayer meetings in the middle of the week were designed to keep the faithful from backsliding between Sabbaths. As he sat rather restlessly listening to prayer after prayer he thought of his mother and her deep desire for a church in the valley. "Wish they hadn't put in such hard seats," he muttered just before the last hymn as the ladder-straight backs cut into his shoulder blades. "Wish I'd stayed home."

A bright-faced girl from the tenth concession came when the weather was good. Leonora MacDonald's family had lived in Paris near his Uncle Asa's house before they had decided to turn to farming. The two daughters had had a year at boarding school when they had finished the eight grades of elementary school. Leonora intended to go to Normal School in Toronto in a few months just as Daniel Harding had done.

One night Newton drove Lee home. They crossed the road from the church to the Harding barn just south of the house. As he hitched the horse, she waited quietly in the light of the lantern hanging over her head. He put a hand under her elbow to assist her into the buggy. Then he backed out the horse and sprang in beside her.

Lee sat primly as the horses clipclopped along the road that led out of the valley up the hill. Newton was going the long way around to her home but she had not protested when he turned the horse south instead of north.

"What did you think of the meeting tonight?" she asked.

"No duller than usual, I guess," Newton answered. "Old Geordie French spouting the same old things, turning his cap around and around in his hands till you'd think he'd wear it out. Wash me till my sins be whiter than snow. Old Beulah Land. God save the country, the Queen and the heathen."

"You're supposed to close your eyes when someone's praying, not watch him twisting his cap."

"I looked at him before he started. If his hair gets much longer he'll soon have ringlets."

"Wish my hair were as curly as his. I just relax when he starts to pray. I like the sound of his voice rising and falling. He could charm the stones to listen, like Orpheus with his lyre."

"Yeah, I've read about Orpheus but I wish old Geordie wouldn't pray the same thing week after week."

The moon shone white on the dirt road that ascended the steep hill in a series of S turns. The horse's head bobbed and his shoes slipped on the gravel as he climbed steadily. The trees on either side of the road tossed gently.

"Did you see any passenger pigeons last spring when they went through?" asked Newton. "Before I went to the States I saw them fill the fields and half the trees. I took a stick and knocked down a dozen easy. Mother made a pigeon pie."

"They went through again, but not nearly so many. I think it's a shame to kill them, they're so pretty."

"Aw, pigeons are stupid. Serves 'em right to get potted."

"I read in my history book that under the feudal system only the lords could keep pigeons and the peasants hated them because they ate the freshly-sown seed. Then in the winter when food was scarce only the landowner could eat them."

Newton laughed. "Now we're all poor farmers together, or millers, or whatever, so it doesn't matter whose grain the pigeons eat. I could do with a good feed of pigeons. We caught some now and then when I was with the army."

"That must have been exciting, but what are you going to do now? Are you going back to school?"

"Not much chance. Costs a lot."

"I liked geography when I went to school and I guess I'll like teaching it."

"Which country do you like best?"

"The South Sea islands. They say there are fish there that are coloured purple and gold and green and silver, not just gray like the pike in the river here. I put a map of the world over the table in the kitchen and when I'm washing dishes I think of the places I'd like to go to. It makes the washing-up go faster."

As Newton opened her kitchen door he said to her parents, "No, thanks, I won't come in, it's late." He saw the map on the wall and thought, "I won't be satisfied with a map on the wall. If I can't get work here or go to school, I'll take off again."

A few flakes of snow were beginning to fall and the ruts on the road were stiffening into ridges edged with frost as he drove back the short way to Harding. His father was waiting beside a lighted lamp.

"High time you were home. Mind you don't do any sparking. You're a long way from earning your own living, let alone some one else's."

"Aw, pa, don't get upset over nothing. I only drove Lee MacDonald home. Her brother didn't want to wait for her."

They climbed the circling stairs together and went to sleep in the country-quiet house lulled by the sound of the river across the road.

[Harding] . . . 1863

Alonzo I often think of you have written twice once last spring from Detroit once since some time past. I received a letter from you have thought of answering it every day but neglected to do so. you write about trade in reference to the lot and thought it would be well to do so in some shape when I was in Cleaveland in the spring and I received $40 from Cartwright in your act I don't know whether you have had any proposals to purchase the lot David Bogart is in Cleveland studying medicin he writes me there is two parties wants to buy one if Dr. Palmer offers $2800.00 can pay $1500 down the ballence in 3 anual instalments or will pay $2500 down for the full. as the value of money is so uncertain I could not advis the best unless you thought the money turned into pine lands in Michigan would be better.

I suppose you would like to know what I am doing with all the rest. I have just finisht the dishes and swept the house Newton has done about six days work for George Dawson haveing but little notion of doing anything about home but eat his meals and run around on special busines for the temple and to see if the girls are all in order sometimes haveing to run colts and carriage for their special benifit verry difficult to get up to breckfast this state of things not being quite plesant for me to continue to furnish the table and general equipage for such high life. I thought it best to change the program perswaded him to take Mans lath mill to run by the thousand which I thought if he did not make so much would confine *him to steddy habits as he must be on hand. he bords at Rob Dawsons at the mill hires two boys pays 12$ per month for them 2$ for bord has 1$ per thousand finds strings files and oil has worked 2 weeks had difficulty getting it to go right but has cleared his expences with prospect of doing better. can clear 1$ a day to himself if he sticks to the work . . . I wish you to write me all about your affairs the paper is full*

Enos [Harding]

Alonzo
I do not pay postage on this as it may not reach you I am working at astronomy

It was true that Newton was restless. He had no special aptitude for the mill. At home his father was becoming increasingly absorbed in his researches into astronomy. Newton considered it a waste of time because his father was working entirely alone and somewhere out there Newton was sure some one had already solved problems that were plaguing his father. His own mind was filled with formless searching as he listened to the preacher's words on Sunday or the repetitious prayers on Wednesday. Though he did not show it outwardly, he was still numb from the shock of Alfred's death. He missed his school books. He drove to see his sister Melissa in Woodstock and saw the new Institute where her husband Heman was finishing his ministerial studies. The rows of books in the library excited him and the introduction to the principal, Dr. Fyfe, with his air of assurance and erudition, challenged him. "What am I without more education?" he thought.

He drove Melissa and Heman to a service in a schoolhouse on Governor's Road. The speaker had a depth of understanding of his subject, Psalm 23, that filled him with humility. It had only been words to Newton before but this man made the whole situation seem close and real, not far away and academic. "He leadeth me beside still waters"—he explained that the sheep would not drink if the water flowed too swiftly. "Yea, though I walk through the valley of the shadow of death"—the shepherd in the land of the Bible must have courage to lead his flock through a narrow passage into the safety of the valley and in the evening must retrace the same perilous route. "Surely goodness and mercy will follow me all the days of my life . . ." May be, thought Newton, the real death that took mother, Daniel, Jasper and Alfred can be surmounted if we take goodness and mercy and hope for a better world as our inspiration. He knew the hopelessness of making a war-torn world better but then it came to him that at least he might keep it from going backwards.

"Look into the blackness of your hearts," the minister was saying. "Let the Lord be your shepherd. Let goodness and mercy attend you like handmaidens, guiding your steps."

Newton was shaken. How black my heart is, for I am purposeless. Where shall I look for guidance?

Enos' letter reached Alonzo in Rolla, Missouri, where he had been lured by the attractive $60 a month pay. He had taken a half dozen wagon trains hither and yon, most of them drawn by mules, some of which he had to break before he could use them. The army was finding horses too expensive for draft work. An army wagon laden with ammunition weighed about half a ton. On the rough and muddy roads horses that had been "doaped" for sale or shipped sight unseen by an unscrupulous jobber collapsed from the strain or had to be shot because of broken legs. The strong but stubborn and unpredictable mule was the answer. As winter set in, the armies were becoming less active but men still had to eat and supply trains had to move.

The number of mules multiplied. They coughed incessantly, keeping the battle or work-weary men from sleeping. Someone said they would keep quiet if cans were tied to their tails. It took just one night for the mules to find they could clank the cans together. Most of the teamsters were accustomed to horses, not mules. When they drove the beasts from a station to a corral the mules dallied along sidewalks, looked into doors and windows, investigated shoppers' bags, immune to pushing or pulling. The curses of the mule skinners could blister the toughest of ears, let alone Alonzo's Baptist ones. It was a relief when some Mexican "greasers" appeared in Rolla. They led an old horse through the first mess of mules they encountered and the mules followed docilely out of town.

As he broke raw mules or organized trains Alonzo listened to tales of battles elsewhere. He sat on a box in the sunshine one day, leaning against a shed, talking to a soldier on crutches with wounds still healing. Wilson had been at Chickamauga. "For miles," said Wilson, his voice choking, "the road was full of dead horses and mules, not to mention bodies waiting to be buried. One night after dark when the fighting had stopped, I went to the creek to fill my canteen and coffee pot. Stood on a log jutting into the stream. Next morning I went back for more water. I'd been standing on a dead mule the night before. September in Tennessee is hot and the mules began to bloat as soon as they died. I'd been drinking dead mule soup. Nice thought."

Alonzo was silent, then, "How many were killed there?"

"More than any other battle, they say. I guess you know that

Chickamauga is just south of Chattanooga, a southern supply depot, and Bragg and Longstreet wouldn't give it up without a struggle."

"Who was our general?"

"Rosecrans. Old Rosie is pretty good but he couldn't have won without General Thomas, the Rock. After they won at Chickamauga they kept right on till they chased Bragg out of Chattanooga. But then the Rebs still held Lookout Mountain and Missionary Ridge and not one supply train could get through."

Alonzo wondered what he would have done had he been ordered to run such a gauntlet. What he and Wilson did not know was that already the men besieged in Chattanooga were down to quarter rations. Three cobs of corn was the daily ration for a horse, and guards had to be stationed around them when they were fed so the men couldn't steal the corn from the horses.

"Well, back to work," said Alonzo. As Wilson hobbled painfully away, he wondered if he should be doing more to bring the war to an end— maybe even volunteer. He wondered even more when he heard that General Halleck in Washington had despatched Fighting Ed Hooker with two corps of the Army of the Potomac to go by train to the rescue of Rosecrans and the Army of the Cumberland and Billy Sherman's Army of the Tennessee. Hooker's men hooted at Sherman's unkempt and slouching backwoodsmen and they in turn ridiculed Hooker's kid glove and "paper-collared" forces.

The western situation was desperate. Lincoln now announced that Ulysses S. Grant would be in command of all the western forces. It was one step towards unifying the armies on all the fronts, one more step in the Anaconda plan. "He drinks too much," objected the War Department. "Give the name of his whiskey," Lincoln countered, "And I'll send kegs of the same brand to the other generals." Grant was on crutches because of a wounded leg. He replaced General Rosecrans with Rock of Chickamauga "Pap" Thomas as leader of the Army of the Cumberland.

Would these changes dislodge the Rebels from Lookout Mountain looming over Chattanooga with the Tennessee river curving around it, or from Missionary Ridge, the 500-foot high crescent not far away? The men who came from the north to rescue the starving men had travelled through such desolate country that they were inclined to think that "the Rebs could take their land and their niggers and go to hell" for all they had seen as the cars sped along.

As the generals formulated plans to get the Army of the Cumberland out of its impasse, Alonzo in Rolla, Missouri, was reading a letter from home.

Woodstock . . . 1863

My dear Alonzo

Having a few moments this evening I will improve them by writing to you. . . . I was very sorry to hear that you had gone to war again but I know you are safe there as anywhere, do not forget . . . that it is not all of life to live, there is a future to prepare for to which we are all fast hastening . . . Newton talks sometimes of going south again but I hardly think he will. I should very much like him to come to the Institute but Father thinks he cannot raise the means. . . . Heman will graduate next July and then we shall leave Woodstock, we are not sure yet where we will go. Heman has received a call from the Mount Elgin church but has not decided where he will go . . . We have bought a nice new Melodeon and are taking boarders to pay for it. If you will just step over some evening I will sing you some of the old songs I used to sing when we lived on the farm. It seems almost like being home again. . . .

Your Affectionate [Sister]
Lissa

Roseltha added:

My Dear Brother

*. . . Lissa has been writing and as I am up on a visit before she mailed it, I cannot let it go without saying a word too. . . . Heman came from Blenheim yesterday and they are all well. I came up with him. . . . I wish the war was over; and you home again doubtless there are many such **heart** wishes, all over the land. You must write often, very often because you know "hope deferred maketh a sad heart". Father wrote to you last week. There has been a protracted meeting in [Harding]; and our dear Newton has we trust been brought to a saving knowledge of the truth. "Bless the Lord, O my soul". May the Lord keep him "unspotted from the world". "Go thou and do likewise. . . . James Dawson was down not long ago to see Mr. Landon . . . I have not heard from Uncle Silas for a long time. . . . Here comes Lissa with broom and duster so I must quit. Write very soon.*
Goodbye.

As ever Your Own Dear
Sister Rose

P.S. Heman has just returned from the Post Office with a letter from you

. . .Your Photograph is very natural many thanks for it. . . . Rose is
waiting for me to go up town so I must bid you good-by . . .

Lissa

The evangelistic meeting in Harding, following the effect of the sermon
in the school on the Governor's Road, had had an effect on undecided
Newton. He had been deeply moved by the fervour of the preacher and
the steady bombardment of his plea to have his listeners follow the paths
of righteousness. One night he had "gone to the front," and as the
minister held his hands had declared his determination to follow the
Christian faith. In the summer when the water in the river warmed, he
would be baptized and arise from the symbolic immersion into newness
of life.

"Saved," for a Baptist, meant more than accepting a few religious
tenets. It meant that a person intended to add purpose to his life, to
contribute by conscious action to the betterment of his fellow men. A
declaration was one thing, but how did an eighteen year old translate it
into action? Education might be the way. He wrote to Alonzo for he was
longing more than ever to continue his studies.

Harding . . .

Dear Brother

I received your welcome letter a few days since . . . I am still in
[Harding]. I have not done anything in the money line this winter. I
worked for Geo. Dawson about a month . . . and since then I have been
helping Father to get out logs posts rails etc. I cannot remain here for I
cannot do anything but work in the mill or such work for $12 per mo.
which is very small wages besides very hard work. I was thinking of going
out west to do something which would get a living for me. Father as you
know is very hard up just now and he cannot help me any. I have no
money at all now and no clothes scarcely not having any since last fall.
Father says he is going to Michigan to try and get into Business he does
not think of going to Cleveland. You spoke of letting me have some
means to go to school. I would like very well to go to Cleveland to school
if possible. If you could let me have enough to carry me through, one
year I would be as careful as possible with it and probably I could find
something to do out of school hours which would pay and I would try to
do something in vacation. After the year was up probably I could obtain
a situation of some kind where I could make some money. I would repay
you as soon as possible.

Stationary would not cost me much as I could use the boys old books
and paper etc. would be about the only cost. If you cannot let me have

*the needful means to go to school I wish you would tell me what I had
better do as you know better than I do.*

*. . . . I have not been very well for several days past but I shall come out
all right. . . . I will send some papers soon. Write soon dear Brother.*
While I remain Your aff. Brother Newton

Perhaps Newton's growing passion for learning was being inspired by
his father's consuming hunger to wrest its secrets from the heavens. Daily
he struggled to surmount problems that his tenacious nature refused to
declare insoluable.

Alonzo received a letter from his father.

*You might want to know what I am doing. I have not worked harder for
many years . . . working early and late I have undertaken a verry intricate
piece of machinery which I would Call an astronomical cientific invention
to harmonize the universe with its natural appearance to the history of it
given in the Bible a machinery to exhibit to the world its perfect
movement I have been working at it some four months causing a great
deal of deep studdy to get the proper movements to work to the
fractionals part of time by logg work then the machinery being so
different from any other in use cannot get it cast but have to make it
myself not haveing means to work to advantage gives great labour should
have got half of the machinery in motion last week but I was sick four
days. . . .*

On November 25, 1863, the Federals defeated the Confederates at
Chattanooga and rescued the starving town. Five hundred miles away
Alonzo heard bits and pieces of what happened. He wrote about it to his
sister. "I suppose you have read about what is going on around
Chattanooga but your papers will tell only so much. Soon after Grant
was put in command of all the western forces he sent General Thomas to
get Rosecrans out of the siege and replace him in command. Then
Hooker moved down the Eleventh and Twelfth Corps of the Army of the
Potomac by the cars, 20,000 men in 7 days. On November 25 I think it
was Grant ordered a charge against both Lookout Mountain and
Missionary Ridge. The Rebs just had to be pushed out somehow. In
some places the way up Lookout was sheer rock and our boys had to
climb up by ladders and hoist each other up on their shoulders. But they
got up and silenced the guns on top. Those down below could not see
what was going on because the top was hidden in clouds or mist and the

217

ones who reached the top looked through the clouds raining on the town below. Sometimes when I stood in the cupola at Harding I thought I was near the clouds and I wanted to get above them. I guess I'll have to go to Lookout to do that. While Hooker's men were taking the mountain, Thomas and Sherman were to attack Missionary Ridge that every one was saying was impregnable. Things were going badly for Thomas and Sherman at both ends of the ridge when Grant ordered the Cumberland boys to take the trenches at the bottom of the highest part. They took the trenches, and without any one ordering them, just kept going till they got to the top. Grant and Thomas were watching from Orchard Knob, Grant chewing his cigar and Thomas combing his beard with his fingers as usual I suppose, and Grant asked Thomas who told those men to take the ridge. Nobody, said Thomas. Guess the Cumberlands just wanted to get their flags on top. Bragg's men just turned and ran down the other side of the Ridge towards Georgia and they may be running still for all I know. So now supplies can get into Chattanooga even though Southern forces are still nearby. Remember me to all the folks.

Your affectionate brother Alonzo

1863 was drawing to a close but the war continued. It seemed a long time since three brothers had gone off with the Fiftieth New York in July 1861 to be followed later by the fourth. Two were dead, without even the Presidential letter sent to parents of those who died fighting, the letter that "praised the solemn pride that must be yours to have laid so costly a sacrifice on the altar of freedom."

In Washington the great dome of the Capital had rounded out under the scaffolding and the statue of Armed Freedom had been pulleyed into place to the accompaniment of a salute from thirty-five guns. And thirty-five times replied the guns of the forts from their protective ring around the capital, for that was the number of the states if they should all be united again.

In Harding Newton wrote in his diary:

December 25, 1863. Merry Christmas to all. Hitched the coalt to cutter, went to Mr. Baughtenheimer's to dinner. In afternoon went for sleigh ride with Lavinia after which I came home at 12 o'clock. Very good time. Dec. 31, 1863. Hooked up coalts and drove Lavinia . . . to Gobles to spend New Years. Found a big party there but unfortunately Nellie had gone to Buffalo. Farewell, old year, much as I have loved you. Many pleasures, many hours of happiness and enjoyment, as well as many hours of pain and sorrow. But think no more of the past, but look

*forward to the future, and amend all errors which a review of the past
brings to view.*

Far away in Missouri Alonzo Harding argued with himself. Is human
sacrifice the only way to win freedom? Is the Union worth it? Are the
slaves worth it? Why should a Canadian bother his head about the
outcome? Maybe the war will be over soon for Lee is south of the
Rapidan and Sherman is in Chattanooga. The Peace Democrats are
shouting for an end to the war. Maybe Lincoln is wrong. Maybe I should
go home and let them solve their own mess.

Well, there was another wagon train to send off on its way. He went to
the corral to see that it was being done properly. The mules were braying,
resentful at being pushed around. Two of the black wranglers were
singing as they swung bales of hay.

> We git up in de mornin' so doggon soon,
> Cain't see nothin' but de stars and moon.
> Mmm-mmm, lawdy lawdy lawd,
> Cain't see nothin' but de stars an' moon.
> I looked all over de whole corral
> An' couldn't see a mule wid his shoulder well . . .
>
> Cap'n, cap'n, Nell is sick
> Damn ol' Nell, put de harness on Dick . . .
> Then I run all 'round de whole corral,
> Tryin' to git de harness on Queen and Sal.
> Mmm-mmm, lawdy, lawdy lawd,
> Tryin' to git de harness on Queen and Sal.

There was mail that day. One letter was from a Cleveland friend.
"Lieutenant William Backus is here from Chattanooga recruiting for the
20th Ohio. I may join up. Ohio is pretty important in this war. Grant,
Sherman, James MacPherson, they're all Buckeyes. Why don't you leave
those old mules in Missouri. A lot of three-year volunteers are getting out
in spite of $400 bounty if they re-enlist. They're recruiting black soldiers
and need white officers to command them. I think the end is near and we
could help out."

That did it. "I'm going back to Cleveland, and then I'll decide whether
I'll stay there, go home to Harding, or join up."

Alonzo threw his belongings into his carpet-bag and took the next
train for Cleveland. On January 12, 1864 he volunteered for the 20th
Ohio Light Artillery, and was assigned to Battery D under Major John
T. Edward Grosskopff.

Chapter 18

Enough For Another Killin'

So there he was in the army—Alonzo Harding, light brown hair, blue eyes, five foot eight, age twenty-two, 20th Independent Battery Ohio Volunteer Artillery, for three years. In no time at all he and the other new recruits were whisked by train to Chattanooga, Tennessee, the main supply base for the armies in the South. Morale in the camp was high for the capture of Lookout Mountain and Missionary Ridge were major advances that presaged the beginning of the end. If Alonzo was on low soldier's pay of $13 a month, he would soon receive the first $60 instalment of his $300 bounty money and he knew what he intended to do with some of it—help his young brother Newton get an education. And who knew? He might even be an officer soon, for there were many negro regiments in the vicinity.

The Emancipation Proclamation of a year ago had barely gone over the wires when Adjutant-General Lorenzo Thomas appeared at General Thomas' headquarters in Tennessee to announce the recruitment of negroes. He knew very well that many of the northern soldiers were violently opposed to the new policy. The negro won't fight, they said scornfully. General Sherman himself considered they were still only fit to hew wood and draw water. Lorenzo Thomas addressed the army: "I have the fullest authority to dismiss from the army any man, be his rank what it may, whom I find maltreating freedmen. . . . Soldiers, when you return to your quarters, if you hear anyone condemning the policy announced here today, put him down as a contemptible copperhead traitor."

The transformation of attitudes would not come easily to either whites or blacks. Slaves had to be taught to act like free men. They came into the camp in rags, slouching, shuffling, afraid to look a white man in the eye.

"What's your name?" asked the lieutenant.

"Henry."

"Henry what?"

"Henry."

"He has to have a last name. Call him Henry P. Banks."

There were fights. One ended in a white pinning down a black. "Call me massa and I'll let you up."

"Nebber. I die 'fore I call any man massa agin."

Some blacks could not stomach war any more than the Peace Democrats. "I sure wished lotsa time I nebber run off de plantation. I was at Lookout Mountain and Missionary Ridge. I begs de Gen'rl not to send me on any more battles, and he says I'se a coward and sympathize wid de South. But I tells him I just couldn't stand see all dem men laying there dyin' and hollerin' and beggin' for help and a drink of water and blood ebbrywheres you looks."

Some came with whip scars on their backs, some with a propensity for stealing or disappearing when assigned to a task. When they were cleaned up and clothed in Uncle Sam's uniform, told to stand straight, punished fairly for infractions of rules, taught to read and write by the chaplain or a fellow soldier, given pride in the regiment in which they served, they could begin to act like free men. If suspicion lingered in many minds that the negro wouldn't fight, there was a new song now:

So rally, boys, rally, let us never mind the past.

We had a hard road to travel, but our day is coming fast;

For God is for the right, and we have no need to fear—

The Union must be saved by the colored volunteer.

The blacks were in it now as deep as the whites. Lorenzo Thomas had recruited over one hundred black regiments proudly known as U.S.C.T., United States Colored Troops. In the 54th Massachusetts some recruits were black Canadians, because there were not enough blacks in Massachusetts to fill the ranks.

Lorenzo Thomas' oratory did not mean that the negro was to be treated as an equal when it came to pay; three dollars of their monthly ten dollars was deducted for uniforms. They could not be officers. They would be commanded by whites. They were not even entirely free, for the Fugitive Slave Law had not been repealed.

Alonzo Harding was assigned to the commissary department. Part of his duty was to see that stores dumped by the railroad tracks so that the cars could return north as fast as possible were not looted and that the stores in camp were not tampered with. He chatted with his helpers. "How did you get away?"

"My massa tole me to look after his property. De sojers come and take food. I hide. When massa come back he whup me and say I tole you look after my property. I say yes, massa, I did. I'se property and I'se wuth $1500. Den I run 'way fer good and come here. Now look at me. Free."

His logic was incontrovertible and there were more stories like that one. Alonzo came upon a negro sunning himself in front of his tent. "Enjoying yourself?" he asked.

"Yes, suh, better'n fightin'."

"So you've been in a fight?"

"Yes, suh, Fort Donelson. Didn't like it much. De leafs caught fire, burn dead and wounded on de groun'. Had enuff. I run."

"That wasn't very courageous of you."

"I'se not a sojer. Cookin's my perfession."

"What about your reputation?"

"Reputation's nothin' side o' life. Self-perserbashun am de fust law wid me. My life's not in de market."

"But if you lost it, you'd have the satisfaction of knowing that you died for your country."

"What satisfaction dat be w'en de power ob feelin' gone?"

"Don't you think your company would have praised you and missed you if you had been killed?"

"Maybe not suh. A dead white man ain't much to dese sojers, let alone a dead nigga. But I'd have missed myself, and dat's de pint wid me."

Alonzo laughed. At the moment he was fairly safe in Chattanooga, but there was fighting all around and a new element of fury was added now that negroes were fighting on the side of the North. On April 12 there came the news that the Confederates had re-captured Fort Pillow nearby and had massacred the negro soldiers. A week later at Poison Spring, Arkansas, the First Kansas Colored suffered the same fate. A week after that at Mark's Mill, Arkansas, no quarter was given. One Confederate said, "No threats or commands could restrain their vengeance." As they went into battle, white Northern officers tore off the badges that said they commanded colored regiments for fear they would be turned on as well.

This slaughter appalled Alonzo. Battle losses were bad enough but this was vile. His mind went back to the nights when he and his brothers had climbed the stairs in Harding Hall with *Uncle Tom's Cabin* tucked under their arms to read in bed. It restored his thoughts of humanity to write home.

Chattanooga

My dear Sister
I received your letter yesterday evening and am much obliged for your prompt answer to my last letter. We are still in Chattanooga and the

*probabillity is that we will remain for some time to come. There is not much excitement here at present with the exception of rebel deserters who are flocking in by the hundreds, something over two thousand have come inside of our lines, at this point, since I came here. If they continue to come in as they have for two or three months longer, I do not think we will have many "Rebs" to fight. Our troops had quite a sharp skirmish day before yesterday on the old battle ground at Chickamauga quite a number of the wounded arrived here last evening. troops are leaving daily for the front. I think you will hear of a hard battle before many days. Chattanooga was about the size of Brantford before the war, but there are but few buildings left, most all have been either burned or torn down, there are about twenty families living here and they are supported by the Government. there are no stores and the "Sutters" charge just what they please for their goods. Butter is worth 85 cts per lb, cheese 75 cents, Tea $3.00, eggs 60 cts per Doz, and everything else in proportion, so you see it is out of the question for a soldier to indulge in many luxuries at $13 per month. I suppose you are having cold weather way up there in Canada, while we are having splendid summer weather down here. all I am afraid of is that when you are having your nice weather, we will be suffering with the heat. Gen. Thomas tells us to keep up a good heart for we will be on our way **home** by the fourth of July, but "I can't hardly see it." We have been busy the last two weeks in fixing our camp, putting up shades and getting in readiness for warm weather. If we should be fortunate enough to remain here during the summer we will have good times. I mailed a letter to Father the same day I mailed your last, but have not yet received an answer. I am writing to Newton and Lissa today as well as yourself. Do not let Newton go to St. Louis by any means, it is the worst place for him to go. is Father going to Cleveland in the spring to live, if so Newton had better go with him and go to school. I will pay his board and clothing for one year. it would be better and cheaper than at Woodstock, and besides he might be able to help Father some if he went into business there. Please answer as soon as convenient you don't know how much good it does a soldier to get letters from home. Kind regards to all the folks. I still remain your affectionate brother*

Alonzo

Now that he was in the army there was urgency to write more often.

Goble's Corners, March 15, 1864

My dear Brother
    Your letter came more than a week ago. I was up in Woodstock visiting Lissa; and found it waiting for me when I came back. . . . It is

*snowing and blowing today like a real Canada winter . . . I wish I could send you a nice piece of maple sugar. I wrote to Uncle Silas last week. I wish they could make us a visit. It was four years last fall since they were here and I think a visit to our **dear peaceful Canada** would do them good.*

*. . . Canadians prize their country and institutions better than they did before the war. When will this terrible war end? Not long since the Federals suffered a defeat in Florida. I have not heard of a battle since you wrote. I saw the skirmish you spoke of at Chickamauga in the papers. General Thomas was spoken of. Who are your officers? and what are your duties? I just wish you were home; but you are not so I will just try and look on the bright side and trust and hope and pray. I have not been to [Harding] for a long time, it storms every time we make arrangements to go. I do not think it very likely Father will go very soon to Cleveland to live. He cannot dispose of his [Harding] property. Your offer for Newton is a very generous one. It hardly seems right for him to go to School on your hard earnings. If he had what money he invested in property then from his Washington earnings it would pay his way for some time. I hope something may open for him. I will do all I can to prevent his going to St. Louis. I have not seen either him or father since I wrote you before. I want to see them and have a talk about the matter. It makes me very sad when I think of our **old home circle** broken, but God knoweth best. I would submit submissively to His decrees. Lissa has a nice Melodeon, it seems so like old times to hear her sing. I hope you may be able to stand the heat this summer, it will be very oppressive to Northerners I fear. You must write very often and that will allay our fears. Good Bye dear Brother, As ever*

Your affectionate Sister

Rose

Eva wants me to write that she went to Woodstock and saw little Ida and she sends her love and a kiss to her precious Uncle Alonzo and wants to write something else to you but she will have to wait this time.

And still they died. On February 1, 1864, the government ordered another draft of 500,000 men and inexorably in March another of 200,000. Then on March 12 the whole army knew that Ulysses S. Grant had been made commander-in-chief of all the Union forces. His prowess as commander in the west had earned him the right. Grant was called the butcher of Shiloh but Lincoln was facing re-election at the end of this year. Lincoln believed that at last he had found the man who would pursue and bring victories. The government must have victories and Grant was the one who said: "Some people think that an army can be whipped by waiting for rivers to freeze over, exploding powder at a distance, drowning out troops, or setting them to sneering; but it will always be found in the end that the only way to whip an army is to go out and fight it."

Grant was summoned from his army camp to Washington and presented with the stars on his shoulder straps that made him lieutenant-general, leader of all the federal armies. Grant knew how Washington had softened his predecessors in command, McClellan, Pope and Halleck. On the night when it was proclaimed that the new lieutenant-general would accompany the President to a grand performance at Grover's Theatre where Edwin Booth was playing, Grant was already on the cars headed for Nashville to say farewell to his troops. The seedy-looking man with the stump of a cigar in his mouth and his headquarters in an army wagon and tent was now the commander of a million men.

Neither the President, nor the War Department, nor the blabbing Washington newspapers would interfere with this man's decisions. His decision was to advance on all fronts simultaneously and keep going till the South could fight no more. Two sizeable Southern armies were still in the field—Lee's army of Northern Virginia south of the Rapidan protecting Richmond, and Joe Johnston, quiet but deadly, protecting the road to Atlanta. Grant ordered the Army of the Potomac to prepare to cross the Rapidan and the western armies to advance into Georgia. The anaconda coils were to be tightened beyond release.

Ulysses S. "Unconditional Surrender" Grant made his headquarters with Meade and the Army of the Potomac that was to go against Lee, for it had always been that army which had stopped short of annihilating the opposition. "Sure," said a Potomac private scornfully when they realized that Grant was going with them in the field instead of staying back in Washington, "he thinks he knows it all but he's never been up against Lee."

Grant placed William Tecumseh Sherman in charge of the western front with just one terse order: "Get Joe Johnston." Under Sherman were three armies: the Army of the Ohio with General John Scholfield; the Army of the Tennessee with "Old Tecump" himself; and the Army of the Cumberland under General George H. Thomas. Alonzo Harding was now serving under "Pap" Thomas.

Get Joe Johnston. Though Alonzo had reported that Rebels were deserting right and left, there were still enough men in Johnston's army that only merciless attrition would conquer them. General "States' Rights" Gist, who had commanded a division of Bragg's army at

226

Chickamauga, had changed neither his name nor his beliefs, and states' rights meant slavery. In Atlanta, Georgia, a young subaltern was writing, "The only solution to slavery is to exterminate the negroes." At Missionary Ridge fifteen year old Southern lads had fought in cotton suits and bare feet, their zeal for the cause burning at high flame. It would be no easy task to get Joe Johnston and his indomitable Southerners.

As he planned his strategy, General Sherman was under no illusions about the easiness of his task. He wrote to his wife, "No amount of poverty or adversity seems to shake their faith: niggers gone, wealth and luxury gone, money worthless, starvation in view . . . causes enough to make the bravest tremble. Yet I see no signs of let-up . . . some deserters, plenty tired of war, but the masses determined to fight it out."

Gobles Corners April 9th 1864

My Dear Brother,

I received your letter mailed March 28 last Monday April 4th and this is Saturday. I intended to write last evening and send this morning but we had company and I did not get it done. I am so afraid you may be away from Chattanooga and not get your letters so regularly. . . . The Daffodils and a few early plants are beginning to peep above ground. . . . I had a letter from Uncle Silas a week or two ago. They are all well. He said a number of Lexington boys are in Chattanooga some had been home on furlough and just returned again he asked them to look for you. He wishes you to write to him so he may know how to send letters to you. You had better write soon. He thought they might visit Canada another year. Father has gone to Cleveland and is going to look about in the Northern part of Michigan for some business to get into. Shingle making or something of that sort. Newton is very anxious to go to School. I think it will be cheaper at Woodstock for one term while Lissa is there than at Cleveland. She will board him for $1 one dollar per week and Heman has books he can let him have. Tuition is about $8 per term. The Term commences next week and will end in July. There will be less inducement to spend in Woodstock than in Cleveland besides much less danger of bad Company. We could look after his mending etc. He thinks if he can get the necessary qualifications he could teach and so earn money to continue his studies. The School in [Harding] will be vacant in September he thinks he could get it if he could get a Certificate. I dont know how far he is advanced or whether one term would fit him to teach. We have only thought of this plan of his going to Woodstock since Father went away. I dont know what he will say or whether he will agree to it he thinks it not right for Newton to go to School on your hardly *earned gain. I dont like the idea either but should hope in a few years he would be able to repay all you advance now. I think a little less than $40 will take him through at Woodstock till July including clothing. He needs a suit of clothes. He must get plain Tweed or something that is not very expensive. Perhaps $30 would be enough. I wish I knew just what was best about it. He cannot get anything to do in [Harding]. The term commences so soon and he ought to begin with it. I wrote Father in Cleveland the first of the week, asking him what he thought of it and to answer him immediately. Hartley Laycocks wife has been very dangerously sick but is I believe getting better. I wish I knew just what you are doing now I think very, very often of you and hope and pray the "Great Father" to take care of you. I wish you were home. . . . Write soon My Dear Brother. Excuse bad writing etc.*

Ever your loving Sister Rose

Morning Monday April 11th
'Tis too bad I could not send the letter I wrote Saturday till this morning it seems such a long time to keep it. I have sent you a few papers we do not take any Political papers except the "Leader" and that is so thoroughly a Southern Sympathizer, I do not think you will like it. Newton Goble was home a week ago. . . . He is a fireman on an engine on the Buffalo Road.

This is a miserable pen and I must conclude. . . . How fervently I wish this war would end. How hateful sin and National wickedness is in the sight of a Pure God that it needs such fearful cleansing. When will it be **enough.** *Good Bye and God bless you My Darling Brother is the earnest prayer of Your affectionate*

Sister Rose

His purpose clear and his heart's desire for education fulfilled for the moment, Newton wrote happily:

[Harding] April 14th

Dear Brother,
I have concluded to go to Woodstock instead of Cleveland to school. Rose thinks it would be much better, cheaper, etc. The term commenced yesterday but as there will not be anything of any account done except arranging the classes until next Monday [18th] I shall not go until then. I have no money but there is some three or four dollars owing me here which probably will do until you can send me some. I will board at Lissas this term at $1.00 per week. Tuition is $28 per annum but I can manage till I get some money. I would have written sooner if I had intended to go to Woodstock but I thought of going to Cleveland till this week Rose

228

persuaded me to go to Woodstock. Will you send the money here in Treasury notes or have it changed before sending it? Write soon for I will kneed the money as soon as possible as ½ the terms fees should be paid in advance. We are all well. Father is still in the states we have not heard from him since he left. . . . times are dull here the watter has been very high for two weeks the mills and everything has been stopped but they have started today. All send their kind regards to you.

Your aff. Brother Newton [H.]

Direct to Woodstock C.W.

Gobles Corners April 20

My Dear Brother,

 I received two papers from you yesterday and suppose you were still in Chattanooga when they were sent. . . . Newton came over last Saturday and went up to Woodstock Monday and commenced going to school . . . I think he will improve his time. He is so anxious about it. He is pretty short of clothing but can do for a time. I helped him what I could and gave him two dollars. . . . Father was here Monday he was just from the West. He came through Woodstock but did not see Newtie he was at school. He gave me $10 for Newtie . . . If you send money for his Tuition I will spend it for clothing if not I will pay on his Tuition with it. He will be just as little expense as possible he says he had learned the worth of money this winter. I hope you are well and not exposed to danger. I almost fear to open your letters lest something should have happened you but I trust in God and pray you may be spared. . . . All unite in love and best wishes for my Soldier Brother. I will expect a letter from you soon. Good Bye. Ever your loving

Sister Rose

And again she wrote:

April 29/64

. . . I am very glad you write so often. Continue to do so My Brother for it removes a load of anxiety. . . . May God protect you my Brother for O! how vain is the help of man. What a terrible work to rebury so many poor soldiers. It must be very unhealthy. . . . Newton is at Woodstock . . . cheaper than Cleveland. There would be a good many incidental expenses there that we can avoid here such as washing, mending and making, that would amount to considerable besides board is $5 per week there now everything is much higher than when you left. . . . Board and tuition this term of 13 weeks will be about $22. . . . There will be a vacation of 6 or 8 weeks and he must earn something then to help

another term if he goes again. He can perhaps get work in Harvest if nothing else. . . . I think Father said he wrote you from Detroit or somewhere while he was away . . . Do you have opportunities of attending Church? . . . Eva is teasing me to let her write to Uncle Alonzo. . . . Adieu.

Dear Uncle Alonzo

The "Old Hen" flew at me yesterday and scratched me because I went to see her chickens. I wish Pa would kill her. I wish you would come and see us if they can spare you and stay a long time. I am 4½ years old. I am making a quilt. I got a nice little garden with two beds in it and a lot of Johnny Jumpups and one daisy, and I am going to have to play house this Summer. I am sorry you have to be away in that naughty war. Our little bird Dicky is dead. I wish you would come home. The nice summer has come. I wish you would come and hear Elder Patton preach. Good Bye.

From little Eva

When Alonzo read letters like that he almost wished he had not enlisted and could go home, but he was young, the cardinals were whistling, the mocking birds were bursting their throats, the white clouds were blooming like cotton balls over the crests of the hills and he had received the first instalment of his bounty money. He did not mind sending part of it to Newton. It was almost a year since Alfred had died, never to return to school as Newton ought to be able to do.

Canadian Literary Institute
Woodstock May 7th 64

Dear Brother:

Coz James Dawson called here last Thursday bringing your letter from Rose. . . . I have been engaged in my studies three weeks now and get along very well. I have been slightly ill this last week but I have lost only two resitations thereby. My Studies are the following

Arithmetic—Sangster's
Grammar—Clarks
Senior Reading—Sangster's Standard Speaker
Dictation—Coutrie's
Geology
Phonography
Mental Arithmetic
Composition and Declamation
Drawing

Also I have joined a debating society. My studies occupy all my time. I have not received any word from Cleveland yet. My tuition remains unpaid. My time is limited. Nellie Goble sends her love to you. Also Lissa and all. While I remain Your

Affect. Brother
Newton [Harding]

Newton was settled for the time being and Alonzo was already a corporal but the comparative lull that surrounded Chattanooga was coming to an end.

Chattanooga, Tennessee
May 10th 1864

My Dear Sister

We are in considerable of a flurry here just now and have been for the last ten days on account of the army moving. We have received marching orders no less than six times the first week and have not got away yet. This morning we turned over all our horses and guns to another Battery so I guess we will have to stay although we are all anxious to move. The weather is getting very warm too warm for comfort it is very unhealthy here. I do not think there would be any more danger in going to the front than to stay here, for my part I prefer the chances of battle than disease, although I have so far enjoyed the best of health. We have received good news from Virginia I hope it is true. You will probably hear the news there quicker than we can. I look forward to great changes within the next thirty days and a great deal of hard fighting. I have a strong presentiment that this falls campaign will wind up the "Rebellion." I sincerely hope it may be the case. There was an order issued yesterday to stop the mail but it was countermanded. I do not know what we would do if the mail was to stop, it would be nearly as bad to stop rations as the mail. I just wish you were here when the mail arrives it would do your heart good just to see the boys make a charge for it. I have often kept back to watch them as they return to their quarters. I can tell just as soon as I see their faces whether they have received any letters or not, those that are the lucky ones will look cheerful and walk briskly to their quarters smiling or whistling, while the others look as though they had not a friend in the world as they returned with slow and measured step. very often you would hear the exclamation well I guess my folks have forgotten that they have any friends in the army or well I wont write any more letters till I get some if never and so on. You have doubtless received my last letter before this, could you use U.S. money for Newton or is there any chance of getting it changed there. We expect to get paid in a few days and if I thought it would be any use I would send some. I

*have written to Cartwright to send twenty-five dollars in Canada money.
I suppose that will do him for the present. I would prefer to send the
money from here than Cleveland if you could get it changed without too
much trouble. Give my best respects to all the folks. Write soon.*

From your affectionate brother
Alonzo

The flurry Alonzo described meant that the big push was beginning. On
May 4 they knew that all three western armies would move with
Sherman, leaving behind just enough to hold Chattanooga. They had
orders to travel as light as Stonewall Jackson's men when they had come
down the valley of the Shenandoah back in '61 with the handles of their
frying pans stuck in their muskets. Sherman's men would not even carry
the government issue candles. The night before they set out every soldier
took his candle, stuck it on a tent pole, wedged it on the end of a bayonet
or simply held it in his hand and waved it like a flickering firecracker.
Across the miles of tents the little lights glimmered in a ghostly display as
cheers went round and round till the myriad tiny flickers died down. Next
morning over ninety thousand men struck out across Georgia to get Joe
Johnston.

Simultaneously the Army of the Potomac crossed the Rapidan. This
time it would not stop till it had conquered Lee, the general renowned for
moving his army like a whiplash and getting away again. As the long blue
stream of men moved across the river in the bright May sunshine with
the dogwood blossoms shining white among the trees, they never guessed
that for the next month they would have no time to bathe or change their
clothes, would barely have time to eat or sleep.

No lessons learned from Prussian officers on the parade ground would
help them in the wilderness of Virginia. Wherever opposing Confederates
would be found, there they would do battle. They sewed their names on
their backs because they were never going to turn around. They carried
their spades with them, no time to put them on the wagon. They just dug
themselves in, fought, and kept on going. In terms of the horrifying loss
of men, 17,000 in one engagement, the Battle of the Wilderness was
defeat after defeat for the North—only they refused to retreat. They never
turned back to Washington.

No lessons learned at West Point taught Grant what to do now. At
Westpoint tobacco and cards were forbidden. Church was compulsory.
Grant never swore. No vulgar word ever escaped his lips. But he could
send men to their death in order to bring the war to a close. On they

went—Spotsylvania, Bloody Angle, Pamunky, Chickahominy, Cold Harbour. They lost as many men as Lee had in his whole army but Grant the butcher, Grant the supreme commander, just smoked cigars, whittled wood and ordered his men ON. This was unprecedented, a commander who was defeated but kept on going.

As Grant battled towards Richmond and Sherman surged towards Atlanta, Alonzo and the 20th Ohio Light Artillery were among those left to guard the supply base at Chattanooga. Alonzo was acting quartermaster now, for the former head had been killed in a skirmish with a daring Rebel cavalry raid two weeks before.

The letters from home were his link with normality.

Gobles Corners May 19th 1864

Dear Brother

I received your letter yesterday Morning dated 10th Inst. . . . I hope the mails will not be stopped. It would be too cruel. I have been anxious to hear from you these eventful times just now. Not knowing where you might be sent, or what might be in store for you. . . . May the "Great Father" preserve you from disease. Could we send you a box of medicines or vegetables prepared or anything of that kind. If so write what you would like and how we had better send them. Pickles and preserved fruit would keep. There is not much fruit now, but we could get something. . . . Be as careful as you can of your health. Bathing in the morning would be beneficial I think, be sure never to do so when you are very warm or fatigued. Cleanliness is conducive to health. Newton wrote you a week ago. He is getting on nicely with his studies going quite ahead of most of the Students I hear . . . We have not received the money or the Trunk from Cleveland. I am getting uneasy about it. . . . The $25 will be enough for this term, and the next will not begin till the middle of September. . . . I dont know what we can do with U.S. mony here but think we might change it with business men who trade on the other side. Father will be over in two or three days. I will ask him and write you again. My health has not been good this spring. . . . Adieu

Sister Rose

Woodstock, May 25th

Yesterday being the Birthday of Our Gracious Queen we like loyal subjects came to spend it here, and I remained a few days with Lissa and Newton. Newton is not feeling very well he has been studying very hard. He has a very long Geology lesson to get up this morning in a short time and has not time to write to you now. I expected to see Father on Sunday and ask him about the U.S. mony but he did not come. Newton says to send it on we can do something with it. . . . I have been waiting till the Trunk should come and see what he would need, but I must go up town this Morning and get him a summer coat and some shirts he cannot do without. We have heard of a great deal of fighting lately and fearful of men both North and South. The last account we had they had been fighting in Virginia 8 days and nights and they were not done. We cannot depend on the News we get they vary so much; but think the North from superiority of Numbers have had the advantages. . . . Yesterday was a fine day, and people in general seemed to enjoy themselves. There was a considerable Military display in the Morning various amusements such as catching a pig, grinning through a horse-collar etc. in the afternoon. We attended a picnic and fireworks in the evening. All united heart and hand in honouring "Our Noble Queen". "Long May She Reign." I hope you may be at Chattanooga still I am sure there cannot be so much danger there as in Battle. 'Tis fearful to read of Regiments of so many going into battle and coming out so sadly less. When will the cup of wrath meted out to that so lately prosperous land be full. When will it be enough. And Judgement be mingled with Mercy. May the shield of the Infinite be round about you My Brother and your life preserved in the midst of death. I have written very hastily this morning I am in a hurry to go down Town and do my shopping. I have a good deal of sewing to do while here and must improve my time. Lissa and [the twins] are well. Accept our United love and prayers for your safety. I remain as ever Your

Affectionate Sister Rose

Newton was busy and grateful.

Canadian Literary Institute May 26

Dear Brother

Your welcome letter came to me last evening, and, as I have a few moments leisure time, I hasten to answer it. I am studying as hard as I can and in consequence of that get along first rate. My health has been very good since I came here except about a week back I have had a very severe pain in my head but on account of three hollidays [Saturday Sunday and 24th] I feel much better now and I think I can continue my studies without interruption through the remainder of the term. I have not heard a word from Cartwright . . . I think I can use Treasury notes here, although I have not had time to inquire. Mr. Brown the flax man of [Harding] will change them, I am sure, as he trades in the states. I have kneeded the clothes and money very much. I have been wearing my winter clothes notwithstanding it has been very warm and I have almost

*roasted. Father gave Rose [4.00] four dollars for me yesterday she bought
a coat [3.50] and some socks which will help greatly. But I am getting
along as well as possible. I spend no money **foolishly at any rate** for I
have none to spend either wisely or foolishly.*

*I am getting along finely with my studies. I have taken up another
since I wrote it is Geology the hardest of the whole lot. Rose was up to
the Inst. the other day and several students told her they "wished that
(Harding) had stopped at home for he was always ahead of them all." I
presume Rose has told you all about the celebration of Her Majesty's
Birthday. I did not enjoy myself much. There were about five hundred
vol. here among them Capt Cole with about thirty of the [Harding]
Rifles.*

*As regards the news I do not have time to look at a paper although
there are some 20 or 30 in the reading room of the Institute. All are well
. . . I remain*

Your affectionate Brother
Newton [Harding]

Though there were daily battles and skirmishes as Sherman inched his
way towards Atlanta, Alonzo remained in Chattanooga, receiving his
mail regularly.

Gobles Corners June 3rd/ 64

*. . . we have received both mony and trunk from Cleveland. It was paid
except for 50 cts duties. Wednesday June 1st the people of the River
Church gave Heman a Donation party. . . . Father was there and all the
Old friends. Mr. Young was there . . . the years sit very lightly on his
brow. His sister Charlotte . . . is wasting away with consumption. . . . Old
Mrs. Young was there and James and many others that seem like Old
landmarks in that neighbourhood. Lissa said the clothes in the trunk
were a good deal mussed up and smelled pretty musty but were not
injured. They will do nicely for Newton. . . . He seems to be studying well
and is determined to stand second to none at Examination. When we
came home from the Donation we stopped at the Express office in
Princeton and found the mony. $25 in Canada Bills. Cartwright wrote
that he had been waiting for the discount to go down it was so high but
when he got Newton's letter had sent it at once. I sent $11 up and have
the rest till Lissa needs board. The tuition for the term will be over $9!
and he has taken Phonography an extra study which will be $1 more.
Then there is 50cts. Incidental expenses for those who board out of the
building. . . . Newton keeps an accurate a/c of his expenses, and seems to*

*be very saving. . . . Father is studying Astronomy I believe . . . The result
of the Donation was $36. . . .*

> *As ever Your affectionate*
> *Sister Rose*

> *Can. Lit. Inst. June 18th/64*

Dear Brother
   *. . . The weather is extremely warm now and it is very hard to study.
. . . I have paid my tuition, bought a coat [3.50] paid Rose what I
borrowed to get books etc.*

Tuition	*6.70*
Incidental expences	*.50*
Phonography lessons	*1.00*
Books and stationary	*4.92*
Clothes (including coat 3.50)	*6.92*
Other little items	*2.05¼*
Total expenses thus far	*22.09¼*

*I have not paid any board yet. There is [8] dollars due now. The school
is a very good one and I like it much more than I did at first. Dr. Fyfe
the Principal is a very nice man as are all the teachers. There have been
about 8 or 9 pupils left this term on account of poor health.*
   *In a great measure I have gained the good will of the teachers and I
can get along better as they take a greater pleasure in showing me
anything that is difficult. It will be about four weeks before vacation
which is [9] weeks long. . . . I think I shall go work for Geo. Dawson at
Carpentry as I cannot stand it in the harvest field.*

> *Your affectionate Brother*
> *Newton [Harding]*

By June 18, the day on which Newton Harding was cataloguing his
expenditures of his brother's army pay, Grant and the Army of the
Potomac were crossing the James River to come upon Richmond from
the south. Gone were the days of "Old Fuss and Feathers" Winfield
Scott, of "Young Napoleon" George McClellan and his grand parades, of
"Old Brains and Paperwork" Henry Halleck. Ulysses S. Grant had
conquered the Wilderness and was on his way to Richmond.
   At Petersburg, twenty miles from the capital of the Confederacy, Grant
was forced to stop and lay siege. Inside Richmond, Jefferson Davis and
his cabinet tossed peanuts into their mouths as they wondered if they
were doomed. Two thin railway lines from Atlanta were the only way of
procuring supplies and Sherman was after those. There was little to eat in

the capital now and federal officers in Libby prison, a converted tobacco warehouse beside the James River, were half starved.

At the beginning of July Lee despatched General Jubal Early with the Confederate Sixth Corps into Maryland to create sufficient diversion that Grant would remove his men from the siege of Petersburg. Wily as Lee, Grant refused to budge.

As Jubal Early came closer and closer to Washington, Lincoln himself went to Fort Stevens to watch. Fort Stevens was one of Washington's guardian forts. It was so close to the city that the 7th Street trolley almost reached it. As Lincoln stood on a parapet, his tall black hat towering conspicuously, a sharpshooter could have picked him off in a minute. General Wright almost had apoplexy before the President could be persuaded to leave. Only when urgent and more urgent telegrams indicated that Washington was indeed in jeopardy did Grant despatch three brigades of his crack VI Corps to relieve the pressure on Washington. It arrived just in time to force Early to retreat into the fertile valley of the Shenandoah in Virginia. Once again Washington was saved and Grant had not moved a mile from Petersburg, twenty miles from Richmond.

As Grant continued the siege of Petersburg, Sherman was marching 100,000 men towards Atlanta. His raucous, jaunty veterans deferred to no one. They cawed lustily whenever an officer rode by on a skinny horse. They baaed like sheep when "Forced March" Bla-a-ir came into sight. Their rangy legs lapped up the miles. They could size up enemy fortifications at a glance and dig themselves in with a tough spirit of preservation. They would have marched their legs off for Sherman and were beginning to spoil for a real engagement, a knock 'em down and out fight. Sherman, trying in vain to catch Joe Johnston and his 60,000 men off guard, sent Thomas one way, Scholfield another and dashing young General James B. McPherson another, feinting and dodging.

Between Johnston's army headquarters near Dalton, Georgia, and Sherman was a gap in Rocky Face Ridge known as Buzzard's Roost. A road ran through it like a door of death, for high on the heights Johnston took his stand and slaughtered the force sent to dislodge him. Sherman mourned the men who perished in the attempt. He returned to his flanking manoeuvres with daily skirmishes and digging in. Back and forth the deadly dance proceeded, but foot by foot Johnston was being pushed closer to Atlanta.

Marching, marching, living on hardtack and bacon, Sherman's men began to come down with scurvy. Black-mouthed and loose-toothed, they longed for the three weeks' rain to stop, for some good food and rest, or for another showdown, anything to end the stalemate.

Alonzo, still with the quartermaster's department in Chattanooga, fared better. On June 21 he could sit down to read another letter from his sister.

. . . It has been so dry vegetation is suffering for want of rain. . . . You have certainly been favoured since enlisting notwithstanding the weariness and ennui of having nothing to do. I am sure it is better than the fatigue of Marching and the terrible uncertainty of Battle. I have heard no fresh war news lately. . . . Newton was home last week a few days. Dr. Fyfe sent him home to recruit, he had been studying hard, and his health seemed suffering. About his going next term I dont know what is best. It seems too bad to make such a sacrifice on your money. . . .

Alonzo returned to his duties with the supplies. As long as the single track railway from the north to Nashville was safe, supplies would continue to come. Every foot of it was guarded but no one knew when Nathan B. Forrest's cavalry would swoop in from the night to destroy it.

Joe Johnston was now securing his men behind log parapets on top of Kenesaw Mountain, south of Dalton and north of Atlanta. It was a vital part of Atlanta's outer defense. On June 27 Sherman attacked the mountain. Again Johnston's artillery blew to bits three thousand men of Sherman's assault column. The only good result of this debacle was that Johnston was removed from command because he had failed to defeat Sherman. Bottled in Richmond with Grant almost on its outskirts, Jefferson Davis was desperate. He ordered General John B. Hood to replace Johnston.

Pugnacious Hood, with an arm crippled at Gettysburg. Gambler Hood, one-legged after Chickamauga. When he learned of the change in command, a Federal colonel told Sherman, "I seed Hood bet twenty-five hundred dollars with nary a pair in his hand." Now Sherman could surmise that Hood might be the attacker and he the defender. How should he deploy his armies now?

On July 20 Sherman crossed Peachtree Creek, five miles from the centre of Atlanta. His men fought fiercely but Hood saved both his army and Atlanta. While Thomas and his men were burying their dead, Hood wheeled and struck at McPherson and his Army of the Tennessee a few miles away at Decatur. McPherson was killed but his army held its position.

McPherson was young, handsome, brilliant and likeable. Sherman wept openly at his death. When she heard the news, McPherson's fiancée in Baltimore went into her bedroom and did not come out for a year. Her family gave her no sympathy for the loss of her lover because they espoused the cause of the South.

About the same time, when a chance shell was lobbed into Richmond from Grant's army, it killed a bride who had just murmured, "I do."

A week after, thinking he had detected a weakness in Union lines, Hood attacked at Ezra Church, just west of Atlanta, but for the third time he failed to drive the Union army away from the city. After the battle, a Yankee picket called out to his Confederate counterpart, "How many of you are there left, Johnny?"

Thin but defiant the Confederate answer came back, "Just about enough for another killin', Yank."

John Brown, is there never to be an end?

Chapter 19

Damn The Torpedoes

While armies circled, crackled, killed and were killed from Maryland to the mouth of the Mississippi, Alonzo Harding and his buddies speculated how long the 20th Ohio Volunteer Light Artillery would be held in Chattanooga to ensure that Sherman's supply line to the north remained open.

"Guess we'll just have to hurry up and wait,"

"Shut up, we'll get it soon enough."

"Here's the mail," called Alonzo.

"Confound you, Harding, you always get some. Lucky Canuck."

Yes, Harding was luckier than many. Though she did not know it, Roseltha had written on July 20, 1864, the day gallant McPherson was killed at Peachtree Creek.

. . . It is very warm and exceedingly dry. The crops are many of them failures for want of rain. We have not had such continual warm weather since . . . before Daniel died in Walsingham. Seven years ago . . . How the time has flown since then and sadly the others are gone too. . . . School closed last week . . . Newton did very well while he was here he stood in division A in every class at the examination. . . . He has failed in getting employment except what he can pick up in [Harding]. . . . Father is very busy setting up Globes etc. and studying astronomy. He is going entirely to subvert the present theory of Astronomy and get up "Something new".

[Mr. Goble] is very busy in the harvest besides we are having a new kitchen and woodshed put up and Mother has gone to Illinois to visit Emma all of which account for my being so busy. The Raspberries are ripe and we have been out gathering. I forgot to mention the ring in my

*last letter. Eva is perfectly delighted with it. It fits her nicely. She will
keep it a long time to remind her of her Soldier Uncle. . . . You must not
delay writing if you do not get our letters. Be assured we sent them.*

Ah yes, the ring. Alonzo tried to visualize the pleasure of the little girl
he had not seen for over a year. The baby blonde of her hair would be
darkening by now and she was old enough to hold up the ring on her
hand and admire its ruby sparkle. He would never tell her how it had
come into his possession. They had been clearing up dead bodies. The
ring had fallen from the pocket of a young man just old enough to have a
child the same age as Eva. Was he carrying the ring as a keepsake, or had
he looted it from some house to take home to the little girl he would
never see again? No sense leaving it on the battlefield to be trampled
under when the next firing swept over it. He washed off the caked brown
blood and sent it home to his little niece.

The stone in it was as red as the juice of the raspberries Roseltha said
she was picking. He thought of the pies his mother had baked when they
were all at home. Once she had set them out on the stoop to cool for
dinner and a blackbird had pecked at the crust of one. "Shoo, scram, get
away from there," he had shouted as the fragrant bright juice oozed up
from the middle. And young Newton had called, "I borrow the piece that
the blackbird pecked!" Alonzo's mouth watered, then he re-read what his
sister had written about his father. Wonder if father's astronomy work is
any good or is he just fooling himself?

Far away in Harding Enos was struggling happily with the stars. There
were always small sums of money coming in from some source or other
even if he had no major business at the moment. His forays into the
mysteries of the heavens engrossed him so deeply that he could forget his
earthly problems. He was certain that there was some pattern to it all,
and alternately he studied the Bible and whatever astronomical books he
could lay his hands on as he travelled outside his little backwater of
Harding.

He opened his Bible at Genesis: And God made the firmament and
divided the waters which were under the firmament from the waters
which were above the firmament. He thought "There are three heavens
and I think they're under the waters that are above the firmament,
though the Bible doesn't say so in so many words."

He stood up and looked through the cupola window to the winding
waters of the Nith and then up into the fathomless blue above him. *"The
wondrous heavens,"* he said under his breath. *"How can I penetrate their
solemn harmony?"* He turned to his writing paper.

The first heaven is the atmosphere which surrounds the earth below the

242

orbit of the moon where the birds fly. The second heaven is the circle that surrounds the atmosphere where the sun, moon and stars are placed, and the third heaven is above the circle of water which surrounds the firmament; and this is the place where God resides with his saints or redeemed from the earth.

His pen flew on, sometimes sputtering blots on the paper with the intensity of the push of his mind behind his laggard hand.

Then according to the word of God, the eternal abode of the unrighteous will be in the space which this world now occupies, that their troubled spirits may always behold the enjoyment of the righteous who inhabit that boundless space that surrounds this universe.

He stood up and stretched. "The Creation story doesn't mention the planets, just the sun and moon and stars. Yet the planets are there and I'm making a machine that circles them around the sun. What does this textbook say?" He copied onto the paper: *"The sun is 4,500 miles in diameter. Mercury's orbit is 18,000 miles in circumference and revolves once in 88 days. Venus's orbit is 38,000 miles and revolves in 225 days."* "And so on. I wish I had more books. Maybe this one isn't right."

Night had fallen. He stepped out onto the balcony and the words he had written a week before came softly to his mind.

It is in the stillness of the night hours when all nature is husht in repose, when the hum of the world ongoing is no longer heard that the stars rule and shine and the bright stars dropping through the deep heavens speak to the willing spirit that would learn thare misterious being.

Above him the planets winked in derision. "I'll wrench your secrets from you yet," he muttered. A whip-poor-will called from across the river, crisp as an elastic band. A robin stirred in the maple tree below him. He ran his fingers through his hair.

"The waters above the firmament—I must think about that. Are they important? The Bible wouldn't have mentioned them if they weren't. Can I reconcile the Bible with what the scientists are telling us? 186,000 miles per second light travels, they say. I must talk this over with Roseltha. I'll drive to see her tomorrow. I wonder where Alonzo is tonight?" A flash of sheet lightning eliminated the stars for a fleeting moment. He turned and circled his way down to the kitchen by the light of his flickering lamp.

He set the lamp in the window, made a quick trip to the backhouse, looking up fiercely at the Milky Way as if to pierce it with the force of his will, then washed his hands in the soft water from the cistern pump. He turned down the wick in the lamp on the kitchen table to a jagged glimmer.

"No use waiting up for Newton. Young pup, he should have been home long ago." Picking up the other lamp he made his way up the circular staircase to bed. An owl hooted softly in the maple tree outside his window. "Maybe the scale of a thousand miles to one inch on the globes isn't right," he worried as he fell asleep.

Still the war to strangle Richmond pursued its bloody way. Though the South had no steel or rolling mills with which to replace the rails on damaged railway lines, some supplies still reached the beleaguered capital. All but one of the railways that brought them passed through the little city of Petersburg on the south bank of the Appomattox River, ten miles from its junction with the James, twenty miles from Davis' stronghold. Lee's winning strategy had always been to strike like a whiplash and get away. Now Grant was immobilizing him between wily, wiry General Phil Sheridan (whose volleys of oaths were setting his little army at cleaning the Confederates out of the fertile Shenandoah valley) and Grant's own Army of the Potomac that was approaching Petersburg.

Grant's army included nearly 20,000 blacks transferred from the southern and western fronts to join other coloured troops recently recruited from points closer at hand. These coloured volunteers were enrolled in nine regiments of the fourth division of Burnside's Ninth Army Corps, eight regiments of the third division of the Tenth Corps and thirteen regiments, one of them cavalry, of the third division of the Eighteenth Corps. When they left their training camp in Annapolis, they had been reviewed by President Lincoln himself as they passed under the balcony above the entrance to Willard's Hotel. This was Lincoln's first review of blacks in the blue Union uniform. The question was still in many minds—would the negro fight?

It was not long before they had the chance to prove themselves. On May 5 they captured Wilson's landing on the north side of the James and held it. On June 15 a coloured brigade consisting of four infantry regiments, two of cavalry and two batteries took a slope at Baylor's Farm, clearing the way for the entire corps. They fought till after dark. The Fourth U.S.C.T. alone lost almost half of its 600 men, but they captured nine out of fifteen pieces of artillery and 200 out of the 300 prisoners taken. They had "displayed all the qualities of good soldiers."

Their general, in spite of a full moon, did not follow up his advantage but bivouacked for the night. This gave the Rebels time to mount twenty guns and force Grant to dig in for a siege of Petersburg.

If Grant's army was safely ensconced behind breastworks where their muzzle-loaders and artillery could hold off an assault, Lee's army lay just as safe behind similar fortifications. The stalemate began to be frustrating to Grant's men for the only excitement during the impasse was dodging intermittent Rebel cannon balls. At one point their lines were only 150 yards from the Rebel's main line, but in front of them projected a fort that had to be reduced before an advance could be attempted.

In Grant's Ninth Army Corps there was a regiment of the 48th Pennsylvania that was composed of former coal miners. Digging was second nature to them and as they peered over the breastworks they had a bright idea. If a tunnel could be dug under the open space between the two opposing lines and seeded with explosives, a great hole would be blown in the Confederate defenses and the Union forces could rush triumphantly through. On to Richmond! Hang Jeff Davis to a sour apple tree!

When the miners presented their plan, Grant and Meade were sceptical but Burnside wanted to try it. The miners set to work and for five weeks they tunnelled, raising a mound of earth at its mouth that was beginning to rouse the curiosity of the Confederates as they watched Union movements through binoculars. Before the Confederates could act on their hunch that the barely disguised heap must be earth from a tunnel, the tunnel had reached the required length of 500 feet and had been planted with 8,000 pounds of gunpowder in 320 kegs. At daybreak on July 30 a match was applied to the long fuse. There was a sickening delay as they waited for an ensuing roar but none came. A daring sapper was sent in to replace a defective fuse and apply another match. In a trice there was a great roar, then a sickening sight of men, guns and caissons catapulting into the air and a 150 foot crater appeared in the Rebel lines.

For several weeks before the completion of the tunnel the black division of the Ninth Corps had been groomed to lead the assault after the charge exploded. Again and again they had gone through the drill of forming double columns and charging. Their pride in being chosen to lead was at fever pitch. The decision to allow them to lead had been made by General Burnside but General Meade questioned Burnside's plan. The negro troops were not sufficiently seasoned for the job, he argued, or else, if the plan failed, they would be criticized for putting the coloured troops in the forefront as though no one cared if they were killed. At the last minute the order went out that the U.S.C.T. of the Ninth Corps would not lead the assault. Who would?

When the crater appeared and the soldiers in the trenches were supposed to advance through the confusion, they found they had been provided with ladders too short to get them out. They scrambled out here and there, hoisted by their comrades or using hastily-scooped toe-holds and then stood uncertainly, waiting to be commanded. Were they to go straight forward through the crater or detour around it? General Burnside was safe in his tent well to the rear, and the division commander who was supposed to be on the spot was in a dugout drinking commissary whiskey.

The first the opposite side knew of the event was a deafening roar as four Rebel companies were buried under the debris. When their commander rushed to reconnoitre, a half-naked soldier ran past him shouting as he disappeared down the road, "All hell's busted."

At the same time the Union batteries opened fire with 110 cannons and 50 mortars, and the First Division was ordered to charge. As they reached the edge of the crater they tumbled into it. They huddled aimlessly in the great pit, sometimes helping to dig out buried Johnnies while they waited for reinforcements or fresh orders. At the last moment Burnside sent in a division of coloured troops, some of whom by-passed the crater, some of whom willy-nilly joined the mass of men below. As the sun rode higher in the July sky they were parched for water, and if they did succeed in reaching the rim of the great hole, they were picked off by the Confederates who by now had rallied and filled the gap in their lines. The result of the Battle of the Crater was several thousand dead, a gain of one yawning acre of ground and the most gruesome debacle of the whole war.

When the news reached Canada Rose wrote:

Gobles Corners Aug. 6th
We read of terrible suffering before Petersburg. A train of powder was fired and thousands perished. When will the end come? . . . Newton is in [Harding] doing what he can. When you write urge him to perseverance he is so easily discouraged. He is trying to get back to saw in Mr. Mann's Mill near [Harding]. . . . He does not seem strong enough for very hard work. Father was here two days ago. He is working almost day and night at his new Astronomy theory. I fear it will not amount to much. . . . George Dawson Jr. was very sick he was sunstruck last week. . . . Mrs. Goble is still in Illinois . . .

After the failure of the Battle of the Crater Lincoln wrote despairingly, "It seems exceedingly probable that this administration will not be re-elected," but nothing could shake his conviction that only war to the end would be effective. With wry humour he summed up his situation: "Two men were chased by a hog. One climbed a tree to get away. The other grabbed hold of the hog's tail and shouted, "Come down and help me let go of this hog's tail."

Then just a week after the failure of the Crater, on August 5, a bright spot appeared in the gloom. It came from far away at the mouth of the Alabama River in the Gulf of Mexico. David Farragut, a sixty-three year old admiral who would acknowledge that he was aging only when he could not turn a handspring on his birthday, was assembling his fleet near Mobile Bay. Mobile Bay was the Confederacy's last point of entry for the blockade runners on the Gulf coast, its last main supply line from the outside world. If Admiral Farragut would get past Fort Morgan into Mobile Bay at the mouth of the Alabama River, the fort would be isolated and fall. The Mississippi as a supply route had been put out of commission since the fall of Vicksburg the previous year, but the Alabama was still open.

The Confederates had laid a line of mines that would force invading ships to pass within range of Fort Morgan's guns. If any succeeded in running that gauntlet they would be finished off in the bay by an ironclad monitor named the *Tennessee*. Farragut waited for an ironclad of his own before he dared attempt entrance to the bay. Finally the *Tecumseh* came lumbering up.

On August 5 the *Tecumseh* led the fleet to the assault. Wooden frigates with a gunboat lashed to each side followed it. Farragut's flagship, the *Hartfold*, was second in the column. As the *Tecumseh* entered the mine field it was blown to bits. The frigates reversed engines to retreat but the incoming tide made them jostle in confusion and swept them towards the fort. Smoke and flying debris rendered visibility poor.

"What's going on?" shouted Farragut and scurried up the rigging to make sense of the disarray.

"Torpedoes. The *Tecumseh's* gone. Let's retreat."

"Damn the torpedoes," exploded Farragut. "Full speed ahead."

As he steamed past the fort into the bay a torpedo-mine scraped his keel but failed to go off. He passed the gauntlet of guns from the fort only to come face to face with the fire from the ironclad *Tennessee*. Ramming its iron carcass with wooden ships created not even a dent. Was there no Achilles heel to this invincible creature? Then out of the pounding of guns from all the ships that had crowded into the bay one found its mark. It shattered the ironclad's steering gear that was mounted on deck instead of being safe below. Disabled and defeated, the monster ran up the flag of surrender. Then all ships' guns were trained against Fort Morgan. The Alabama river as a supply line for the South was sealed.

Victory at Mobile Bay or not, there were many forces working against the Republican President. That month the Democrats met in Chicago to choose their candidate for the presidency. Clement Vallandigham had returned daringly from his exile in Canada to urge cessation of hostilities. He was defeated by General George McClellan, the displaced hero, but he too was a soft-war man.

Two days after the victory at Mobile Bay a meeting took place in London, Canada West, between three commissioners of the Confederate government and representatives of the Knights of the the Golden Circle. Though Canadians entering the United States were now obliged to produce passports, Americans were allowed to enter Canada at will. The Knights of the Golden Circle was a secret organization whose object was to separate the northwestern states from the Union and form a second rebelling confederacy. That would complicate things for Lincoln, to say the least, and Lincoln would soon be seeking re-election.

That was not all that was going on in Canada. There were "peace meetings" organized by confederate George Sanders from his room in the Queen's Hotel on the waterfront in Toronto. In Toronto also, young golden-haired Thomas Hines was organizing Southerners to proceed against the North using Canada as a base. His secret code was so simple that the U.S. telegraph office deciphered it easily, but who knew what other messages went undetected. When ex-Mississippi Senator Jacob Thompson arrived in Quebec under an assumed name, he was received by Governor-General Monck. What did that mean? As Thompson passed through Montreal he opened an account in the Bank of Ontario there and took to Toronto the rest of the $900,000 that Jeff Davis had given him to establish a base for Confederate operations in British North America. Any trouble caused by these Southerners would bring a Northern army running.

More than ever, Canadian politicians were beginning to think that separate existence was dangerous. In unity lay strength, above the border as well as below. As Sherman's army advanced on Atlanta, Maritimers Joseph Howe, Dr. Charles Tupper and Sir Leonard Tilley were about to host a conference of three provinces on the subject of confederation.

The uneasy 1841 union of Canada West and East had reached a legislative deadlock with English and French both seeking ascendancy. When they heard of the Maritime conference, John A. Macdonald, George Brown, Georges Étienne Cartier, John Galt and D'Arcy McGee asked permission to participate. A Canadian nation stretching from sea to sea was seeking birth. The country to the south had been born in blood and, bathed in blood, it was struggling to survive. Whatever could be done to keep Canada from the same fate—if 'twere done, 'twere best done quickly. The Charlottetown Conference set a date for a second meeting in Quebec to discuss a union of five provinces.

In spite of both covert and overt opposition to his undying determination to continue the war to the end, Lincoln was re-nominated as Republican candidate for the presidency. All soldiers, whether United States citizens or not, were eligible to vote in the coming presidential election. As Alonzo Harding went out from Chattanooga on one foray after another, he knew where his sympathies lay and was not afraid to express them.

Chattanooga Tennessee Aug. 14th

My dear Sister

This has been a gloomy disagreeable day it has rained since early this morning without ceasing . . . We have just returned from "Gordon's Mills" twenty miles south of this place, there was a squad of 300 Reb cavalry bold enough to venture that far from their main army and we were sent out along with a small squad of infantry to drive them back we got there about ten o'clock in the evening and waited patiently for daylight to appear, but the "Johnnys" had no notion of making themselves a mark for our twelve pounders so they were taken with a dose of digout some time before morning and when daylight appeared and we went where they were they did not happen to be there we followed them about five miles and did not get sight of them so returned to Chattanooga. The weather has been very warm this month sometimes I think it will almost melt me down . . . I have not heard much war news lately of any consequence there has been some pretty hard fighting around Atlanta and there have been a great many wounded sent here also quite a number of prisoners. I look forward to considerable changes about election time. I do not think there is a doubt but what Lincoln will be reelected. I am entitled to a vote and shall give "Old Abe" the benefit of it so help him all I can. How fast the time flies . . . my three years will soon pass and then I shall be free again, I have never regretted having enlisted and think if I was out of the army today tomorrow I would be into it I want to see the end of it . . . We have just received marching orders and I must quit.

From Your Aff. Brother
Alonzo

In Harding, Canada West, Enos sat at his work. He looked again at the words, "And God divided the waters which were under the firmament from the waters which were above the firmament. How far up are the waters He said were above the firmament? He couldn't have meant just the clouds. What did He mean?" Enos wrote:

It could be then that the waters that God placed above the firmament are like a belt or concave of water that like a molten mirror of glass makes a vast reflector for the sun, throwing its beams of light with great power over all the universe below. The sun is not the source of heat to the earth but it is a property entirely belonging to the earth and the rays of light from the sun are the agency to draw the warmth from the earth.

"Might this be correct? Have I found a new theory of the universe that reconciles the Bible with science? If the planets follow their orbits beyond the sun, they must circle under this concave of water." For a moment Enos forgot the limitations this theory imposed and let his mind soar again.

Suppose a man were to go out from the sun as if he could travel through endless space. At a mean distance of 485 million miles he would cross the orbit of Jupiter. Continuing on to a distance of 87 million miles he would come to and cross the orbit of Saturn. Then at the distance from the sun of 1,800,000,000 miles coming to the orbit of Uranus and after this still going off in space would come to the limits of discovery to the planet Neptune . . . even travelling at the speed of light it would take a man of great age to return and report. I'm beginning to think the mind of man has outreached his measuring line.

"I must read some more in this book by Dr. Dick, *The Christian Philosopher,* but this is enough for tonight. If I only knew more about mathematics, I could be more certain about the revolutions of the planets I'm setting up in my orrery. But it's beginning to work, and it will, I know it."

Ten miles away his doubting daughter was writing to Alonzo.

Goble's Corners Aug. 29th '64

My Dear Brother,

. . . I am vainly wondering where you may be to-night, and what may be your circumstances. When you wrote you were just ordered to March. Where have you been, and how have you fared and are you still among the living; are questions I'm vainly trying to ask myself. . . . We are all well and everything goes on in the same "old nice way." It would not perhaps suit you but I love quietness and peace. . . . We are having nice

Tomatoes and Melons now, better than usual. How far is it to Atlanta? It seems by our news that the latter place is still possessed by the Rebels. . . .

As ever Your loving
Sister Rose

Yes, how far was it to Atlanta? How much longer would it take to "Get Hood?" Bit by inexorable bit Sherman was extending his lines south and east of the city, cutting railway connections wherever he could and bending the rails into "Sherman's knots" so they could not be used again. On September 2 he and his army entered Atlanta.

Most of Atlanta's population of thirteen thousand had evacuated the city. Sherman ordered his men to destroy factories, railways, anything that might be of use to the enemy. Thinking to prevent unnecessary destruction he said, "Let no fires be set except in my presence," but it was useless and fires swept out of control.

Lincoln's tenacity was paying off. General Thomas, usually sedate, lost his dignity, combed his whiskers with his fingers, skipped and almost capered. Lieutenant-General Grant ordered a one-hundred-gun salute with every shot aimed at Petersburg.

But Hood had not gone down with the city. He and forty thousand men were off and away, circling to the south preparatory to converging on Chattanooga and escaping northward to assist Lee against Grant and save Richmond. It was no easy task to get Gambler Hood. Hood was now after General Thomas, and Alonzo Harding was part of Thomas's army.

Chapter 20

Prisoner Of War

After the big push to capture Atlanta, Sherman took three weeks to pull his army together and exchange prisoners, then he set out to get Hood. Hood refused to do Sherman the honour of allowing himself to be snared easily. He circled and feinted. Sherman complained about Hood's elusiveness. "I cannot guess his movements as I could those of Johnston who was a sensible man and did only sensible things." But Grant had telegraphed, "If we give the enemy no peace while the war lasts, the end cannot be far distant."

With Hood on the rampage, Alonzo Harding's easy garrison life in Chattanooga came to an end. General Thomas was ordered to move south, leaving only enough men to guard the railway to Nashville, their source of supplies from the north. With Hood were two armies, his own and General S.D. Lee's. Sherman still commanded three, his own Army of the Tennessee, General John Scholfield's smaller Army of the Ohio and General George H. Thomas' Army of the Cumberland. Their strategy was to snare Hood in the middle of the three prongs. Hood could hope for few reinforcements from the depleted manpower of the South but Sherman could draw on the latest draft order for 500,000 Northern men. The victory at Atlanta had given Lincoln and the War Department the courage to proceed with more draftees.

Corporal Alonzo Harding, set off with Battery D, of the Twentieth Ohio, of the Third Division under Captain Backus, of the Second Brigade under Major Francis Shaklee, of the 17th Army Corps under Brigadier General T. Ransom under Major General George Thomas of the Army of the Cumberland. Some of the units might expect a little rest but not Battery D for it was an independent battery that served wherever it was ordered.

They were going south to catch Hood. They went on foot because the railroad in many places had been broken up by Nathan Forrest's cavalry. Sometimes they ate well according to what the foragers brought in or if their supplies reached them. Sometimes there was very little. The enemy was all around. They were waiting beside the guns on top of a little hill, everyone quiet but alert. They were hungry. They heard a rustling in the bushes, tensed, then a Barred Rock hen came picking its way out, head bobbing. Aha, fresh meat!

Alonzo crouched and held out a hand. "Here chook, here chook," he coaxed quietly. The hen came closer, its silly little eyes glinting. "Chook, chook, chook," he coaxed, then grabbed for it. But in a gabble of frightened clucks the hen fled into the bushes where they could not crash after it. "Well, anyway, if we had caught it, there wouldn't have been more than a mouthful for each."

"Looks like good forage over there for the army cattle if they can come up to us," said Alonzo's buddy Joseph Fitzgerald, a Canadian from Millbrook, Canada West. "Maybe when they catch up with us we'll have fresh beef."

"Don't think so. I saw them herding the cattle over to the west where the fields are better. Anyway, we won't get mule, 'cause they weeded out the poor ones and sent them back to Chattanooga."

"We ate better there but it's more exciting here."

"Watch out, they're coming at us from the left."

"Postions," yelled the lieutenant. "Double quick."

They sprang to their posts, for by now the battery worked like a precision team. In no time at all they could unlimber the guns and ammunition and be ready to fight. Sight a twelve-pounder cannon towards whatever was coming at you or wherever an enemy emplacement was aiming at you. Ram in some shot, then a cannon ball (that you'd used for a pinball game two hours before), light the fuse, hold your ears if there was time, watch it land if you could see, cool the bore with water if there was any handy, count the ammunition, run for another box if there was any extra, pray if there wasn't. Limber up after the fight to move your line ahead—or back if they had pushed you. Count the colours captured, if any. Bring in the wounded. Bury your dead.

They never knew when a detachment of Hood's or S.D. Lee's men might appear. No matter how good the scouts were, they could miss a couple of Confederate guns hidden on a hilltop, ready to create cover for infantry as they advanced in the confusion. Then the reports would go to headquarters: a brief skirmish, a lively exchange of fire, a demonstration. Downplay for the official report the terror and uncertainty and grief for a dead comrade.

When the 20th Ohio reached Dalton, Hood's former headquarters, Dalton was in ruins. Everything that could be burned for campfires was gone—woodpiles, trees, furniture, flooring, wainscotting, frame houses. Outside the town, one day a bridge was there, next day torn down or burned. One day a railroad was usable, next day the rails had been twisted and the wooden ties burned or axed. One day there was a wooden area for cover. Next day the trees lay hacked down across the roads to stop the enemy advance. "Be ready to strike in any direction the enemy may be seen moving," ordered General Sherman.

Hood was driving north on every possible road. Allatoona, Cassville, Resaca, Rome. The names melted into confusion.

Snake Creek Gap, Dug Gap, Tunnel Hill Road, Spring Place, Sweet Water, be prepared for anything.

Van Wert, Stilesborough, Big Shanty, King's Mill, Turkeytown. Change your strategy.

Decatur, Powder Springs, Pumkin Vine Town. Deploy your units again. Send despatches and hope the riders get through. Send telegrams and hope the lines will not be cut. Write reports to be sent to headquarters hoping they'll not be stale by the time the general gets them: *"Sept. 30, 10 a.m. Have had considerable skirmishing in my front this a.m. on Camp Creek; have driven the rebel cavalry across the Sweet Water. They are now barricading the fords on that stream. Had 2 men killed and 5 wounded, and lost several horses killed and wounded. I have 100 men on the opposite side of the river watching Sweet Water. I have very few people to guard so long a line; my pickets from Mount Gilead Church to the left should be relieved by infantry; 150 men will be sufficient; can they not be spared?"*

Or Oct. 9: *"I have encountered the rebel cavalry under Ferguson . . . I am having a pretty severe fight. . . . Scouts report none of our cavalry at Dallas, as I was led to suppose. I would not have advanced so far had I known this sooner. It is now 2 o'clock in the day. I cannot withdraw in the face of so many cavalry without a fight. General Morgan's brigade of cavalry, 700 or 800 strong, is at Villa Rica. I am afraid they may attack me in the rear . . .*

Very respectfully &c . . ."

Or: *"Oct. 10. General Hood left Van Wert on Saturday with his army at 9 a.m. . . . The entire rebel army 36,000 strong, encamped last evening in the neighbourhood of Cedartown. . . . Prisoner taken today reports that General Beauregard crossed the Chattahoochee on Moore's bridge on Friday last . . ."*

Or more desperately; *"Send me support . . . send me 75,000 elongated ball cartridges calibre 57 . . . turn the cattle towards Resaca . . . the river is too high to cross . . . no news from the courier . . . no news from General Rousseau . . . my men took food from women and children . . ."*

The deadly juggling continued without abate. Hood seemed to be omnipresent, coming from all directions at once. Sometimes the fate of a whole army was in the hands of the signalmen flapping their puny flags.

The telegraph line between Kenesaw and Allatoona had been destroyed. Lieutenant Fish was in charge of the signal post on Little Kenesaw with orders from General Sherman to hold out at any cost. Sherman himself was on the top of the mountain all one day, communicating with seven different stations through signallers. For five days the signal corps held out, weary to the point of exhaustion.

"At 9 a.m. the enemy had us surrounded on every approachable side and the engagement became general. As soon as I could I sent them a message stating the arrival of our reinforcements &c. . . . The message was flagged under a sharp fire, and I wish to make special mention of the coolness and bravery of J.W. McKenzie, acting sergeant Lieutenant Allen's party, and Frank A. West, of the signal corps . . . West was on his way to join his party at the front, and happened to be detained here on account of the railroad being cut. I was not aware of his presence until I saw him voluntarily get up on top of the works and relieve McKenzie at the flag. The message was of some length and was flagged with remarkable coolness and accuracy by these two men . . . I have not a word of censure for any man of the detachment . . ."

Sherman himself thanked the signallers. "What you did for me was worth $1,000,000."

Nearer and nearer Hood was coming to Dalton. On the eighth of October his army took up its position between Big Shanty and Kenesaw Mountain. On the tenth he made a forced march to Kingston, thirty-eight miles with scarcely a halt. He had crossed the Coosa sixteen miles away and was proceeding to Resaca and Dalton with his entire army, and then might proceed on Rome, who knew?

The Northern Army of the Ohio was moving with the Army of the Tennessee. General Ransom with the Seventeenth Corps that included the Twentieth Ohio took a crossroad that was muddy, rough and difficult for wagons. There was a tense and brief engagement towards evening.

"Whew," said Alonzo to Joe Fitzgerald as they lit a little fire that night. "That was a close call. Bit different from Chattanooga."

"Don't know which is worse, waiting or fighting. Guess we don't have much choice, sitting here with Hood all around. Wish I were back in Millbrook."

"At least we're getting reinforcements, even if they are draftees. Hood can't get anymore."

"Wish Hood had that one," said Joe, pointing to a new arrival with a face like a pinched Simian. "He's no bigger than a flea. Might as well be home looking after chicken coops."

"He's wiry. He'll do in a pinch and that's where we are now."

A picket came in from duty. "Any cornmeal left?" They handed him a plateful. "Mush, mush, nothing but mush, I'm sick of mush. I was sitting on a log out there when a Reb picket called to me, he was so close. We talked things over for a while. If we had anything to do with it, we'd have settled the war in half and hour. Nice fellow. Hope I don't have to kill him tomorrow."

Another man approached the fire. "Anybody need a watch?" He was the kind who would play wounded after a battle and then rifle the pockets of the dead, either friend or foe. This time he had two watches and some letters.

"Here, Harding, you're always looking for letters. Read these." He thrust the letters into Alonzo's hands and went off to peddle the watches elsewhere.

Alonzo looked distastefully at the two battered envelopes knowing where they came from if Rube had brought them. Then he opened one, thinking he might write the senders, Southern or not, and let them know the certain truth, not wait on tenterhooks.

"Dere Chet, I feel like a lonesome dove that had lost thair mate rose is red the villets blue an hant gives me narry present that is nice like you my pen is bad my ink is pale my love for you shall never fale. Molly

The other letter was a never-finished reply.

Dere Molly butiful thou art and have my hart my only welth is the love I bare if nothin happens more one thot from you will cheer my dropping mind if I had the wings of an eagle to the i would fly but alas I am a soldier we are within four miles of Yankees.

The mud on Molly's envelope obscured the address. Alonzo put one corner of the sheets into the fire, watched them blacken, flame, then fall into the fire. "Hope no one finds my letters the same way even if I'm not writing to a sweetheart. Wish I had one. Wonder what that Lee

MacDonald is like that Newton says he sees sometimes? Or the others Father says he drives around?" He searched out as dry and smooth a spot as he could find and shook out his blanket. "Wonder how many miles tomorrow?" He rolled his blanket around him. "Girls. Wonder what one looks like? I'd probably drop dead if I saw one, a nice sweet girl, not like the banshees in bonnets with hate in their eyes like those we saw last week."

There was continuous fighting now, a constant shifting of advantage. One day there might be butternut uniforms behind a breastwork, the next the blue would be firing their muskets from the same shelter. No matter how much they were on the move the mail seemed to come.

[Harding] Sept. 11th   64

Dear Brother
    Father was out to Mr. Goble's last week and Rose had recd your letter
. . . I have looked in vain for your letter. You have had a narrow escape
and I am glad you came off unharmed. May the same good fortune
always follow you is my earnest prayer. I'm at present running a lath mill
at Mr. Mann's saw mill. I can get one dollar per thousand. . . . Father
has been quite unwell for a few days but is better now. . . . O! how I wish
I was with you! I have almost made up my mind to come several times
but they dont want me to. If this business pays me pretty well I shall
continue at it all winter and go to the States in the spring and go into
some kind of buisiness probably in the state of Michigan in the lumbering
district. . . . The leaves commenced to assume the autumnal yellow some
ten days ago. Heavy frosts.
    You must write to me right away and give me all particulars of your
engagements etc.
    While I remain your

Affectionate Brother   Newton

To A [Harding]
20th Ohio Battery
U.S.A.

Gobles Corners Sept 12th 1864

My Dear Brother,
    I received your last letter a week ago, written from Dalton, you had
been in battle and escaped unhurt, bless the Lord for his preserving care,
surely He hath covered your head in battle. . . . Nellie Goble is going to

*Woodstock to-morrow to School again. The Term commences this week.
Newton cannot attend this term. He is working in Mr. Mann's mill on
the 9th Conc sawing lath . . . Father is working at his "New Astronomy
theory", but is not so sanguine of success as at first. If he fails he talks of
going away somewhere in the fall. . . . Heman and Lissa were here over
Sunday, they expect to move to Port Burwell. He has charge of a church
there and is to have $400 per year. . . . I hope you have succeeded in
getting a new boot for it cannot be very comfortable to go with one. I do
not know what the present war news are. It is reported that Atlanta has
been taken by the Federals, and also that Grants Army has been blown
up at Petersburgh or a part of it. How terrible these things are. I suppose
soldiers who are constantly surrounded by blood-shed and the sad effects
of war, become accustomed to it and do not mind it; but after all it is
very-very sad. . . . Good Night My Brother. May angels guard your bed.
Write often.*

As Ever Your Aff. Sister Rose

They were resting in front of the campfire before turning in. There was
no sense trying to conceal their whereabouts from the enemy whose own
fires were flaming in plain sight. "Wonder which direction we'll be
shooting in tomorrow?" Alonzo asked himself. "Anyway we're on a hill
now."

This was the hill they would have to hold tomorrow when they'd be
rushed by Rebels trying to grapple with the gunners and plant the Stars
and Bars where the Stars and Stripes now flew. "Of course, another unit
might open fire and get the Rebs before they come at us . . ."

Alonzo reread his letters, then folded then carefully into their little
envelopes and tucked them in the kit bag he never allowed to leave him,
for it was a kind of amulet against danger. "Good night, Joe," he said as
he settled himself to sleep.

Dawn came. The long roll sounded and they ran for their positions.
Another skirmish. Nothing decided on the Dalton front yet but one thing
was slowly becoming evident. The 14th U.S.C.T. was at Dalton, with
every one doubting their ability to stand fast under fire. Captain Davis
sent to see how they were performing. He reported to General Stedman:
"The regiment is holding dress parade under fire" so well were they
acting. This was the first engagement in which negro troops of the Army
of the Cumberland had participated. It heightened confidence in them,
but they still had to face a major battle and so far Hood was dodging too
well for that.

If there was a temporary stalemate around Dalton, the North was moving ahead elsewhere. On September 19 Northern General Philip H. Sheridan finally defeated Jubal Early in the valley of the Shenandoah. Never again would the South be able to draw food from the rich valley. Never again would anyone be able to taunt the Lincoln administration about "the valley of our national humiliation."

Atlanta had fallen, the Shenandoah valley was safe. Two down and two to go—Lee in Richmond where Grant still lay siege to Petersburg, and Hood jockeying his forces around three Northern armies that themselves were being shunted so fast that a unit hardly knew which army it was fighting in.

Some news of this activity filtered through to Roseltha and Newton.

My Dear Brother . . . I have received no answer to my last letter. . . . We have just received news that Sheridan has gained a great victory on the Confederates. May it be so; and hasten the close of this war. . . .

. . . I feel very thankful that you have been able to withstand the heat all Summer, while so many have sickened and died. . . . Jasper Goble saw Newton last week at Drumbo Fair. I was not there. . . . Granpa Goble is dead. He died the 14th of this month. He was nearly 82 years old. and like a Shock of Corn fully ripened was gathered into the "Great Garner". His last end was peaceful and full of hopes of a Glorious immortality beyond the Grave. May we my Brother like him be ready when the "Reaper" comes. . . .

Ever Your Sister   Rose

I suppose you are still at Dalton. The last letter I had from you was written from there. I send this to Chattanooga.

[Harding] Oct. 6th 1864

Dear Brother

I recd your welcome letter . . . about ten days ago. In my last letter I told you that I was running Mr. Manns lath mill but I left it a day or two ago as I could hardly make my board and Mr. Mann would not give me any better site. I shall run Mr. Lovetts lath mill prabely all winter at [$20.00] twenty dollars per mo. It will cost about nine dollars for there is no chance of doeing any better here this winter. You spoke of getting a situation for me. I wish you could. . . . Times are awful hard here now. No work at all scarcely and everything dreadful high. The country is swarmed with "skeddlars" they are perfect nuisances—will work for almost nothing and board themselves. Father is here yet and doeing nothing. . . . We are keeping "Batch". There is a Mr. Camp here from Dundass, talking about renting the south half of the house to live in and *the barn for a carriage shop but I don't believe he will. He "hums and haws" and don't know what he wants.*

. . . There has been nothing thought of for the last two weeks but fairs—Drumbo commenced and was followed by Woodstock Ayr Brantford and Hamilton. There was not one single prize from the provincial fair at Hamilton brought into Blenheim.

Last week some one poasted a lot of hand bills up in Windsor Sandwich and Maudlin stating that the militia of Upper C. would immediately be put on an efficient footing and some sent to India to do garrison duty and that all fugitives from the United States would be enrolled also. It had not been up twenty-four hours before hundred of "Skeddlars" "skeddelled" back to Yankeedom but soon returned on finding that it was all a "take in".

It is awful lonsome here the old house seems like a barn. Curreys are tottering on their last stump and I guess the first little breeze will blow them over. Jim hardly shows himself any more. You must write soon and give me all the particulars how you live if you have plenty of "salt horse" etc. If it had not been for Rose I should have come down there and inlisted this fall but she don't want me to. . . .

Your aff. Brother   Newton

Battery D was still in Dalton and Hood was all around. Let no one underestimate General John B. Hood whose intention was to separate three armies and force the individual surrender of all Yankee posts, one after another. By October 12 he had worked his way to Resaca, just ten miles south of Dalton.

Resaca was the headquarters of the Second Brigade, Third Division, Fifteenth Army Corps with a mixture of the Eightieth Ohio Infantry, Tenth Missouri Infantry, Seventh Kentucky Cavalry (or was it the Sixth, since in the squeeze it was hard to know) and a battery of four guns. They were covering a line of fifteen miles on the Western and Atlantic Railroad. By 3:30 p.m. on October 12 the Confederates had invested the town and sent a flag of truce to the colonel. Surrender was refused and firing continued, but on the 14th the colonel withdrew to a safer place. Hood held Resaca.

Six miles from Resaca at Tilton 300 men were holding a blockhouse. They held it till an enemy cannon ball made a lucky entrance through a loophole, filling the blockhouse with so much smoke that it was untenable. Its garrison had delayed the enemy nearly eight hours but Hood now held Tilton.

In between the two a small force was defending a construction camp of materials for bridges, breastworks and pontoons. For five hours the

261

Federals maintained a desparate resistance then the captain was wounded, and they were forced to yield when overpowered by the Rebels. Yes, Hood was moving fast and the next day on the Villanow side of Dalton he would be attacking the battery of the Twentieth Ohio and the Fourteenth Colored Infantry.

Dalton was laid out roughly north and south with a road running through it coming from Tilton to the south and forking on the north to Tunnel Hill and Cleveland. At right angles to this road coming from the east was Lower Spring Road. Colonel L. Johnson placed his 700 men on a hill on the north side of Lower Spring Road. It should have been an advantageous position except that on the west side of Dalton there was a higher hill and on the other side was another hill fifty feet higher still.

Reports were coming in fast and furious. The railroad track one mile north of Resaca was burning. The bridge at Tilton was on fire. Union cavalry rushed in saying they were being pursued by a large force, whether infantry or cavalry or both, they had not waited to find out. Then the enemy began to occupy the hill north of Dalton and place guns on the hill across the road from Johnston's redoubt.

Alonzo and Fitzgerald looked at their meagre arsenal. They shrugged. "Looks hopeless. Think we're done for."

"Lets fight," said a coloured soldier. "Won't be worse than capture for us."

Hood knew he had the Yanks surrounded but he balked at wholesale annihilation. He ordered a cease-fire and sent an officer under flag of truce with the confident communication:

> *Headquarters, Army of the Tennessee, CSA*
> *In the Field, October 13, 1864*
>
> *Officer Commanding U.S. Forces*
> *Dalton, Ga.*
> *I demand the immediate and unconditional surrender of the post and garrison under your command, and should this be acceded to all white officers and soldiers will be paroled in a few days. If the place is carried by assault, no prisoners will be taken.*
>
> *Most respectfully, your obedient servant,*
> *J.B. Hood,*
> *General*

Twice Colonel Johnson refused to surrender, stalling for time, hoping for rescue or for better terms. Then from his hill he saw approaching a dense line of infantry two miles in length, reaching from Tunnel Hill to the lower Spring Road and enforced by several batteries. He heard cannonading from Buzzard's Roost gap, and was informed that a division of cavalry occupied the Cleveland Road, that the railroad north of Dalton was burning, that the guard at the first bridge north of Dalton was captured, and that the rebels were shelling the blockhouse at the second bridge north of Dalton. Then the Captain of the Seventh Kentucky Cavalry came in. "I've ridden the entire length of the enemy lines. They have enough men to eat us up."

Fully aware that he could hold out for only a short time in what would be a total massacre, Johnson asked permission to inspect the rebel forces. If he considered that he was actually overwhelmed, he would evacuate if safe conduct to another post was granted, he said. Hood himself showed him 25,000 men and thirty pieces of artillery already in place on the highest hill. "You're wasting my time," he said, "I cannot restrain my men and will not if I could."

Johnson looked around at his coloured soldiers. He had no way of notifying forces in either direction that he was surrounded. He had 700 men to protect and he knew that a division commanded by General Cleburne, the man who had not restrained his men from masscring negro troops at Fort Pillow, was in Hood's immediate rear and was spoiling to get at "the niggers".

At 3 p.m., October 13, he surrendered on the condition that officers and white soldiers were to be paroled, officers to retain their swords and whatever private property they could carry. The infantry privates, that is, the negroes, would go south. His white officers said they would go south with their men but this was refused. All slaves belonging to persons in the Confederacy would be returned to their masters.

Dalton and the country south of Villanow were now in rebel hands. Among those men surrendered was one section of the Twentieth Ohio Battery, about twenty enlisted men, one of them Alonzo Harding. The guns the battery surrendered were one 12-pounder Napoleon and one damaged 3-inch Rodman. They had left only 150 rounds of ammunition. No, they could not have held out for long.

Alonzo Harding submitted with as much resignation as he could muster. He was now a prisoner of war.

Chapter 21

Nashville

"**N**ice howdy-do!" Alonzo sat down on the Napoleon as the order for surrender spread along the lines. Joseph Fitzgerald looked more sad than mad. "I'm hungry. Anything in your knapsack?"

"Water in my canteen. Couple of hardtack. Think we'd better save them. The Johnnies are likely starving and only a loaves and fishes act would provide enough for all of us to eat."

"Wonder what they'll do with us now they've got us?"

"Maybe they'll exchange us the way they did after Atlanta —you know, four privates for one lieutenant and so on. We've enough prisoners to make another deal."

"That might do us some good, but I don't think they'll do much exchanging among the negroes. Not here in Georgia." Alonzo looked at the black soldiers sitting dispairingly around, waiting for the worst.

"Maybe they'll send us to Andersonville."

"My God," Alonzo burst out, breaking his rule of no blasphemy. "I hope not."

Tales of the horrors of the prison at Andersonville, 170 miles south of them, had already reached them. More than thirty thousand men packed into a twenty-six acre stockade designed to hold ten. No shelter from the blistering sun but tents. One little stream running through it for drinking and washing. One hundred and fifty dying each day. Insufficient food. Dysentery rampant. Scarce cooking utensils rented out for profit. Desperate attempts to retain decency. One man wrote in his diary, "I pray to God to purify my heart and elevate my desires . . . but this evening I sinned by getting angry." Another made comic attempts to joke—"I wish all the guards would get the measles." Or they tunnelled to escape boredom and the camp. Once they miscalculated the distance. The

265

tunnel ended in the middle of a guards' fire and when the prisoners broke through, the guards fled, thinking red-hot devils from hell were after them. And none of them knowing that Lieutenant-General Grant forbade any exchanges out of Andersonville because release of Southern prisoners would endanger the success of the overall cause. Andersonville, presided over by Captain Henry Wirz.

"Andersonville—not Andersonville! Anything but that," said Alonzo again.

"Well, we won't be sent to Libby prison in Richmond, that's for sure. It's only for officers. Even there things aren't much better, except they have a roof."

"I'd rather die than go to Andersonville."

"Cheer up," said Joe, "maybe you will. No love in those eyes coming at us."

The approaching Rebs were not going to kill. They were systematically seizing all the prisoners' clothes except their underwear.

"What'll you do with a blue uniform, you crazy Reb?"

"Put it on under this here butternut stuff. Keep me warm at nights instead of you. Gimme them boots quick and keep your mouth shut or I'll take your drawers too."

Joe and Alonzo looked at each other in their underwear. "They didn't even leave us our swords to keep us warm."

"Shut up. This is no time to joke. Maybe if we'd had swords they'd have let us keep our clothes. Now I know another reason why I'd like to be an officer."

"Don't be too sure. Look how they're treating Lieutenant Johnson and Captain Markle. Cursing them and taking their boots and coats."

"Fall in for marching," came the order. Then they learned that they might be paroled; and meantime they were to be moved to Villanow while Hood figured out what to do with them.

Alonzo patted the Napoleon goodbye and started to sing "When this cruel war is over."

"Shut your trap," yelled a Southern sergeant. Major Grosskopff came up. "Just cooperate, men, till we get a few things straightened out."

Alonzo lined up with the rest of his battery. If the situation had not been serious, he might have burst out laughing at the sight of so many men in their underwear. He looked at the pile of confiscated muskets ready to be loaded into Rebel wagons. If he and Joe could only get a couple, they might make a getaway when night came. One of the guards looked at him as if he could read his mind. Another group of guards came marching up.

"You niggers, get up on your hind legs. March. You're going to tear up the railroad."

266

"No suh, not goin' to," roared one.

A Reb pointed a gun at him and the negro changed his mind. "Anyone else don't want to pull up rails?"

No one spoke. All moved forward.

They stayed at Buzzard Roost that night, hungry and shivering. Alonzo and Joe shared a hardtack between them. At noon they were ordered to march.

"That's Racknor over there. He's too sick to march."

Racknor stumbled and fell into a heap. Some of the Northern men quietly ranged around others of the sick, supporting them on the march to Villanow. As they went, they passed hundreds of Rebs resting in camps beside the road.

It was after dark when they arrived at Villanow. A small ration of cornmeal and beef was issued, the only food since surrender.

"Where's Jackson?" said Joe.

"Sh-h, he got away a while back. Good luck to him. And the ones who were out foraging got away too."

They sat morosely. "How many regiments of Rebs do you think we passed?"

"Somebody said they counted 170 and fifty pieces of artillery. Maybe one of them was our good old Napoleon."

"Someone said there were a dozen generals too. They didn't look hungry."

"Where do you think they'll head next?"

"Maybe Blue Mountain. Maybe Tennessee."

"Maybe Hood thinks if he can get past us into Kentucky he'll get some recruits there."

"If he captures any more of us, he'll get there. Wonder if the government will honour our parole, or if we can get back into action."

"There are parole camps somewhere, I've heard. Hope they aren't like Andersonville."

"I'd commit suicide before I'll go there," said Alonzo.

"I'll keep you company, if it's any comfort."

"Maybe we can escape, like Jackson."

Joe looked at his underwear. "At least we won't get our clothes dirty if we can."

They put their knapsacks under their heads and lay down back to back for some warmth in the chill October night. Alonzo felt the edges of his little bundle of letters, and finally slept.

Next morning came an order to line up. It was true that they were to be paroled. Hurriedly pieces of paper were pushed in front of each man as he came up to the tables. Alonzo took a quick look at what he was being asked to sign:

I,   *20th Ohio Bat'y*
                 Regt   Brig
                 Div   USA
being a prisoner of war in the hands of the CSA do solemnly swear that I
will not bear arms against the Confederate States or aid or assist anyone
so doing until regularly exchanged.
                 Attest
                    L. Joemme
                    Col   44th USC   I
                 Attest
                    By comd Genl Hood
                    E J Hami
                    Col & Insp Gen, A T

There was a blank for the signator's name.

"Hurry up, just make an X."

"I've been to school. I can write," Alonzo said indignantly and signed his name over the X. He looked at the fine script on the parole paper and thought, "That writing looks as good as Alfred's. Over a year since he died."

"Move along! Next!"

Joe broke into his thoughts. "So we're paroled. Guess we won't have to kick the bucket. That's a cheery thought for a fine afternoon."

"I'm wondering when we get more clothes."

"Maybe we can go home since we've promised not to fight."

"Fat chance. It said till regularly exchanged. We may be back in soon."

As Alonzo was being freed on parole in Villanow, the desperate South was increasing clandestine activity in Canada. In Toronto, Lieutenant Bennett Young, a twenty-one year old escapee from a Northern prison, outfitted thirty fellow ex-prisoners with long overcoats that concealed Confederate uniforms, took them in pairs to Montreal, then over the border to St. Albans, Vermont, twenty miles south. At three o'clock in the afternoon of October 19, 1864, Young brandished a pistol on the porch of his hotel and declared, "In the name of the Confederate States of America, I take possession of St. Albans!" The rest of his gang proceeded to rob three banks, not omitting to sell to a local financier some of the gold they had just stolen. The townsfolk formed a posse to pursue the raiders who were heading for safety across the Canadian border. Only cool heads on both sides averted an invasion of vengeance-bound Northern soldiers who claimed that Canada would allow any kind of plot to be hatched within its bounds.

With this crisis overcome, all attention now returned to the armies jockeying for ascendancy south of Nashville. As Chattanooga would likely be Hood's next objective, reports flew thick and fast between General Thomas at Nashville and his generals in the field:

> Oct. 13. *"The First Brigade started from Athens at 10:30 today, the Second Brigade at 3 p.m., and the Third Brigade follows this evening. Call in troops from Tunnel Hill and Ringgold. . . . should you be attacked all the defenses between Chattanooga and Bridgeport must be held to the last extremity . . ."*

The generals around Dalton reported that they would do the best they could with "the fragments" under their command and the others would move as fast as rail transportation permitted.

> Oct. 15. *"Hood's army left Villanow at daylight this morning . . . Tunnel Hill is safe . . . The rebels are living on parched corn . . . There are no troops between Nickajack Gap and Villanow . . . Wagon trains are here—rebels don't know where . . . These men were placed here in accordance with General Thomas' orders and I will not feel authorized to move them without General Sherman's orders. . . . I am instructed by General Sherman to keep harassing the rear of the enemy. . . .*

The messages flew around like grapeshot. October 16, the day after Alonzo was paroled, was so busy that Sherman in Rome sent this to a general in Atlanta: *"Look out for yourself and hold Atlanta. You have plenty of grub, and I will turn up somewhere."*

> W.T. Sherman,
> Major-General, Commanding

Then Thomas in Nashville was able to send Sherman the welcome news: *"Reinforcements are arriving at the rate of one regiment a day."* At five o'clock that afternoon Sherman replied wickedly: *"I want the first positive fact that Hood contemplates an invasion of Tennessee; invite him to do so. Send him a free pass in."* In other words, Come into my parlour, said the spider to the fly. Would Gambler Hood, successful at Resaca, Tilton and Dalton, still try to get through the web of three armies?

As Hood swung his men to the west of Dalton to enter Tennessee and from there get across to Lee at Richmond, the Twentieth Ohio was being refitted with clothes and arms in Chattanooga preparatory to joining the harrassment of Hood's rear. Hood had lost this gamble. The Northern generals had not honoured the parole of those who had surrendered at Villanow.

Morale in the armies here was at fever peak. On November 8 the soldiers had crowded into every polling booth that could be pre-empted for the presidential election—tents, ambulances, houses. After a sharp debate in Congress every soldier, American citizen or not, could now vote. When the national count was completed Old Abe had won again.

"Now we can finish the job, and it can't be too soon," said Joe Fitzgerald to Alonzo when the vast hurrahs had died down. It was only a matter of strategy from now on.

"Old Tecump" Sherman had his ideas of how to proceed. He was trying to convince General Grant that the quickest way to make the South and her probable allies overseas realize that the jig was up, was to march straight through Southern territory. He was determined to take his Army of the Tennessee right through Georgia to the Atlantic Ocean and then up the coast through the Carolinas to join Grant at Petersburg. That should cook Lee's goose!

On November 15 he started out, leaving Scholfield and Thomas to cope with Hood. It was just as he suspected. The seemingly invincible South dissolved before him. At Milledgeville there was one brief attempt to stop him. When the engagement was over and Sherman's soldiers began to gather up the dead and wounded, they found to their horror that they were all boys and old men. Every Southern man of fighting age was with Hood or Lee.

Sherman's "bummers" were on their way, advancing in a swath sixty miles wide, feasting on hams and sweet potatoes that no railroad could take to Richmond, raiding the smoke houses, digging up fresh "graves" that concealed buried provisions, not a body, feeding oats to their horses out of drawers from heirloom dressers, singing, hollering, hooting:

Hurrah! hurrah!
We bring the Jubilee.
Hurrah! hurrah!
The flag that makes you free.
So we sang the chorus from Atlanta to the sea,
While we were marching through Georgia.

On they went in easy fifteen-mile marches a day, past the hate and scorn in blue eyes, followed by a ten-mile long column of freed, ecstatic negroes. Sherman wrote to Washington: " . . . *they call me vandal, barbarian, a monster. All I can pretend to say is, on earth as it is in heaven, men must submit to some arbiter. I would not subjugate the South but I would make every citizen of the land obey the common law— . . . to be sure I make war vindictively; war is war and you can make nothing else of it."*

Because he was not one of those who were disappearing almost incommunicado on their junket to the sea, Alonzo Harding continued to receive his mail. Their contents lagged far behind the swift movement of events around him.

[Harding] Nov 6th 1864

Alonzo your letter to Rose of the 18th was received allso to Newton verry sorry to hear of your reverse fortune but glad to hear it is no worse than it is yet it is uncertain what a day may bring fourth life is so uncertain death is sure to come sooner or later but when and in what way we can not tell we may bee well today and ded tomorrow we are all well at present . . . I am still living alone . . . Newton . . . is now hired to Lovett $20 per month doing better it takes me a good deal of my time to cook and do my chores. I am still working what I can at my machinery . . . I am not certain if I can sell my horses I shall go to Ohio this winter you rote me you had instructed cartwright to settle the mortgage on the house the rent I expect will not do it by that time he will probably have to use some of your other money to take it up have you done anything about exchanging part of the lot to make it square If I can arange things here in canada so that I can leave I think I shall seek some place for business in the states soon What kind of a country is it whare you have been for a person not subject to military duty to do business in I think you had not better keep much of your means you get with you more than you kneed from time to time as you are so subject to loos every thing and if you live to get through the war you may want what you have and if you get in difficuilty and destitute you may get it sent to you but I hope you will have better luck for the futer I think Newton while he can get 20$ per month and bord himself he had better stick with it as Canada money is worth more than greenbacks I some times think I will go over to Kentucky this winter and see Silas and see if thare is any thing to do in the shape of business in that country farewell

from your effectionate Father
Enos [Harding]

My Dearest Brother

I cannot tell you how glad I was last Friday morning to rec. a letter from you. I am very sorry that you were taken and obliged to undergo such hardships but I am thankful you were not obliged to remain in a southern prison as some have for months. I wish you could come home. Can't you get a furlough—you once said you could. It would be so much better, now the cold, rainy weather is coming on, if you could come North if only for a few weeks. . . . I am still at work very steady. I have acted upon your suggestion and allowed myself $8.00 for board $2.00 for clothes $1.00 for pleasure [tobacco included] and $.50 for other unavoidable expenses per mo. and I will try to keep within these bounds.

How are we going to settle the account between us. Will you let it go on the money I payed on the Cleveland property or shall I give you my note for it. Probably we better come to some definate understanding as soon as possible. . . . There is to be a wedding here shortly and I will have the pleasure of standing up with the couple, . . . Father is well and working away at his astronomy as usual . . .

Your aff. Brother   Newton

Gobles Corners Nov 17th 64

Mr Dear Brother

. . . I have heard there is some prospect of a General exchange of prisoners taking place . . . What a hard time you had of it among those rebels tis well it did not last long or you could not have survived it. I was very anxious to hear from you for we had heard of the capture of Dalton and wondered what had become of you. It was such a relief to get your letter. You must have been glad to get back to Chattanooga again. Were you clothed up again by Government? and how are your feet? If you can get a rest for a few months it will not be so bad after all, being taken prisoner. If you come to Cleveland I suppose you will come home and make us a visit. I hope so. Well Election is over and Lincoln is President I suppose it will not make much difference in the war. How I wish it might cease. Just now is an interesting time in Canadian Politics. A Delegation of all the Provinces have been in Session some time, [and are through now] conferring about the Union of all the Provinces, both Canadas New Brunswick Nova Scotia Newfoundland and Prince Edward's Island under one chief Governor. The result will not be made public till each individual Legislature has been confered with. Various names have been proposed for the New Confederation. Arcadia, Acadia, Stadacona, New Britain, Britannica, Borelia, Tuponia, Quebec and Canada, are among those proposed. I wish you could get papers. . . .

*Father is keeping house, . . . Newton boards with Father. I guess they get
a little lonely some times. I wish I was nearer so I could help them some
times. We are all unusually well. Eva sends Uncle Alonzo a kiss and
wants to write a little letter, but there is not much time this morning. . . .
I have written to Uncle Silas. . . . I feel much obliged to you for your
regularity in writing me. Good Bye My Brother*

As Ever

Your Loving Sister

Rose

Tuponia, Borelia, Arcadia, or whatever name might be chosen if the
union of five Canadian provinces went through were far from Alonzo's
mind at the moment. If Roseltha only knew how hard it was to be
regular in writing! Sherman's men might be rollicking unmolested to the
sea but Thomas's men, left behind to prevent Hood from reaching Lee,
had little time for singing. Thomas could hardly gather together the
scattered regiments that were supposed to be under his command. One of
his three corps had to come by rail from Missouri and would not reach
him till November 30. Sherman could have left behind at least 12,000 of
his 60,000 bummers to give Thomas the numbers necessary to move
immediately against the mercurial Hood but Sherman hadn't. The Rock
of Chickamauga would have to prove his mettle alone.

Hood had plenty of kick yet, even though his men were now refusing
to fight without breastworks. Hood grumbled about them, saying that
cautious Joe Johnston had destroyed the old get-up-and-go that had
characterized the Southern soldier. As he circled around, edging towards
Tennessee, he feared that Sherman might abandon his southward march
and return to bolster Thomas.

Thomas sent Scholfield towards the Georgia border to delay the
enemy's advance. By a fast flanking movement Hood moved to
Scholfield's rear and set his men on the top of a hill, a victory move if
there ever was one.

"Look at the Rebs there. What do you think the general will do?" said
Fitzgerald to Alonzo as they were allowed a brief rest.

"I hope he gets us out of here darn fast," Alonzo wheezed. Young as he
was, he was exhausted.

"He has us trapped, same as Dalton. Better prepare to meet Thy
Maker."

"Not for a while yet. Not as long as I have this dee-licious salt pork
and this superb hardtack to keep me going."

"Ugh," said Joe, "that would gag a maggot on a gut wagon."

"If Hood hasn't come on us by now, I'm beginning to think he doesn't intend to. Look, they're starting to light their fires and rest."

"Holy mackerel, I think you're right. Maybe we can roast our pork at one of them, they're so close."

Whatever possessed Hood, gambler Hood, to rest his men at that moment? He had this Northern army within his grasp. There it was, at arm's length. He rested his men. Had he ordered them into battle again, it would not have been the first time a general had pushed exhausted men into action trusting to the adrenalin of desperation to see them through. He let his men rest, and they settled down to eat and sleep.

When the Northerners realized that fate had played into their hands, down the lines the order passed from one officer to the next—keep quiet and get moving. All that night the Union army, eleven miles long, marched past the Rebel fires, running when they could, eating on the run, walking to catch their breath, but never stopping. Never a Rebel stopped their eerie march through the darkness. Never an order to fire.

"The sun's coming up. Do you think we're in the clear?"

"I think we're safe. The Rebs are behind us and we'll soon be in Nashville where it's fortified. Hood muffed his chance to get us."

Alonzo was wrong. Hood's main army was behind them but if the infantry was not moving, Nathan Forrest and the cavalry were. Nathan Bedford Forrest, the fanatic who would later found the Ku Klux Klan. Nathan Forrest, superb cavalry man.

"Look out, here they come. Unlimber the guns," came the shout. The infantry fixed bayonets. The battery primed its guns.

What chance had cavalrymen coming at full speed against artillery at close range. If he could have, Alonzo would have closed his eyes to what was happening. A head fell off one side of a horse and the body on the other. The horse ran around nickering for its master, then it too fell, screaming its agony. A rider fell from his seat with his foot caught in one stirrup, was dragged and trampled to death. Wounded horses fell on their riders. Blood and slaughter till Forrest was driven off with what remained of his gallant contingent.

Swiftly the battery loaded the caissons again and kept on to Franklin on the south branch of the Harpeth River. They could not cross to safety for the Rebs had burned the bridge. They would have to build a new one before men or guns could cross.

"Wonder if Hood'll follow, or wait a bit?"

"I think he'll come fast. He let us go last night, God knows why, but he won't let it happen again."

274

The two friends were right. Hood, haggard with sleeplessness, was coming fast, not even waiting for his artillery to catch up with him. He had to prevent Scholfield from joining Thomas. Scholfield barely had time to dig in his men in front of the river when Hood's army flowed through a gap in the hills to the plain around Franklin. There he faced a hastily constructed long crescent of trenches and barricades, its convex side facing him.

It was four o'clock in the afternoon. The sun shone in a clear blue autumn sky. Rank on rank, in perfect order, 18,000 Confederate infantrymen were advancing. If they defeated the Yanks now, it would be on to Kentucky and Richmond and well the Yanks knew it. They had to stop Hood.

But could they? Hood broke right through the centre of their line. The Rebel yell could have been heard in Washington. "Fill the Gap," came the shout, and the Ohio troops with the Wisconsin and Kentucky poured over. "Give 'em hell, boys, give 'em hell." They fought with bullets, with bayonets, with clubbed muskets, with fists.

They gave them hell. Six thousand Confederates were slain in the most desperate hand-to-hand fight in the whole war. Utterly beaten as darkness fell, the last ones begged, "Don't shoot, Yanks, for God Almighty's sake, don't shoot." Among five generals who lay dead after this great Northern victory at Franklin were negro-hating Cleburne and States Rights Gist.

At midnight the engineers finished the bridge and the dog-tired Union troops marched across, leaving two thousand casualties, but not their guns and wagons. All the rest of the night they marched, almost walking in their sleep, for it was their second sleepless night and a battle between. They reached Nashville, eighteen miles away, before they stopped— Nashville with its forts and fortifications, for it had been in Union hands for three years. Nashville with hot coffee, food and sleep. Nashville and Thomas's army.

"Lieutenant John Burdick was killed," said Alonzo when he awoke from his exhausted sleep.

"So were Jacob Bender and Sam Braine and Pearson Sorter," answered Joe. "Jake and Pearson were twenty-one, same as us, and Pearson only enlisted in the 20th Ohio the end of August."

"Somebody from Cleveland said that Peter Graff who was taken after Chickamauga last year died at Andersonville in September. Well, I have to write home." Alonzo tore a page of lined paper from a record book. Who knew—if Hood came upon them again, it might be his last letter.

In camp two miles from Nashville
Dec. 4th, 1864

My dear Sister

I should have written sooner but it has been impossible. We have been moving from place to place and building breastworks as well as fighting occasionally so that I have had no time to do anything. I expected when I wrote to you last that I should soon go north, but the Government would not recognize our parole so we were ordered to report for duty, in the meantime the Battery had left Chattanooga and I started for the Battery on the 30th of October and joined it at Pulaski on the 6th of November where we remained till the 23rd when Hood flanked us and our army had to evacuate the town. We marched to Columbia where we fought them three days. There was no very heavy fighting chiefly artillery duelling. Again Hood forced us to move further north as far as Franklin where we arrived on the 30th at noon and our Generals determined to make a stand, and threw up breastworks, at four o'clock the Rebs came on to us in full force and there ensued one of the hardest fought battles for the time it lasted there has been since the war commenced. The rebs seemed determined to conquer or die they made thirteen desperate charges, several times they planted their colors within ten feet of our cannon and our men would knock them down with their muskets or the artillerymen with their sponge staffs or handspikes. Our Battery was in the centre of the very hottest of the fight we lost nearly half of our men and came out of the battle commanded by a sargeant, I never dreamed that men could fight with such desperation. I never expected to come out alive but was fortunate, I was struck twice once in the cheek the ball just grazed my face and cut through the skin it bled freely but did not amount to much, and once in the hip the ball cut through my pants drawers and shirt and made a slight wound but not enough but what I attend to my duty. About ten o'clock the rebs withdrew and our army started for Nashville bringing the wounded along but the dead were left lying. I never realized what a battle was, the roar of musketry and thunder of artillery was deafning, it was full as dark ten minutes after the battle commenced as when it ceased. the only way we could tell when night come was by the stars. Hood is now within four miles of us but I do not think he will venture to attack this place he got whipped too bad at Franklin. I can form no idea what our loss was but it was heavy and the rebs must have lost four times as much as ours the ground was covered as far as I could see with their dead. I will write again in a few days when I have a better chance and give you full particulars.

Your brother   Alonzo

Direct to Chattanooga as before. Write soon, Kind wishes to all

When death thins the ranks, promotions come quickly. The next letter
he wrote had the proud return address—Lieut. Alonzo (Harding),
Bat. D., U.S.C. Art (Heavy), Nashville, Tenn. He was now a white officer
over coloured troops. He wrote his acceptance of the commission on a
half sheet of paper:

> 20th Battery O V A Nashville Tenn.
> `   Dec. 17th 64
>
> *I have the honor to acknowledge the receipt of an appointment as 2nd
> Lieut. in 9th U S C Art [Heavy] and accept same.*
>
> *I am [21] years of age, was born in the town of Blenheim Canada West
> and my present residence is 20th Battery O V A*
>
> *I am very respectfully*
> > *Your Obt. Servt.*
> > *Alonzo [Harding] Corp.*
> > *20th Battery O V A*
>
> *To Maj. E. Grosskopff*
> *Comdg 9th U.S.C. Art. Heavy*
> * and 20th Battery O V A*

"I made it. I'm an officer," he said triumphantly to his friend Joe
Fitzgerald. "It'll soon be your turn."

Hood had indeed been whipped bad at Franklin but he was not yet
finished. Is he to be castigated or admired for his determination? He dug
trenches facing the strong Union line around Nashville and set siege to it.
Would Thomas attack or would he suffer the siege? General Grant at
Petersburg, still in siege position himself, was not given to jitters but
when he heard that Hood was still on the offensive he now came close to
it. He bombarded Thomas with orders, demanding that he attack Hood
at once. Move, move, move, he commanded.

Thomas was not ready to attack. Square of body and square of jaw, he
let the messages roll off him. He sat grimly waiting for the strategic
moment to move. Again Grant sizzled the wires. If Hood spirited himself
away some night, Grant could see all of his commander-in-chief war
plans shot to pieces. He was smoking twenty cigars a day now. He was
holding Lee immobile, waiting for Sherman to get to the sea and turn
north up the coast to join him. The last thing Grant wanted was for
Hood to get on the loose into Kentucky. What was going on in
Nashville? Still Thomas refused to budge for his army was not ready.

It began to rain. The rain turned to sleet, the sleet to ice. Thomas's men looked at each other in their tents, shivered, slipped and slid if they went outside. Under their frozen crust the guns were lumpy and still.

Grant could stand it no longer. He dispatched Major-General John Logan to relieve Thomas of his command. Grant himself went to Washington and from there he intended to entrain for Nashville to oust a general who suddenly refused to fight. Before either Logan or Grant arrived, the four day's ice began to melt. On the night of December 13, George H. Thomas gave the order that the attack would begin the next day. "Call me at five in the morning," he said as he went to bed.

The commander could sleep till five but the men were ordered up at four. In the cold muddy December dark they ate breakfast. The night before, one hundred rounds of ammunition and two day's rations had been issued to 55,000 Union men. The companies fell in. The colonels sat on their horses in front of their divisions. They dismounted, bowed their heads, and the chaplains asked the blessing of the God on whom their lives depended. Then they all moved off in the chilling fog, leaving their tents standing. There would be no retreat. This battle would settle the fate of the war in the west. They had to win and those who were left would have standing tents to return to.

The IVth Corps, the XXIII, XVI, and Alonzo Harding's XVII and Wilson's cavalry all moved out, passing at times some companies already standing with stacked arms, some beside flagstones taken from a garden and tilted up for protection, some eating jam and jelly taken from a cellar. The hogs in the yards were too weak to squeal unless they leaned against a fence.

A brigade of five negro regiments was assigned to lead the feinting movement on Hood's right flank that was to open the assault and trick Hood into thinking that the major attack was to be concentrated there. General George H. Thomas was a Virginian but he was putting his faith in eight negro regiments to fight valiantly for their cause, in spite of opposition to his decision. A small black imp who had readied an officer's breakfast of hardtack, beans and sugarless coffee called him with a flourish, "Suh, de feast awaits."

All day the fighting raged. A sergeant was following his captain. A bullet lifted the captain's coat and pierced the sergeant's heart. Another bullet severed a lieutenant's shoulder strap. He shrugged. "Who knows, the next might go through my head," and it did. The minié bullets flew around like angry hornets, emissaries of the god of battles.

Behind the smoking Napoleons Alonzo and Joe laboured and ducked, too busy to feel fear, yelling, shouting, hollering, cursing with words that they never would have believed would sully their tongues. They were pushed back, they moved forwards, they gained a little ground. All day they fought till the cold wet dark fell and they were told to remain at their posts. Hood had been pushed back six miles but he was still there.

In the dark they counted their companions in the battery. Astonishingly, none were even hurt. What good angel had protected them while all around were perishing? "Let's not think about it," said Joe, "tomorrow's coming." And another, as he tried to make himself comfortable in the mud, improvised grimly:

> Now I lay me down to sleep
> In mud that's fifty fathoms deep.
> If I should die before I wake
> Just hunt me out with an oyster rake.

Dawn, and Hood obstinately began a second day of fighting. Again the desperate charges, the hand-to-hand fighting, the courage and the carnage. One huge black colour bearer in the 4th Louisiana waved his standard to bring his fellows forward till he fell, pierced by a Southern bullet. A diminutive drummer, "I can drum right good, suh, I learned it in the Firty-fird Gawja," beat them on. His drum straps had been shortened so his drum would not drag on the ground. On the Southern side the officers sneered, "The Yanks must have made the niggers drunk to get them to fight like that."

Alonzo shoved another shell into their gun. He heard a cry above the turmoil. He looked around to see blood streaming down Joe's face. He dropped the shot he was about to ram in after the shell, and ran to him.

"Back to your place," yelled Lieutenant Backus but Alonzo ignored him. This was his friend who was hurt and bleeding, and had not his friend Mose helped him back at Antietam when he needed it? "Are you hurt bad?"

Joe staggered, holding both hands to his head. "I can't see for the blood."

Alonzo took a rag from his pocket. "Sit down. Let me look." He wiped Joe's eyes. "Hold your head back." Then he saw the cut just above the hair line. He remembered that his brother Jasper had been hit with a board that fell out of a tree when they were building a tree house. The blood had run all over his face in a frightening stream but when Harriet had washed him it was only a small cut.

"It's not deep, Joe. You'll be all right. Head wounds always bleed a lot. Rest a bit behind the emplacement." He threw his blanket over his friend.

"Harding, get back on the job," shouted the lieutenant. And Alonzo returned to his gun.

The fighting raged till dark when finally the Union forces broke through the Rebel lines and planted their colours the whole length of the

279

Confederate trenches. Hood was in full retreat down the Franklin turnpike, his only route of escape. It was the only time in four years of war, said the sorrowing commander, when a Southern army fled a field of battle. The Union had lost 387 killed and 2,558 wounded compared with 4,462 Confederates killed and wounded and 13,000 prisoners. Hood's army had been effectively destroyed. After Nashville only 9,000 men gathered around him.

"Dang it to hell," exulted Thomas, "didn't I tell you we could lick them?" Then his face sobered as he looked at the negro dead, "And didn't I tell you that the negro could fight?" It was cold comfort for those who had died to prove it.

The news of the victory reached Grant in Washington at Willard's Hotel. "I won't be going to Nashville now," he said with satisfaction and ordered the guns at Richmond to fire a 200-gun salute, double the usual victory signal.

Alonzo wrote home. "I won't get home for a while yet, but I like being a lieutenant at $75 dollars a month."

Hood was out of the picture and on December 17 Sherman reached Savannah. "A Christmas present for the nation," he commented.

Only Lee remained to be finished off and President Jefferson Davis would not concede peace unless the sovereignty of the Confederacy was acknowledged. This the Union and the blood of many men refused. Sherman's men left Savannah to march to join Grant's army, still besieging Richmond at Petersburg. It had taken a long time for John Brown's soul to reach the sea, and Richmond had still to fall.

Chapter 22

With Malice Towards None

Lieutenant Alonzo Harding was again in charge of the commissary—no small task since marauding bands were active all around Nashville in spite of Hood's defeat. Joe was now a lieutenant too. He came in waving his appointment paper in front of Alonzo and the two whooped with pride. "All right, cut the cackle and let's get to work."

Alonzo's black soldiers still needed guidance but the fame of their exploits in the recent two battles had reached Canada.

Dec 28th 1864

My Dear Brother

I received your letter yesterday and although hardly strong enough yet to do so I must answer it to-day. I am so glad and thankful to hear from you in health and safety. I have read of the fighting about Nashville and supposed you would be in it all; and had tried to make up my mind to the worst that might happen. It was a great relief to get a letter in your own handwriting. I am glad too the North are being successful and hope it may be the beginning of still greater victories and that the end of this war may not be far distant. Now I must tell you of something else. We have a little girl baby. A precious tiny thing that we of course think a great deal of. We have named her "Clara Emma." She is two days old and begins to grow finely. Eva is very much delighted with her little sister.

There has been a good deal of excitement and anxiety the last few weeks lest the peace of Canada should be seriously disturbed; and warlike preparations have been going on, which we seriously hope may be the means of preventing instead of causing trouble. 30 Companies of Volunteers have been called into Service. Newton Goble and our Newton have both gone. Some 25 or 30 went from Princeton 12 from [Harding]

281

*and a good many from Woodstock. They have gone somewhere below
Montreal, and we believe the "Regulars" are to be stationed at various
points along the lines to prevent the incursions or excursions of lawless
men. There is a reward offered for the apprehension of the St. Albans
raiders. I hope they may be taken. We have not heard from the boys yet.
They left Woodstock last Monday. They will write as soon as they reach
their destination. They are to get $18 per month and found, better than
many of them can do at home. If they are only careful they can save
something. I am very, very glad at your improved prospects. I am sure it
is better to be an officer over coloured men than only a private in many
ways, but best of all if you can get a discharge, sometime and leave of
absence to make a visit home, and then you get so much more pay,
besides the honour of promotion, but I dont think so much of all this if it
only please "The Great Ruler" to keep you in safety and bring you to rest
in hope of an inheritance beyond these scenes of earth's unrest. I see by
our papers that one of the most brilliant charges during the last fighting
was made by the coloured regiments. If so you need not be ashamed of
your command. Father was here to dinner last Sunday [Christmas] he is
all alone, now in [Harding] . . . How did you spend Christmas? May you
have a Happy New Year My Dear Brother. I must conclude, my paper
and strength both fail. Write soon. May God bless you.*

Ever Your Sister
Rose

*. . . I received your photograph . . . I really never thought you were so
ancient looking. Its that mustache.*

Though the negro had proved his worth at Franklin and Nashville,
many were still technically slaves. The previous June, 1864, Congress had
finally repealed the Fugitive Slave Law, yet after the capture of Dalton,
negroes had been sent south again to their former masters. Not till
January 30, 1865, would Congress ratify the bill that declared all slaves
free. For the first time since the nation's founding all Americans, on
paper, were free. The Toronto *Globe* celebrated the occasion with an
editorial: "Four million men will cease to be chattels and attain the
dignity of human beings."

Still the war continued. Joe Johnston, so recently removed himself,
had replaced Hood after Nashville. Grant had still not captured
Richmond. Lee left his army headquarters in front of Petersburg and told
Davis and his cabinet that his army needed food. They still refused to
listen to Lee, or to a peace delegation from the North that would not
include in its proposed terms the independence of the South. Lincoln
called for three hundred thousand volunteers and the hated draft was still

in force. Some Canadians went as paid substitutes. Canada continued to guard its border.

LaPrairie C.E. Jan 26th 1865

Dear Brother

You will be surprised to hear from me under the present circumstances. There was a call for Volunteers to go to the Frontier and I was the first one to leave [Harding]. We were not forced to go but volunteered our term of service ends on the first of May next when I suppose the militia will be called out and take our places. There has been a ballot and almost all who remained at home were drafted to serve in the Militia but I was not. I am in No 1 company of the 3rd Administrative Batalion of Canadian Vol Rifles stationed at La Prairie C.E. nine miles south of Montreal on the south side of the River St. Lawrence and some thirty miles from the lines. Our duty is not hard and although some grumble a great deal I think we have good times the only trouble is the inhabitants cannot speak English and we cannot speak French so when we want any thing we are obliged to make signs or if this wont do get an interpreter or do without the article. Our drill and duty consists of Company drill in the morning and Battallion drill in the afternoon of one hour each and twenty four hours guard duty about every five days and patroll about every five days.

The cause of this move is to put a stop to the raids which are conducted by Southern sympathisers for the purpose of bringing disturbances between the two government which would be the most effictual way of assisting the South. There are bright prospects now for a settlement of the war and it is to be hoped it will be soon ended for I am sure every one is hartily sick of it.

Newton Goble is here and Sile Dawson . . . It is extremely cold here the river being frozen over forming a beautiful bridge to Montreal nine miles below. I am glad you have been promoted it will be better every way. I cannot write anymore now as it is about tattoo when we are all to "turn in" putting lights out. Write very soon while I remain your

aff. Brother
Newton

Roseltha now had two soldier brothers to write to.

Feb. 28th 1865

My dear Brother Newton

. . . I made a little cake for you and a little cushion. . . . We have no girl and I have been very busy. . . . I was fearful your cold might settle in

your lungs. . . . Jasper took the box to Princeton today. . . . It will only go by Express as far as Montreal and be forwarded from there. We have no map of Railroads in C.E. and could not make out the name. Marked it Ver Cent R.R. . . . Try to be patient my Brother do your duty faithfully and all will end well. Make your Motto always "Duty before pleasure." How much are you saving of your pay? I received the $5 all right and will keep it safe for you. . . . Adopt Alonzo's plan of just spending so much and no more however great the temptation may be. Dr. Bent's son has sent home $12 after supplying himself with clothing and I believe one of Mr. Horton's boys has sent home $20 . . . Last night was the Grand Annual Ball at Princeton. We did not attend. . . . How do you get your washing done?
. . . As ever

> *Your affectionate Sister*
> *Rose*

Then Corporal Newton Harding wrote to Lieutenant Alonzo Harding from Company No. 1, 3rd Adm. Battalion, Phillipsburg, C.E., on March 3, 1865:

"We have moved from La Prairie to this place 1½ miles from the lines and are having good times not much to do and fifty cents per day and board. We are billeted in hotels and private houses and live on the fat of the land. You can imagine my disappointment better than I can describe it, on receiving your letter learning my loss in not getting the situation you spoke of. I will be clear May 1st and then I think I shall go immediately to the U.S. . . . I was a fool for coming here at all for I could make as much if not more at home and besides be free. . . . I am trying to save a little money but there is so many things to eat it up. They require us to have a full regular Kit which they issue to us and take it out of our pay. Then we furnish our own underclothes, socks, boots, stocks, forage caps, oil, blacking to black our accutrements every day, etc. which counts up fast besides many unnecessaries which I am going to dispence with for they do not pay except out of pocket.
Father, I believe is till in [Harding] doing nothing it appears that he cannot get anything any more . . . There is quite a quantity of U.S. troops just across the lines among them are a detachment of the 14th U.S. regulars. The passport system is in full force again and creates some little excitement. . . .

> *I remain Your aff. Brother*
> *Newton*

The day after Newton wrote to Alonzo, President Lincoln's second inaugural took place. The day opened with heavy rain and Pennsylvania awash with mud, but just in time the sun emerged so that Lincoln could take his oath in front of the great crowd assembled there. Then he spoke:

"... One eighth of the whole population was colored slaves ... localized in the southern part. ... Fondly do we hope, fervently do we pray, that this mighty scourge of war may speedily pass away. Yet, if God will it continue until all the wealth piled by the bondsman's two hundred and fifty years of unrequited toil shall be sunk, and until every drop of blood drawn with the lash shall be paid by another drawn with the sword, as was said three thousand years ago, so still it must be said, "The judgments of the Lord are true and righteous altogether."

With malice toward none, with charity for all, with firmness in the right as God gives us to see the right, let us strive on to finish the work we are in, to bind up the nation's wounds, to care for him who shall have borne the battle and for his widow and his orphan, to do all which may achieve and cherish a just and lasting peace among ourselves and with all nations."

Never was there such a mixture of implacability and tolerance. Some of his listeners shed a tear, some spat. Could Lincoln hold in check those who wanted to wreak vengeance on the South as soon as Richmond fell? How much longer was Grant going to sit in front of Richmond whittling, smoking? The men he was pitted against were men who still sang:

I hate the Yankee nation and everything they do.
I hate the Declaration of Independence too;
I hate the glorious Union, 'tis dripping with our blood."
I hate the striped banner. I fought it all I could.

As Grant waited for the strategic moment to move against Lee, and Lee contemplated trying to burst out and join Joe Johnston who was moving into North Carolina to stop Sherman's advance northward, Alonzo Harding fell ill in Nashville. As the fever mounted he thought with anguish of Alfred's death from smallpox just two years before. Mother, Daniel, Jasper, Alfred. Will I be next? He was moved to the hospital as the spots broke out. When he had some strength he read Rose's recent letter.

Gobles Corners March 6
"... I received your letter saying you had the promise of a furlough of 20 days in Feb. ... We are all well except Nellie. She had a tumour taken from her side in Jan. This operation was very severe. ... Newton ... moved from La Prairie to Phillipsburg two miles from the Vermont line. Newton said he had been sitting with his right leg in Vermont and the left*

285

one in Canada and both Lance Corporals. Do the duty of Corporals and get the pay of privates but are next for promotions . . . I guess they get the pay of Privates and spend as officers. . . . sent $5 in his last letter . . . Baby Clara was very sick a few weeks ago, but is well now and grows nicely. . . . We hear smallpox is in Kingsville. Heman was in Houghton last Sun. he stopped at Mr. Bridgeman's where Daniel boarded when he taught school seven yrs. ago this winter . . . Goodnight. May angels guard you.

The doctor came in. "You're over the worst. You'll be better from now on." Alonzo grinned weakly. Maybe tomorrow my head will stop aching.

On the evening of March 23 outside Richmond, General Grant too suffered from a splitting headache. The policy of attrition that was wearing down Lee had cost him 72,000 men. If it takes all summer, he muttered, I'll get him, I'll crack him, I'll crumble him, but he wanted it to end sooner and at last had issued orders for all to make ready for a great assault.

If Davis and Lee would not face reality, the common soldier, more expedient, knew the end was near. One night recently an officer checking the Confederate trenches found them strangely empty. Johnny Reb was in the Union trenches opposite his, playing cards with Billy Yank.

So Grant nursed his headache and wished that whoever was playing the out-of-tune piano on the first floor would stop banging on it because every note vibrated painfully through his noggin. What if there was something wrong with his preparations? Sheridan and Sherman were near enough for support and the President himself had visited the front so the men could say they had seen the President himself.

As Grant added more hot water to his footbath, reports were brought to him that all sectors of his elongated front were ready for the grand push. His headache vanished. The waiting was over. Morning could not come soon enough.

He attacked first on the left flank, then on the right, then he broke through the middle. Lee retreated first into Petersburg, then into Richmond. On April 2, Davis fled from the city. On April 3, Lee withdrew from Richmond.

A regiment of negroes was first into the fallen capital. Then Abraham Lincoln, the President of the United States of America, drove through the streets, the lines on his haggard face smoothing out. Richmond was no longer the capital of the Confederate States of America. Erstwhile

President Jefferson Davis was fleeing for his life and Lee had led his tattered hungry army to Appomattox, about forty miles southwest of the evacuated city.

In a modest farmhouse at Appomattox there lived a man named Wilmer McLean. Four years before, Wilmer McLean had left his farm at Bull Run to get away from the war, because his house had been used as army headquarters and his barn as a hospital for the first fresh-faced young men wounded at Manassas. Four years later, with grizzled veterans of two armies around him, he and his house were to witness the end.

When at last Lee considered further resistance useless, he went upstairs in McLean's farmhouse, put on a fresh uniform complete with hat, sash and ornate dress sword, and sent a white towel as a flag of surrender to Lieutenant-General Ulysses S. Grant in his battle-worn private's clothes with a Lieutenant-General's tabs tacked on the shoulders.

Grant was ready with peace terms. Merciless in war, he was not vindictive in peace. The Southerners could keep their horses since they were needed to plough the springtime furrows for a harvest to feed a devastated people. Officers could keep their swords. The terms included no independence for the South, no separate government for states that were separate no longer.

Lee asked for 25,000 rations for his hungry men. Till they could be provided, Union men shared the rations in their haversacks with their recent enemies. The generals shook hands. Lee mounted his good horse Traveller, iron gray, with black mane and tail and an obedient mouth, sixteen hands high, said a sad farewell to the men who had served him and the cause through thick and thin, and cantered away into civilian life.

Grant patted his horse Cincinatti, then boarded the cars for Washington where Secessionists still nursed their hatred for the President who had never wavered in his resolve to settle the questions of states' rights and black freedom once and for all.

When Alonzo was beginning to feel better he received another letter from home, written two days before the meeting at Appomattox had ended the war.

Gobles Corners April 7, 1865

My dear Brother
... The water has been very high and a good deal of damage has been done to bridges etc. ... Newton has been promoted to full corporal and gets ten cents more per day. He sent $1 making 49 he had sent since he went there ... Father was over three days ago ... People here think Richmond has fallen and the war will soon close. Canadian politics and

affairs seem unsettled . . . I wish you would send me when you write a nice lock of your hair. I am going to have some hair flowers made. . . .

Ever your loving Sister
Rose

It was a nice, newsy letter designed to make a soldier feel comfortable.

Yes, Richmond had fallen and every one could relax. Late in the afternoon of Friday, April 14, President Lincoln walked from the War Department to the White House to dine before going to the theatre as a little celebration over Lee's surrender. At Ford's Theatre on Tenth Street the play that night was a comedy, *Our American Cousin,* starring Miss Laura Keen.

Lincoln was late, for his afternoon callers had been numerous and the play had begun as he entered the presidential box. As there were empty seats in the box, his bodyguard left his post outside the door and sat inside where he could join in the laughter, which was very gay tonight for the double occasion of a comedy and a victory celebration.

There was one who was not relaxed. Actor John Booth, who knew the theatre well and who was known to the employees, was coming stealthily up the stairs. He reached the unprotected door. Throwing it open, he fired pointblank at the President, and in the thunderstruck confusion over what had happened, he jumped to the stage and made his getaway before those backstage knew what had taken place.

They carried the President across the street to an obscure boarding-house and there died the man who had said, "Whenever I hear any one arguing for slavery, I have a strong impulse to see it tried on him personally."

Gobles Corners April 28th 1865

My dear Brother

I received your letter this morning . . . I felt sure that if you were able you would write and so I imagined all sorts of unpleasant things; and dreamed about you at night and all such nonsense. Did you have that terrible disease very bad? and did you have good care and medicinal attendance? . . . The murder of the President and the attempted murder of Secretary Seward and others excited a great deal of attention here and still continues to do so. Last Wednesday the Funereal day in Washington was observed throughout Canada. Business was suspended from 12 till 2 and funereal services were held in all the towns and cities. Churches draped in mourning and sorrow felt generally. That so good and honest a man should fall is untimely; and in so dreadful a manner. I hope the strong sympathy expressed by Canada in this their time of grief may be a means of binding the two nations together in a common brotherhood. God grant these sad events may not be the means of perpetuating the war. . . . The Volunteers passed here to-day on their way to Woodstock. We saw Newton and Newton G. on. . . . Newton G. intends going to the Military School in Hamilton while he is home and if he gets a certificate will get a Commission when they return. Father was here last Sunday night. Left Monday morning for he hardly knew where was going to Walsingham and then West. He is trying to sell his horses and carriage, thought some of going to Michigan if he could not sell them in Canada; and maybe going to Kentucky and perhaps to Nashville to find you. . . . There is some Small Pox here this spring. One man in Brantford died and some at Princeton have it, But not severely I believe. . . . May you be spared to return in safety . . .

Rose

All over the States came cries for vengeance against the South. How frail was the thought of "malice towards none" in the midst of the hysteria, and not only the Confederates might bear the brunt. Secretary of War Edwin Stanton claimed that the assassination plot had been hatched in Canada. Though Secretary of War Frederick Seward lay recovering from an assassination attempt on the same night that the President died, no one had forgotten that he figured the annexation of Canada would compensate the North for the losses sustained in the war with the South. How adequate for the crisis would be the new President Andrew Johnson? Would the confederation of five Canadian provinces bring strength and cohesion to that somewhat uneasy land?

Chapter 23

Mustered Out

A little shaky, Alonzo returned to his work in the commissary. The war was winding down but an army of a million men could not be puffed out of existence as easily as a candle. Lincoln, the kingpin, was gone, and who knew what direction the reconstruction period would take—revenge or acquiescence. "Mr. Stanton," Lincoln had once said, "if you have an elephant by the foot you had best let him go." How far would his wisdom be accepted?

Alonzo and Joe talked as they kept track of barrels of flour and sides of meat.

"Lincoln's funeral train has left Washington. It will be going through Cleveland on its way to Springfield. There's a large portrait of Lincoln mounted on the cow-catcher."

"Fighting Joe Johnston surrendered at Greensboro."

"Jeff Davis is in chains."

"They shot Booth."

"Sherman's marching his men to Washington for the Grand Review. They say that some corps commanders have wagers who'll get there first."

"They should be sending them by train. They'll drop dead in Virginia's heat."

"There's to be a Grand Review on May 24th in Washington. Wish we could be home for the Queen's Birthday or else in Washington to see the review."

For the great day of the Grand Review Washington replaced its black mourning crepe with the red, white and blue bunting of peace at last. Miles deep around the city camp fires leaped red and shining and house after house in the city filled its windows with candle flames of happiness. In brilliant sunshine President Johnson and Lieutenant-General Grant

291

took their places on the reviewing stand. Around the corner of the Capitol came Sheridan's cavalry, filling Pennsylvania Avenue with the sound of the crisp clop of hooves. The Ninth Corps, the Fifth, the Second, sixty men abreast, followed with military precision, tight-fitting coats buttoned high, bayonets bright in the sun. The flags of the Army of the Potomac had flown at Bull Run, Antietam, the Wilderness, Gettysburg and on to Appomattox. Tramp, tramp, tramp the boys are marching.

On the second day it was the turn of Sherman's men, the Seventh, the Fifteenth, the Twentieth, the Fourteenth Corps, rangy westerners in loose blouses, slouch hats and wornout shoes. Their tattered flags had led them through Vicksburg, Chattanooga, Atlanta and Nashville. As W.T. Sherman with his grizzled red beard rode by, the band played "Marching Through Georgia." When he took his place on the reviewing stand and Secretary of War Stanton extended his hand, Sherman flushed and turned away. He could not forget the times he had asked for more support and been refused.

When Johnny comes marching home again, hurrah, hurrah,
The men will cheer, the boys will shout,
The ladies they will all turn out,
And we'll all feel gay when Johnny comes marching home . . .
—all but the million dead.

At the end of two days of forgetfulness, the bivouac fires burned down, the bands packed up their instruments, the dust and manure on Pennsylvania Avenue settled and war was no more.

In Nashville nineteen year old Joe said to Alonzo, "I'm resigning and heading for home double quick."

"I'm staying another month or so to help with the clean-up. Take this letter to mail in Canada. I wish you'd have time to go to see my sister."

"I'll probably head straight for Millbrook. That's near Peterborough, you know."

June 2nd 1865

My Dear Brother

. . . We are just in the midst of that bane of civilized society—house-cleaning; . . . I received your letter sent by Lieut. Fitzgerald mailed at Toronto he has not been here; I would have received him with pleasure. . . . I hope it will not be long before we welcome you back in Good Old Canada. . . . Father came home two weeks ago. He was in Cleveland and Detroit. . . . He has been having some trouble with some old Walsingham debts. Newton is in Hamilton attending the Military School. . . . He can go three months and if he gets a 2nd class certificate he draws $50. A 1st

class $100. They are boarding at the American Hotel. If you should come through Columbus, Ohio, if possible call at Dr. P. Goble's . . . I wish you would come by Lexington and see Uncle Silas. . . .

Love from all
Your own dear Sister

After the constant kaleidoscope of dead, wounded, sickness, fighting, eating on the run, life in Nashville was now routine. For Alonzo it was a kind of buffer between being a soldier and becoming a civilian again.

June 20th
. . . You speak of it being a long time since you heard from Canada till my last letter. Father wrote and I sent one or two letters that must have been lost. I hope we will not write many more letters to you but see you instead which will be infinitely preferable. . . . Yesterday a man was sunstruck in Brantford. . . . plenty of strawberries and a profusion of flowers lading the air with perfume. . . . And now, my dear brother, that you have been spared through battle and sickness, remember . . . God hath truly cared for you through many dangers.
. . . Newton is at home. He staid in Hamilton two weeks and came home. His letters are in for admission in the school in Toronto. He found when he applied to enter the School in Hamilton he could not without new papers. He did not succeed in getting them till he got tired of waiting and came home. Perhaps it is as well he has not written because he is anxious to get something to do before he writes. Poor boy he wants to do something but does not seem to have the faculty of helping himself. He left home so young he never had proper training. 'Tis sad when young children are left motherless. . . . Jasper is taking out stumps with a machine and has not come in yet. I like these long bright summer days. . . . Love from all.

Sister Rose

And again she wrote, August 1.

. . . You said Lieut. Fitzgerald had resigned and would call on his way home. We have seen nothing of him yet . . . I fear lest having escaped the perils of war something yet might befall you. . . . There is a good deal in the papers about the Conventions lately held in Detroit and "Reciprocity", "Tariffs," etc. I read Mr. Horne's speech and whatever yankees may say think it excellent . . . Newton is in [Harding] he has been working in the Harvest. . . . All unite in sending love . . .

The pull of home was strong. In July, twenty-three year old Alonzo left the army and went to Cleveland where the veterans had marched triumphantly down Superior Avenue. The 20th Ohio had lost during service one officer and five enlisted men and through disease one officer and seventeen men.

He looked at the house he and his brothers had built. "Maybe if we applied only half the rent to paying off the mortgage and let Newton have the other half to go to school with—I'll speak to father about it." He said his goodbyes, then boarded the cars for home.

The train sped on, then suddenly he was at Princeton, Canada West, and they were all there to meet him with the carriage, red velvet lined, and laden with food Roseltha had prepared for the reunion in Harding. Through the town they went, waving to friends. Along the Drumbo road they drove, guiding the horses around the jogs at every corner where the early surveyors had failed to measure correctly because some of their chains had worn thin, and down the eighth to the top of the Big Hill. Through the trees, there was the Nith winding serenely through the valley and the cupola of Harding Hall. The horses picked their way down the hill, bracing their haunches to hold back the loaded carriage, their hooves slipping on the gravel, sometimes striking sparks on the stones. Past the schoolhouse and around the corner they went, chatting happily because Alonzo was home.

After the huge southern mansions he had seen, Harding Hall looked strangely small, but the winding stair was just as inviting as ever when he stepped through the doorway.

"Let me carry your bags to your room. A hero shouldn't have to do it himself." Newton bumped the bags up the stairs, and into their bedroom with its big walnut bed, its prickly horsehair sofa and its door open onto the north balcony with bird songs outside. Then down to the living room full of laughter. "Tell us all about it."

Alonzo took a deep breath. Tell about the blood and burying half bodies or ones with no heads? Tell all the things he hadn't put in the letters? "I hardly know where to begin, but there were lots of funny things depending on your point of view. We were marching along a road when a lieutenant had his foot blown off because the Rebels had buried torpedoes in the road. We had some prisoners, so the major put them marching in front. You should have seen them stepping along as if they were walking on hot coals."

"Not very funny for the lieutenant."

"Then there was the time some of our unit were caught in the rain and wanted to surrender because their powder ammunition was getting wet. They sent a message to the major and the major sent back, 'Hold out.

The enemies' ammunition is just as wet as yours.'"

"Tell us more, Uncle Lon," coaxed Eva.

"I remember shooting across the river at the Johnnies one day and the next day when there was no fighting we traded newspapers across it like old friends. I gave one man some tobacco."

"I thought I smelled smoke on your breath," cried Roseltha.

"Well, I guess if I'm old enough to have a mustache I can have the odd cigar. I promise I won't smoke in the house."

"How could you shoot at them one day and be friends the next?" asked Eva. "I think that's dreadful."

"We were just doing what we were ordered. War's a strange business." He wanted to stop thinking about the logic of a child's mind so he changed the subject. "Before I joined up I was in charge of mule trains in Missouri. "Somebody made up a parody on *The Charge of the Light Brigade* because once some mules stampeded into the Rebel lines and they thought they were being attacked by cavalry and ran away. It goes like this:

> Half a mile, half a mile,
>   Half a mile onward,
> Right through the Georgia troops
>   Broke the two hundred
> "Forward the Mule Brigade!
> Charge for the Rebs!" they neighed.
> Straight for the Georgia troops
>   Broke the two hundred.
>
> Mules to the right of them,
> Mules to the left of them
> Mules right behind them
>   Pawed, neighed and thundered.
> Breaking their own confines,
> Breaking through Longstreet's lines
> Into the Georgia troops,
>   Stormed the two hundred.

"There's more but that's about all I can remember."

They all applauded. "More, more," begged Eva.

Alonzo sobered, "Once, at Chattanooga, up on the mountain outside it, I stood above the clouds. I remember one day, Rose, when we were high up in the cupola and the clouds seemed close enough to touch, I said I'd like to be above the clouds, closer to the sky. You said the mountains were too far from Harding for me to get my wish. Now I've had it. It

295

wasn't high enough to be a real mountain but I've been above the clouds."

"What did they look like?"

"Well, it was raining that day same as the day when we captured Lookout and they were just ragged and gray," Alonzo said ruefully. "Maybe if the sun had been shining they'd have looked more—" he searched for a word, "more ethereal."

"Time for bed, Eva, come and wash." Then as the child protested that she never was allowed to stay up late, "I'll let you carry the candle upstairs."

"What's going to happen in the States now that the war is over?" asked Enos.

"It's half and half—vengeance or reconstruction. Sumner wants vengeance. Johnson still isn't sure. What's happening in Canada?"

"There's bad blood between the North and Britain over the *Alabama,* that ship that slipped out of England where she was being built for the Confederacy. She preyed on Northern shipping till she was captured. The North says Britain let her escape on purpose and is claiming huge damages. But I don't think they'll fight over it."

Newton broke in. "Now that the St. Albans crisis is over, we're afraid the Fenians may come in from New York to try to capture Canada. The Irish hate the English still. Our defense policy is all confusion as I found out when I went to Hamilton. So here I am working in the harvest fields and hating it, but I may be needed again by the militia."

"I think we should be able to do something about letting you go to school," said Alonzo. "Maybe we could arrange for you to have Alfred's share of the Cleveland house, or part of the rent."

"I'll wait to see about the Finnegan-Fenians. When I left the militia I was a corporal."

"Make your own decisions, but remember what I said about Alfred's share. Anyway I hardly know what I'm going to do myself. How about you, father?"

"Let's not be too serious tonight. Come and look through my telescope in the cupola. The sky is clear."

Alonzo looked at the dead pocked face of the moon, wonderful, marvellous, but sinister somehow with its sterile shining. He gazed at the rings seen faintly around Saturn and the double star in the handle of the Dipper. He felt now some of the fascination astronomy was exerting over his father and knew that, striving as he did in a little village, it was lonely work but mentally rewarding.

"That's enough viewing for tonight," said his father. "What wonders there are yet to be discovered! The heavens are proof of God's might.

Now come and see the orrery I have in the back kitchen. At last I have it working well."

"Oh father, save something for tomorrow," Rose interrupted. "Alonzo needs sleep after his journey."

"We're sleeping in the same room," Newton said. "No sense mussing two bedrooms when we're batching it."

With a great sigh, Alonzo slept with the murmur of the river in his ears and no guards marching up and down, and no alarms.

Chapter 24

Persicos Odi

In the morning Alonzo raced Newton down the circling stairs to the kitchen where Rose was cooking breakfast. He lifted the lid to look at the oatmeal porridge simmering in its iron pot, smelled the bacon crisping in the pan. Then they gathered around the dining room table where happiness whetted their appetites.

"This is sure better than the army. We used to say that army soup was made from the shadow of a chicken that had died from starvation." He was almost going to tell them the story of the mule soup but thought it would spoil the taste of the ginger cookies.

"What are the negroes going to do now that they're free?" asked Rose.

"A lot of them will have a hard time. Some learned to read and write. If they come north looking for work, it'll be tough but many want to stay and raise their own corn and cotton if they can."

"Some of them," said Newton, "think they won't have to work any more.

> Niggers learnin' Greek and Latin,
> Niggers wearin' silk and satin,
> Niggers gittin' mo' like white folks every day.

They'll need a deal of learning before they get to that stage. Can't say we're at it either."

"All right, boys," said Enos as if they were still youngsters, "now that we're together again we'll have family worship."

He reached for the big Bible, selected a passage, and pushing back their chairs they knelt beside them, remembering those who were not kneeling with them. Then smiles came as they rose and looked at each other, hardly believing this much was true.

Enos cleared his throat. "Come on, Alonzo, time to look at my orrery.

Eva can help her mother with the dishes."

The men went into the back room where Enos had his books and instruments. There Alonzo looked at his father's work, a home-made orrery with metal rods and balls of varying sizes with some central wheelwork. Enos gave it a little twirl and the balls began to move slowly about the biggest one.

"The big one is the sun, of course, and the rest are planets. The ancients thought that the earth was the centre of the universe and sun revolved around it, but in the sixteenth century Copernicus said the ancients were wrong. The sun, not the earth, was the centre."

Alonzo counted the little balls. "There are eight planets then revolving around the sun, and the ninth is our own earth. What is this little one called?"

"That's Neptune. It was only discovered in 1846, three years after you were born. Maybe some day we'll discover another."

"This is pretty interesting, father."

"Father takes the orrery down on the river bank on clear nights to explain planets to people. The school teacher sometimes brought her pupils. They call it Harding's planet pointer. You ought to meet the teacher. She's nice."

Enos shuffled some pages together and handed a few to his son. "I'm writing a paper on my studies."

Alonzo took a quick look at them. "I'll take time to read these later," he said for he could sense that Newton was growing restless.

"Come on, Lon, let's go down the street and see who's around. Might see a few girls anxious to meet the hero returned from battle."

Girls, thought Alonzo, girls. Harding, here I come.

"Yes, you can come with us, Eva," said the young men to their niece as they rushed through the kitchen. "See you for dinner, Rosie. I can hardly wait for more of your cooking."

"Raspberry pie for dinner," sang Eva as she grasped Alonzo's hand.

"Eva," he said, "you're wearing earrings. You've had your ears pierced. Didn't it hurt?"

"No, Uncle Lon, it didn't hurt. It just surprised my ears. And look, I'm wearing the ring you sent me."

How normal life seemed now. How pleasant it was to walk through the quiet village along the well-known plank path. There was a new yellow brick carriage shop on the corner where the main street forked to go up the hill. The blacksmith shop on the side street with sparks flying from the anvil was as fascinating as ever. Flax was lying in the pond on the far fields, spread to ret under the hot sun. A bandy-legged old man was walking down the road from the bridge.

"Why, that's old Jake," exclaimed Alonzo. "Hello there, Jake."

Jake spat a brown stream. "Well, boy, finished with the killin'?"

"Come now, Jake, don't be that hard on me. Takes a long time to make some people see sense."

"There's ways and ways of makin' people see sense, is all I kin say. Some day countries will find another umpire besides war." Jake rolled on his way, wrinkled, brown and gnomic.

"If he gets any thinner, he won't even cast a shadow."

"Don't worry about him. He's looked the same for years. Want to go to look at the schoolhouse?"

A horse and buggy was tied to the hitching post in front of the school. "That must be Lee's. Wonder what she's doing? School doesn't start for a week."

A little figure in bonnet and long skirt was bending over the flower bed by the fence. She straightened as she heard them coming. Eva began to swing on the squeaking turnstile.

"This is my brother Alonzo. I told you he was coming home. Alonzo, this is Miss MacDonald."

Alonzo looked into eyes as blue as flax flowers. "How do you do, Miss MacDonald," he managed to say.

"Didn't expect to find anyone here," said Newton, pulling a couple of weeds.

"Nobody else looks after the flowers so I have to. School will soon be open and I'll have no time then."

Alonzo was tongue-tied. Where had he seen those blue eyes and the dark brown curling hair? He didn't want to appear flashy with a silly remark like "Haven't I seen you somewhere before?" but the thought that he had was teasing him.

The young lady was speaking to him. "Welcome home, Mr. Harding. Your brother has told me all about his adventures in Washington and yours away off in Chattanooga and Nashville. I followed the progress of the war on the map."

"I didn't see much of it. I was mostly stationed in one place." Alonzo was no boaster.

"I've never been farther than Brantford and Woodstock. I used to live near your Uncle Asa in Paris. I think you visited him a few times."

Then it came to Alonzo—the girl who hopped on the path to the tune of that strange Latin chant.

"Now I remember where I've seen you before," he said with relief. "You knew a Latin rhyme, Persicos something or other. That meant Persians."

"You remember that? Like to hear it again?"

"Yes, yes." Anything, as long as he could look into those blue eyes.
"Here goes."

> Persicos odi puer apparatus,
> Bring me a chop and a couple of potatoes.
> Displicent nexae philyra coronae,
> If I can't have that I'll have cheese and macaroni.

"But you used to hop to it. Do that too."

A mischievous look appeared on her face. "Oh no, Mr. Harding, I'm not a little girl any longer. I'm the schoolmarm."

Yes, even though she came only to his shoulder, she was grown up. "What a pity," said Alonzo, "that adults aren't supposed to play any more."

Newton was beginning to feel left out. "Do you have a key? May we go in to see our old desks?"

"Just as long as you don't carve your names in them! Heavens to Betsy," she exclaimed as they passed through the little vestibule into the schoolroom, "look at the dust."

Eva began to draw pictures on the "blackboard," the front wall painted with black paint. Alonzo looked at the desks, the small ones in front graduating to large ones at the back, and wondered how he had ever fitted into any of them. "How many pupils are you expecting in September, Miss MacDonald?"

"About thirty-five, all grades."

"That'll keep you busy. Not much time for play."

"Oh, I get to prayer meeting, if you call that play. And the corn roasts and the skating parties on the river and the sleighing down the Big Hill."

"Will you be at prayer meeting tomorrow night?" he asked quickly.

"Possibly," she answered, twinkling.

"Come on, let's go," Newton broke in. He hadn't realized his brother was such a fast worker. He had no actual designs on the school teacher himself but he liked her. "The sun's high, it's dinner time. Rose'll be waiting for us."

"I'm ready to leave too," said Leonora. She locked the door, they untied her horse and with a flick of the reins she was off. The two young men clattered down the wooden walk after Eva, single file among the Queen Anne's lace and chicory that bordered it.

"Where are you going to look for work now, Lon? There's not much doing around here, as I've found out."

"What's the rush? I've just come home. Come on, Eva, let's see who gets to the raspberry pie first." They burst breathless through the kitchen door.

Newton dropped into a sound sleep as soon as he hit the bed that night but Alonzo lay awake. What *was* he going to do? His father, except for his engrossing hobby, seemed to be at a stalemate. The venture in Walsingham and the death of two wives and three sons had sapped his vitality. The rents from the store and mill were not sufficient to keep him properly. "I'm now the eldest son," Alonzo thought, "I should be able to come up with some solution. Besides," he hardly dared acknowledge even to himself what was forming in his mind, "maybe I've travelled around enough and should settle down." Eyes as blue as flax flowers appeared before him. "Harding should be as good a place as any." He slept, but awoke still thinking.

"Yes, we have to get back home today. Sorry to leave you bachelors but we must." Roseltha put her hands on Alonzo's cheeks and kissed him. "I sleep better knowing that you're home safe." She picked up baby Clara. "Come, Eva, papa's finished hitching the horse. Come to see us as soon as you can."

"I'm going up to Stevenson's farm to see if he needs help. He's going to slaughter pigs." Newton bounded down the street. Enos went to his workroom to correct a wobble in the orrery.

Alonzo walked through the house to the north verandah and stood looking towards the river. A freight train on the tracks across the flats on the other side of the cedar swamp sounded its insistent, intermittent whistle. Who-o-o whoo who-o-o. Again it sent out its message, a long, a short and a long, a warning to people on the nearby crossing to wait till it had passed. Wait, thought Alonzo. Wait. I don't want to wait to get started at something, but what *am* I going to do now that I'm home?

He looked down the street, so quiet a dog could lie in the road and not move for half an hour. The village sounds came to his ears—the faint clang of the blacksmith's hammer, a cow bawling for her calf, a hen clucking triumphantly after laying an egg, a child's voice calling, "Come play catch with me, Georgie."

He crossed the road where it rounded the corner of the house and brushed his way through the weeds to a little rise where he could look across to the high bank beneath which the Nith flowed, invisible from where he stood. He'd walked there the day before and knew it was pitifully low because of the dry summer. In some places it barely gurgled over the gravelly bottom. There was not enough water to turn the mill wheel. Yesterday the miller had stood at the loading door, idly chewing a straw. "Pasture's dry. Farmers need feed but I can't grind today. Don't look like rain neither," he said, squinting skywards.

Alonzo looked at the brilliant sky. No rain today. "I've my bounty money and a good part of my pay. Should be able to put it to good use, but how?" He heard a faint hoot from the train as it rounded the bend. Then it came to him. "I have it. Railway ties—cedar from the swamp. It's father's land. Cut in the fall when it's dry, rent a team of horses and skid them out in the winter. The railway pays cash and they always keep piles in reserve. I'll get the money by spring and—and." In the confusion of his thoughts all he would say to himself at the moment was—"and there's lots of room in the big house."

He hurried back for noon dinner, leftovers from his sister's cooking and milk cool from the stone cellar. As soon as he could he went back into the hot sun towards the river. "If the river weren't so dry the mill could run every day, maybe even day and night."

He studied the lay of the land. He walked along the bank and over stones that should have been deep under water. There was a natural line of hummock curving between what had been a previous high bank of the meandering river and the flats where it now ran. He'd seen the army repair a dam or throw a bridge across a river in record time. "There's no mystery to making a dam. If I build a dam here," he said to himself as he walked back to the bend where the river turned south, "it will hold the water back to run into a storage channel. I can make a dike running along there and another dam opposite the house with gates to release the water into a mill race. Open the gates, let the water run into the race and there's a head of water to run the mill. I'll have enough money by spring to do it. Then I'll run the mill myself." Breasting the mullein and teazels and skirting the thorn trees as he went, he hurried back to the house. "I'd better think some more before I say anything."

Sunday came and afternoon church, for Harding was the second stop in the minister's three-point charge. Alonzo tried hard to concentrate on the sermon and keep himself from turning around. The last prayer died away, and yes, there she was, just a few seats behind them.

"I think I'll ask Miss MacDonald to go walking with me," he said hastily to his father and caught up with her as she stepped outside.

"Would you, would you come for a walk with me?" he said, tipping his hat. "It's a nice afternoon."

"I'd like to. Wait a minute till I tell my parents."

They walked through the village slowly, chatting inconsequentially. Then Alonzo spoke up, "Would you like to walk around the river? It's not muddy today."

They turned back up the street past Harding Hall towards the river. The cows on the flats stared, then resumed cropping.

"I'm glad these are tame," said Leonora. "Some get a little wild after they've been loose all summer."

"I walked here a few days ago. I've been getting a few ideas about what I should be doing now that the war is over." He held out his hand to help her over a log. She lifted her long skirt slightly with one hand and put the other in his, then withdrew it after she had stepped over.

"I've been thinking that if the mill could only run all the time, instead of spasmodically in the dry spells, there'd be a good profit from it."

"Maybe a rain dance to get water?"

"More reliable than that. When I was in the army I was mostly working in the commissary, but when we were on the march I could see how they ran mills and dammed up water and built swing bridges. You see this bend in the river, and that ridge of high ground over there."

"Yes, I see them. That ridge holds the water in the frog pond and in flood time there's some water on the other side."

"Exactly. If there's water in flood time, there could be water there now if a dam was across here. That would keep all the water from going down this channel. Then if there was another dam opposite the house, it could be closed off with gates. We'd raise a head for the mill. There'd always be water to run it."

"I think that much water would erode the banks and spoil your plan."

"We'd have to do some piling up here and there and, I have it, I'll plant willow trees all along and the roots will hold the soil. I'm starting now." He took out his pocket knife, reached up and cut a switch off the willow tree above them. He walked a few rods along the ridge and stuck it in the ground. "There, that'll begin to grow with the first rain."

"Let's plant some more. Lend me your knife." Together they ran along the ridge, planting a dozen.

"I've some money saved up from the army," said Alonzo, astonished at hearing his voice say what was on his mind. "And I'm going to take out cedar logs from the swamp this winter to sell to the railroad for ties. Then I can think of building the dams in the spring. Father'll be glad to let me run the mill instead of renting it."

Leonora swung her bonnet by its ribbons. "That sounds like a good plan, but won't you find Harding a bit dull after the army?"

"No, I've made up my mind to stay here. I won't find it dull—with you here."

Leonora gave a little gasp, half pleasure, half confusion. "It's time I was getting back home."

"I'll drive you home. Newton's not using the buggy this afternoon."

He said nothing to his father or brother about one of the reasons for his bursting energy. In a week he had the promise of a team in the winter. Then he took Newton into the swamp with him to mark trees for cutting, in good locations for skidding out.

"You going to stick around here for the winter, Newton, or are you going to try to go back to school?"

"I don't know what I'll be doing. There's still talk of the Fenians coming over to take Canada away from the Queen."

"I'll be glad when Confederation goes through though they seem to be taking their time about it. It'll make the country stronger."

The Fenian threat increased. The Volunteers were called up again and Newton went off with them. His brother's thoughts were all with the school teacher and his father's with the stars. Why should he hang around the village?

Oak Grove Barracks
Sarnia, Nov. 30th 1865

Dear Brother

... There is quite a stir about the Fenians here. There are some two or three hundred ruffs over in Port Huron a few of which visit this town nearly every night and in their drunken sprees cause some trouble. Last Monday evening a gang of them collected in a hotel and drawing their revolvers took possession driving out the inmates in haste who brought the alarm to the barracks of the Toronto company who turning out went down town on the double but by that time the gang was in the river steering for Yankeedom. Last night they entered a store in town and stole a few things and stabed a man who tried to arrest one of them. Tonight we will have a piquet of twelve men, corp, Sergt. and officer of the day to patrole the streets all night. We are drilling hard the awkward squad drills about four hours per day.

Your Brother
Newton

While Newton was chasing "ruffs," Alonzo had a goodly pile of logs ready to be skidded out when the snow was deep enough to pack a road. He kept Leonora informed of his progress and now was invited regularly to her home for Sunday supper. Sunday supper in the country was simple—fresh bread, home-churned butter, home-preserved peaches, cake and tea—but the simple grace with which it was served made it a feast.

Newton's life was livelier.

Oak Grove Barracks
No. 2 Co Western Administrative Battalion
Volunteer Militia
Sarnia December 22nd 1865

Dear Brother

*Not having heard from you since I arrived and not knowing why you have not answered my last letter, I want you to write **immediately** if not sooner, if you wish to retain your peace of mind and save yourself the trouble of receiving and me the trouble of giving you an awful "blow-up." I presume you are so deeply engaged in the seder swamp that you cannot think of anything else. I really hope you will not loose yourself entirely in the swamp and give me the trouble of coming home to attend to the Girls. We had a rout last night. At 2.30 the Bugle at the Toronto Barracks sounded the alarm and our sentry hearing it warned the Barracks and in just 3 minutes after the Corporal of the Guard woke me we had 53 men under arms and I had commenced proving the Company. We waited about five minutes and the Majors, both Captains, Lieut. and Adjutant came doubling down and had the goodness to turn us in telling us that the Finians declined coming at present. We are getting along swimmingly here and are looking for the river to close up entirely when they say we will have some work to do but no one knows. . . . I have been attending the Temple here for the last four weeks . . . Sarnia is the dulest place I ever was in. There is no amusement here at all not even as much as there is in the famous city of [Harding]. When you write let me know what is going on in the village and how many logs you have cut. Have you heard from Father lately? Where is he? and what is he doing? Give my love to Bruce and all friends.*

Your aff. Brother
N. [Harding]

Enos had passed through Walsingham on his way to Detroit to investigate prospects there. When he finally wrote he mentioned that the husband of Abigail Becker, the heroine of Long Point, had perished in a snowstorm while walking from their cabin to the nearest house. Enos had not yet decided what to do.

Sarnia Feb. 2nd '66

Dear Brother

. . . Have you heard anything about the "Finegans" lately? The people here are all or at least some of them ready to leave town. One family actually left yesterday to find a place of security in the interior of the

country. Night before last the Sarnia Volenteers were called out and placed on guard at the station and a detachment of them joined Me on the main guard. What the cause of the excitement was we do not know but the Mayor recd a telegram no one knew what it was but he immediately called out the col. and made out a roll of all the able bodied men in town and warned them to prepare what arms they could get their hands on and hold themselves in reddiness to answer the sound of the bugle. Rumors of every kind were rife in the town and a great many changed their silver at the brokers for bills in order to facilitate a precipitate retreat before the advances of an imaginary foe. Many of the stores are closed the merchants and clerks preparing for War! Many forget to sleep the streets very full all night. Parties who have arrived from London report equal excitement there. While all this was going on in this mighty city we very quietly went to bed and slept as usual well knowing that if there was anything wrong we would know it in time to wake us up or if we slept too long they would kindly wake us up. All this I believe to be humbug. However time will tell. I was promised a pass to go home Saturday for my birthday but they have not recd orders to issue no passes. The fright some are in is enough to make one kill themselves with laughter. Tell the ladies they better commence picking lint. Yours till finegans find me or I'm carried away by force of war. . . .

Your aff. Brother
Newton

If father and brother were restless, Alonzo was content. The February sun cast crisp shadows on the snow as he worked, thinking of Sunday supper with Leonora on the farm a mile and a half from the village.

The moon was going to be full the next Friday night. There would be a skating party on the river with a bonfire on the shore near the bend in the river where he and Leonora had planted their willow wands the previous summer and watched them take root. He had said he would supply wood for the fire and he set logs in place for the skaters to rest on as they ate or warmed themselves.

He harnessed Phoenix to call for Leonora in the cutter. The runners squealed as he pulled out into the frozen snow, the horse's breath trailing white behind him. He tucked the buffalo robe around Lee and leaped in beside her, their skates at their feet. They could drive the horse off the road and onto the river near the party.

Soon a fire was leaping high and a rink was cleared though the wind had swept most of the snow from the river. The ice stretched black and mysterious away from the firelight, inviting exploration. Leonora and Alonzo crossed hands and skated away into the moonlit night, skirting snow patches, swinging in rhythm, skimming over the white ridges where the snow lodged in the cracks. Sometimes the ice boomed fearsomely as they passed but they were accustomed to the temper of the river and paid no heed. The moon sat above them in the heavens, smiling like a Cheshire cat. It was almost too cold for talk. It was enough to be skating along together. They stopped for breath, still holding their crossed hands.

"Look, I can see the moon reflected in the ice." And there, indeed, was the moon below them mirrored in the clear black shining depths.

"Time to go back now. The wind will be against us. You're cold." Alonzo said.

"It's worth being cold on a night like this." She looked up at him.

Alonzo could wait no longer. He took off his mittens and framed Leonora's cheeks between his hands. In the moonlight her eyes were blue-black, her hair frosted like a Marie Antoinette maiden.

"My work's going well. I can start the dams in the spring when the flooding's over. It won't be easy but there's room in the big house for both of us. I love you. Will you marry me?"

"Yes, I know. Yes, I will." Lee felt her words so deeply that tears came to her eyes caused by more than the cold.

He bent towards her. Their first kiss trembled on their lips. She rested in his arms against his bulky coat. They felt a life-time together ahead of them. Then filled with wonder and wordless, they turned and swung back down the river, breasting the wind till they reached the bright circle of the firelight and their friends with their many-coloured tuques and scarves.

Chapter 25

Beulah Land

They were keeping their commitment to themselves for a little while. Leonora taught the children in a haze of happiness. Alonzo struck down cedars as if they were matches. He had little thought for his brother who was away fighting ephemeral Fenians.

> *Sarnia Feby 23rd 66*
>
> *Dear Brother,*
>
> *As usual you have not answered my letter yet. . . . We are all right and are not eaten up by those dreadful "Finegans." Our duties are the same old routing.*
>
> *I wish you would see Ted Groves and see if he will not come up and take my place. If he will come up soon he can get the position of Sergeant. You must not tell him I am sick of it but tell him I want to get away for I have good prospects of going into the oil business if I can get away. . . . I have lost too much time with the humbug now and want to get out of it if possible. I will pay his fare up if he will not come without . . . In haste*
>
> *Your aff. Brother*
> *Newton*

Enos was back home again, engrossed with his books and tools. He was making progress with his writing if nothing else.

> *"Gravitation is a potent power suggested by Sir Isaac Newton who is called the father of astronomy. It is a name given to some invisible unknown power which no man has ever seen or handled. Philosophy teaches us that matter must also have a creative power if it is not governed by some infinitude of wisdom foreign to itself. It has neither life*

311

nor spirit nor reason therefore we must give that power which is called gravitation to the spirit and power of God the creator of heaven and earth for with no effort but His mind He brought this structure into existence. With the same mind He sets the whole universe in motion and by His eternal unchanging mind holds it in motion."

"Well, that's enough for tonight. Maybe I'll read a little to Alonzo when he comes in. I'm glad Newton is safe with the militia in Sarnia. Don't think the Fenian scare will amount to much."

At Easter Alonzo and Leonora were ready to announce their wedding day.

"Can't say I'm too surprised," said Enos, kissing Leonora on the cheek. "You've had stars in your eyes as big as Venus for some time. When will it be?"

"The middle of August."

"Welcome to the family, my dear," he answered, concealing a pang because of what he lacked in his own life.

Now Alonzo revealed what he was planning. "Father, I'll soon be finished with logging in the cedar swamp. I'd like to take over the mill myself and I've plans for running it so that we don't have to stop when the water's low in the summer."

"Oh, now, what would your plans be?"

Alonzo launched into his scheme for building two dams.

"Quite an undertaking but I'll help you all I can. Maybe I can sell my railway stock and maybe Newton can help you too when he's finished in Sarnia."

Newton came home a few weeks later. "Sure I'll help you but I may not be around much longer. I'm through wasting my time. I'm going back to school. I'll find the money somehow."

"You're nineteen," Alonzo reminded him, "and I'm glad you've seen the light at last."

"I've seen the light, and since I'm older I'll be better."

"What'll you do with schooling?"

"Maybe be a minister. Maybe be the principal of the Canadian Literary Institute. Maybe it will be called Woodstock College some day. When I finish there, I'm going to the University of Toronto to get a degree."

Alonzo was flabbergasted. "You can't even spell. And you smoke. They'd never let you."

"Maybe the Lord will help me stop smoking. No use asking him to help me spell."

Enos recovered from his astonishment. "Guess you take after your grandfather, Preacher Harding. You may not be good at spelling, but you can be a spellbinder like him."

Newton was slaphappy over his decision. He sang out a Spoonerism, "When kinquering kongs go forth to war."

"You'd better be serious, Newtie. What would you teach if you ever did become principal of any school, let alone the Institute?"

"I'll teach mathematics, maybe astronomy. How about that, pa? I might get some rich fellow to donate a telescope bigger than yours, maybe an observatory. I've lots of other ideas too. I think gentlemen's sons should be able to work with their hands as well as with their brains. Why couldn't they teach carpentry or cabinet-making at school? Manual training it would be, working with your hands to relax your brain after studying."

Father and brother looked at Newton with the colour mounting in his cheeks and his eyes sparkling with enthusiasm.

"It sounds far-fetched, but can you stick with it? You've not done much except bounce from one thing to another."

"This time I'll stick with it. And as for money, the mortgage on the Cleveland house is nearly paid off and maybe you'd let me have the rent from it to pay my way, or else sell it when the price is right."

"If you stay with it, we'll see you through somehow. I think that at last you're serious," Enos assented.

Alonzo wrote to his sister to tell her his plans.

Dear Brother,

*I am glad you are to be married and hope your fondest anticipations may be more than realized. I am anxious to see my new **Sister**, give her my kindest congratulations, and earnest best wishes of "Sister Rose" and may you both be happy in your new relations. I can have no better wish for you than that your married life may be as happy as ours has been, no cloud has ever rested on it. . . . We are going to London to celebrate the Queen's birthday. We have tickets at this Station at reduced fares. Come up to Princeton . . . on the Accommodation. We will leave in the morning. . . . I must conclude with much love to all at the "old Home."*

Your affectionate
Sister Rose

Alonzo Harding and Leonora MacDonald were married on a Saturday afternoon in August under the gnarled Sheepnose apple tree in the garden. Newton had joked that a couple of Isaac Newton's apples might

313

be impelled by the power of gravity to fall on their heads as they said "I do" and upset the gravity of the occasion.

When the wedding breakfast was over, Newton threw his carpet bag into the Goble's surrey for he would stay in Goble's Corners with his sister till the opening of term at Woodstock College. The last of the guests departed.

"Glory, glory, hallelujah," sang Alonzo. "Howdedo, Mrs. Harding." He caught Lee in a bear hug. "How does it feel to be living in Harding Hall? Come on, let's go up to the cupola for a few minutes before it gets dark."

Up the circling steps they climbed, the laughter with which they had begun the ascent diminishing as they reached the first landing to murmurs of contentment as they reached the second and to near silence as they climbed the third narrow flight to the top.

They gave two startled gasps as they saw Enos standing there with his hands in his pockets, a tuneless whistle on his lips, looking to the north where one dam was already roughed into place.

"Father, what are you doing here?"

"Just thinking of your plans for working the mill."

"You don't like them after all?"

"Yes, I do, but I think you should be the one to finish them. I've decided to go to Kentucky. Silas needs help with his business and mail routes. I wrote him a month ago. I'm beginning to live too much with memories. A change will do me good. I'm only fifty-five. I've lots to do yet."

"Are you certain that's what you want?"

"Yes, I'm sure. I'll take my telescope and astronomy books with me. I intend to visit the Observatory in Cincinnati on my way. You'll make a success of the mill, I know. I'll come back to visit."

He looked through the windows with the curly little flaws in the panes. Then he spoke again, jingling the coins in his pocket. "Once I filled this house with children. Now it's your turn." Then he added with sad irony. "Lately all I've seemed to fill is the cemetery." He paused. "I'll leave in a couple of days. You can drive me to the station in the carriage. And maybe, Leonora, after I get away you could sew some fresh cushions for it. The red velvet is getting pretty worn."

"Father," was all two voices could say as he hugged them both, then ran briskly down the stairs.

The two young people looked at each other. They moved closer together, two pairs of eyes brimming with sadness for the goodbye and happiness for the present.

Through the open door of the cupola there came the sound of children's voices ringing like bells through the clear air. The setting sun spread its glory over the sky. The river coursed on its green-brown ruminant way. Alonzo could almost hear his mother's voice rising from the house below, "O Beulah Land, sweet Beulah Land." Now there was Leonora. Tomorrow there would be singing once more in Harding Hall.

Epilogue

Some years after he left Wolverton, Enos returned to live in the house he had built. By now he was experimenting with electricity in what he called his laboratory. His hearing-aid was run by batteries that required sulphuric acid. Over the objections of the family he kept a bottle of acid on his bedside table. He put a bottle of cough medicine there as well and one night in 1893 drank from the wrong bottle.

Alonzo lived to change his sawmill to a grist mill, then a flour mill. He also exported butter and eggs to England. When the mill burned, he and his son built a larger mill, 400 barrels a day capacity, exporting after World War I to Cuba and Germany. Respected and beloved, he died in 1925. His wife received a widow's pension from the American government till her death at the age of ninety.

Newton graduated in mathematics from the University of Toronto in 1877 in a class of ten men and was soon ordained as a Baptist minister. He became principal of Woodstock College, instituted the first class in manual training in Canada and helped to set up a meteorological observatory there. In 1891 he became principal of Bishop's College, Marshall, Texas, a college for blacks. Moving west later, he was treasurer of Brandon College, Manitoba. In 1907 he was accorded an honorary LLD from MacMaster University. He died in Vancouver, B.C., in 1932.